*He glanced at her while he continued to paint.
"Yes. We seem to be on intersecting paths. Or a
collision course."*

How could two people share a potent kiss, Kay asked herself,
and not even mention it to one another the next time they
met?

"Do you like hot stuff?" she asked, and could have thrown
the coffee in her own face when she heard herself.

He glanced up, dark eyes assessing her, trying not to smile.
"Of course," he answered, letting the double entendre linger
between them. "Do you?"

"I..." The single syllable came out high and broken. She tried
again. "I was going to recommend the Jalapeno Burger."

"Sounds good. Thanks for the recommendation."

Kay reached for the door and was about to escape into the
hallway and gasp for air—and suddenly hated herself for her
cowardice. She took a sip of her coffee and walked back into
the room.

"You're not going to bring up the kiss?" she asked. Her tone
was pugnacious. She couldn't help it. She was spoiling for a
fight.

Jack felt the crackle of tension that seemed to charge the air
whenever he saw her. He steeled himself against it—against
her. There wasn't room for this in his plan.

And Julia still filled his heart.

Dear Reader,

The editors at Harlequin and Silhouette are thrilled to be able to bring you a brand-new featured author program beginning in 2005! Signature Select aims to single out outstanding stories, contemporary themes and oft-requested classics by some of your favorite series authors and present them to you in a variety of formats bound by truly striking covers.

We plan to provide several different types of reading experiences in the new Signature Select program. The Spotlight books will offer a single "big read" by a talented series author, the Collections will present three novellas on a selected theme in one volume, the Sagas will contain sprawling, sometimes multi-generational family tales (often related to a favorite family first introduced in series) and the Miniseries will feature requested, previously published books, with two or, occasionally, three complete stories in one volume. The Signature Select program will offer one book in each of these categories per month, and fans of limited continuity series will also find these continuing stories under the Signature Select umbrella.

In addition, these volumes will bring you bonus features...different in every single book! You may learn more about the author in an extended interview, more about the setting or inspiration for the book, more about subjects related to the theme and, often, a bonus short read will be included.

Watch for new stories from Janelle Denison, Donna Kauffman, Leslie Kelly, Marie Ferrarella, Suzanne Forster, Stephanie Bond, Christine Rimmer and scores more of the brightest talents in romance fiction!

We have an exciting year ahead!

Warm wishes for happy reading,

Marsha Zinberg
Executive Editor
The Signature Select Program

SAGA

MURIEL JENSEN

SEASON OF SHADOWS

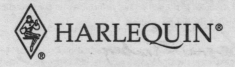

HARLEQUIN®

TORONTO • NEW YORK • LONDON
AMSTERDAM • PARIS • SYDNEY • HAMBURG
STOCKHOLM • ATHENS • TOKYO • MILAN • MADRID
PRAGUE • WARSAW • BUDAPEST • AUCKLAND

ISBN 0-373-83652-X

SEASON OF SHADOWS

www.eHarlequin.com

Printed in U.S.A.

PROLOGUE

Entry, Julia Keaton's diary, January 12

Am now certain Ron is bilking clients. Have traced M & S Money Management's income over the last three months, and have discovered that only a small percentage of investments have actually been made. Statements have gone out to clients, claiming that their money is in high-quality, low-risk investments, and in gold. But I can find no evidence to prove the claim, only hundreds of thousands of client dollars unaccounted for.

I've listed names and addresses of the clients I know came to us with their money following our investment seminar at the library. Will stay late tonight on the pretext of catching up on correspondence. Will actually make copies of the last quarter's statements and our investment record, which appears to me to be full of holes and lacking documentation to back up Ron's claim. Tomorrow, I'm taking the information I've collected to the District Attorney.

God, I wish you were here, Jack. Talking to you in my journal and telling you all the things I can't say in my letters to you helped at first, but now that the news from Iraq is filled with horrible stories of ambush, kidnap and butchery, I'm terrified for you. Plus, I've taken a job with a complete crook. All of this is challenging my determination to be strong for you.

I'm truly frightened for the first time since you brought such courage and light into my life. The children brighten my world, but beyond them I feel such darkness. I know you'd hate to hear that and would remind me of the powerful Love that always surrounds us. I don't think I'm experiencing a loss of faith. I just have a very solid grasp of my reality.

But I'm sure things will look better to me tomorrow when I can take action against Ron. Then one more month and you'll be home! I can't wait! I'll let Amanda and Paul have you all day, then I'm going to send them to your mother's and ravage you all night long. I told you that in the letter I wrote you today, but I want to say it again just for me. I am living for the day you walk into my arms again. Good night, Jack.

News story on page 5 of the **Burlington Eagle,**
January 13

Julia Keaton, 31, of Haverstown, was killed last
night when the SUV she was driving left the road
at Allan Falls and plunged into Lake Champlain.
She leaves two young children, and a husband,
Lt. Commander John Keaton of the Naval Reserve, serving as chaplain to a Marine Corps unit
deployed to Iraq from 29 Palms, California.

CHAPTER ONE

AT FIRST, KAY FLORIO thought the smudge of red on Maple Hill Lake was the bobber on a fishing line. Then she realized there was no boat, no fisherman patiently waiting for a bite. She put the camera to her eye and let the autofocus do its thing. The zoom lens she was using to get pictures of the community Labor Day celebration going on at the head of the lake brought in a clear image of the calm water.

She scanned back and forth, up and down, looking for that spot of red. It appeared suddenly in the center of the frame, a shock of sopping red hair atop the head of a small child whose little face was screwed up as she screamed soundlessly for help. Then the small head disappeared into the water.

"Oh, my God!" Kay's exclamation also carried no sound as the high school band struck up a Sousa tune. She tried anyway, shouting, "Help! Somebody!" and pointing to where she'd last seen the child.

But everyone gathered for the annual celebration in Maple Hill, Massachusetts, was focused on the music being played in the newly installed bandstand. She noticed absently that the bright sunlight flared off the polished instruments, off the chrome and windshields on all the cars parked in the lot and on Lake Road, off soda cans, sunglasses and watchbands.

She experienced one instant of denial. She saw Betsy's face superimposed on the little redhead's, and felt all the old terror, guilt and inexplicable misery rise up to clog her throat and start that thumping in her head that would take days to quiet.

Then the need to help *this* little girl forced that aside. Kay held the camera against her chest as she ran up the paved road until she was parallel to the child. She whipped off her camera, put it down in the grass and cursed the extra minute required to pull off her hiking boots.

As she did that, a figure burst out of the trees nearby and leaped into the water. Kay caught a quick glimpse of a man in khaki shorts, a white T-shirt, big, bare feet. And a slight limp. He sliced neatly through the water at considerable speed, diving under like a cormorant near the spot where the little red head had disappeared.

Her heart and her head thumping, Kay yanked up her camera and focused on the spot, waiting, praying. Her whole body trembled in anticipation, awash in the old memories she always thought she'd accepted—until external factors brought them up again and made her wish she'd died instead of her little sister.

Water spewed in all directions as the man shot up out of the lake, the little girl in one arm. Kay snapped the shutter.

One boot on, one boot off, she steadied herself for another shot as the man turned onto his back, clutching the seemingly lifeless child to his chest, and began to swim to the shore, his free arm pumping strongly.

Kay was knocked off balance as a veritable wave of humanity raced past her, crowded around her. Someone at the celebration must have seen the man go into the water and alerted everyone else.

Her view of the drama completely obstructed, she tried to elbow her way through the crowd. It was impossible. She heard a woman's voice raised in fear, shouting, "Misty! Misty! Oh, my God! Oh, please!"

Looping the camera around her neck, she got a foothold at the base of a sturdy maple, reached up for a low-hanging branch and pulled herself into the tree. As she climbed, thanking heaven for her aerobics class and good muscle tone, she heard the crowd directing the man.

"Here! Over here! Lift her up!"

Holding tightly to the tree with one arm, Kay leaned through the leaves, her camera held as steadily as possible, and waited for a shot.

The man appeared suddenly in the viewfinder, wet hair plastered to his head, face set in anguished lines. He raised the limp little body in long, strong arms. Kay shot again as another man dangled over the bank, supported by bystanders, and took the child from him. She snapped the shutter on the dangling man, wondering if his grim expression identified him as the little girl's father.

That question was answered for her when a young

blond woman, still crying out, "Misty!" knelt beside him on the bank as he leaned over the little body. "She's dead!" she shrieked. "Yale, she's dead!"

"Watch out. Let me have a look." Randy Stanton gently pushed the mother aside. Kay recognized him as an EMT with the Maple Hill Fire Department, though today he'd been a civilian manning the barbeque for the community picnic.

Randy put his ear to the child's lips, then to her heart. He tipped her head back slightly, held her nose closed, and breathed twice into her mouth. One long-fingered hand applied compressions high on the small body, then he breathed into her mouth again.

The crowd fell silent while he worked, three pumps on the tiny chest to one breath. The only sounds came from the breeze in the trees, the distant whoosh of traffic on the highway and the flat call of a duck somewhere on the other end of the lake.

Then out of the relative quiet came a little gasp, a cough, the screech of a child now fully awake and screaming to the world her indignation at its treatment of her.

The mother held her close, sobbing hysterically. The father wrapped his arms around Randy. Kay kept shooting.

She scanned right, looking for the rescuer, her journalist's brain already making up the front page, placing photos. She had to have the rescuer, but he wasn't there.

She dropped the camera to her chest and pushed a branch aside for a better view of the water, certain she hadn't seen him climb onto the bank. Nothing.

People were now following the parents and the weeping child back toward the parking lot. There was the distant wail of a siren. Kay watched the crowd go, searching it for the man's wet head, for square shoulders in a sopping white T-shirt, but she saw no sign of him.

Cursing the undeniable truth that climbing out of a tree was much more difficult than climbing into it, she finally swung from a bottom branch and landed with a bone-rattling thump on her unevenly shod feet.

Was Misty's rescuer a shy hero? she wondered. The little girl's parents hadn't noticed him in their concern for their daughter, but Kay was sure once a doctor declared the little girl healthy, they'd want to thank him. And his identity was critical to Kay's story.

All right. This could be good. She had a mystery, something else to think about so that all her memories of her little sister didn't come crowding in and make her hate herself all over again. Once a day for the last eighteen years was certainly enough.

"Kay!" Haley Megrath, the publisher of the *Maple Hill Mirror* and Kay's boss came running through the retreating crowd toward her. She wore a blue-and-white Hawaiian print top over white cropped pants, her long, dark hair caught up in a knot. Except for the bright little girl bouncing up and down in her arms as she ran, Haley looked more like a surfer than the publisher of the local paper. But she'd proved time and again that looks were deceiving. "Did you get a shot?" she asked hopefully, stopping a foot from Kay. Henrietta, her little girl, gave Kay a big baby-toothed grin. "Tell me you got a shot."

Kay held up her camera. "Got it." She capped her lens, then patted it. "That was front page stuff, Haley." She smiled at the toddler, who spent a lot of time in a playpen in the *Mirror*'s office. "From the man jumping into the water, to him handing her to her father. At least, I think that was her father."

"That was her father." Haley swept one hand in a gesture of helplessness and hoisted Henrietta a little higher onto her hip. "I missed everything. I'm trying desperately to make some headway in Henrietta's potty training, and took her to the ladies' room. By the time we heard the commotion and found the crowd, the ambulance arrived and everyone was heading for the parking lot."

"So, you know the little girl?" Kay asked, taking a small notebook out of the large leather tote that served as purse and camera bag.

"Misty O'Neil. Her father worked for Hank for a while, but I think he's employed by the city now. Jackie would know."

Hank was Haley's brother, Hank Whitcomb, former NASA engineer turned local entrepreneur. Four years ago, he came home to start Whitcomb's Wonders, a unique collection of men who provided various skills required to maintain a home or business—plumbing, wiring, painting and papering, gardening, janitorial services. Most of the men he employed worked part-time because they were finishing an education, raising a family or fulfilling other pursuits.

As Kay recalled from a story she'd recently done about the service, Hank had also added a security team just two years ago.

He was not only a business success, but a personal one, as well. After returning from NASA, he married Jackie Fortin, his high school sweetheart, and together they were raising four children from her previous marriage—a big job considering Jackie was also mayor of Maple Hill.

"The big mystery," Kay went on as they started back toward the group at the head of the lake, "is who jumped in after Misty. I've never seen him before, and he just disappeared."

"That was Jack Keaton," Haley said.

"How do you know that," Kay asked, "if you weren't even here?"

"Because as I was running this way, I overheard one of Hank's guys say that Jack Keaton jumped in to save Misty."

"Jack Keaton." Kay repeated the unfamiliar name. "What's he do?"

"He works for Hank. Painting."

"Okay. I'm going to pay a call on him and see if he'll let me get a picture, give me some personal information."

"Good. I'm up to my ears with the back-to-school feature. This is great front page stuff, especially since it all turned out well. Can't beat a hero story."

"Yeah. I got some good shots of Randy at work, too."

At Haley's blank look, Kay explained, "Randy Stanton did CPR on Misty, brought her back. You really did miss everything."

"That's what motherhood does to you."

Kay was grateful motherhood wasn't in her future.

Haley excused herself and hurried off to meet a beckoning friend. Kay hung back and uncapped her camera lens again to get a few shots of the lake, now quiet as people packed up their blankets and picnic baskets and streamed toward their cars. The close call had apparently dimmed the holiday mood.

She took pictures of two ducks paddling lazily through the late-afternoon sunlight on the lake. Haley was bound to need a change-of-season shot in an upcoming issue.

Kay had missed Maple Hill so much when she'd lived in New York after college. There was something to be said for the excitement of living in a big, lively city, but she'd so loved the summers she'd spent here as a child.

Kay's parents loved returning to Maple Hill every summer for the Florio family reunion. Her father and his brothers and sister were the offspring of a Portuguese father whose great-grandfather had come from the Azore Islands to open a fish market. Their mother had been French-Canadian from New Bedford.

Kay and her sister, Betsy, enjoyed spending the month of August with their Uncle Manny and their older cousins, Rachel and Charlene. Uncle Manny, their father's eldest brother, lived in the old family house on the lake. It was torn down ten years ago when she was a teenager. A doctor from Boston bought the property and built an elegant log home on the site.

She'd been startled and a little saddened by the change, then surprised that once she accepted it, it didn't affect how she felt about the place. Her memories still lived there, the lake was the same, the town the same, the people still those she knew and loved.

She went to Boston College, was hired as a copywriter upon graduation for Rush and Pfeifer Advertising. She had been well on her way to a corner-office position when she'd stood by on a reading for a fruit-juice account and looked into the face of a redheaded little girl— a last-minute replacement for the little blonde she'd originally chosen who'd come down with the chicken pox. The child, a professional already accustomed to auditions at the tender age of seven, had introduced herself to Kay and taken her hand. She'd looked and behaved so much like Betsy that Kay had done the unforgivable. She'd run away from the shoot, left her assistant to take over, gone home to sedate herself with a bottle of Drambuie and turned off the telephone.

That was the point at which she knew she had to go away and write her novel. It had been surfacing in her since she'd become an adult. She'd been taking notes for a couple of years and had done a lot of research on Portugal, where she intended to set her story about the failing marriage of a pair of wanderers, looking for something they couldn't find. It excited her to think about finally creating her characters and sending them off on their adventures—and it helped bury all the things she didn't want to think about, like the traumatic loss of her little sister.

She'd sat up most of that night, working through the idea of leaving New York. At first it was hard to consider abandoning the big-city success many young women dreamed about, but it was time to get herself in hand. She was twenty-five. She should do it now while she was still young enough to work full-time to support herself, then work on the book at night.

When she considered where to go, Maple Hill was the obvious option. She had family and friends there, it was beautiful and the relative quiet of small-town life would be conducive to creativity.

She went to work the next day, apologized for her behavior, claiming a sudden migraine, then gave two weeks' notice. She drove to Maple Hill the next weekend to hunt for a job and found that the publisher of the *Maple Hill Mirror* was looking for a reporter. Kay applied and was hired.

That was a year ago. So far Kay had discovered she was a much better reporter than she was a novelist. She'd deleted the first forty pages several times and was now floundering somewhere in chapter four of draft number three.

In her own defense, she'd learned that a weekly newspaper office was far busier than she'd imagined, and repainting and wallpapering the old home she'd bought a few months ago was far more difficult than she'd anticipated. Almost everyone in town lived in old colonials or Victorians, and she'd been seduced by the charm of the homes.

She bemoaned her increasingly full schedule, but it succeeded in accomplishing something important. The novel allowed her to live someone else's life, reporting the news involved her in other people's problems and successes, and hanging wallpaper in a house that wasn't square was so frustrating that it required her complete concentration.

She had the perfect formula for ignoring the past. The present kept her far too busy.

CHAPTER TWO

JACK KEATON stood under a hot shower and let the water beat between his shoulder blades. He was still shaking. Not because a little girl almost lost her life, but because she didn't—God had intervened attempting to prove to him that no matter how far away Jack strayed emotionally, he was never out of His reach.

He'd been painting the frames of the new windows in Cam and Mariah Trent's living room when he'd straightened up to flex the muscle in his bad leg and saw the little girl. He couldn't believe it was a child at first, until he saw her puny arms flail and watched her disappear below the water. He wasted a valuable few seconds wondering how on earth she'd gotten so far from the celebration at the head of the lake, then a father's instinct took over and he ran out of the house and through the trees into the water.

She'd been easy to find underwater, her white shorts and shirt billowing, beckoning him like a beacon. Now that it was over, he could analyze what had happened and know that if he hadn't stood up to flex his leg, *she might have drowned.*

If Cam hadn't hired him to paint his window frames and there'd been no one with this particular vantage point on the lake, *she might have drowned.*

If Julia hadn't died, and if he hadn't been distracted by grief and injured in a firefight the day before he left Iraq then lain in bed for five months with a shattered femur, reading her diary in his unabating misery and need to be near her, he wouldn't have known about Ron Milford cheating his clients, wouldn't have found Julia's safety deposit box key taped between two pages in her diary, and he wouldn't have followed Milford to Maple Hill to exact his revenge.

And he wouldn't have been here, painting the Trents' window frames—*and the little girl might have drowned.*

It was proof that God was ever vigilant, ever in charge, ever merciful.

At least, that's what he used to believe. If this had all happened to someone else two years ago when he'd been Pastor Jack Keaton, he'd have told them they'd been part of a miracle. All the other ugly things surrounding it couldn't be explained. They should be accepted as the workings of a God who always knew what He was doing.

Now—after a year in Iraq as a chaplain, the death of his wife at the hands of some arrogant bastard trying to abscond with other people's money, months of excruciating physical and emotional pain—he found it hard to believe that this had all been part of some wise plan. He had two motherless children, a heart far more damaged than his leg and a whole host of friends and comrades lost forever to their grieving families.

And a plan in play to avenge Julia and send Ron Milford to jail—or hell—he wasn't sure which.

Finding Julia's boss had been the driving force behind Jack's recovery. When he'd been released from the hospital two months ago, his first step had been to check his safety deposit box. In it was a square white envelope with his name on it. It contained a CD without a label. He opened it on his PC at home and found photos of the dubious bookkeeping Julia had mentioned in her diary.

Julia had taken the job with M & S Money Management after he'd left for Iraq, as a way of getting out of the house a bit, while helping to make ends meet. Jack had never met anyone she worked with, so he'd checked the company out on the Internet.

His first hurdle was that both partners were named Ron—Ronald G. Milford, and Ronald W. Scieszka. Nowhere in the diary had Julia mentioned a last name. And it seemed to be only a two-man operation.

Unsure if the partners were both responsible for her death, Jack looked into their activities in the past few months.

Ron Scieszka lived in a 4200-square-foot house in Haverstown, had four superachiever children—three in college, and one working in Europe—a wife well-known for her charity work, and he still ran the company.

Ron Milford, on the other hand, had retired since

Julia died, spent several weeks in Spain, bought a boat and a new BMW, and retired to Maple Hill, Massachusetts. And one of the documents she'd photographed—some report Jack didn't understand except to see that it had been altered from the photo of the original report beside it, had Milford's signature on it.

The high-end purchases and the move were incriminating.

The signature was damning.

During the early days of Jack's painful recovery, he'd considered murder. The hideous year of separation from Julia in Iraq, his homecoming shattered by her death before he could see her or hold her again, then the discovery that it had been no accident had filled him with such darkness that taking a life had seemed a viable option.

Then things changed. He'd intended to leave his children with his parents and follow Milford on his own to mete out a swift justice. But his father had a minor heart attack six weeks ago, just before Jack's move to Maple Hill. It was a warning, the doctor had said, to live a healthier lifestyle and relax. Jack's parents had taken care of Amanda and Paul during his seven months in the hospital—not an easy challenge for a couple in their early seventies.

So the plan evolved. What had been a dark rage evened out into a cold determination that filled every waking moment, a decision to find and watch Milford, get to know him, find a way to prove him responsible for Julia's death and let the State of Vermont supply the justice.

Jack turned off the shower and shouted at God in the ensuing silence. "Don't try to draw me back with Your miracles. Leave me alone. I'm lost to You!" His angry voice reverberated in the confines of the shower. Lost to You. Lost to You. Lost to You.

He was, of course, very happy the little girl survived. But if God wanted to impress him with His miracles, He could give him Julia back, erase the year in Iraq from his memory, breathe life into the friends he'd lost there.

No, he didn't really believe that could happen. But neither did he want to be charmed by the things God was willing to do. He was happy for the little girl's parents, but he wasn't happy with God. He felt as though he'd been betrayed by a friend behind Whom he'd thrown all his love and support.

Now his mind was filled with the last pages of Julia's diary, with the knowledge that she'd been frightened, disillusioned, and all alone because he'd gone to war to minister those fighting for their country.

He had to live with the painful fact that his wife had died alone and probably in terror on some dark and icy road—maybe calling his name as the car left the road and fell into the lake.

He screamed at God again when he thought about the sound of Julia's fear-stricken voice shouting for him. Swallowing a knife would probably feel just like this—as though everything inside had been cut open and laid bare.

Glancing at the clock, he pulled on briefs and a pair of jeans. The kids were due home in fifteen minutes, and

Calpurnia Jones, the nanny, was the most punctual human being he'd ever met. He needed a Scotch to mellow him out enough to hide his anguish from a five- and six-year-old, but that was not an option with his children coming home. He punched his way into a T-shirt as he went to the kitchen for a cup of strong coffee.

"Daddy!" Amanda always hit the front door, shouting for him. His mother maintained that it was because she'd been without him for so long that now that she had him back, she needed to know he was at least within earshot. But he thought he detected a particular excitement in her voice this afternoon.

"Coming!" He hurried toward the living room, then stopped short at the sight of Amanda with an armful of black puppy. She knelt beside it because it was too big for her to carry. Paul was clutching its long black tail and was forced to move with it as it wagged.

"Look!" Amanda was illuminated. She had dark gold hair like her mother, bright blue eyes, as though she brimmed with summer sky. Her smile always brought his smile in return, even when he'd thought there was nothing anywhere to be happy about. "We went to visit Glory, and she said we could have this puppy if you said it was okay 'cause somebody else bought him but they couldn't keep him because he ate their car. Can we keep him, Daddy?"

Glory was part-time nanny to the Whitcombs' children, and was married to Jimmy Elliott, who worked part-time for Whitcomb's Wonders, Jack's employer. He was also a Wonder and a fireman who raised Labs. Cal was Jimmy's aunt.

"His name's Buster!" Paul said breathlessly. "Glory says he's gonna be really big!"

"He ate their *car?*" Jack asked Calpurnia, certain that couldn't be true. Although the dog was obviously young with innocent brown eyes and a soft muzzle that begged to be rubbed, his gangly body was already tall and long. Puppy was almost a misnomer for something that size.

Cal, a rotund, bighearted woman with close-cropped, curly gray hair and a preference for jeweled T-shirts, smiled fondly at his happy children. "Only the bumper," she said, as if this would take all the horror out of the claim. "It was one of those fiberglass things."

Well, that explained it. Fiberglass was so digestible.

"And your bumper *isn't* fiberglass," she reminded him.

That was true. He had an old Dodge truck. Godzilla would have difficulty eating that.

"And he had to always be in the garage." Amanda clutched the puppy's neck, convinced he deserved better accommodations.

"That's 'cause he ate the sofa!" Paul interjected, delighted again by the dog's appetite.

Amanda glowered at him. "Not the *whole* sofa," she told Jack, realizing her brother's arguments were doing their case no good. "Glory says he needs to be with people."

Jack considered how to let his children down easily,

certain that the last thing in this world he needed was something that added chaos to an already barely controlled situation. They weren't even supposed to be with him on this mission to build a case against their mother's killer. Add a dog to the mix, and the situation took on a comic-opera tone.

Then Amanda cajoled, "I think he wants to be with us." She put her face to the dog's and he kissed her from chin to hairline. Paul stuck his face in between them and got the same treatment.

Jack opened his mouth to plead for reason, but knew that was never an arguing point with little children. And his own case for logic was eroded by the sound of Amanda's and Paul's laughter. It was loud and riotous and he hadn't heard it in a long time.

Jack squatted down in front of the dog. Apparently realizing Jack was the one to whom he should make his case, the puppy shook off the children and leaped on him with two remarkably big front paws.

Caught off balance, Jack fell backward and the puppy came with him, standing on his chest and kissing him enthusiastically. The children piled on, laughing.

Cal leaned over him. "Don't worry about a thing, Jack," she encouraged. "We can cope. I'll go to the store right now and buy everything you need for him."

"Have you ever had a dog?" he asked her, his voice strangled by the many legs standing on his chest.

"A Chihuahua," she replied. "About…thirty years ago."

A Chihuahua.

Thirty years ago.

If he was still a praying man, he'd start now.

KAY SIPPED at a paper cup of coffee and waited for directory assistance to find Jack Keaton's telephone number. He hadn't been in Maple Hill long enough to be listed in the phone book.

Things were quiet in the *Mirror*'s office at 7:45 a.m. Haley wouldn't be arriving until nine o'clock, and Jed Warton, who sold advertising, was probably already calling on clients. Priss Adams, who did office work and sold subscriptions as part of the high school's work experience program, wasn't expected until early afternoon.

"I'm sorry," a polite voice said on the other end of the line. "At the customer's request, that number is unlisted."

"Thank you." Kay hung up the phone, then opened the computer's subscriber databank, wondering if Keaton received the *Mirror*. He did! She jotted down his address in her notebook and glanced at the clock. Technically, it was too early to visit, but if she didn't do it now, he'd be off to work, and he might be less willing to talk on the job. The fact that he'd disappeared right after the rescue yesterday proved he was either shy or modest.

She checked her purse for her camera, dropped her notebook and pen inside, then hurried out to her car.

Maple Hill was just beginning to stir. The *Mirror*'s office faced a common around which most of the business in town was conducted. Many buildings left over from the eighteenth century remained shoulder to shoulder with newer construction built to look period appropriate. The town had been founded in 1702 and had a population of just over four thousand.

On the square was a bronze statue of Caleb and Elizabeth Drake, who'd fought off the British. Near them was a pole with an American flag waving proudly above an old colonial flag with thirteen stars in a circle, representing the original colonies. Globed streetlights stood around the common, which was surrounded by a low stone wall.

Kay made a superhuman effort not to be distracted by the heavenly aromas from the bakery as she went to her cyber green VW Beetle.

She was intercepted by her cousin Charlie.

Kay was a little surprised to see her. Charlene Florio taught English literature at Maple Hill High School and should have been starting first period by now on this first day of school. She looked happy.

"Hi," Charlie said breathlessly. She had long, wavy, carrot-red hair—too long for her weight, Kay had always thought, but she loved her dearly and would never tell her that. Freckles stood out on her plump-cheeked face. Her eyes were soft brown under eyebrows she never darkened and lashes she never made the most of. Her warm and open personality showed through, though, in a cheerful smile. "We're starting an hour late this morning, giving kids time to find their lockers and homerooms. Thought I'd take fifteen minutes to go to the low-carb store. I'm bringing a cheesecake to Aunt Agnes's tonight. You'll be surprised at how good it is!"

"Great. Were you able to talk Rachel out of making garlic and onion pasta?"

Rachel, also a cousin, was a nurse and devoted to a low-fat diet. She and Charlie were always at odds over what and how much to eat. Considering Rachel was forty, ten years older than Charlie, and still looked spectacular, Kay would have leaned in her favor if she ever considered watching what she ate. Fortunately, so far, it didn't seem to matter. She chased all over town for her work, put in long hours and was remodeling an old saltbox in her spare time. She never gained an ounce, though everyone she knew was happy to tell her that her bad habits would catch up with her one day.

"I didn't even try." With a prayerful look to heaven, Charlie added, "You know how she is. I'll just eat it and keep my mouth shut."

"Won't that make eating difficult?"

Charlie groaned. "You and your literal sense of humor. You'd think a brilliant journalist could come up with better stuff. Off on a story?" Her life was filled with teenagers, preparing classes, grading papers and little else. She considered Kay's life exciting.

Kay had tried to enlighten her on that score, but to no avail. Usually, her job was about council meetings, birth-and-death records and the police blotter, seldom exciting in Maple Hill.

"I'm trying to get a picture of the man who saved little Misty O'Neil yesterday. According to Haley, it's somebody named Jack Keaton."

"I heard about that. Everybody's talking about him this morning. You were there?"

"Yes. I was covering the celebration for the paper. I was pulling my boots off to jump in when this man came flying out of nowhere and went in after her."

Charlie's gaze narrowed on Kay. "And…you're all right?"

Kay pretended not to understand the question. But Charlie was used to dealing with teenagers. Nothing fooled her. "You know what I mean. It reminded you of Betsy and upset you, didn't it?"

"Betsy didn't drown, she was kidnapped." She tried to sound unaffected and in control. She thought it worked. "Not the same thing at all."

"No, but anything involving little girls in danger upsets you."

"Little girls in danger should upset everyone!"

Charlie nodded. "So, you don't want to talk about it."

"No." That would never have worked with Rachel, but Charlie was more respectful of Kay's space. "And why weren't *you* at the picnic? You promised to stop hiding at home and start getting out more."

"I… I…" Charlie stammered for a moment, then pulled herself together. "I was busy packing up my stuff in the guest-room closet, if you must know, so that Rachel can have more room. For someone who wears a uniform to work, she certainly has a lot of clothes."

Rachel had recently left her husband, a Maple Hill police officer, and moved in with Charlie. Rachel was grateful for the place to live, but privately complained to Kay about Charlie's relaxed approach to housekeeping and the kind of food she bought for her low-carb diet.

"There's no such thing as sharing a food budget," Rachel had said the last time Kay had seen her at their Monday-night dinners at their aunt's apartment. Because of the Labor Day holiday, this week's dinner was tonight—Tuesday. "So each of us spends more than we should because there's her food and my food. That's so wasteful."

"Rachel, if it works..." She'd begun to argue, then smiled at Rachel's impenetrable logic and stopped trying to explain. Her cousin was a nurse with a scientific turn of mind. She would never see sense in the thought processes of a literature freak or a reporter-cum-frustrated novelist.

"Maybe Jack Keaton is on the run," Charlie suggested in a quiet voice. "That's a common theme in stories of rescue where the hero is trying to keep a low profile because he's escaped from prison or is on the run from killers. Forced to rescue a child or a woman, he ends up in the public eye—the very thing he dreads."

"Hmm. I doubt it'd be anything that exciting in this town, but you never know. See you tonight."

"Okay. I'll have good news."

Kay had been about to slip into the car, but straightened again. "What kind of good news?"

"I'll tell you tonight."

"But I'll worry."

"No, you won't. You're always so focused on your work. And anyway, I said *good* news. Nothing to worry about in *good* news." And Charlie took off down the street, generous hips swaying under the hem of a big loose sweater pulled down over a long skirt.

JACK KEATON'S neighborhood was located on the east end of downtown in an old residential area lined with trees. Their leaves were just beginning to turn color, the comblike ash leaves yellow tipped, the sumac's dipped in red, and the giant maple leaves were just lightening to gold. Soon the street would be a riot of color, and people would come from all over the county to look at the picturesque old houses with their front porch tableaux of scarecrows and leaf-stuffed figures surrounded by gourds and squash. In the magnificent embrace of the surrounding trees in their autumn dress, it was powerful stuff.

Kay parked a few houses back and across the street from Jack's address. A big older model blue truck, and a little red American midsize car stood in the driveway. She took that as proof that he was still at home. She was gathering up her things, mentally preparing what she would say, when the front door opened and a loose-limbed black dog shot out of the house. With great strength and considerable speed, it headed for a small woods at the end of the block. A long leash was attached to the dog's collar, the other end of it held firmly in the hand of Kay's quarry. She wasn't sure she recognized his features, but the slight limp in an otherwise graceful stride was familiar.

The dog dragged Keaton to the middle of the fortunately quiet street, headed for the trees. Keaton shouted an order the dog ignored, then shouted it again, planting his feet and pulling on the leash so that the dog was forced to stop. When the dog turned to look, Keaton said firmly, "Buster! Come!" and slapped his knee.

The dog interpreted that as, "Leap on me and grab my pant leg."

"No! Down!"

Kay, hanging back, wanted to tell Keaton that "Down!" was for "lie down" and the wrong command, but she was sure that would do her mission here no good. She waited. He pulled in all the leash's slack so that the dog had no choice but to stay with him, and led him toward the woods.

When man and dog came out a few moments later, the dog was leaping in the air, in pursuit of a drifting leaf. Keaton smiled at his antics. He looked as though he didn't want to, but couldn't help himself.

"Good morning," she said cheerfully.

Keaton looked up and Kay was struck by the perfect symmetry of his face. He had straight, dark gold eyebrows over bourbon-brown eyes, a strong straight nose separating subtle cheekbones and a pleasant mouth with a thin upper lip. His hair was dark blond and closely cropped.

Those handsome features were sharpened by a jawline that spoke of pain or unresolved anger.

She offered her hand with a little trepidation. "I'm Kathleen Florio," she said, "with the *Maple Hill Mirror.*"

He gave her a firm, brief handshake. "Good morning."

She sensed his withdrawal instantly. But, getting the story despite a subject's reticence was what good reporting was all about. "I was hoping I could talk to you about your rescue of the little girl at the lake yesterday."

He shook his head once. "Nothing newsworthy, really. She's wanted swimming lessons, her parents couldn't afford them, and when she saw the lake, it was more than she could resist. But, staying afloat, like most things in life, was harder than she thought. I saw her and went in after her."

Kay dug into her purse for her pen and notebook. He headed for the house. She stayed with him, making notes. "See, now, Mr. Keaton? Her wanting swimming lessons gives the whole story that personal touch that *is* newsworthy. How did you know all that? Are you a friend of the family?"

He stopped with a long-suffering sigh. The dog whined at the interruption of his excursion. "Her father called me this morning to thank me. He explained how she happened to be in the water." His jaw tightened further. "You will have the grace to leave out that they couldn't afford…"

"Of course, I will," she assured him, a little annoyed that he asked. But she kept that annoyance to herself, feeling what little cooperation he had shown her slipping away. "Will you let me get a photograph?" She was pulling out her camera as she spoke.

"No." The word was quietly spoken but in a tone that suggested no negotiation. He started away, and she pleaded, "Mr. Keaton. People love their heroes. They…"

He came back over the few feet that separated them and said sharply, "People have 138,000 heroes in Iraq. They risk death every day. Go take their pictures."

The journalist in her wanted a detailed explanation for that personal reaction. The novelist in her made them up. He'd lost someone there. He'd *been* there.

"You're absolutely right," she agreed. "Reporters are risking their lives right beside them to make sure the whole world knows what's going on there. I'm just reminding the people in *our* community that we have heroes at home, too."

"Then put Randy Stanton's picture in the paper. He's the one who really saved Misty's life."

"I intend to. But if you hadn't gone in to get her, he wouldn't have been able to bring her back."

"No picture." The dog strained against Keaton's tight hold on the leash and Keaton let him run to the end of it to inspect a windblown candy wrapper.

"Okay." She put the camera back in her purse. "Then, can you tell me a little bit about yourself? I know you're new to Maple Hill. Your neighbors would be interested in…"

"No."

There were times when simply keeping your cool was what good reporting was all about.

"All right, then," she said with a civil smile. It was the best she could do. "Thank you for your time. I…" Her wish that he have a good day was aborted when the dog spotted another spiraling leaf and went in pursuit. She watched in fascination as the leaf made a circular flight around her body, encompassed Keaton's and turned again. The dog had her and his master bound tightly together by his leash in a matter of seconds, Keaton's knees to the middle of her thighs.

Kay instinctively grabbed his arm as they rocked precariously. Her fingers made contact with warmth and muscle that caused a weird little fluttering awareness in her chest.

JACK HAD KNOWN he was going to pay for that moment of weakness in succumbing to Buster's charm. He just hadn't expected it to be so soon. He was tied to the nosy reporter so tightly that he could feel softness and curves and her anxious indrawn breath. Her breasts pushed into his rib cage then retreated as she tried to fight their confinement.

Her hand bit into his arm for balance. He held on to hers to steady her and tried to encourage the dog to retreat while he unwound the leash. He knew it was hopeless, even while he did it.

"I'm sorry," he said. His life had once precluded body-to-body contact with any woman except Julia, but here he was, literally bound to a woman so that he could feel everything she possessed in close contact with everything he owned.

It was...unsettling.

He guessed his body reacted to the almost two years of celibacy. The fact that he'd been a man of God didn't mean he hadn't been very much a man on his own terms.

Still, that part of his life died with Julia. His reaction was a surprise.

He reached around the woman to put the leash in his other hand and encouraged Buster to retrace his steps. The distance the reporter was trying to keep from him made that difficult.

He drew a steadying breath—not a good idea because those breasts bumped against his ribs again—and put a gentle hand to the back of her right shoulder. "You'll have to move in," he said, "or I won't be able to get the leash around us."

"Okay." She took that well, if with an unflattering lack of enthusiasm. She drew closer, both arms curled up between them, her head bent so she wouldn't have to look at him. That made her forehead touch his chest.

He worked as quickly as he could, turning her with him as he moved clockwise and unwound the leash the other way. The moment they were free, she backed up a few steps, expelled a breath, and nervously ran a hand over her hair. It was short and dark with curls that couldn't decide which way to go. Some curled under in glossy bubbles and others stuck up as though she'd slept on them wrong. Since the effect was attractive he guessed it was deliberate. Wary brown eyes looked him over.

She wore a pale yellow sweater over a short black skirt, black stockings on trim legs disappearing into big black shoes. Really ugly shoes that looked like doorstops.

He hadn't studied a woman this closely in a long time. He couldn't wait to get rid of her. The last thing he needed was someone telling the world, or even just Maple Hill, all about him. He didn't need Milford figuring him out before he was able to build a case against him.

Jack had arrived six weeks ago only to discover that the Milfords had left on a cruise. They were due back any day. Jack didn't want Milford reading a headline that said a widowed minister just back from Iraq had left Vermont for Maple Hill. Julia's boss had figured out that *she* had his number. If he read that Jack Keaton was in town, he might draw the obvious conclusion that Jack had come after him. Jack didn't want to have to follow him again.

"Just stay out of my life, Miss…?" He couldn't remember her name. And he heard his own words in some surprise because that hadn't been what he'd intended to say. He'd wanted to put her off, but not that harshly.

"Florio," she provided coolly. "And I wanted your photograph for my story, Mr. Keaton, not my name on your checkbook." She gave him a dark look then ruffled the dog's ears. "And to make Buster stop jumping up on people, the command is *Off!* not *Down! Down* is to make him lie down."

"Thank you, Barbara Woodhouse." She didn't look at all like the deceased doyenne of dog training, but he wished she'd mind her own business.

She shrugged away his sarcastic reply. "I just thought you might want to get him under control before you no longer can. He looks like a field Lab, not a show dog."

Field Lab? He didn't know the difference. She seemed to see that and was happy to straighten him out.

"My father had Labs all the time I was growing up. Field Labs aren't for showing, they're the dogs that go hunting with you. They have to run and swim, so they're bigger, stronger." She gave him a small smile he didn't understand. "And they read your mind, so you'd better be careful."

He hated to keep her there another minute, but he had to know what she implied. "What do you mean by that?"

"You're obviously a very…private person. But dogs are amazingly intuitive—Labs, particularly. This dog's going to figure you out. I just thought you might want to be prepared for that. Have a good day, Mr. Keaton."

He didn't know what to say to that and simply stood there while she walked away. He hated his speechlessness. He'd always been praised for his sermons, stood on the pulpit with ease and could talk off-the-cuff about whatever the current moral challenge was. Of course, being tied body to body with a strange woman wasn't exactly a pulpit situation.

Buster galloped ahead of him up the walkway, apparently already happy to be home. "I know dogs are supposed to be babe magnets," Jack told him, "but you don't have to do that here, okay? Just protect the house and the kids and put your head on my knee when I'm feeling lonely. The only thing in my future is settling the score with Milford, then raising my children. And you, too, if you promise not to eat my truck."

"When do we get to walk him, Dad?" Paul asked fifteen minutes later. He and Amanda sat opposite each other, eating cereal at the small table in the middle of the vast kitchen. Jack had rented this house because Julia had always loved a big kitchen, insisting that the children could play in it while she prepared meals and that togetherness was good for a family.

He stopped thinking about that before the darkness took control of him again.

"Maybe when Buster understands his commands. He's too big and strong for you to handle if he won't listen to you."

Buster had already found his food and water bowls in a corner of the kitchen and was eating heartily.

Cal watched him. "The bag said two and a half to three and a quarter cups for twenty-six to fifty pounds. I gave him three. You think that's about right?"

"Sounds good to me."

"Eggs and bacon, or cereal for you?"

Not only had he been fortunate to find a rental house with a big kitchen, but he'd also been lucky to meet a recently widowed grandmother whose children and grandchildren were all at the other end of the country. While Cal wanted to maintain her own residence, she'd told him at their one-and-only interview that she could be at the house by 7:00 a.m. and could stay as late as he needed her. He'd hired her on the spot.

It wasn't Providence, he knew. Providence hadn't given a rip about him in a long time. It was simple good fortune.

"Eggs and bacon sound good. I'm going to finish that meeting room in the rectory today."

Cal laughed. "You'll need your strength to deal with Father Chabot."

"How come you call him 'father'?" Amanda sported a milk mustache and a little flowered apron Cal had put on her over her school clothes.

"Because he's a priest," Jack replied. "He takes care of a church."

"But…didn't we used to have a church?" she asked.

"Yes, we did."

"But people didn't call you father, did they?"

"Father Chabot is Catholic. That's what Catholic people call their priests instead of reverend or pastor."

She seemed to consider that answer acceptable. He was relieved. In her childish innocence, she had a way of asking questions that went deeper than his ability to answer.

"Are we gonna have a church again?" Paul hardly remembered before Jack went to Iraq, but he always provided backup to Amanda's interrogations.

"No," Jack replied simply. "I'm a housepainter for now."

"How come?"

"Because I like it."

"I think it's cause Mommy's not here," Amanda told Paul.

"Well, why don't we call her and tell her to come home?" Paul dropped his spoon into his half-empty cereal bowl. "I *want* her to come back."

Jack had explained to his son a dozen times that his mother couldn't return, but it was hard to blame him for failing to understand what even adults resisted.

Amanda, who had stopped asking for her mother about the third time Jack had explained, said, "She can't, Paulie. I told you. She's gone forever. Forever."

Paul began to cry.

Jack would have given anything to be able to leave the table, but his loss of faith hadn't affected his love for his children and his sense of responsibility. Jack beckoned his son, who came to wrap his arms around him and climb into his lap.

"Mommy can't come back," he said. It was always hard to find that tone of voice that was gentle but held out no hope. "I know you love her and you miss her. She loves you and misses you, too, but she's gone to heaven and she can't come back. She's in your heart, though."

Jack put his hand over Paul's delicate little rib cage. "She'll always be there. You can think about her, and tell her all the things you'd tell her if she was here."

"How can you talk to somebody who isn't there?"

"She's there. You just can't see her."

"I don't get it."

Jack held him tightly. "I know. It's very hard to get. What if you told *me* the things you wanted to tell her?"

Paul thought about that, then ran the back of his hand across his nose. Jack handed him his napkin.

"Okay," Paul sighed. "But I'd really like to *see* her."

Amen, to that. "Right. But that can't happen, so we have to live with things the way they are."

Paul smiled suddenly, unexpectedly. "Amanda said she thinks Mommy sent Buster."

Amanda looked at Jack, waiting for a reaction. He knew that in the intuitive way of children, she knew something had changed in her father since her mother's death, but she wasn't sure what. Jack thought she suspected it had something to do with God and prayer, but her young mind couldn't analyze it.

He encouraged the children to say their prayers, certain Julia would want that, but where he'd once talked to them all the time about the wonders of God's universe, he never did that anymore.

"I think she's right," Jack replied. "I think that's Mommy's way of talking to you."

Paul smiled at Buster, who gobbled up the last bite of food. "That's kinda neat," he said.

"Yes, it is. If you're finished with breakfast, why don't you go brush your teeth. Mrs. Whitcomb's going to be here in ten minutes." Jackie, his boss's wife, had agreed to come for Paul every morning and deliver him to preschool along with her twin sons. Cal would drive Amanda to kindergarten, then pick up both children at noon, though Jack intended to take her himself today.

Paul scampered off, grief diverted, at least for now, by the large black puppy.

All right. Maybe taking the dog in had been a good move after all.

Jack scanned the *Boston Globe* headlines while Amanda carried her empty bowl to the sink.

"Daddy?" she said.

"Yeah?"

"I think Buster's still hungry."

"He got three cups," he answered absently, running through headlines, trying to get a sense of the world's condition before he went to work. "Cal followed the directions on the bag of dog food."

"Okay," she said in a skeptical tone, "but he's trying to eat the bowl."

CHAPTER THREE

AGNES FLORIO was tall and slender at eighty-three years old. She had her hair colored light auburn once a month at Clea's Beauty Shop, applied makeup every morning whether she left the apartment or not, insisting that tips learned from Perc Westmore himself, the famous master of makeup for film stars, should not be wasted.

She wore pink because Lauren Bacall had told her it did a lot for her complexion. That had been on the set of *Key Largo* in 1948. A signed publicity still from that Bogart and Bacall film had pride of place on the mantel in her living room. She'd been a script girl for a major Hollywood studio from the forties through the seventies. Signed photos of the film stars from the period and memorabilia from their movies decorated the walls of her apartment.

It was rumored that she had Marlon Brando's motorcycle from *The Wild Ones*, but Kay knew that wasn't true. She'd sold it to a collector when Kay was just a child.

In those days, Agnes flew into Maple Hill from Hollywood every summer for the yearly Florio family reunion. She was Kay's father's older sister and always arrived with exotic gifts and stories of love affairs and wild goings-on that Kay and her cousins had found so exciting. She'd fussed over her nieces, driven them to Boston shopping and to take in the theater. They'd stayed overnight at the Ritz-Carlton and marveled at the life she knew.

Then she'd fly back to some faraway movie set and summer settled back into its comfortable but far less dramatic routines of long, lazy days punctuated by clambakes on the beach on Sundays. Rachel was old enough to date, while Charlie and Kay only talked about boys and imagined futures of great romance.

Now Agnes suffered from arthritis, a mild heart condition and growing dementia. As their resident medical expert, Rachel took Agnes to all her doctor's appointments, and filled her weekly pillbox. Kay and Charlie shared the duties of running her errands and getting her groceries. The three of them met at Agnes's every Monday night to prepare dinner and catch up on each other's lives. She was the oldest but the last living member of the Florio siblings.

Agnes always loved a dinner party, and had thrown a few in her day that had made the pages of *Variety*. When the cousins arrived on Monday she always had the table set as though she expected royalty.

Tonight, she'd put her best linens on the apartment's small, round table, used the Limoges table settings she'd bought while working on *An American in Paris*, the Lalique wineglasses that had been a gift from Lana Turner.

The silver was the set that had been used in *Guess Who's Coming to Dinner?*

When Kay arrived, Rachel already stood at the counter cooking, elegant in lavender fleece. Her pale blond hair and blue eyes were the legacy of her Norwegian mother. She worked over onions and garlic on a chopping sheet, while olive oil warmed in a deep frying pan. Kay hugged her aunt, who poured water into glasses in the corridor kitchen.

"Have I ever told you," Agnes asked with a cool hand to Kay's cheek, "how much you remind me of Jean Simmons? Except that she was more petite."

She told her that every time she saw her. "Yes, you have," she replied, "and I'm very flattered."

"She was married to Stewart Granger, you know."

"Yes, I do."

"And you're not married to anyone." That little jibe marked one of Agnes's lucid and witty moments.

"I noticed that," Kay replied. Every time one of those moments happened, she hoped it meant a reversal of the effects of old age and a return of the familiar Agnes. But, of course, it didn't. Kay turned away from the sadness of the thought and put her spinach salad in the refrigerator. "But if he was married to her, he couldn't very well be married to me, could he? In fact, hasn't he gone to his reward?"

"I know. I just want you to have someone when I go to *mine.*"

"You can relax, Aunt Agnes. I'm not letting you go anywhere."

A quick knock sounded on the door and Charlie let herself in, a pink cake box on the flat of her hand. "Hi, guys!" she called cheerfully. Her cheeks were pink, her wild hair all over the place. "What a day! Starting a Chaucer unit in my classes, and being named the school's liaison with the Fall Festival Committee shouldn't happen to anyone in the same day."

The Fall Festival was another of Maple Hill's annual celebrations and the one Kay loved the most. It was an excuse for pumpkin carving contests for the children, pumpkin recipe contests for the adults and other food, crafts and games for everyone.

"Hi, Charlie!" Rachel called from the kitchen. "What'd you bring?"

"Low-carb cheesecake," Charlie replied, stopping to hug Agnes on her way to the kitchen. She opened the refrigerator door and groaned at the filled shelves. Kay had just been shopping for Agnes two days ago. Charlie balanced the box carefully on top of Kay's salad.

"How can cheesecake be low carb?" Rachel asked.

Charlie rolled her eyes at Kay. "Because it's made with cheese and cream and a sugar alcohol sweetener," she replied patiently. "And has no crust."

"What's the fat content?"

"High."

"You're clogging your arteries."

"Rachel, please," Charlie said. "I'm going to eat your pasta without beating you up about it. You can have a small piece of my cheesecake."

Rachel tossed the chopped garlic and onions into the olive oil. The aroma was wonderful. Then she checked the boiling pan of water and tossed in a pound of angel-hair pasta. "Okay, okay. It's just hard to respect a diet where a piece of cake is legal and a bagel isn't."

Charlie swung on her, growing impatient. "That's not what I said. I said a piece of cake had less grams of carbohydrates than a bagel. I don't intend to eat either one."

Rachel cast a glance up and down Charlie's body in the oversize sweater and skirt. "How much have you lost so far."

"Twenty pounds," Charlie said smiling. "I'm very encouraged."

Rachel nodded, stirring the contents of the frying pan with a wooden spoon. "That's very good. But you should have your cholesterol checked when you get a chance."

"I know. You've told me before."

"What's your surprise?" Kay asked Charlie, desperate to change the subject before her cousins came to blows. She sometimes wondered how mankind could ever hope for world peace when two women could get hostile over what to eat.

Charlie beamed. "I've been named Assistant Principal. With a pay raise, and everything."

Feminine squeals filled the small kitchen. Even Rachel turned from her cooking to wrap Charlie in a hug. "Congratulations! That's wonderful, Charlene!"

"You deserve it, darling." Agnes took Rachel's place. "Will you still have time to do my shopping?"

"Oh, I'll be much too important." Giving her long hair a toss, Charlie assumed an air of busyness. "Kay and Rachel will have to do everything. I'm sure parents will want to consult me on their children's futures, and the school board will want to know what I think on all sorts of issues. The White House may even name me to a…"

"Whoa!" Kay shouted, flicking water into her face.

Charlie stopped and pretended to pull herself together. "Okay. I'm all right now. I got a little drunk with power there, but I'm back. Of course I can do your shopping, Aunt Agnes." She wrapped Kay in her sturdy embrace. "But, it's so cool, isn't it?"

"It's very cool." Kay was delighted for her. Charlie was a dedicated teacher, and one of the hardest-working women she knew. "Does it mean you have to put in more hours?"

"I think so. I'll be a sort of liaison between the school and the parents, and it's my job to make sure every student feels welcome and comfortable. I'll just have to get a little better organized."

"You'll have to get a *lot* better organized," Rachel corrected. "Sounds like a big job."

Charlie made a strangling motion behind Rachel as Rachel drained the pasta. Kay covered a giggle with her hand. Timing of dinner was now critical, so they all worked to put things on the table while Rachel tossed the drained pasta into the sautéeing garlic and onions.

Over dinner, Rachel, who'd been on duty at the hospital the previous afternoon, talked about Misty O'Neil.

"No ill effects?" Kay asked in surprise.

Rachel shook her head. "None at all. Doctor Dawson was on call and she said it was remarkable. It helped that Misty was brought out of the water right away, and that Randy Stanton got her breathing so quickly. There was no sign that she'd been deprived of oxygen."

"Happy endings are such a miracle." Charlie sprinkled more fresh Parmesan on her pasta.

That had been a lucky happy ending for little Misty, Kay thought. Though she resisted the thought that followed, it formed anyway and knocked on her brain for attention. Betsy hadn't been so lucky. Betsy hadn't gotten a miracle.

Kay's brain played a little joke on her lately whenever she got to thinking about Betsy. It made her wonder what her little sister would look like now, at twenty-four. She'd been a beautiful child, so undoubtedly, she'd be a beautiful young woman. She'd had their mother's vivacious personality and their father's auburn hair. She could have been an actress and a television personality like their mother.

Then Kay wondered what things she and Betsy might be doing together if her sister had lived. She imagined shopping with a grown-up Betsy, meeting for lunch, planning vacations, talking about men.

"Stop it!" Rachel said sharply, bringing Kay out of her thoughts.

Kay turned to her in surprise. "Stop what?"

"Thinking about Betsy. It's written all over you. It

wasn't your fault she was kidnapped. You are not responsible, end of story. You were eight years old, for God's sake. She was with you, but it wasn't your fault. If you're going to torture yourself for the rest of your life over every little girl that gets hurt or…or…disappears, you're going to go insane. So, stop it."

Kay wondered sometimes if she wasn't already insane. How could one be expected to go on after such a horrendous event? And yet you *were* expected to. Kay hadn't died, so she just had to keep going, day after day, wondering if anything would be different today if she'd been holding Betsy's hand in the candy store, if she'd heard something when she'd been picking out her candy and turned around, if Betsy had called out and gotten Kay's attention when the man grabbed her.

But that served no purpose because time ticked relentlessly forward and there was no going back.

Rachel pointed her fork at Kay's plate. "You're letting my pasta congeal."

Kay knew Rachel's heart was in the right place. She saw suffering and death every day and simply had a different perception of it than other people. She probably had to or she wouldn't be able to do her work.

But there'd been times when Kay would have killed for an embrace from her, an expression of sympathy. She'd been like a big sister to Kay, but the summer after Betsy was lost, Rachel had told a suffering nine-year-old that it had been an awful thing but life went on and she had to, too. Rachel had been twenty-three and already married to Gib Whittier.

Charlie had cried with Kay, but then Betsy hadn't been her sister. Charlie had been able to go off to the movies with friends or go to the lake. Kay's mother sent her along with Charlie a few times, or made other play dates for her, and though Kay went without complaint and did what she was expected to do, an image of Betsy was always there behind her eyes the moment the distraction was over.

The family had gone for counseling, and Kay had had sessions alone. Eventually, a more adult perspective on the situation had helped her survive her day-to-day life, but when all was said and done, she still felt responsible. Even when the vagrant who'd committed the crime had been found and sent to prison for life, she remained convinced that it had all been her fault. And she doubted that anything would ever change that for her.

That was why she remained single. She knew she'd never be able to be a mother and not be driven insane by all the awful possibilities that could befall a child. Inflicting a childless future on a husband didn't seem fair. And, conversely, she didn't want a man who didn't want children. She'd observed that most men who were fathers were by necessity more fun, more open, less rigid. She could allow that that wasn't entirely reasonable, but so little in life seemed to be.

"Have you seen Gib this week?" Charlie asked. Kay suspected the diversion was to get the heat off Kay and bring up something that would quiet her usually aggressive cousin.

"He's always around," Rachel replied, stabbing her fork into her salad. "But, no. I haven't talked to him."

"Don't you think you should?" Kay suggested. "The two of you have a lot of time and love invested in your marriage, two brilliant children…"

"Apparently he considered his investment worth risking." Picking up the bottle of Riesling, Rachel added more wine to everyone's glass. "That's what happens when you gamble. Sometimes you lose everything."

"Rache, this isn't just money," Charlie said reasonably. "This is your marriage, the stability of your children, the rest of your life!"

"The kids are fine."

That claim appeared to be in dispute when Rachel downed half the contents of her glass in one swallow, and glowered moodily at nothing. "They understand. Jerry's on my side."

Jerry was nineteen and an art student at New York University.

Kay was able to guess what she didn't add. Rachel and Gib's twenty-one-year-old daughter Marissa was in her last year at Dartmouth on a scholarship. She was beautiful and smart and a real daddy's girl. Charlie couldn't seem to help saying the obvious aloud.

"Marissa's on Gib's side?"

Instead of being offended that Charlie had said the words, Rachel nodded bleakly. When she didn't take the opportunity to find fault with Charlie, it meant she was worried.

Kay put a comforting hand on Rachel's arm. "She'll come around. All girls defend their fathers. It's some basic, electra complex. And all girls fight with their mothers. How can you have lived within viewing distance of my mother and me and not accept that?"

Rachel examined her half-empty glass. "When Marissa told me how she felt, I asked her how she could side with Gib when he'd been unfaithful to me." She downed it and put the glass down precisely on a woven circle in the lace tablecloth. "She said she wasn't surprised that he went somewhere else for love and affection because I'm always such a bitch."

Charlie opened her mouth to speak. Fearing she intended to agree with Marissa, Kay sent her a silencing glare. Charlie kept eating.

"Gib was a rat to turn to Princess Barbie," Kay said sympathetically. Barbara Grand, Rachel's former neighbor, was so called because she held her head as though she wore a crown. It didn't hurt that she'd been a dancer, and had a body that made everyone take a second look—men and women alike. "But I think the whole situation was one of those things where both of you were under a lot of pressure and probably not at your most patient or logical."

Rachel turned to Kay with hurt and anger in her eyes. "You're saying I'm partially to blame?"

Kay knew Rachel's fierce look. She met it intrepidly.

"I'm saying—and I apologize in advance for the cliché—there are two sides to every story. At the same time you were working full-time and getting your degree and only four hours sleep a night, Gib was on the gnarly Bosworth case and doing all that domestic violence training. He probably wasn't getting much rest, either, and had a lot of ugly things on his mind."

"I had a lot on my mind and I wasn't unfaithful to *him*."

"Women stand alone better than men do. And while you were working yourself ragged, his emotions were probably being beaten down by the ugly details of that case, and then the nature of the training he was doing. The photos and the facts of what they work with are depressing. I covered his class for the paper."

The Bosworth case had involved a middle-aged drug addict confined to a wheelchair several years ago after an automobile accident. Susan Bosworth had been asked to leave every care facility in the county at one time or another for her abusive and nonconformist attitude and at the time of her death, was being looked after by a husband and wife, who'd been neglecting her completely and collecting her disability and a small stipend from her sister to support their own drug habits. A couple of fishermen found Bosworth in the lake, tied to her wheelchair, a victim of her caretaker's complete disinterest and neglect except for what her money could provide them. Gib had responded to the 911 call and had worked the case.

"I was there when he came home at night," Rachel said.

"With your nose in a book and all your own anxieties on the surface. He needed someone to comfort him and in a weak moment…"

"I don't need a man who has weak moments." Rachel began gathering plates.

Kay tried to hold her in place, but felt her resistance. "He was wrong. There's no doubt about it. I just wonder if talking to him about it would be such a bad thing. Explain how you feel, listen to his…"

"It *would* be a bad thing," Rachel interrupted, "because if he said something to annoy me, I'd beat him with his own baton." Drawing her arm away, Rachel carried the stack of plates to the sink.

Charlie focused on helping herself to more salad.

"Tell us about your novel, Kay," Agnes said. She leaned forward interestedly, apparently unaware that there'd been conflict at her table. The drifting nature of senility wasn't all bad, Kay thought.

Kay stood on the pretext of helping Rachel. She hated to talk about her novel. It had been her reason for changing her life a year ago, for moving to Maple Hill to be near her cousins and her aunt, to observe and record insightful things as a reporter, and to learn about real life as a human being. She'd always felt the events of her own life had been so out of the ordinary that they didn't qualify as a basis for popular fiction.

"Oh, it's going," she said, glancing apologetically at Charlie, who looked up at yet another cliché. "But not very quickly. I don't understand people as well as I thought I did. And when I try to put words into their mouths, they sound forced and ridiculous."

Charlie threatened her with her fork when she reached for her plate. "Haven't you been listening to our conversation? Forced and ridiculous is pretty common when people talk."

Kay sighed and put down the plates she'd collected. "I want to write good Hemingway-Steinbeck dialog, Michener descriptions, create James Patterson plots. Instead, my stuff sounds a lot like *The Simpsons*."

"*The Simpsons* are very popular!" Rachel called from the kitchen. "Maybe you have something."

She was sure she didn't. Her fictional divorced woman who'd lost her baby and sent her husband away because she didn't know what to do with him was talking drivel and behaving even worse.

When Kay had gone home for lunch today, she'd deleted the last ten pages she'd written and was giving serious thought to excising a large portion of the three chapters that remained. She couldn't seem to understand her character, to gain any momentum in reeling out her life.

"You'll figure it all out, Kathleen." Agnes smiled sweetly at her. "You were always good at noticing what other people didn't see. You were the one who first suspected that something had happened to Charlie, remember?"

Silence fell on the room as though a door had been closed and they were suddenly cut off from the rest of the world. Rachel froze near the table with the bowl of Parmesan and the salad dressing in her hands. Charlie paled, and Kay struggled to maintain a neutral expression.

She always hated it when someone learned about her abducted and murdered sister and made a big deal of it. It was a big deal, but someone else's attention on it only served to enlarge it and make the reality of it more unmanageable.

She'd always imagined it was the same when a girl was raped by her mother's boyfriend—the kind of awful, life-altering event you didn't want trotted out for all to discuss.

Charlie's father had been sickly all his life, and died of a heart attack when Charlie was ten. Aunt Sylvia, Charlie's mother, had gone from man to man for years after Uncle Joe died, trying to recapture what she'd had with him. One of the boyfriends, a trumpet player with a band in town for the summer, raped Charlie while her mother was at work the summer Charlie was fifteen.

Kay had been the one to notice the way Charlie had withdrawn, the way she would surface occasionally with the most miserable expression on her face, as if some horrible revelation was on the tip of her tongue, but never voiced.

Kay remembered telling her parents, then all the family got together to talk to Charlie. The man had been prosecuted and sent to jail, and the Florios had absorbed and dealt with another major blow.

Desperate to neutralize the charged atmosphere, Kay turned to Rachel. "Well, aren't you going to yell at her the way you yelled at me?"

Rachel didn't understand. "What?"

"Tell *her* to stop it."

"Oh. Right." Rachel pointed the salad dressing at Charlie. "Stop it, Charlie. It was not your fault. You are not responsible. End of story. If you're going to torture yourself every time the subject comes up, you're going to go insane. So stop it."

They all listened to Rachel's repeated lecture and Charlie was forced to smile.

"You just said that, Rachel, dear," Agnes admonished with concern in her eyes. "I'm sure I just heard you say that. You're beginning to repeat yourself."

Rachel laughed and went to lean over her aunt and hug her. "Yes, I am. And that's because no one ever listens to me the first time I order them around, so I usually have to do it twice, sometimes more often. Whipped cream on your cheesecake, Auntie?"

Agnes patted Rachel's cheek, her eyes sparkling. "Of course. And Irish Cream in my coffee."

Irish Cream in their coffee had become a ritual at these dinners. "Coming right up. Charlie, you want to cut your cheesecake, or do you trust me to handle it?"

Charlie grinned at her. "I'll do it. Just keep your carbohydrate-laden hands off of it."

"Oh, now, come on. Wasn't that the best pasta you've ever tasted?" Rachel put an arm around Charlie's shoulders and they walked together into the kitchen.

Kay watched them go and thought it was no wonder her novel sounded like some adult cartoon. When she was with her cousins and her aunt, she was living one.

WEDNESDAY AFTERNOON Father Charles Chabot looked around the now terra-cotta-colored meeting room with its stark white trim, and shook Jack's hand.

"Beautifully done," he praised. "I'm sure had the Sistine Chapel been painted without all that fuss, it would have looked a lot like this."

Jack appreciated the priest's sense of humor. Father Chabot had dropped in on him at various times throughout the day with a cup of coffee or a snack and stuck around to chat for a few minutes. He had a long repertoire of jokes, and a few relating to God that one had to be on good terms with Him to tell.

Now Jack was trying to leave for the day, but the priest seemed determined to learn some things about him.

"I understand you have two little children?"

Jack was surprised he knew that.

"My new housekeeper is a friend of Addy Fortin's," the priest explained, "who's the mother of…"

"My boss. Yes. Yes, I have. A boy and a girl."

"Ah. Widower?"

"Yes."

"Are you…seeing anyone?"

That seemed an odd question from a priest. Although

Jack remembered when he'd been in the prime of his pastoral work, he'd been known to match make.

"No, work and the children keep me pretty busy. Well, if you'll exc…"

"Because I have a list of eligible young women," the priest said, following him to the door, "that I'm matching up with a list of eligible young men."

Jack stopped on the top step. "I'm not Catholic, Father."

"It's an ecumenical world, my son." Father Chabot clapped him on the shoulder. "A good man is a good man in any religion. What are your interests?"

Jack smiled politely and glanced at his watch. "Right now, getting home for dinner. But, thank you, Father. I appreciate your concern about my social life. If I ever feel the need to see a good woman socially, I'll call you to set me up."

"You do that," the priest grinned. "eHarmony.com has nothing on me." It was amazing, Jack thought, to know a priest who claimed to have more influence among his flock than an online dating service.

Jack stopped at Perk Avenue for a double shot Americano on his way home. If he couldn't have Scotch, caffeine would have to do. Tonight after he put the children to bed, he was going to spend some time going over his notes on M & S Money Management. When Milford came home, Jack was going to need a reason to introduce himself, and getting some investment advice was the obvious way to do it.

The unfortunate truth was that, as a minister, he'd

never had anything to invest, so he knew little about it. He needed a book from the library, and to pay more attention to the financial section of the *Boston Globe*.

With those studious pursuits on his mind, he stepped aside as someone walked out of the coffee bar, not realizing it was Kay Florio until she spoke his name.

She wore the same dark skirt and stockings, the same doorstop shoes, but she'd pulled on a short, black leather jacket over her sweater, and he noticed a gloss in those odd in-and-out curls that he hadn't observed this morning. For a moment he was distracted by the movement in them as she spoke.

"Mr. Keaton," she said, smiling. "You've changed your mind about letting me take your photograph and you've tracked me down to tell me?"

He also saw something behind the smile, he thought; something he recognized, but couldn't define. Some subtle something told him she wasn't as collected inside as she appeared to be on the surface.

He didn't know if it was the old pastor in him, seeing into another soul, or if this was some personal connection he made because he used the same trick on the world. No one tried to pity you or commiserate with you if you looked as though you had it together.

He smiled back. "Nice try, Miss Florio, but no. Unless the fact that I have a weakness for very strong coffee would help your story? I'm going to have to work overtime to pay for my twice daily Americanos."

"Well." She seemed pleased about that. "I have just

the person to help you with that." She pivoted and swept a hand back toward the man who'd been following her out of the coffee bar. He was medium height, average build, dark hair and eyes—just an ordinary man with a coffee in his hand and a salesman's smile.

Jack recognized the face instantly, though the stranger sported a sweater and slacks rather than the three-piece suit he wore in the photo on the bulletin board in Jack's home office.

Jack's mouth went dry and he tasted metal. His heart punched the back of his rib cage.

"This gentleman," Kay Florio said brightly, "recently retired to Maple Hill, and after a month on a cruise, has decided he's had it with downtime. He's opening an office in Porter Building II next door to the *Mirror* and going back to work. Trust your money to him, and he can help you pay for those Americanos. Jack Keaton, I'd like you to meet Ron Milford."

CHAPTER FOUR

NOW CONFRONTED with the moment he'd awaited for months, Jack found himself frozen in surprise. He hadn't anticipated how hard it would be not to smash a fist into Milford's smiling face. A killing rage filled him as the man affably offered his hand. It was tanned and without blemish, not a working-man's hand. Jack willed his own fingers to stop trembling as he took it.

"Mr. Milford," he said, forcing a genial tone. His voice came out a little strained, he thought, but no one seemed to notice.

"Oh, please. Call me Ron. When you handle other people's money, you have to be on a first-name basis." Milford had an easy confidence Jack guessed was a natural result of knowing how to get what you wanted without bothersome moral boundaries.

"Keaton." Milford repeated the name thoughtfully. Jack watched him roll it over in his mind. Before Milford could think about it long enough to make the connection, Jack smiled and made himself relax. "No relation to the famous actor," he said. The success of his plan depended upon getting to know this man and learning the intimate details of his life and business. And the busybody reporter was handing him the opening he'd been looking for.

"It's a pleasure to meet you." Jack injected a little pulpit confidence into his voice. "Is there a 401K or something that'll make enough to allow me four-dollar coffee drinks a couple of times a day? On a house-painter's salary?"

Milford laughed and held up his own drink. "I understand. I have a weakness for double mochas. I guess the trick would be to invest in Perk Avenue so that every purchase you make comes back to you."

Jack knew the suggestion was made in jest, but he was getting into his role of eager money-management student. "I'm a humble tradesman, remember."

"There's a way to make money work for just about anyone," Milford assured him. "We just have to find the system that's best for you." He dug into a pocket and handed Jack a business card. "I'm having an open house a week from Thursday. There'll be an ad in the *Mirror*. Invitations have already gone out, but please consider yourself invited. I'll be talking about plans and making appointments."

"Great." Jack pocketed the card. "That sounds like what I've been looking for."

Milford smiled and shook his hand again. "Well, if you'll excuse us, Ms. Florio is interviewing me for an article. And much as I hate to be closed up in my office with a beautiful woman, it has to be done." He pretended an air of long-suffering, then smiled again. "I'll look for you at the open house."

"I'll be there," Jack promised firmly.

He drove home, unable to believe how beautifully the meeting with Milford had fallen into his lap. It was going to happen. After months of thinking and planning, he was actually going to get close to Milford and prove that he'd killed Julia.

He felt alternately jubilant then grimly determined. He decided to go with jubilation for tonight. There'd been so few reasons for celebration over the past two years. He was going to take the children for pizza and ice cream. They, of course, had no idea what he was up to, but he was sure they could use a break in their routines, also.

Five minutes later he pulled into the driveway and let himself into the house. He was surprised to find the kitchen empty, no aroma of dinner cooking, no sound of the television and the six-o'clock news Calpurnia usually watched while she worked.

There were no children running to greet him. There was a piece of paneling from the basement lying near the doorway to the living room, and a kitchen chair pulled away from the table. He couldn't imagine what that meant.

He walked into the living room. At first he was certain that the heaven he no longer believed in had somehow materialized before his eyes. There were white clouds all over the floor.

No. On closer inspection, he realized it was the guts of his sofa. Then he saw it, all three blue-and-gray roughly woven pillows on the floor. They were lifeless shells, their innards all over the carpet. It struck him that they were a weird metaphor for his own existence.

A few children's books were strewn around, all with teeth marks on them, and he found a teddy bear that looked as though it had been mauled by a lion. Cal's purse lay nearby, destroyed.

"Cal!" he shouted. "Hey! Guys?"

Calpurnia shouted from the top of the stairs. "Up here, Mr. Keaton!"

Jack took the steps two at a time and found Cal knocking on the bathroom door. She looked miserable, her usually maternal and serene expression vanished.

"I'm so sorry!" she said, turning to him. "I took the kids with me to get some things for dinner, and I thought he'd be all right if I closed him in the kitchen, so I got a piece of paneling from the basement and pushed it in front of the door with a kitchen chair to hold it in place." She made a self-deprecating face. "It never occurred to me he'd be able to move it, but he managed to knock over the chair and chew off enough of the paneling to worm his way through."

Jack was still having trouble making sense of everything. At least it was now clear that by *he* she meant Buster and not Paul.

Calpurnia closed her eyes and shook her head, still apologizing. "He's a tornado of destruction, Mr. Keaton, eating everything in his path. I'll buy you another sofa. I'll…"

He raised both hands to stop her. "Where *is* Buster?"

"Locked in the bathroom," she replied.

"You locked him in there?" The tub was probably safe, but there were all those edible cabinets, shower curtains, bath rug.

"No, Amanda locked herself and Paul and the dog in there and she refuses to come out. I've tried everything I can think of."

"Are the kids all right?" he asked.

"Physically, yes," she replied with a commiserating pat on his arm, "but they're very upset about the dog. They're sure you're going to send him to the animal shelter."

He drew a breath. Considering all he'd lost over the last couple of years, the sofa was negligible. He walked Calpurnia to the head of the stairs. "I have a Fall Festival meeting tonight. Forget fixing dinner and we'll go out for pizza."

Cal smiled wryly at him. "You have to buy. Buster ate my twenty, and I think some of my change."

"I'll replace it. Let me just talk to the kids…"

She blinked at him. "I was afraid when you saw the living room that I'd be done for good."

"I don't blame you for that, Cal. I'm the one who said the children could keep the dog. We'll have to get a crate for times when you have to leave him alone. We were just unprepared. That's nobody's fault."

She smiled, then she hugged him tightly. "I'll try to tidy up while you get the children out of the bathroom," she said, and started down the stairs.

He went to the door and knocked. "Amanda?"

A tearful, reluctant voice answered, "Yeah?"

"Buster's not going to the shelter. You can come out."

There was a moment's silence. "But…did you see the sofa?"

"He ate *all* of it!" Paul added with a note of admiration.

"I saw that. But, I said he could live here and I meant it. He has to have some training, and we're going to get a dog crate to keep him in when we have to go out."

"What's that?"

"It's a big box. He can see out, he'll be comfortable, I promise."

Paul opened the door. Amanda sat on the small square of carpet in front of the bathtub, her arm around the dog, who sat up as tall as she did. Amanda's round face was blotchy and tearstained. As Jack bent down to pick her up Buster leaped at him and kissed his face.

Amanda wrapped her arms and legs around him. "Thank you, Daddy," she said, her voice strained. "He was really, really bad."

"But he's part of the family now," he said, taking Paul's hand and heading for the stairs. Buster ran on ahead. Jack felt a compulsion to hurry and follow before the dog ate something else along the way. "Nobody gets kicked out for doing something bad."

"'Cause God loves all of us, even when we're bad?"

That was what he'd taught her from the moment she could understand.

"Yeah," he said. It was a good thing he didn't believe that anymore or he'd have to wonder where God stood on the issue of revenge. "How about pizza for dinner?"

The suggestion was met with unanimous approval. Jack looked around himself at the destruction and modified the plan from eating out to having the pizza delivered.

KAY AND CHARLIE sat together in the back row of folding chairs in the Bank of the Berkshires public meeting room waiting for the weekly Fall Festival meeting to be called to order. Built to resemble an old colonial building, the bank had every amenity, including kitchen facilities.

Charlie closed her eyes and groaned. "Oh, God. Someone's microwaving popcorn. Can you smell that?"

The aroma was wonderful. "We just had burgers and salad. You're fine. You don't need popcorn."

"I know." Charlie's eyes were closed as though that somehow blocked her olfactory sense.

"Way too many carbs."

"I know, I know."

"You've lost twenty pounds," Kay reminded her. Charlie appeared to be on the brink of some carb-craving explosion.

"Twenty-one."

"Charlie, that's wonderful!"

Charlie opened her eyes and gave Kay a jaded glance. "Yeah. Only forty-nine to go."

"It's a good start," Kay insisted, "and you'll get there. Now stop thinking about popcorn and tell me…" She stopped talking as Jack Keaton walked into the room with Evan Braga and Hank Whitcomb. Evan was in charge of the painters who worked for Whitcomb's Wonders and Jack's immediate boss. Evan slipped down an aisle to talk to someone, Hank waved at Kay, causing Jack Keaton to look in her direction. He acknowledged her with a brief, perfunctory nod.

She returned the nod, feigning the same lack of enthusiasm he'd shown, hating to admit how much his disinterest bothered her. After she and Ron Milford had run into him a few days ago, she'd been haunted by recurring images of his brooding face. That was very unlike her. She wasn't usually attracted to men of mystery. She liked a straightforward man with a strong work ethic and a good play instinct. That didn't mean she was going to fall for one; marriage was out of the question. But someone fun with whom she could fool around was something else again.

Jack Keaton didn't look like fun, so she didn't know why she was even interested.

"Tell you what?" Charlie asked, interrupting her self-analysis.

Kay needed a moment to assimilate the question. Keaton had followed Hank to the front row of chairs and taken a seat. He looked back over the room as though searching for someone. She wondered if it was his unobtrusive way of spotting her again.

"Who is that?" Charlie demanded in a whisper.

"Who?"

"The man you're staring at lustfully."

Kay elbowed her cousin. "There is no lust in me. Only interest. That's Jack Keaton, who saved Misty O'Neil."

"Mmm. Wow." Charlie's voice held respect and awe. "That is one seriously good-looking man."

"Mmm." Well. Who could disagree with that?

"Did you get your photograph of him?"

"No, he refused. He was even a little hostile about it."

Charlie nodded, as though that proved her point. "I'll bet he is on the run. Though he doesn't look like a criminal." She smiled as she speculated. "Maybe he's a prince who's tired of his responsibilities."

"Oh, yeah. These days a prince's responsibilities consist of racing automobiles, skiing in the Olympics and dating supermodels. Who'd want to run away from that?"

Charlie continued to stare. "There's a hunted-hero look about him," she said, leaning forward. "Jean Valjean in a Celtics T-shirt."

"Hello, ladies." Two men in Maple Hill Police Department sweatshirts moved into the row in front of Kay and Charlie. Gib Whittier, Rachel's husband, turned to give them his charming grin. He was six feet four inches of handsome self-assurance—though Kay thought that had dimmed a little since Rachel left him. "How are the cousins tonight?"

When they assured him they were fine, he introduced the young man who accompanied him. "Kay and Charlene Florio, I'd like you to meet Sam Cavalleri. He's from Boston. New to the Maple Hill force. Sam, these are my wife's cousins, Kay and Charlie Florio."

Sam, a few inches shorter than Gib, had impressive shoulders, curly dark hair and hazel eyes. "Gib wrecked a car two days ago," he said, shaking Charlie's hand, then Kay's. "So we got the Fall Festival duty. My misfortune to be his partner." The police force always sent a team to help plan the event.

"Was it a pursuit?" Charlie asked.

He turned to her. Kay saw the moment's hesitation in him before he replied. "No," he said finally. "He'd just ticketed this kid on a motorcycle. We'd pulled him into the Maple Hill Store's parking lot. When we were ready to leave, Gib backed into a light pole, crumpled it and sprang the trunk."

Gib frowned at him. "Where was all this detail when we were filing our report. I had to stay late and do it."

"You were driving. It was your report."

"Then you could let me tell the story."

"You'd leave out the good stuff." Sam smiled from Charlie to Kay. "It's a pleasure to meet you both. Made coming here worthwhile after all." He sat down in front of Charlie.

"Did you have to go to the hospital?" Kay asked Gib, pointing to the small bandage on his forehead. If so, she wondered if he'd seen Rachel.

He shook his head. "Patched myself up. Rachel was on, and she'd have taken too much pleasure in stitching me up without sedation. She working again tonight? I thought she was off."

"She's subbing for somebody." Kay had guessed she'd taken the extra shift purposefully to be able to miss tonight's meeting and seeing Gib. She was the hospital's liaison to the event, but Kay had promised to fill her in on what was decided.

"The woman holds a grudge," Gib said darkly.

Sam had turned around to speak to Charlie. Since they were both distracted, Kay took the opportunity to tell Gib what she thought.

Kay leaned closer to him. "You cheated on her with another woman. That might be acceptable in some circles, but not with the Florios. I know you were having a tough time, but so was she. Expecting her to simply forgive and forget is unrealistic."

"I know, I know," he said, a pained pleat on his forehead. "I didn't mean that to sound careless, I just don't know how to get her to even talk about it."

Kay felt a certain sympathy toward him, felt fairly confident that he was a good man with generally good intentions. But her loyalty was to her cousin. "She's very hurt," she said. "There's no easy fix here. You have to be willing to work on it."

"To grovel, you mean," he put in grimly.

"If that's what it takes."

"I'm sure it will. She makes us all grovel."

A firm feminine voice called the meeting to order. Gib winked at Kay, then faced the front of the room. Kay turned on her tape recorder and prepared to take notes, as well.

Claire Bell, wife of the bank manager, stood at the head of the aisle in jeans and a red turtleneck. She was petite and youthful for a woman pushing sixty, and always made Kay feel like an awkward giant. She had a gift for organization and a positive outlook, and was therefore a good choice to lead this event. Everyone loved her but braced themselves for her progress report. Claire had been a kindergarten teacher for twenty-eight years before retiring four years ago, and often forgot she wasn't dealing with six-year-olds.

"This is where we stand right now," she said, leaning eagerly toward them with a wide smile, both hands joined together at her waist. "Mrs. Whitcomb has agreed to let us block off the streets around the Common as usual, and Kiwanis will be available to help set up booths and pavilions." She giggled. "And please don't forget to anchor them this year with sandbags or water-filled plastic jugs. We don't want a repeat of last year when the pavilion around Glory Elliott's jewelry booth took flight and had to be chased halfway to Boston."

The giggle became laughter at her own joke. She found Glory in the audience and waved. Then she asked, "Booth chairwoman, are you here?"

Mariah Trent stood up, waving a clipboard. She was a gifted painter and a Wonder Woman, the community's affectionate term for the wives and girlfriends of Hank's men.

"How's the sign-up coming?" Claire asked.

"Very well," Mariah assured her. "We have more than enough to surround the square and will probably have to add another row. Booth deposits stand at…" She named a figure and there was a round of applause.

"All right!" Claire said, still clapping. "A gold star for you, Mariah! Kay?"

"Yes?" Kay handed the tape recorder to Charlie and stood, notebook in hand.

"How many cakes?"

One of the festival's favorite features was the Cake Walk, a circle made with chalk in the middle of the street. At two-foot intervals, smaller circles were drawn, each identified by a different number. Participants paid fifty cents to play, marched in a circle to music with other participants, and when the music stopped, the booth tender drew a number. The player standing on that number won a cake.

Because the game was so popular, getting enough cakes donated to keep the booth going for the length of the event was a major feat. But all in all it was easier than many of the jobs needing volunteers and Kay had snapped it up. Her job, her novel and preparing for her own booth of dried flowers and herb gifts left her little free time.

"None," Kay replied fearlessly. When everyone laughed—except Claire—she added quickly, "But everyone knows I can make them look bad in print, so they'll be eager to help." She pointed to Glory. "If you don't want that blown-away pavilion story to surface again…"

Glory pretended horror and raised her index and second fingers. "Two cakes!" she promised. "German chocolate and cherry chocolate chip!"

Kay wrote that down. "Two cakes, Madame Chairwoman," she said. "Any other promises while I'm taking notes?"

While half of the audience laughed at the tactic, the other half shouted out promises that she quickly added to her list.

"Well," Claire said when Kay finally sat down to applause, fourteen cakes promised, "a gold star for you, missy."

"Well, aren't you a hotshot," Charlie teased under her breath. "You're helping to carb-poison an entire town and its little children."

Kay knew her cousin's weaknesses. "I'll save you the German chocolate."

"Thanks. I'll freeze it until I'm a size seven."

Claire chirped her way through several other committee reports, then frowned sadly upon arriving at Entertainment. Everyone sat up curiously, probably thinking, as Kay did, that Cinda Scavullo, the pop icon who hailed from Springfield and was second cousin to Rita Robidoux's nephew, was a done deal.

"I'm afraid Cinda had to cancel," Claire said

mournfully. "She broke her ankle during rehearsal for a dance number and is in seclusion on Long Island. Does anyone else have a celebrity connection they'd like to share with the class? The group?" she amended.

There was silence, then someone offered, "My neighbor's a magician."

"Thank you, Robert," she said with an apologetic little bow. "No aspersions cast on your neighbor, but we're hoping to get someone who'll attract visitors to Maple Hill, and hopefully, media, too. Any other ideas?"

Charlie elbowed Kay.

Kay gave her what had been known in their childhood as "the death-ray look."

Then someone else spoke the dreaded words. "What about Brenda Florio?"

An Ohh! of approval went up and Claire stood on tiptoe to find Kay at the back of the room. "Kay? Can you charm your mother into helping us out?"

Kay could feel everyone's eyes turned toward her.

"I…" she began.

"Having one of the Food Channel's most beloved chefs would be such a great boon!" Claire looked directly at Kay expectantly. "Could you do that for us?"

Kay could imagine the few days her mother would be here. They'd be determined to get along, have one cozy meal catching up on friends and family, then her mother would tell her her hair lacked luster, or her skin looked dry, or that she was wasting her youth on work and pipe dreams, and Kay would know she really meant that she'd let some monster steal her little sister, ruined the entire family's life, and she'd never be forgiven for it.

"She's…usually very busy," Kay said faintly. Then she looked at all the hopeful faces and added with a falsely cheerful attitude, "But I'll do my best."

She was applauded again and Claire beamed.

"Want to go to the Barn for pumpkin pie?" Charlie suggested as they walked out to her car.

"Can you have that?" Kay asked.

"If you don't eat the crust, it's only twenty carbs. Not bad for a dessert."

"Sure." She was going to need an entire coconut cream to be able to deal with her mother.

But Charlie's old Plymouth wouldn't start. It was a joke among Kay and her cousins that the Reliant— wasn't. Charlie had intended to replace it for years, but there was always another financial crisis involving some life necessity more important—a new roof, a summer at Boston College updating her credentials, an opportunity to go to Rome with a group of other teachers sharing expenses.

Within two minutes of the motor grinding but refusing to turn over, Kay and Charlie stood beside the car while five men who'd also attended the meeting conferred under the hood and one sat behind the wheel, turning the key in the ignition.

"Your fuel line's clogged, and your pump's not working," Clete Morrison finally diagnosed. He owned a towing service and had recently bought a small garage on the west edge of town. "This isn't taking you anywhere tonight. I'll take it to the shop and call you in the morning with an estimate."

"Thanks, Clete." Charlie looked worried.

"I'll take you home," Sam Cavalleri volunteered. He was speaking to Charlie, who stared at him in disbelief. Kay had noticed that he'd found reasons to turn and speak to her several times during the evening. Charlie was unaccustomed to such attention.

"Ah...well...we'd appreciate that," she said, clearly flustered.

"Actually—" he smiled apologetically at Kay "—I have a two-seater—an MG."

"Oh. I couldn't..." Charlie began to protest, catching Kay's arm as though afraid she'd desert her.

Kay gently disengaged her hand. "You go ahead. Gib will take me home."

Gib shook his head. "I rode with Sam, who's heartlessly abandoned me. But I'm on graveyard tonight anyway. I'll just walk to the station."

"Jack will take Kay home." Hank also apologized to Kay. "I'd do it, but my van's full of brush I was supposed to take to the dump this afternoon, but I got tied up. Is that okay with you, Jack? You two know each other?"

"We do," Jack replied, less reluctant than she'd expected. "If you promise not to take my picture," he said to Kay, "I'll be happy to drive you home."

Kay appreciated his attempt to be polite. "I promise," she said.

Actually, she felt a major stirring of interest in him as they stood together under a streetlight. There was great anguish in him, she guessed, judging by the careful distance he kept so artfully. Those around him didn't seem to notice, or maybe it was just that other men didn't care. They didn't need the intimacies, the confidences women needed from one another.

The clever way he kept himself apart suggested experience; he'd been doing it for a while.

Then he took her arm in a casually chivalrous way and pointed with the other hand to the old truck she remembered from his driveway. A touch on her hand or her arm always reminded her of Betsy being led away and she snatched her arm back.

They stood still for a moment, looking at each other. He didn't seem hurt, as she might have expected, but more curious, even concerned.

"I'm sorry," she said, completely off balance emotionally. "You surprised me."

His truck dated from the days before remotes and he went to unlock it with a key.

"Not a problem," he said, holding the door open for her. They were in a puddle of darkness and she could see only the planes of his face, the pale blond highlights in his hair and the gleam in his eyes from passing headlights. "I've had a few bad surprises lately, too."

CHAPTER FIVE

"EAST OR WEST?" Jack asked as he turned the key in the ignition. He was uncomfortable—an unusual condition for him. He knew it was this woman. He didn't dislike her; the nosiness was probably just part of her job. But he had a feeling she could mean trouble for him where his plan was concerned, and he wasn't going to let anything get between him and his mission to prove Milford guilty.

And here he was confined with her in the small space of the front seat of his truck. Instead of the usual gas and oil smell complicated by the pine-scented cardboard tree dangling from his radio knob, the scent of something tropical filled the cab.

"East, please," she said, buckling her seat belt. He watched her movements and thought how feminine they were. The belt in place, she turned to look at him and he could see that she was uncomfortable, too. Or wary. His attention was snagged by a curl at her left temple that rolled under and into the curl beside it, that stuck out. Once again, he was transfixed by her unruly hair. And couldn't imagine why it was so appealing. "Do you know where the Bargain Basement is?"

He nodded. "I bought a desk there."

"I'm right behind it, two blocks up the hill. Adams Street."

Thank goodness. Not far at all. He drove in that direction, turned up the hill at the secondhand store and found Adams.

Kay pointed through the windshield. "Fourth house on the left. The old saltbox with the overgrown forsythia bush."

"Well, I wouldn't know a forsythia bush if it tackled me, but I can count to four." He pulled up to the curb in front of the house she described. It was set back behind a broad lawn, a narrow walkway leading up to it.

He had to walk her to the door. His proper Yankee parents would frown on him if he didn't. But her discomfort seemed to be growing proportionate to his and he was anxious to get home to the relative sanity of his children and his dog.

He reached for his door handle. She put a hand on his other arm to stop him. He drew away from her the same way she'd pulled away from him.

"Sorry," he said quickly when she looked alarmed. "This time *you* surprised me."

She nodded. "That's all right. I was just going to tell you that you don't have to get out of the truck."

Presuming she wouldn't understand if he told her that he did have to, he simply did it and walked around to pull open her door.

"Trained by a mother determined to raise a gentleman, huh?" She smiled and waited while he closed the door. She fell in beside him as he stepped up on the curb and started up the walk.

He put his hands in his pockets. "How did you know?"

"Because my mother tried to raise a lady. I never chew gum outside of the house, never shout across the street to get a friend's attention, always send thank-you notes for gifts or kindnesses."

"But you're reluctant to invite her to the festival?"

He couldn't believe that he had actually asked that. Her relationship with her mother was personal and none of his business. It's just that she'd looked distressed during the meeting when someone had suggested her mother as the celebrity draw. Old habits did die hard, he thought. In his former life, he'd have wanted to know what was behind that look so he could offer to help.

"I love my mother," she said firmly. Then she sighed and one hand swiped the darkness. "We're just two very different people and we can't spend an hour together without arguing about something."

So. As he suspected, she wasn't as together as she liked to appear.

"Your fault or hers?" he asked.

She considered that a moment, then replied with that same firmness. "She was indulged as a little girl, my father adored her, and every man and woman in America who watches the Food Channel thinks she's the best thing to have happened to a kitchen since the range replaced the woodstove." She turned to face him as they reached her front door. "She's also very beautiful. Consequently, she's supremely confident, a bit of a diva, and thinks she should be able to run my life as well as her own."

"Ah." He could understand that. His mother tried to cut his food when he was in the hospital. His father made her stop. "I guess it's hard to stop being a parent, even when your child is grown."

The expression in her eyes was pitying. It asked him how he could possibly think he understood. It told him that her pain was thick and dark and coated her life like a layer of mud.

But she smiled thinly and said, "That must be it," obviously hoping to get rid of him. "That must be it. Thank you for the ride home."

She turned to put her key in the lock and the minister he used to be wanted to ask her to explain her pain. He fought the impulse, knowing she wouldn't appreciate it and he didn't need to add someone else's grief to his own. Particularly, the nosy reporter's.

But when she looked at him, he saw a desperate need there, saw her try to check it then lose the battle as she opened her mouth to speak.

He took an encouraging step closer even as he thought he should say good-night and walk away. He waited for her to share what was on her mind, but even as he watched, the connection they'd almost made evaporated before it could form.

"Good night," she said, and let herself into the house.

He felt relieved and weirdly deflated. "Yeah," he said to the lonely darkness. "Good night."

THURSDAY WAS Kay's day off. The *Maple Hill Mirror* and most weekly papers went to press with their valuable grocery store ads early Wednesday afternoon. It was a print tradition as old as the *Mirror* itself.

Kay worked on her novel on Wednesday afternoons, and all day Thursday, unless something newsworthy happened and she took off in pursuit of the story. Or unless the words refused to come for her, then she worked on her wreaths and herb gifts for the Fall Festival.

She'd awakened this morning with a strange feeling that she was going to make sense of her novel today. Which was odd, considering how little sense her life made. Jack Keaton had plagued her mind for two days. She had an image of him in her brain, leaning toward her on the walk in front of her house, looking as though he wanted to listen or help.

But she'd have to be serious about him to share what troubled her, and she didn't want a serious man in her life. She often thought it would be nice to have one she might fool around with, but she had a suspicion no one fooled around with Jack Keaton.

After dinner she rewrote the first chapter so that Greta, her heroine, was more confused, less angry. Anger seemed to restrict movement, while confusion left more options open for action. She ended the first chapter with Greta encountering Tom, her ex-husband, when her car collided with his on the road to his sister Diana's villa. Greta had decided to stay in Portugal after their breakup, and because she and Tom's sister were good friends as well as relatives by marriage, she'd been invited to Diana's husband's surprise party. She closed with what she hoped were several lines of sparkling dialogue as the couple exchanged barbs for the first time in four years.

Feeling as though the book was finally on the right track, she was emboldened to call her mother.

"Brenda Florio's Fantasy Foods," a pleasant voice answered.

"Hi, Margie, it's Kay. Is my mother available?" Margie Newman had been Brenda Florio's personal assistant for the last five years. She was Kay's age, a small, blond organizational dynamo without whom her mother had said over and over she couldn't function. Kay was sometimes jealous of Margie's ability to get along with her mother and could have hated her for having earned her mother's respect and affection, if Margie wasn't so unfailingly kind and cheerful.

"Kay!" Margie always sounded delighted to hear her voice. "Are you still happy out there?"

"Out there" was only one hundred miles from her mother's Boston office. "I love it. The job's great and it's fun to be near my cousins."

"That's terrific. Hold on. Your mom was on a call with Jacques Paumier and she wandered out onto the patio with the cordless."

Margie put her on hold and Kay waited.

On a call with Jacques Paumier, the great French chef. Her mother had mentioned in a note in Kay's birthday card that they had talked about collaborating on a book. Since Kay's father had died, her mother had devoted every moment to her career and it had flourished. She'd sounded excited at the prospect, and Kay had written back in a thank-you note that she was happy for her. Her mother had the Midas touch where her career was concerned. In Kay's lifetime she'd gone from a well-respected local chef with a restaurant where reservations were booked months in advance, to a Food Channel maven with book deals and celebrity appearances that never stopped—and all that with a tragedy under her belt that would have withered a lesser person. Kay admired that, but didn't understand it. She felt as though she carried the anvil of Betsy's loss every day.

Of course, her mother hadn't been the one responsible for it.

The line opened and a smokey voice said cheerfully, "Hi, Kay! What's up?"

"Hi, Mom," Kay replied, matching her mother's tone. "Is it a go with Jacques Paumier?"

"It is! And guess where we're meeting to plan the book?"

"Ah...doesn't he live in Provence?"

"Yes, but he has a vacation home in Gstaad."

Kay had visited Provence when she spent her junior year in France, and thought it such a perfect, pastoral landscape. It was hard to imagine the Provençals needing to get away somewhere else.

"All right! You'll get to wear that new ski sweater you bought at Filene's last year." Her mother could afford to shop anywhere, but she considered the yearly sale at Filene's in Boston a test of her mettle and always invited Kay to go with her.

"The annual Fall Festival is coming up," Kay said, deciding a direct approach was best. "Cinda Scavullo was supposed to be our guest, drawing visitors from far and wide, and tantalizing the press into giving us publicity and possibly even national attention."

"Ah, yes. I saw her at the Emmys. Quite a little tart."

Brenda Florio had several food show Emmys, and knew her tarts.

"Didn't I read in *Variety*," Brenda asked, "that she had an accident? Broke her arm, or something?"

"Her ankle," Kay corrected. "The chairman of the committee asked me if I would impose upon you to come and be our people and publicity draw."

"Oh!" The simple word had a wealth of stroked ego in it. Her mother loved flattery. "Give me a date, and if you'll hold on a minute, I'll check with Margie."

"You can take a couple of days to think abo—"

"I'll be happy to do it if the date's clear. It's still a weekend thing, right?"

"Yes. Second weekend in October."

"Okay, hold on."

The line went quiet again and Kay waited, going over in her mind all she should do to make her home presentable.

"Kay? I'm free! I'd love to come."

"Great. There'll probably be a small honorarium, but they can't afford…"

"Oh, pooh! I'm happy to do it for you. For them."

Her mother might be the only woman in the world who still said, "Oh, pooh."

Happy that the conversation had gone so smoothly, certain she could brace herself over the intervening time to be an unflappable hostess, Kay opened her mouth to sign off. But her mother stopped her with, "Can you make reservations for me somewhere for the weekend? Or give Margie some numbers."

Kay drew a breath for patience. Her mother loved to pretend she didn't want to put her out, when she really loved special attention. "I'd like you to stay with me, Mom."

"Oh, darling, no you don't. You know you'll be yelling at me within an hour of my arrival."

That was likely to prove true, but their standard method of operation was to pretend they got along well and undertake mutual projects. That way the arguing didn't start until they were actually together.

"You haven't seen my new house yet," Kay coaxed. For the past several months her mother had been in Rome, doing her show from famous inns and restaurants. Kay hadn't seen her since she had helped her move into the apartment Kay had occupied her first few months in Maple Hill. "It's old and needs a lot of work, but a descendant of the Drakes—you know, the people whose statue we have on the Common?"

"Of course."

"Well, Philomena Potter, their oldest daughter, once lived in it." They were one of the families that founded Maple Hill and helped defend it from the British during the Revolutionary War.

"That's fascinating." Her mom loved historical recipes, and anything that had a story.

"I'll even let you sleep in Philly's bedroom."

"Philly?"

"Philomena Potter. She was quite a force. You'd probably relate to her. I researched her a little bit when I bought the house and have some pages of her diary you can read. There's even a recipe from Abigail Adams."

"I'd love that!"

Kay was privately congratulating herself on having handled her mother well when her mom asked, "Have you met anyone yet?"

The eternal question. Most mothers of single adults hoped for romance in their children's lives, but her mother was particularly obsessed. Or maybe Kay was particularly sensitive.

"I've met lots of people, Mom. I'm a reporter. Getting to know people is what I do."

"You know what I mean. Have you met men people?"

"A few."

"Are you dating?"

"I don't think they even call it that anymore. Today you 'hang out,' or you live together. And no, I'm not doing either. With my job, my book and my house…"

"You should never be too busy to welcome people into your life."

"There are people in my life. I volunteer in the reading program at the school, I'm helping with the festival, and Rachel and Charlie and I get together all the time."

Brenda sighed. "Yes, Kay. I'm sure you're doing good work at the school, but that puts you in an environment that's mostly children and women. And I'll bet everyone involved in the festival is married or otherwise connected. Your cousins are wonderful company, but they're as socially…"

Kay felt defensive. This was the predictable result of most of their conversations. "What?" she asked. "Inept? As I am?"

"You wouldn't be a good reporter if you were socially inept. I was trying to say that you're afraid of social contact. Well, Rachel's married and she sees people all the time as a nurse, but she functions only from a position of power. If she's in charge, she's fine."

"Mom," Kay gasped in disbelief. "That's the way *you* operate!"

"I'm loud and I talk a lot and I cajole," Brenda disputed, "but I don't bully. There's a difference. And Charlie's afraid for obvious reasons, and does her best to make herself unattractive so no one will pay attention to her...."

"She's a beautiful woman. And anyone who doesn't see that, doesn't deserve *her* attention."

"Of course she's wonderful, but you know what I mean about Charlie. You've said it yourself. You just want to argue about it because I'm saying it."

That might be true, but Kay's cousins were everything to her and defending them was a lifelong habit. Kay's mom was quiet for one pulsing moment, then she said in a tone that combined pity and accusation, "And you claim you don't want to get married because you want to dedicate yourself to this novel, but I think it's because you are so afraid someone's going to love you."

Well, damn it. Her mom had a knack for zeroing in on the truth. "Mother..."

"That's all I have to say."

"Good." All she had to say was always too much. But now that their small outburst was over, Kay felt compelled to smooth the gap between them. "When are you planning to come?"

"You're sure you still want me?"

She did, but she had to make herself say it. "Yes. And the festival committee will be counting on you."

"All right." She was amenable again. "I'll be there Friday afternoon in time for the opening festivities."

"I'll have your room ready."

"Don't fuss. Promise?"

"I promise." That was a lie, of course. She was going to do her best to make everything as perfect and difficult to criticize as possible. "I'll wait until you get here to buy groceries."

"All right. I'll make chicken livers in Madeira sauce while I'm there."

Kay had a weakness for her mother's favorite dish and succumbed to it. "I'll look forward to that. See you soon."

"I love you, Kay."

"I love you, too, Mom."

Kay and Brenda ended every conversation with that claim, but Kay always wondered if it was true. It was true on her part, though her mother made her insane. She couldn't help but feel that her mother was driven by some sense of obligation. But she'd been Betsy's mother, too. And Betsy was gone. Because of Kay.

"You are so afraid someone is going to love you," she'd said. Kay was a little surprised that her mother had been that insightful. She didn't want to be loved. Love would get in the way of making up for Betsy.

Kay hung up the phone, feeling as though she'd climbed Mount Everest without oxygen.

CHAPTER SIX

JORDIE SLOCUM stared hard at the words in *My Little Red Storybook.* He was in second grade in a remedial reading class in which Kay volunteered once a week. He looked closely at the picture of a black-and-white dog climbing into a child's wagon, mischief obviously on the dog's mind. In the dog's mouth was a stuffed rabbit. Knowing the words related to the image, Jordie pronounced the single word under the picture. "Bunny!" he said.

"You're just guessing," Kay scolded gently, pointing to the consonant that began the dog's name. "That's an *F*. Does that sound like the beginning of Bunny?"

"F…" Jordie said dutifully. Then added the *l* that followed. "Fl…"

Kay waited patiently. When she'd decided to volunteer at the school, she'd asked to be assigned to a little boy. Little girls were precious, but too hard on her memories. Little boys kept her brain nimble.

"Fl…ip," He puzzled over that, then made the sounds again more quickly. "Fl…ip." He turned to Kay with a frown. He was a beautiful seven-year-old with big blue eyes, dirty blond hair, and clothes that probably hadn't been washed in a week. She wondered where he found the energy to try so hard when he was clearly a victim of neglect. Ms. Langevin, his teacher, had provided his breakfast today as she did most mornings.

"His name," Jordie asked Kay skeptically, "is Philip?"

Okay. So the sound-it-out principle didn't always work. Kay wrapped an arm around his shoulders and squeezed. "Flip. The dog's name is Flip. Probably because he jumps around like dogs do, and looks like he's flipping."

He turned a page. "What happens to the bunny?"

"You have to keep reading."

On the next page, the wagon fell onto its side and the dog leaped out, losing the stuffed bunny in his mouth.

"Oh, good!" Jordie said. "The bunny gets away!"

A bell rang loudly, announcing the end of the reading session.

"You did very well today, Jordie." Kay pinned a large yellow paper star with his name on it to the pocket of his shirt. "We want all the other kids and your mom to know how well you did."

"My mom's on vacation," he said. "But I'll save it so she can see it when she comes home."

"On vacation?" she asked. Zoe Langevin had called Children's Services several times about the condition in which Jordie arrived at school, but the boy's mother always had a reason why he left without breakfast. Zoe and Kay never believed them, but understood that the caseworker had to have physical proof in order to take steps against Jordie's mother. They'd made it their mission to find some. "Where'd she go?"

"I don't know. She said it wasn't very far."

Some tavern, Kay guessed, and the apartment of one of a long string of boyfriends.

"When's she coming home?"

"I don't know," Jordie replied. "But Derek knows." He held a hand high up over his head. "He's really big and he knows everything."

Derek, she knew from the few months she'd spent helping Jordie at the end of the previous school year, was his older brother. She typed up information on him for the "Police Record" column of the paper, usually under the lead, "Juvenile arrested for..." He'd stolen several cars since she'd been reporting for the *Mirror*, and had a penchant for riding his motorcycle at excessive speeds on downtown streets after dark.

"It's nice to have someone around who knows a lot of things. Did you get to practice your reading over the summer?"

He shook his head. "Mom doesn't have any books. Derek has some magazines, but he says I can't see them till I'm older. I think there's naked boobs and butts and stuff."

She nodded understanding, grateful Derek had enough sense to keep his reading material away from his little brother. "Well, what if I got you some books to read at home?" she suggested. "Because I think you're already reading better than you did last year. I'll bet if you get to practice, you'll do even better."

"Awesome! Is there one about Spider-Man?"

"I'll find one. Here's your reward for trying so hard today." She gave him a small bag of trail mix combined with chocolate candies. He loved the treat.

Jordie wrapped his arms around her, his odorous little body clinging as she hugged him back. He ran back to his class, turning at the door to wave at her.

She went to the teachers' lounge in the hope of finding a cup of coffee. She was surprised to discover that it was empty of teachers, but filled with half a dozen little boys clustered around—she looked again, unable to believe it—Jack Keaton. He had to be pretty interesting stuff to keep fourth, fifth and sixth graders in the building during recess. He was painting the inside of a window frame with a remarkably steady hand while fielding questions. The piano and several bookcases and tables were covered with tarps. The walls, she saw, were a new, sunnier shade of yellow.

"What's the paint made of?"

"What's the brush made of?"

"How come you like the Red Sox?"

Jack concentrated on an overhead swipe of the brush that changed the inside of the window frame from beige to crisp white. "I've been watching their games since I was your age."

"How old are you now?" another little boy asked. "Sixty?"

Jack grinned but held the brush threateningly. "I could paint your hair white and make *you* look sixty."

The other boys laughed. "Did you go to college?" somebody asked.

The sixth grader nudged him punitively. "Don't ask personal questions. Maybe he didn't have money to go to college."

Jack glanced at the boy, then went back to finishing the top of the frame. "I went to college in Maine," he said.

"Did you graduate?"

"Yes."

"Then…how come you're a painter and not a lawyer or a CEO or something? My dad says you can be those things if you finish college."

Jack nodded. "Your dad's right. But I want to be a painter."

"*My* dad says you were in Iraq." That was Josh Northrup, a sixth grader. Kay knew his father worked for Hank. "That's why you have a limp. Your leg got messed up."

The other little boys gasped and Kay, too, was taken aback. A military stint in a war zone might explain the pain she saw in him.

Jack stopped to nod at Josh, though he looked surprised. "That's true. How does he know that?"

Josh shrugged. "He always knows everything. But he used to live in Haverstown, Vermont, when he was little, so Grandma sends him the paper. He recognized your picture."

Big brothers and dads, Kay thought wryly. How wonderful it must be to inspire such confidence in the children in your life.

Kay realized suddenly that the conversation had stopped and that Jack Keaton and his audience were looking at her. Then a little boy with a flushed face appeared beside her and shouted, "Are you guys coming out? We're having a contest for who owns the monkey bars!"

Certain the playground supervisor was going to have something to say about that, Kay flattened herself against the doorjamb as the boys raced past her. Silence fell over the room with their retreat.

"Hi." Jack smiled. His quick gaze seemed to assess her, just as her brief study of him reminded her of what Charlie had said about him having the look of a hunted man. Something in his eyes reached for her—touched her.

She took a step back before she was tempted to reach for him.

"I came looking for a cup of coffee," she said. "And…here you are."

He went back to painting. "Yes. We seem to be on intersecting paths. Or a collision course." He lowered the brush to dip it in a plastic container he held in his other hand. He angled his chin toward the corner of the room. "Coffeepot's still going. Teachers have been in and out for it, but they moved their sofa and chairs into the conference room temporarily. Do you teach here?"

"No. I volunteer in the reading program." She pumped coffee into a paper cup, then looked over her shoulder to ask, "Would you like some?"

"No, thank you." He made a neat, steady swipe with the brush along the bottom of the window frame. "I'm meeting a few of the guys for lunch at the Barn in about ten minutes."

"Do you like hot stuff?" she asked, and could have thrown the coffee in her own face when she heard herself.

He glanced up, dark eyes assessing, interesting mouth trying not to smile. "Of course," he answered, letting the double entendre linger between them. "Do you?"

"I…" The single syllable came out high and broken. She tried again. "I was going to recommend the Jalapeño Burger."

"Ah." He kept a straight face. "Sounds good."

"The fries are also seasoned with jalapeño and cheese." She was backing toward the door. "I have to go."

"All right. Thanks for the recommendation."

"Okay. Have a good day."

"You, too."

KAY SAT IN HER CAR a moment later, both energized and mortified by the rapid beating of her heart. How pathetic was she, she wondered, that a few sentences exchanged with a handsome and mysterious man made her flush like an adolescent?

Wasn't she always reminding herself that she *didn't* want to get involved with a man? Why wasn't her body listening?

She wasn't reacting to her mother's psychoanalysis of her full schedule, she was simply…what? Letting herself feel this unresolved attraction to better handle the dispute between her hero and heroine?

Yes. She liked that. Because last time she'd seen Jack Keaton, she'd gone home and written furiously. And she could feel the dialogue forming in her brain right now. The man was bad for her peace of mind, but good for her novel.

Comforted that she'd justified her actions, she turned on the motor and started home. She'd driven less than a block when she heard the wail of a siren. She glanced in her rearview mirror, saw a motorcycle racing toward her and pulled over, sure she was about to get a ticket. For what? she wondered. For imagining Jack Keaton's kisses? That translated to reckless endangerment if anything did.

Then the bike raced past and she realized it wasn't a state policeman at all but simply someone on a motorcycle trying to elude the police car racing in pursuit. From the number on the car, she knew it was Gib and Sam.

The moment they were past her, Kay drove after them, reaching for the camera that was always in her purse on the passenger seat beside her.

At the crossroad to town, the bike took the road into the woods, Gib and Sam followed, siren blaring, red light rotating. The pursuit was over quickly when the bike presumably hit something in the road. All Kay saw was the cops' sudden brake lights, then the gleam of sunlight off a helmet as the biker flew into the air.

Sam leaped out of the car and ran to the biker, Gib also jumped out of the car. "Bike's had a 1216 half a mile up Rabbit Road. Checking for injuries now," he reported, staying in touch with Dispatch with rock-star radio technology looped over his ear. He hurried to the side of the road where the biker lay groaning while Sam brushed gravel out of his face.

Kay focused for a shot and recognized Derek Slocum.

"You made me break my arm!" Derek accused with a groan.

"You broke your own arm." Sam opened Derek's collar. "If you can't ride a bike any better than that, you shouldn't be breaking the speed limit and eluding the police."

"Send an ambulance," Gib told Dispatch. "The victim is breathing and talking. Believes he has a broken arm."

Kay took a photo of Sam leaning over Derek and of the downed bike. Then when the ambulance arrived, she got several shots of the EMTs working on him, then putting him in the ambulance. Gib and Sam followed the ambulance to the hospital.

Generally, motor vehicle accidents weren't the kind of news the *Mirror* preferred, but local weeklies dealt with what interested their subscribers. Fortunately, this didn't look as though it would have an ugly ending—except that Derek Slocum, who should have been in school, was courting a life of crime and wasting his potential.

Kay followed Gib and Sam to the E.R., remembering that Jordie had told her his mother was on vacation. She passed that information on to a nurse, who could relay it to the E.R. doctor. She could only hope that the hospital being unable to reach Derek's mother would help build the case to take Jordie and Derek away from her.

"Aren't you off today?" Gib followed Kay, standing outside the hospital, his sunglasses dangling from one ear while he made notes for his report.

"Like cops," she said, heading back to her car, "reporters are never off." Then she added under her breath, "Heads up. Here comes Rachel."

Kay waved at her cousin, then went back to her car and sat a moment, watching Rachel and Gib. She wished she could hear their conversation, but had to be happy with trying to read their lips.

The discussion began calmly enough. Kay guessed Rachel was asking Gib about Derek's mother. Rachel nodded grimly. Everyone in town was familiar with the Slocum boys' situation. They talked for a while and Kay could tell the moment the conversation became personal. Rachel's expression turned cold while Gib seemed to be pleading passionately for something to which she shook her head.

There were broad arm gestures, Gib's shaking head, Rachel's finger pointed at his chest. He turned around and walked away. Rachel stormed back into the hospital.

Kay turned the motor on in her little VW and headed home, grateful to be single.

No matter how attractive Jack Keaton was.

Kay drove to the Maple Hill Store for Agnes's groceries. She had a standing list of things she picked up for her every week, and Agnes sometimes called and added to the list. It always amazed Kay that her aunt could remember to do that, yet forget other things that had happened only hours earlier. But that was the complexity of dementia.

An hour later, Kay clutched two grocery bags to her chest and extended her index finger to ring her aunt's bell. Agnes opened the door wearing a pink Dior gown Kay knew she prized, and a diamond earring and broach set that were worth a small fortune. Her smile sparkled as brightly as the diamonds when she pushed open the door to admit her and said, "Liz, how lovely to see you again. I'm so glad you…" She stopped abruptly once Kay was inside, studying her as if she'd suddenly morphed into someone else.

That also was the nature of the problem—a mind that perceived things one way one moment in its demential disguise, then in the light of reality the next moment when dementia slipped aside to lie in wait for another opportunity to confuse.

"Hi, Auntie," Kay said, pretending there was nothing unusual about her aunt's appearance, or the fact that she'd mistaken Kay for Elizabeth Taylor, one of her aunt's preferred guests at her table in the old days. "How are you today? I picked up one of those painted pumpkins you like to put in the middle of the table."

Then Kay noticed the dining table, set for six with fresh flowers and her black-and-white dishes and cut crystal.

Agnes pulled a chair out and sat down, looking confused and upset. Kay hated this part more than anything. The confusion could be dealt with. Agnes's pain and embarrassment when she realized she was confused was difficult to bear.

"I was having a party," Agnes said, twisting the large emerald on the third finger of her right hand. "I think. I mean...Liz was coming with Richard and Roddy McDowell." Then she frowned as she thought and looked into Kay's eyes. "But you're not Liz."

Kay sat at a right angle to her. "I'm Kay, Auntie," she said, patting her hand. "Your niece."

Agnes nodded. "I know that. Now. But before..."

"Well, if they're not coming, I'd love to stay. What's for dinner?"

"Um..." Agnes rubbed her temple. "I think...ah..."

There was nothing in the oven, but three pans filled with water were on the stove.

"What if I make omelets and salad so you don't have to cook?" Kay suggested, remembering the sharp and vibrant woman who used to inhabit Agnes's body. She remembered also her kindness and her generous indulgences, and happily put the groceries away and began to cook, even though she'd be back on Monday with her cousins.

At home several hours later, her fingers flew over her computer keyboard as Greta and Tom Stratton stood in the middle of Diana's fragrant garden and blamed each other for their broken marriage.

> "You stayed at the office so you didn't have to come home and deal with me and a house without Jacob in it," Greta accused.
> "You never left the house because you weren't dealing with anything—at all. You made a shrine of Jake's room and lived in it all day."
> "He was our baby!"
> "He was gone! He'll live with me forever, but it was time to make another baby, to take back our lives."

Kay stared at those lines of dialogue and wondered where they'd come from. Nowhere in her notes did Tom and Greta have a baby.

She put her fingers tentatively back on the keys. Her couple continued to argue. She remembered the expressions on Gib's and Rachel's faces as they fought in front of the E.R. and used them as she wrote. She felt a flutter of excitement as creative energy built upon itself and gained momentum.

One day, she'd have to invite Jack Keaton to her book launch.

But where had the baby come from?

CHAPTER SEVEN

KAY SIPPED AT HER caramel mocha the following Monday morning as she inserted her key into the lock of the *Maple Hill Mirror*'s office. She was there even earlier than usual today. She'd worked all weekend on her novel then had been so stimulated by the activity—and the coffee that had kept her going—that she couldn't sleep last night.

She got up at 5:00 a.m. to put together the bare bones of a story about the standing of Maple Hill's children in national equivalency tests, then came into the office to see if she could develop a good lead for it while the day was still quiet.

Cursing the workings of her contrary system that had made her wide-awake all night at home and groggy now that she'd reached the office, she dropped her coffee, jacket, purse cum camera bag on her desk and headed for the bathroom in the back to splash a little water in her face and take a vitamin.

In the middle of a yawn, she opened the door that separated the front office from the back. And then she was eaten by a vile creature that trapped her in its closing maw and coated her with its digestive juices.

At least that was how she felt.

Common sense told her better, and yet she was caught in something that had grabbed her arm and the front of her sweater as it tilted to get a better grip on her. She heard an oath in a male voice and a thud somewhere nearby as a thick, sticky substance seeped into her scalp, inside her clothing, into her shoes.

There was a heavy, painful weight on her neck and shoulders, and unable to figure out what on earth had happened, she did the only thing she could think of. She screamed a long string of not very nice words.

"Whoa, whoa, Kay! You're all right. You're okay. Just stand…no, stand *still!*" A male voice she recognized with a sort of bleak acceptance as belonging to Jack Keaton shouted instructions as he manipulated her head and her arm.

"What is it?" she demanded as he lifted the weight off her. The thick substance covered her face and she dared not open her eyes.

"It's just a ladder!" he replied. "Stop pulling. Your sweater's caught in the folding mechanism."

She was about to snap a complaint at him when she felt his hand at her breast. The air left her lungs in a whoosh.

"Take it easy," he said, calm mingled with amusement in the directive. "I'm trying not to ruin…well, it's covered in paint anyway, so I guess it is ruined."

Paint. That was the slimy goop that covered her. Great.

There was a little more fumbling during which she

began to wonder if she and Jack Keaton together caused some disturbance in the cosmic continuum.

"There!" he said. She was suddenly free of the ladder and heard the clink of metal as he stood it aside. Then he added feelingly, "Holy sh—" He stopped abruptly, and she imagined he was getting a good look at her for the first time. "Well, Kay Florio, you're a sight," he said. This time the amusement was mingled with sympathy.

She knew this wasn't entirely his fault, but someone should have to pay for the fact that she'd been attacked by a ladder and covered in paint.

"Is the doorway the best place to put a ladder?" she demanded icily.

"When you're painting the wall above the doorway," he replied reasonably, "and no one's due into the office for another hour, it is. Don't you watch where you're going?"

"I didn't expect you to be there. Haley told me she hired the Whitcomb's Wonders to paint, but she didn't say when."

"You're very early."

"I couldn't sleep."

"Well. I'm sorry my ladder ate your sweater. Come on. You need a shower."

She resisted his hand on her arm though she still couldn't see it. She shouted in the direction of his voice, her eyes screwed tightly shut. "Oh, really! And what am I going to put on when I come out of the shower?"

"Can I run out and buy you something?"

"At 6:00 a.m.? I don't think so."

"What if I went to your house to get you a change of clothes?"

That was a reasonable offer, but she wasn't feeling reasonable. "Thanks, but I don't want you rifling through my underwear drawer."

He laughed, but when she glowered, he stopped. "Okay. Not funny. But when that latex hardens in your hair, we're going to have to cut it off you and it's such great hair."

God. She was so easy. Her anger doused by the compliment, however unconsciously he'd made it, she groaned and pointed in the direction of her desk. She heard paint drip with her gesture.

"My purse is on my desk. Take my keys and bring me back…" She paused to think about what would be easy to find.

"I will, but first, let me help you get the paint off your face." He put an arm around her and physically turned her around.

"I think my eyelashes are stuck together."

"A little mineral oil might help that." He held her tightly to him to direct her steps through the old equipment that filled the back room of the office. In the corner of the room, Haley's husband and his friends had built a beautifully equipped bath and shower shortly after Kay had come to work. With Haley taking Henrietta to work with her so often, she needed cleaner facilities and more room than the old closet-size bathroom had provided.

Jack led her into the bathroom. "Okay, stop. You're right in front of the sink. Are there terry-cloth towels in here instead of the paper stuff?"

"In the cupboard under the sink."

He pushed her back slightly as he reached for one, then she heard the water run. He caught her arm and pulled her closer to the sink and worked on her face in broad strokes of the towel. He rinsed again and swept carefully around her eyes with a corner of the towel wrapped around his finger.

Kay was a quiet puddle of vulnerability. His ministrations were gentle and careful. She felt a little current of power travel along her skin every time he touched her to move her around. She was going to be able to write her little heart out tonight.

He worked gently on her eyelashes, then finally said, "Okay. I think you can open your eyes."

She did it carefully. Water and his work on her eyelashes made her eyes sting, but she could see. It was a great relief.

She focused on a vivid bruise on his right cheek. "What happened to you?"

As she spoke, paint dripped out of her hair onto her face, and he quickly swiped at it again with the towel. Then he tugged gently on her hair to tip her head back. "So you don't get any more paint in your face," he explained, "when you hit the ladder, it knocked me off balance and I jumped off. I hit the edge of one of those machines when I went down.

"The paint should come right out of your hair. What do you want me to bring you back?"

"A pair of pants and a sweater, then you won't have to worry about tights or stockings." It was weird to be talking to the ceiling. "Upper left drawer of my dresser is bras and panties," she said, now grateful she *was* talking to the ceiling. "Socks are in the drawer below, and shoes are in the bottom of the closet. There's a pair of brown boots I usually wear with pants."

"Okay," he said. "Makeup? Perfume?"

"Makeup's in my purse, and I've got perfume in the medicine cabinet here." As he headed for the door, she added, "You should put some ice on that bruise."

"Be right back," he replied.

That was probably silly of her, she thought as she took a newspaper out of a stack they kept in a corner, opened it out on the bathroom floor, and put her paint-smeared clothes on it.

He'd been to Iraq. The bruise was nothing.

She stepped into the shower, made the water hot and set the showerhead to pulse. Though she tried not to think about Jack Keaton in her bedroom, her brain wanted to take creative liberties with the concept.

KAY'S LIVING ROOM was Williamsburg blue with cream and cranberry in the wallpaper border and the fabric on the sofa. It had what might be the original distressed hardwood floor, and an old stone walk-in fireplace with a thick plank mantel that held pieces of folk art and an old clock. He looked through doorways, wishing he'd remembered to ask her where her bedroom was. After her remark about him rummaging around in her things, he didn't want to touch anything he didn't have to.

He saw a kitchen with a stove and refrigerator, but shelves instead of cupboards, and a big, high-backed sink with gingham fabric underneath that probably concealed more shelves.

The living room opened into a sort of parlor where there were what looked like new curtains, but very little furniture, and beyond that, a laundry room.

He climbed the back stairs off the kitchen and found three bedrooms upstairs, one with a brass bed in it, a Boston rocker and a tall dresser. It was painted a soft pink and was pristine, as though no one had ever even walked into it. The second room contained a computer desk and an office chair and several stacks of books and papers. Her home office, he guessed.

The third was obviously the bedroom in use. He smiled. The bed had been carelessly made with a blue-and-yellow flowered bedspread, flannel pajamas with pigs and clouds on them flung across a bottom corner. An antique trunk painted in a Scandinavian or German design stood against a window with drapes in a blue-and-yellow stripe. One dresser drawer was open as was a small closet.

He peered into the drawer and saw a lavender lace

bra. He felt a stirring of excitement but forced himself to focus. Tomorrow night was Ron Milford's open house. He wanted to be prepared and watchful.

He pulled out the bra, saw lavender panties under it and grabbed those. In the second drawer there were easily twenty pairs of socks—athletic socks, boot socks, funny little socks with designs on them. He'd have settled on the boot socks since she'd asked him to bring her a pair of boots, but women's boots were dressier than men's and the thick, woolly socks might not be the right thing.

He explored the bottom of her closet, found a pair of flat-heeled brown boots that did look utilitarian, but too narrow to accommodate the big socks. He took one of the decorated pair and stuffed them in the boots.

Pants all hung on pants hangers at one end of the closet. She had them in every color. Having been married to a woman who coordinated her clothing very carefully, he picked a pair of gray slacks and a yellow-flowered gray turtleneck. He put the underwear in the other boot, and carried everything out to his truck.

When he returned to the *Mirror* building, he was surprised to find the front door open. He pushed his way in and came face-to-face with a veritable crowd of people. There were Hank and Jackie Whitcomb, Evan Braga and Gideon Hale, who ran the security arm of Whitcomb's Wonders. With them was a pretty young woman with a baby.

"Hi, Jack," Hank said. "You're reporting to work early."

"The plan was," Evan explained, "for Jack to get some work done before any of Haley's employees got to work." His eyes went to the clothing over Jack's arm and the boots in his other hand. Evan raised an eyebrow and asked, "You've brought a change of clothes."

Jackie came to look more closely at the boots. Only then did she see the glimpse of a lavender strap sticking out the top of one of them. She took it between her thumb and forefinger and pulled out the bra.

The woman with the baby gasped then giggled and everyone else stared in surprise. Evan came to put a hand on his shoulder. "It's okay, Jack," he said with mock seriousness. "We honor diversity at Whitcomb's Wonders."

Jack was both embarrassed and able to appreciate the absurdity of the situation.

"But you look like you could use the push-up variety," Evan went on, standing back to study his flat chest. "Appropriately called the Wonderbra, if I'm not mistaken."

Hank grinned and nodded. "A boon to science for which I happily take the credit."

Jackie backhanded him in the stomach. "It was invented by a French woman for a Canadian company forty years ago. It didn't have much of an impact on the market until Playtex took over the license in 1994."

The others weren't sure whether or not to laugh at her detailed lesson.

"What?" she asked. "I own four. I was interested."

Jack frowned threateningly at Evan. "If you don't

want to have to digest this bra, just be quiet. This happens to belong to Kay, who is probably freezing in the shower as we speak."

"Kay's here?" Jackie asked. "We've been here for five minutes talking over an advertising plan and had no idea…."

"Never mind that," the other young woman said, readjusting the baby on her hip. There was laughter in her eyes as she extended her free hand. "I'm her boss, Haley Megrath, Hank's sister. Why is Kay freezing in the shower?"

Jack explained about the accident. "She sent me to her place to get her a change of clothes. Now, if you'll excuse me, I'll deliver them."

"Hah!" Evan called after him as he opened the door. "The old pour-paint-all-over-a-woman-so-you-can-get-her-naked trick!"

Jack threatened him with a look and closed the door behind him. He expected to find Kay wrapped in a towel, waiting for him. But she'd probably heard the others arrive and was hiding out, afraid someone might walk in.

"Kay?" he knocked on the bathroom door.

The door opened slightly and a slender hand came out. He put the boots in it.

The hand disappeared with them, then reappeared. "Funny," she said. "There'd better be more."

He had no reason to feel playful, and yet he did. Unless it was the ridiculousness of the entire incident, the silliness of his friends, and the weird fact that he even had made friends at this dark time in his life.

"I'm not amused," she said, the hand groping in his direction. "If you don't want to be punched around by a naked woman, give me my clothes."

There was a joke there, but it seemed wisest to let it be. He turned her hand to put the hangers in it.

"Thank you," she said again, drawing the clothes into the bathroom.

"And here are your keys." He held them in the small opening and she took them.

"Thank you," she said, just her face surrounded by wild wet curls appearing in the space. "I'm sorry about your face."

He shrugged. "It's all right. I've had to live with it all my life."

She giggled. "No, I mean the bruise."

"I'm fine," he assured her. "I'm sorry about your hair and your clothes. And when you're dressed, your boss and the Whitcombs and a few other people are waiting in the office. I'm sure they're going to want to torture you about this, even though I've explained."

"Oh, it's all right," she said with a sigh. He could hear the rustle of fabric as she pulled on her clothes. "Are you going to stay and paint?"

"I'm going to stay and clean up. Then I'm due back at the school to finish the baseboards in the teachers' lounge. I'll finish here tonight after you've all gone home."

"Thanks for everything."

"Sure. Have a good day."

"You, too."

Jack turned to find Evan, Hank and Gideon picking up the now hardening puddles of paint with pieces of cardboard. Jackie held the baby while Haley wielded a squeegee dipped in cleaning solution. The mess was pretty well gone when he reached them.

"Thank you," he said. "I appreciate your help. It was my mess."

Jackie smiled. "It's the code of Maple Hill. Be kind to strangers so you can make them feel indebted and blackmail them later."

"Noble," he said. "See you all later."

He heard their silence as he left. He knew they were staring at his retreating back and wondering just what had happened between him and Kay. He wouldn't be there for anything when she finally came out of the bathroom.

Well. He was doing a fine job of keeping a low profile and blending into the Maple Hill background. So far he'd been front page news, was on oddly intimate terms with an eager reporter and had acquired friends who let nothing slip by them. If he were the old Pastor Jack, he'd think that God was trying to keep him from his objective. But he wasn't that man anymore. This was just a joke played by an unkind Fate to see whether he was determined enough to work his plan on Ron Milford that he could evade all distractions in his path.

He had only to prove that he was. And to wait patiently for Milford's open house and the opportunity to get to know him better, to gain access to his office.

And to stay out of Kay Florio's way.

KAY COVERED a Historical Society meeting at the Maple Hill Museum later that morning, took several photos of the high school band practicing in the new gazebo at the head of the lake, and interviewed a woman who'd come to Maple Hill in 1937 because her doctor had advised her to get out of the city due to her failing health. She was now ninety-six.

Kay's cell phone rang as she waited at a stoplight. It was Rachel. "Where are you?" she asked. "I came to take you to lunch."

"But we'll see each other at Agnes's tonight."

"I know. I was just free and thought it'd be fun."

"Are you at the *Mirror*?"

"Yes. And there's a package on your desk from Prudent Designs." The clothing line was owned and designed by Prue Hale, Gideon Hale's wife. Her work was making a splash all over the East Coast, and, thanks to a spread in a magazine run by Gideon's aunt, she'd captured some interest in Europe, as well.

"What? I didn't order anything."

"Well, it's here, wrapped in silver paper. You'd better hurry before I get into it."

"It must be a mistake." Ten minutes later Kay stood between her cousin and her boss, who crowded close as she pulled a small white envelope from under the lavender ribbon wrapped around the box. She removed a silver note card and opened it.

"Sorry about your clothes," it read in a bold script. "Hope this makes up for it. But next time, watch where you're going." It was signed, "Jack Keaton's ladder."

Rachel already had the lid off but waited for Kay to delve into the tissue. Shocked and touched, Kay drew out a mossy-green shirt jacket with square pockets and a shirt collar.

Rachel and Haley gasped in unison. "Oh," Haley said with deep respect. "You can't let a man with that kind of taste get away."

"What does he mean, 'Jack Keaton's ladder'?" Rachel took the garment from her to look it over.

Kay explained briefly about colliding with Jack's ladder and being covered in paint when she came to work that morning.

"He went to her house and brought her back a change of clothes," Haley added, reverently touching a sleeve of the garment. "And went into the shower in the back to deliver them."

"He did not." Sinking into her chair, warmed by the thoughtfulness of the gesture, Kay defended him. "He stayed politely outside the door and passed the clothes to me."

Rachel held the jacket up and studied it lustfully. "I want one of these. I wonder if it comes in brown."

Haley pulled a brochure off the bulletin board behind her desk. "Here's her catalog. I've always wanted that hooded cloak she makes. I admire you, Kay. The accident was essentially your fault, yet you got him to feel guilty enough to buy you a gift."

"I wasn't trying to."

Rachel put the jacket back into the box and patted her on the shoulder. "There's something about you that makes people want to do things for you. Go with it, girl. Don't fight it."

Unable to determine if that was a suggestion that she appeared weak or somehow helpless, Kay chose not to be offended. Rachel set a strong standard for women and probably thought Kay still suffered too much over Betsy, though she'd never outright said so.

But Jack's gift was so kind, she couldn't be upset about anything.

Kay and Rachel went to lunch at Perk Avenue. Over soup and the salad sampler, they talked about Derek Slocum's accident.

"Was his arm broken?" Kay asked.

Rachel shook her head, adding pepper to her soup. "No, but it was a bad sprain."

"Did you find his mother?"

"No. She hadn't left any numbers, apparently. We got in touch with Children's Services, and his caseworker picked him up when we were finished. She was going to pick up Jordie at school, then take both of them to a foster home in town until she can locate their mother."

"So, Gib didn't arrest him."

"He ticketed him for speeding. The caseworker's angling to get the whole family into counseling."

"The mother's hopeless. She only keeps the kids around to get welfare money for them."

"Everyone who's dealt with her knows that, but their caseworker is young and considers everyone redeemable. She keeps trying."

"Meanwhile, the kids are neglected, and Derek's going to end up killing himself."

"Possibly." Rachel nodded. "But preventing that is Children Services' responsibility, not yours. I know you've grown attached to Jordie, and Charlie's convinced she's going to find a way to redeem Derek. He's been one of her favorites since he hit high school. She says he's smart, but he's never been taught to aim his brain in a good direction. She told me she was signing him up for Father Chabot's weekend basketball camp and he'd better show up or she would tell his caseworker how she spotted him at the Patriot Pub after curfew."

Kay was pleasantly surprised by her cousins' concern for Derek and their crafty plan to help. The priest gathered together troubled teenagers and kids to play basketball with adults from the community. They played for hours every Saturday, then his housekeeper fed everyone dinner in the church's community room. He announced scores and winners from the pulpit on Sunday, and gave the scores to the *Maple Hill Mirror*. Many of the Wonders were involved in the games.

"So, you have a soft spot for Derek Slocum, too?" Kay asked.

Rachel put her fork down, seemingly ambivalent. "I've helped treat him and Jordie for various illnesses and household accidents over the last few years, and I can imagine what their lives are like. They're both smart and have potential, but if someone doesn't turn Derek off this self-destructive course, it's going to be too late. And losing him to injury or jail would devastate Jordie. I guess we'll just have to wait and see if we're too late, or not."

"Do you think he'll show up for Father's basketball games?"

"I hope so. The kid deserves a chance."

Kay let a minute pass, then asked, "What about Gib?"

Rachel looked up from her dissection of the third and last salad in their sampler plates. "What do you mean?"

"Doesn't he deserve a chance?"

Rachel pulled a face, them pushed her plate away. "I don't want to talk about it. It's my business, Kay, not yours, so butt out."

"You're always in *my* business," Kay reminded her quietly while conversation among other diners buzzed around them. "You butt into my life all the time. You're always harping at me that Betsy wasn't my fault. That not wanting to get involved with a man is stupid. That devoting my life to a novel is…"

"Please!" Rachel pleaded in a loud whisper. "I'm older and smarter than you are. I'm allowed to tell you how to live your life. And I'm tired of hearing Gib say he's sorry when it doesn't mean a damn. He ruined my life!"

"You're *letting* it be ruined. That doesn't have to happen. At least meet with him and talk about it. What could that possibly hurt?"

"It could hurt *me!* I'd have to look into the face I've devoted most of my life to and listen to him tell me it didn't mean anything when he made love with that vacuous woman while I was working like a fool to be a better nurse."

Kay sighed, understanding Rachel's position and hating it at the same time.

"It would almost be better if it *had* meant something because then my life wouldn't have been destroyed for nothing."

"Okay, okay." Kay waved a hand for the waitress. "Forget I brought it up. I'm sure one day you'll wake up and realize you're throwing away a man who acted like a jerk for one night in circumstances that were very difficult for him, and that you should do something about it."

The waitress arrived. She was a very delicate, slender little thing with wispy blond hair and wide gray eyes. "Your check?" she asked, pulling her order pad out of her apron pocket.

"Not yet." Kay smiled at Rachel. "We're having pumpkin cheesecake, please. And more coffee."

Rachel frowned at Kay. "Do you know how much fat is in cheesecake? Why did we bother having salads?"

"Because you wanted them and I was trying to indulge you and put you in a good mood so I could bring up Gib. But since that didn't work, we're having dessert. There are only twenty carbs in pumpkin pie if you don't eat the crust."

"But this is pumpkin *cheesecake*."

"Doesn't matter. Negligible carbs in cheese."

"Oh, God. Charlie's taken over your brain."

Kay smiled, even as an image of the beautiful green jacket waiting for her on her desk filled her mind's eye.

"Not true," she denied, then added to herself, *Jack Keaton's taken over my brain.*

CHAPTER EIGHT

JACK WAS READY for Ron Milford's open house. He'd
spent the last couple of evenings poring over the vital
points in Julia's journal, and studying a book he'd bor-
rowed from the library to help him identify terms and
become familiar with types of savings and investments.

He was prepared to chat intelligently with Milford,
make an appointment to discuss investments and write
him a check, albeit a small one. While he'd been in the
hospital recovering from his wounds, his father had sold
some investments he'd made and given the money to
Jack to help him start over. Having always lived in
church housing, he'd had no house to sell when he left
Vermont, and no money of his own, except for a thousand dollars the congregation had given him when he'd
left for Iraq. Julia had managed to save it.

He thought of her with a sharp renewal of anguish.
She'd waved him off without tears and with promises
of all they'd do when he returned home because he'd
needed to know when he left that she was strong and capable. But when he'd read her letters amid the dust and
death of Baghdad, they'd been filled with how much she

missed him, how she longed for him, and delicious details of the love they would make when he returned. That need and lust for him had been just what he'd needed to know when he'd been desperate with homesickness and emotionally ill with the death of friends, innocents and children.

Julia had gone to work to make a living while he'd been gone, and she'd managed to save that thousand dollars so that they could do something special with it when he came home.

"Take the kids to Disney World," she speculated in her letter, "or the Jersey shore, or maybe New York for Christmas."

And that job had killed her.

He felt terrible guilt for having been intrigued by Kay Florio. Not that he'd done anything remotely inappropriate. But he was interested in her, despite the single-mindedness of his mission. He'd even been fascinated, bought her a jacket in apology for the ladder incident. He couldn't stop thinking that somehow he was tarnishing Julia's memory.

He was shrugging into the jacket of his one and only suit when Cal called. She'd gone home to feed her cat and was due back in ten minutes.

"My water heater burst!" she exclaimed without even waiting for him to say hello. "The kitchen carpet is drenched, I have water everywhere, and I…oh, Jack, I'm so sorry, but I can't leave this mess! I don't know where to begin!"

Ha. That Fate again. He knew the drill; he had to forge on anyway. "Don't panic, Cal. Hank Whitcomb's got a crew who can take care of that for you. You stay there and I'll call and see that they send somebody out."

"But your appointment."

"I'll just…take the kids." The invitation had said children and friends welcome.

"Jack," Cal said feelingly, "you're a saint. Or an angel, or something sent from heaven."

It was all he could do not to laugh aloud. Tonight he was definitely from the more southerly contingent.

He made the promised call, performed what his mother used to call "spit-washes" on the children, running a soapy washcloth over them without actually putting them in the shower. They were thrilled at the prospect of accompanying him to a party, and cooperated happily.

Jack put Buster in the kitchen in the crate he'd purchased, and he and the children piled into the truck.

Well, he thought, driving to the Common where Milford's office building stood, he'd sent the jacket to Kay to apologize for the accident the other morning. And that should be the end of it. That would make up for the harm he'd done, and…that would be that.

He saw her chartreuse Bug parked among all the other cars on the street, presumably belonging to other invitees.

The place was packed with people. Milford had a suite of several rooms, one of which he'd filled with toys and children's books. A young woman who introduced herself as Jenny Rowe, his new secretary invited Jack to leave the children with her. Recognizing Hank's kids among the group watching a cartoon video, he agreed. And that was a good thing, because Amanda and Paul were already sitting on the floor in front of it, mesmerized.

Jack went in search of Milford.

He ran into Evan, his wife and Gideon and Prue. Prue gave him a quick hug. "I think you made the right decision with that jacket," she said, looking pleased. "Kay's wearing it tonight and telling everyone it's one of mine, and the funny story of how she happens to have it."

"Really." His mind imagined Kay in it, then he called it back to remember his purpose for the evening. He recalled thinking when he chose it that Julia would have liked it. They'd never had money for elegant things, but she'd had a gift for scouring thrift shops and finding clothes for herself and him and the children that looked as though they'd been found in a designer's showroom. "Well, it was lucky for me that you promised me an item of clothing when I repainted your studio. Otherwise she'd have gotten a bouquet of flowers."

"I'm sure she'd have loved that, too, but you should see how spectacular she looks in my jacket. But, now seriously, Jack." Prue took the lapels of his coat to reclaim his attention as he looked around for Milford. "When I promised you an item of clothing, I wanted it to be something from the new menswear line I'm designing. So you still have that coming."

"Thank you, but I think we're square."

"We're not, but we'll argue about it another time. See you." She waved to a friend and wandered off.

Jack greeted the other two then left them to talk while he wandered through the rooms, which were crowded with people all talking about investments. He found that amazing. Usually such events were an excuse to sip champagne and eat canapés.

Then he was handed a plastic cup of champagne by a white-coated waiter, along with a sheet of questions Milford had apparently prepared. There were questions with multiple choice answers and prizes offered for the guest who had them all correct in the least amount of time. No wonder everyone was staying on topic.

After a quick glance, he felt as he had in Divinity school when the semester final in theology was made up of all the things he'd studied hardest. He found a table in what was probably a meeting room. Though there was a glass on a napkin on the table, the room was empty.

The rooms in this top floor suite all had Palladian windows under high ceilings. Jack wasn't familiar enough with the building to know if Milford had added architectural details when he'd redecorated, but there were picture rails, and elegant molding at the windows and doors.

He took a pen out of his pocket and decided to make sure he was prepared for this meeting. There were dozens of people here who were potential clients, but Milford had asked Jack specifically to come and talk to him about investing, and he was sure this meeting was meant to be. Tonight he would put his plan into motion. He began to check off answers.

He looked up at a sound in the doorway and saw Kay standing there holding an open book, the quiz sheet and a pen in her other hand. The ever-present camera hung over her shoulder.

The jacket did look wonderful on her, and the color of her lipstick matched the imprint of lips on the napkin under the drink across from him. He'd been hoping to avoid her tonight—or if he had to speak to her, to make it a simple greeting and move on—easy to do at this kind of event.

But she looked up and her eyes lit up when she saw him. His heartbeat accelerated. Hell.

"Hi, Jack," she said, her voice calmer than her eyes. She held the book on the flat of one hand and did a turn to show off the jacket. "Thank you so much. It was completely unnecessary, but I love it."

He smiled back, subtlely withholding the strength of his feelings at seeing her. She wasn't the reason he was here, and if his body couldn't remember that, his brain did.

"I thought it was only fair. And it looks as though I made the perfect choice. Now, if you'll excuse me, I'm about to win a free…"

"You may as well give it up," she said, sitting across from him, missing his attempt to discourage conversation. She set her camera on the table. "I'm going to win. I found this book in his office…" She held up *Fundamentals of Investments*. "This has a glossary. I can't remember what ADR means. I took an economics class in college, but…" She frowned over the choices. "It has something to do with arbitrage, I think."

"That's APT, you're thinking about," he said. "Arbitrage Pricing Theory, not ADR."

She looked up at him with a raised eyebrow. Her curls were in order tonight, all going smoothly under. It seemed wrong somehow. He'd have loved to see that unruly one near her temple spring out. "How do you know that? I thought you told him that day in front of the tea shop that you don't know much about investing."

That was true. He thought fast. "I've been…studying. I want to invest, and I don't want to just leave it to someone, I want to know what I'm doing."

She nodded, apparently considering that reasonable—thank goodness. "Then, what is ADR?"

"American depositary receipt. A means of investing in foreign companies."

She smiled and checked the appropriate box. "Thank you. What's a block? 2,000, 5,000 or 10,000 shares of stock?"

He was amused by her obvious belief that he was willing to help her. "Are you aware that I'm competing for the same prize?" he asked, waving his sheet at her.

"Of course I am. It's dinner for two at the Yankee Inn.

If I win, I'll take you. If you win, you can take me. Is it 5,000?" She poised her pen over that box.

"It's 10,000 or more," he said.

She checked that. "Bull market," she read. Then laughed and looked up at him. "It's not lies about how the market's doing, is it?"

"No, it's not."

"It's investors who believe the market will rise. Because things struck with a bull's horns go up, and things hit by a bear's paws go down. A bull market's up, and a bear market is down." She began to check the box, then glanced across the table for corroboration. "Right?"

"Yes."

"Okay, I only have one unanswered."

He pushed his sheet aside and said with exaggerated patience, "Well, by all means, let me help you with that."

"What's Best Efforts?"

He had to grin at that. "Certainly not what you're putting forth."

She smiled into his eyes. "Well, I've discovered that you're more informative than the book. What's the answer?"

He had to pull his eyes away from hers to think. He consulted his own sheet. "It's b," he said. "An offering of securities to investors where the investment banker provides only a marketing effort."

"What does that mean?"

"I have no idea, I just know it isn't, 'trying hard to sell,' or 'making every effort to acquire more shares.'"

"Okay." She looked the quiz over one more time and gave him that smile again that reached right into his soul. He couldn't imagine what had suddenly brought this on. She usually preferred to frost him with a glance, or beat him over the head with clever comebacks. It was the jacket, he concluded. He'd meant only to apologize for being where she hadn't expected him to be, and she'd decided it meant more than that. "You can start planning what you want to eat. Their menu…" She began to rhapsodize about it when Amanda ran into the room.

"Daddy!" she exclaimed. "We're watching *Finding Nemo!*" She was hand in hand with a dark-haired little girl. "This is Moonie. Her American name is Margaret Isabelle, but her Indian name is Moon Flower."

"Hi, Moonie," he said.

She smiled shyly in return, but when Amanda crawled into his lap, a sign that she was about to ask for something she really wanted, Moonie did the same. His arms full, he braced himself for the imminent request.

"Moonie's dad has horses," Amanda said, her eyes bright, her cheeks pink. "And we can buy one from him."

That was just what he needed. "When Buster grows up," he said, squeezing Amanda to him, "he's going to be as big as a horse. Right now, that's all we can handle."

"I could ride him to school!"

"Amanda, that's not a good idea. There'd be cars all around him and pavement that would hurt his feet. We'd have to live in the country to have a horse."

"Well, could we move?"

Amanda always had an angle.

"I thought you liked our house."

"I do. But I'd like to have a horse, too. I bet Buster would like somebody to play with."

"He has you and Paul."

As though the sound of his name had conjured him up, Paul ran into the room, his eyes wide. "Now, we're gonna watch *Shrek,*" he said excitedly, "and we're gonna have ice cream! You better come!"

Both girls slithered out of his lap. "Can we talk about it later?" Amanda asked.

"We can always talk about it." That had been Julia's policy.

Amanda stopped at the door to give him a long-suffering look. "That means no."

"Yes, it does."

Moonie waved at him and both girls took off at a run.

Smiling after them, Jack turned to Kay to apologize for not introducing her, and was surprised to find the warmth he'd been so worried about just a few moments ago completely gone. She looked pale and…horrified? And was pressed against the back of her chair.

He couldn't imagine what had prompted that sudden and complete turnabout.

"What is it?" he asked gently. She looked almost ill. "You don't like children?"

She cleared her throat and pushed out of her chair. "Of course I do," she said, forcing a smile. "I…just didn't know you had…any."

He stood, too. She looked as though she might fall over.

She waved the quiz sheet. "I'm going to turn this in."

"Good idea," he said.

She looked him in the eye, an odd sadness in her expression he didn't understand. "Good night." She started for the door.

"Kay!" he called.

She stopped and turned, that odd sadness deepening.

He held up her camera, surprised that she'd forgotten it, wondering what accounted for that expression. "You might need this."

She stared at it a moment, clearly as surprised as he was. She took the few steps back to claim it, then gave him a quick glance. "Bye," she said, and hurried from the room.

He had the strangest sense that the distance he'd been determined to put between them tonight had just happened with no effort on his part. Amanda and Moonie seemed to have done it.

What the hell did that mean?

And why wasn't he happier about it?

He had little time to think about it when Ron Milford passed by and beckoned to him. "Got your quiz finished?" he asked, motioning Jack to follow him down the hallway. They dodged a woman gesturing with her champagne glass, and a line of people waiting for the restroom.

"Actually, I was helping a friend and didn't get mine finished." Jack's adrenaline was kicking in. This guy-to-guy connection was the reason he was here. "Is my time up?"

Milford laughed. "No, but I'm afraid Jackie Whitcomb turned hers in ten minutes ago and won first prize. There are a dozen other smaller prizes, though. Just submit your quiz before you leave."

They'd reached Milford's office and he ushered Jack inside. The room was decorated as Jack imagined an investment office in Manhattan would look—antique furniture upholstered in what appeared to be gray silk, carved floor-to-ceiling bookcases, a standing globe and several potted ferns on an Oriental carpet. Above Milford's desk was a magnificent chandelier.

"Very impressive," Jack praised as Milford pulled one of the silk-upholstered chairs out for him, then moved around his wide, cherrywood desk to take his place behind it. Privately, Jack thought this had not been decorated on a retired man's pension or Social Security. Every detail looked expensive.

Milford nodded. "I've been spending money like a drunken sailor. Once I decided to open an office again, I thought it should look like I know what I'm doing with money." He smiled ingenuously. "So, have a seat, Jack, and tell me what you'd like to have and do in your future, and I'll try to figure out how we can get that for you."

Jack returned Milford's smile and said to himself, "What I'd like to do is beat the crap out of you, and what I want to have is the knowledge that you're going to jail for a long, long time, and that Julia can rest easy while she watches them lock the door behind you."

But, aloud, he said, "Well, we can start small. We're renting our house, and I'd like to have enough money for a down payment on a bigger one, some money to put aside for my children's education—" he, too, could smile ingenuously "—and a little for those Americanos I'm so fond of."

JACK KEATON had children. A little girl. A little girl about six! On her computer at home, Kay put Jack Keaton's name in the search box on the linked database for the Newspaper Publishers' Associations of America. All newspapers in the country archived their articles in a central database.

While waiting for it to come up with matches, she forked chocolate cake into her mouth and gave up trying to understand herself.

She'd come home an hour ago, determined to work on her novel; encounters with Jack usually helped her to come up with dialogue for her hero and heroine.

Tonight should have inspired some Nora Efron dialogue, Neil Simon dialogue, good old Frank Capra dialogue.

Instead, she'd stared at the screen, unable to even think about her fictional people. Jack had a little girl!

She'd begun to think of Jack as her muse. Nothing serious could come of their relationship, but she'd started to think there was something between them that would have been fun to explore. That would be worth taking down the road in a light and friendly way to see what happened.

And he'd given her that beautiful jacket, leading her to believe that he might be thinking the same thing.

But he had a little girl. Amanda, he'd called her.

That absolutely shut the door on any kind of a relationship for them because she could never got into a light and casual fling with someone who had children. It was too risky for kids to become attached to someone who couldn't stay.

That beautiful little girl with the big blue eyes, the blond curls and the personality that lit the room. She was so much like Betsy had been.

She took another bite of cake as a list of matches came up on the screen. Common sense told her that she should let the whole Jack Keaton issue go since she could have nothing to do with him.

But she was beginning to sense the bones of a story here. Maybe not anything that could ever be front page in the *Mirror*, but something she had to know for her own edification.

Definitely Jack Keaton was different. Charlie had sworn he was a man on the run, a deposed prince.

Kay had seen pain in his eyes and put it down to the time he'd spent in Iraq. And every once in a while she saw a murderous look as though whatever had caused the pain was something he couldn't live with until he righted a wrong—or exacted revenge.

She scanned the matches. Drummer in a grunge band, mayor of a small town in Kentucky, sound technician on an independent film, character in a murder mystery. She checked them all, looking for photos.

The drummer OD'd three years earlier, the mayor was bald, the sound technician was sixty-seven.

She checked out the next four. Someone arrested on a DUI, a minister in Haverstown, Vermont, a doctor on a cruise ship, a high-wire artist with the circus who broke both legs in a fall.

Kay gasped, remembering Jack's limp, and quickly clicked on the high-wire artist. She sighed dispiritedly when a photo came up of the man in a wheelchair in the middle of his wife and six sons in a leafy neighborhood in Adelaide, Australia.

Maybe the doctor on the cruise ship. Perhaps he'd unwittingly harmed a patient and Charlie was right—he was running away from an investigation. But he turned out to be platinum blond and in his late twenties, photographed between two bikini-clad women for the cover of a men's magazine.

She took another bite of cake, prepared to spend a long night at the computer, and clicked on the minister. She could not have been more shocked when Jack Keaton's photo came up—Maple Hill's Jack Keaton.

She stared at it in disbelief. There he was in the garb of a clergyman, standing with his arm around a very pretty young woman in front of a small white church tucked into a verdant hillside.

"Reverend John Keaton of Burlington has taken the pulpit of the Path of Light Church in Haverstown," according to the caption under the photo that appeared on page five of the *Haverstown Gazette*. "His wife, Julia, is expecting their first child."

The story that accompanied the photo said that he'd been educated at Bangor Theological Seminary, that he'd played football in college, done two years in the navy, joined the Rotary Club, and that he was looking forward to getting to know the community.

His wife, Julia. He no longer had a wife, did he? Kay hadn't seen a wife, but then she hadn't seen his children, either—until a couple of hours ago.

She erased the search box and put in Reverend John Keaton, then refined the search to Haverstown, Vermont.

There he was again, in uniform this time, a little older and remarkably handsome. He was on the way to Iraq as a chaplain in the Naval Reserve. He had the rank of Lt. Commander, and had been assigned to a contingent of marines.

Then his name appeared in a headline, no photograph accompanying the story. Reverend Keaton Recovering At Walter Reed In Washington. The story said he'd suffered a shattered femur during a firefight in Baghdad the day before he was to return home. He'd been with a marine battalion ordered to seize a presidential palace. A mortar had thrown him fifteen feet into the air, and he'd slammed into the Humvee when he fell down.

Haverstown prays for his recovery, and mourns the death of his wife, Julia, in a single-car accident on Allan Falls Road. The Reverend Keaton's parents are caring for their two children, Amanda, 5; and Paul, 4.

Kay's stomach turned over. A shattered femur. The death of his wife. No wonder his eyes were filled with pain and anger.

Adding that grim knowledge to her collection of information, she went back to the list of matches and found, "Julia Keaton, wife of Jack…" She clicked on it and found the news story about her death in the *Burlington Eagle*.

As she read the story, digesting the facts, she held in her mind's eye the pretty woman standing beside Jack in the photograph. She'd been thirty-one when her car went off the road on an icy night in Haverstown. The car had rolled down the embankment and plunged into the lake. She'd sustained multiple traumas to the head and chest. She left two children, and a husband serving in Iraq. He was being sent home for her funeral, and was involved in a firefight the night before he was to leave.

Kay read the story again then stared at the words, her heart bleeding for Jack Keaton. How horrible was it to be separated from his family for a year, only to lose his wife before he could come home to her? How awful to know that she'd been driving home from work, probably tired and missing him, and slipped off the road.

And Kay had seen his two beautiful children. Had they been her final thought when she realized she was going to die? Had she cried their names? Jack's name?

She imagined Jack fighting for his life in the hospital, unable to attend his wife's funeral. How deep was his agony that even now, all these months later, it still brimmed in his eyes?

She was about to print the information for herself when she realized that the scroll bar was not at the bottom of the page. She pulled it down and found a final paragraph.

"M & S Money Management, Mrs. Keaton's employer," read the last few lines, "made a generous contribution to Families of Our Fighters in her name."

Something familiar in the paragraph nagged at Kay's consciousness. She was reading it a second time when her brain suddenly made the connection. She stopped still for a moment, a strange wariness crawling coolly along her spine. She rummaged frantically through notes on the side of her desk until she found the small stack of yellow-pad pages she'd used in her research on Ron Milford when she'd interviewed him for her article.

She scanned her notes until she found what she was looking for. Ron Milford had been a partner in M & S Money Management in—she checked it against what was on the screen and saw incredibly that the city was the same. Haverstown, Vermont.

Her heartbeat picked up as her well-cataloged brain rifled through facts, memories, impressions. What were the chances, she asked herself, that a man whose wife was killed would end up in the same town as the man who'd employed the wife when she died? She remembered Jack's unwillingness to be photographed. Had that been simple shyness, or had he been afraid of publicity? Afraid Milford would realize who he was?

And why, when he'd met Ron Milford that afternoon she'd introduced them in front of Perk Avenue, hadn't he mentioned that his wife had worked for Ron? As she remembered, Milford had repeated Jack's last name as though he might remember it, but Jack had teased about not being related to Michael Keaton.

Jack had turned up at the open house though he'd admitted he had little to invest. Of course, Ron Milford had encouraged him to go, assuring him he could find a way to help him invest.

She read the story over one more time, looking for the time of the accident—10:57 p.m. Did Jack consider Milford responsible for Julia's death because she'd had to work so late and drove home in dangerous conditions?

She mulled over what she knew about Ron Milford and what she'd learned about Jack Keaton, and thought she saw an unsettling convergence of data.

This could not be a coincidence.

Jack had a plan. She guessed it was revenge of some kind. As she'd been leaving the open house tonight, she'd seen Ron leading Jack toward his office.

Her heart began to thump. Was Milford still alive?

All right, she was letting the novelist in her take over

from the reporter. She'd heard no sirens, and her scanner was always on. There'd been nothing about trouble on the Common.

Still, she picked up the phone and glanced at the clock. It was just after 10:00 p.m. She dialed Milford at home and his wife answered.

"Milfords' residence."

Joanne Milford was a beautiful woman with thick graying red hair and a pleasant personality. She volunteered at the hospital, delivered Meals on Wheels and was a Master Gardener. She'd helped Gary Warren, Hank's gardening expert, design landscaping for the new courtyard at the high school.

'Hi, Joanne," Kay said. "I'm looking for Ron to get a few details about attendance at the open house for the 'City Doings' column. Is he still at the office?"

"No, he just came home. Hold on."

Kay breathed a sigh of relief.

"Hi, Kay." Milford sounded enthused and excited when he took the phone. "It was a wonderful evening. We had so many people come that we might have lost count, but my secretary says 104 signed the guest book, and I made thirteen appointments. I'd call that a successful evening."

"Absolutely." He did not sound as though he'd been threatened or traumatized in any way.

"Remember introducing me to Jack Keaton?" Ron asked.

Kay's breath caught in her throat. "Yes, I do," she finally replied.

"He showed up."

"Yes, I saw him. But I got the impression…I mean, he has two little children and probably not a lot of investment capital."

"Right. But we worked out a deal. I'm renting the single room across the hall from my office that used to be Madame Tatiana's Palm Reading Parlor. Joanne and a couple of her friends have some wild idea about making purses and wallets, like that designer Vera Bradley."

"Yes?" She thought she saw where this was going and began to lose her sense of relief.

"They think they'll be more credible if they have office space. But the place is the most god-awful purple."

"So…Jack's going to paint it for you in exchange for…"

"My services! Right. Good old Yankee barter system. He's a great guy. I'm happy I could work something out for him. And it'll make Joanne happy—always a good reason to do anything. We might be able to use him at home, too. We have an unfinished room in the basement we want to use for a gym."

Oh, God. Kay had a suspicion this could not be good. Milford was safe today, but Jack Keaton had cleverly worked his way into the man's life.

She thanked Ron for the information about the open house and said good-night. Then she spent an hour sipping at a cup of spiked coffee and wondering if she should tell Gib what she suspected.

Of course, she had no proof of anything, just a series

of incidents and facts that were coming together like some Bermuda Triangle moment.

She decided to do what all good reporters did when they had the threads of a story, but no proof. She was going to keep her mouth shut and investigate.

CHAPTER NINE

JACK STARED at the sandal in his hand. Well, it hadn't been a sandal when he'd bought it several months ago. Then it had been a sturdy Doc Martens half boot purchased to celebrate the fact that he was walking almost normally again, except for the slight limp he'd probably never get over.

Now the toe was missing and half the heel was gone—thanks to the footwear artistry of Buster, who licked the hand that held the shoe. When Jack snatched his hand away, the dog backed up, looking surprised and hurt.

Jack growled at Calpurnia and the children collected around where he sat on the foot of his bed. "You're all with him all day and no one saw him eating my shoe?" he demanded.

"We were baking cookies," Cal replied, a hand protectively on each child's shoulder. "You know, the ones you've already eaten a dozen of?"

Jack strained for patience. His favorite pair of fleece-lined slippers had also been the victim of Buster's artistry. "I'm happy you were so productive," he granted, "but if you're going to be busy, can't you make sure he has a toy to play with, or that you put him in his crate?"

"Daddy." Amanda came to put an arm around his shoulder. "You're supposed to do what you told us to do when Buster ate your slippers. Put your shoes away in your closet and close your door when you leave."

She was absolutely right, but he was in no mood to be preached to by his own six-year-old. He was grumpy and out of sorts. He was supposed to connect with Hank and Gideon at the bank in fifteen minutes for the weekly Wednesday Fall Festival meeting and he had no shoe for his right foot. Today he'd painted the principal's office the color he was supposed to use in one of the Lightfoot sisters' bedrooms, and he had no one to blame for the confusion but himself. So, he was going to have to repaint, and that would make him two days late painting the office for Ron Milford.

Not that that would make any big difference to his plan, but now that he finally had it in play, he was anxious to make some headway. He knew he'd get nowhere quickly if he didn't remain calm, but he found it hard to be so close to getting proof of Milford's crooked operation and his involvement in Julia's death. He was impatient to get started.

He was liking this town and the people in it too much. He wasn't going to be able to stay here when this was over. Though he thought this was one of those the-end-justifies-the-means situations, he doubted the locals would feel the same way. They'd welcomed him into their homes and offices, shared their lives and their laughter, and he doubted they'd be pleased that he'd misrepresented himself.

But that was life. Eventually he'd be able to think about where he would take Amanda and Paul so they could all begin again, but now vindicating Julia consumed him.

Amanda, however, looked just like Julia and it was hard to be angry at her for feeding his own words back to him. He pointed her to his closet. "Would you look around in the bottom and see if you can find my old tennis shoes, please?" Half an hour in them and his leg would be killing him, but making this meeting was an integral part of the plan.

"Okay, Daddy." Happy to cooperate, she disappeared into his closet.

Paul came to sit on his knee and Buster tried again to lick Jack's hand. He raised it to pet him and the dog leaped up and pinned him backward onto the bed, exuberantly happy at his forgiveness.

Paul piled on, and Amanda followed, wearing his tennis shoes on her hands.

Calpurnia gave them a moment, then peeled the children off him. "What is it about these two? Whenever you're down, they leap at you like you're weak prey." She dispatched the children to the kitchen and smiled at him as he sat up. "You don't have to hurry home after the meeting. If you'd like to take that pretty Kay Florio for coffee, you're welcome to."

He pulled on his tennis shoes. "I only took her home last week because her cousin's car wouldn't start."

She shrugged. "You should make your own opportunities. Don't wait for machinery to fail."

"You're not trying to do a little matchmaking, are you, Cal?"

"I am. Blatantly so. It's time, Jack. This house needs a cheerful woman in it."

"And what are you?" He glanced at her as he tied the second shoe.

"Happy to be here, but not at all what I'm talking about. Good men need good women. It makes the world a good place."

She was completely serious. She hadn't a clue how filled with hatred he'd become.

He got to his feet, hugged her briefly and left the room without comment. He kissed the children good bye, scratched Buster between the cars and leaped into the truck. He might just be on time.

Hank and Gideon were getting out of Gideon's red pickup when Jack pulled up. Hank grinned at him as they waited for him in front of the bank. "I hear you tried to paint Biff Huxley's office persimmon pink," he said.

Jack rolled his eyes. It was the first major mistake he'd made since going to work for Whitcomb's Wonders. "I'm sorry about that," he said. "I'll be happy to pay for the two quarts of…"

"That won't be necessary." Hank laughed and clapped him on the shoulder. "It's worth it for the harassment value. Next time I need to send a man to represent the Wonders at a community meeting or event, you're him."

Jack pretended distress. "You mean this Fall Festival committee doesn't fulfill my obligation?"

"Hell, no. This is fun. We have to get you involved in one of the not-so-fun ones. Mosquito Abatement, or Friends of the Common."

"Friends of the Common? That doesn't sound so bad."

"It's picking up dog do," Gideon explained, "and cleaning pigeon do off the statue. We call it 'doing the do.'"

"How…quaint." Jack was determined to do his part in the community even while he was planning Milford's destruction, but he was going to manage to be absent for "doing the do."

The festival plans were taking shape. Jack sat at the end of a middle row with his companions. Hank volunteered Gideon's crew for security, told the chairwoman that he was reporting for Jackie that the City Works Department would see that the barricades needed for the streets around the Common were up by 5:00 a.m. Claire Bell applauded in kindergarten-teacher excitement that things were coming together.

"Kay?" she called, looking around. "Are you here?"

"Yes." Jack was surprised when he heard Kay's voice right behind him. He'd have sworn the few times he'd seen her downtown this week that she'd walked across the street to avoid him or simply disappeared as he approached. Judging by the horrified way she'd looked at his children, she wasn't anxious to encounter him again. And he supposed that was good; it was just the attitude he'd hoped to bring about in her. Though her obvious reason for it offended him.

"My mother's agreed to come," she said with a smile.

"In fact, she's excited about it. She just e-mailed me today, wondering if we wanted to advertise that she'll judge a cooking contest using pumpkin as the main ingredient."

Applause again, this time from everyone.

"And she's offered to prepare a couple of pumpkin pies from Philly Potter's journal. They're Abigail Adams's recipe. That should be worth a raffle, don't you think? Maybe at the dinner dance Sunday night?"

There were oohs and aahs. "Okay," she said. "I'll tell her that's a go, then. And I'll take care of advertising the cooking contest. What do you think? An adult level, and a children's?"

Bridget Malone, one of the partners in Perk Avenue, waved from the middle of the group. "I'll be happy to help you work out details," she said. "And our café will donate dessert for the dinner. And two cakes to the cake-walk."

Kay blew her a kiss. Claire was downright tearful.

Father Chabot raised his hand. "St. Anthony's would like to do the jail booth again," he proposed, "if that's all right with everyone."

Jack turned to ask Gideon what that was, but he and Hank were engaged in quiet conversation with Gib, who sat in front of them.

Kay leaned forward, apparently aware of his confusion. "It's one of the biggest moneymakers of the event," she whispered. "For fifty cents you can have a friend put away in the jail for five minutes. For a dollar, you can put them away for ten. Father Chabot plays the jailor and goes looking for whoever you're putting away and hauls them off to jail. If they resist arrest, they have to pay five dollars."

He didn't know what to make of her eagerness to explain the jail to him, or her prolonged study of his face.

"That sounds like fun," he said.

"If you're anxious to go to jail," she said, then she sat back in her chair.

He thought that a strange response, but then even before his children had upset her, she'd been an unpredictable young woman.

She wasn't wearing the green jacket tonight, he noticed. He should never have sent it to her, but her collision with his ladder had been an unfortunate accident that she'd taken remarkably well, all things considered. So, while he didn't understand her, he liked her fuss-less approach.

And he'd really liked her house. If he was going to stay here, that was the kind of house he'd look for—all the amenities of the present with a solid connection to the past.

But he wasn't, so it didn't matter.

The details of the jail booth approved, Ron Milford stood, along with Alan Dartford, a Maple Hill native and a city councilman. They represented Kiwanis and wanted everyone to know that the membership would be available to help with putting up booths and taking them down. Milford said, to more applause, that as usual they would host the meatball sandwich booth.

Jack watched Milford, who looked completely comfortable in this group to which he was as much a newcomer as Jack was, and wondered if he was a true sociopath. What else could explain his ease in cheating scores of clients out of their money, running Julia off the road to keep her quiet, and resuming his life as though nothing had happened.

A murderous hatred welled in Jack, and the impulse to leap across the aisle and beat Milford senseless was almost overpowering. But nothing would come of his plan if he didn't remain calm, bide his time and get the proof he needed to put him away.

So he folded his arms and listened, reminding himself that the result would be worth everything.

KAY WATCHED Jack's profile while Ron Milford spoke and saw a muscle work in his jaw, a pulse tick at his temple. He rested his forearm on the back of his chair, his hand doubled into a white-knuckled fist. Though she saw only one eye in profile, the intensity of Jack's gaze was enough to laser the ground open under Milford's feet. She didn't have to be a body-language expert to recognize fulminating hatred.

She was right about why Jack Keaton was in Maple Hill. Though following him around for the past few days had proved nothing except that he went to work and went home then went to work again, she was sure she'd been right about why he'd come here.

As though aware of her scrutiny, Jack turned to look at her, that hatred for Milford still alive in his eyes. She felt the impact of it but managed to smile and appear innocent. He studied her for a moment with a concentration that made her feel transparent. She felt an instant's panic, then forced herself to calm down. That "I-can-read-your-mind" way he had of looking at people was just some sort of personal power tool. Probably came in handy when he'd been a minister. It didn't mean he knew she was on to him.

As Milford and Dartford talked on, Kay put her right thumb to her fingertips in a "yak yak yak" gesture to prove her innocence.

The men finally sat down; Claire read a list of duties that she hoped to have done by the next meeting and asked for volunteers. Then she closed the meeting.

As Hank and Gideon talked to Cam, seated in front of them, Jack turned toward Kay again. "Where are your cousins tonight?"

"Rachel's working, and Charlie's grading papers," she replied with a grin, reaching to the floor for her purse. "Unfortunately, my job makes me always available for meetings."

"Got a ride home tonight?"

She nodded. "My car's much more reliable than Charlie's. But I left it in front of the office because I'm going back to work." Had he been about to offer her a ride?

"All right, then." He stood to leave and said good-night to his companions. There was a general milling around as people walked toward the doors, stopped to talk, obstructed the flow of traffic. Caught in the congestion, Kay heard Milford's voice behind her invite someone for a drink. She turned with a sense of foreboding just in time to see Jack smile. Afraid of what might happen if they disappeared into the night together, she intruded upon the conversation before Jack could reply.

"If you're going to bestow clever advice on how to get rich without risking your life savings," she said to Ron with the smile that had gotten her an interview with him in the first place, "I think I should be invited along, too. My novel's not going so well and there may not be bestseller, get-rich money in it for me after all."

Ron looked a little surprised by her boldness and smiled uncertainly. He turned to Jack, clearly unsure what to say. If he really did intend to give Jack investment advice, she was placing herself in the middle of some money manager–client privilege thing. She pretended ignorance of that possibility, certain Ron would appreciate her interference if he knew she was shielding him from whatever Jack intended to do to him.

Jack agreed graciously, though his surreptitious glance at her as the congestion broke and everyone streamed out of the building, was knowing and faintly hostile.

The three of them met on the sidewalk.

"What about the lounge at the Yankee Inn?" Ron suggested. Jack and Kay were in agreement and they were all about to head for their cars when Ron's cell phone rang.

"Hi, Jo," he said, smiling in apology at his companions as he took several steps away. "No, the meeting's just finished," he said, still within earshot. Jack and Kay took several steps in the other direction, trying not to listen.

"You hoping to beat the consulting fee," Jack asked, his tone containing that same hostility, "by learning the ropes over a drink?"

She faced down the look. "Were you?"

"He invited me, if you recall," he replied. "I know you must have heard him since you were eavesdropping. And I think he wanted to talk about my painting his basement."

A little embarrassed that she'd misunderstood the situation, she still held her ground, certain it had the potential to be dangerous, whatever Ron had intended to discuss.

"It's a free country," she said, acknowledging to herself that that wasn't biting dialogue. "Are you offended by a woman inviting herself into a meeting of men?"

He put his hands into his pockets and looked her in the eye. "No, I'm not. But I am offended by being followed, and by becoming the subject of what I can only guess is a journalistic investigation."

She felt her mouth fall open. She'd had no idea that he'd seen her watching him.

"If you're going to follow someone," he advised, "don't do it in a chartreuse Bug."

Accepting that he'd caught her, there seemed little point in pretending. She returned his steady gaze. "Technically, according to the manufacturer, it's cyber green," she corrected, then added accusingly, "I know why you're here."

His mouth didn't fall open, but she saw something explode in his eyes. She was suddenly grateful Ron was nearby. Everyone else who'd attended the meeting was driving away.

"Guys, I'm sorry," Ron said, closing his cell phone and putting it in the inside pocket of a dressy leather jacket. "That was my wife. Some friends from our old neighborhood have shown up and she wants me to bring some treats home." He laughed lightly. "I know the two of you would be more fun than the old neighbors, but good manners require me to be a good host."

"Of course they do," Kay said. "You go on. We'll do this another time."

"Thanks for understanding." Ron shook Jack's hand and hugged Kay. "I owe you both a drink."

"I intend to collect," Jack said, waving him off. Kay heard an ominous quality in the promise. "Don't worry."

Ron strode off to his car, leaving Kay and Jack alone on the now dark and quiet street.

Kay, who had walked from the *Mirror* office across the Common now regretted that, wishing desperately that she had a car to jump into. Since she couldn't escape, her only alternative was to pretend she saw no need to.

"Another time, then," she said to Jack politely, as though she hadn't just told him that she could tip his hand. "Good night."

His thumb and index finger cuffed her right arm. "I don't think so, Kay," he said. "You're coming with me."

CHAPTER TEN

PRIDE WOULD NOT allow her to become hysterical. She had mace on her key chain. "People know where I am." She said the words like a threat as he drove through the dark downtown and in an easterly direction where there were deep woods.

He glanced away from the road to shake his head at her. He looked dangerous in the shadowy interior of the cab of his truck. At the moment there was no evidence of the man whose face lit up at the sight of his children. This was a man on a dark and ugly mission.

"I'm sure people always know where you are. You're hardly shy."

"There's a disk in my desk drawer with everything I've learned about you." Her voice was high and unsteady. She hated that and cleared her throat. "If anything happens to me, Haley will find it."

"Would that bother me if you were out of the way?" he asked. The question was so blatantly heartless, she couldn't answer for a moment.

He'd stopped the car. Her heart began to thump against her ribs and her mouth went dry.

"I mean, I'm asking," he said almost conversationally, "since you've admitted to investigating me and you seem to think that that empowers you to read my mind. So, would I care? What's your opinion?"

He seemed interested in her answer. Would it make the difference as to whether she lived or died?

"I guess," she replied, "only you know that."

"Mmm," he said, unbuckling his seat belt. "My point exactly. There's a lot about this that the facts won't tell you, and since you *can't* read my mind, you shouldn't decide what this is all about without really knowing." He pressed the button on her seat belt and it slid across her chest like a snake. "Let's go."

She watched him walk around the front of the truck, certain he intended to haul her into the woods and test the theory himself on whether or not he'd care if she was gone. As he opened her door, she closed her fingers around the mace on her key chain.

Only as he stood aside and offered a hand to help her out did she realize they were in the parking lot of the Yankee Inn.

"Sometime tonight, Miss Florio," he teased as she remained seated, still staring at her surroundings. "I really need that drink, but I have to get home to my children eventually."

She took his hand, hers cold and trembling.

It was startling to realize, Jack thought, that Kay Florio considered him a threat to her life. At least she had for a few minutes.

He'd known he had her worried, but he figured she owed him that after following him around and threatening to upset the plan that had become paramount to his sanity. But he hadn't suspected she really considered her life in danger until she took his hand to step down from his truck and would have collapsed to her knees if he hadn't caught her.

One single sob erupted from her as he supported her weight. Then she straightened, tossed her head and raised large, dark eyes to his. It was clear she'd been traumatized and she was trying to read in his eyes if he'd frightened her deliberately.

"No," he said, without waiting for the question, "I'm not dangerous." His hand on her elbow, he led her toward the Yankee Inn's lounge. "At least not to you."

She was herself again as they settled into a back booth in the lounge decorated like an old New England tavern. The booths were high backed and wooden, though a soft cushion on the seat was a concession to modern comfort.

"I'll have a strawberry margarita," she ordered quickly when a pretty young woman in a short skirt, a short white apron and a dust cap came to take their order.

He asked for Scotch and water and smiled across the table at Kay as the waitress left. "That's a sissy drink," he said, watching her pull off her jacket. "I thought all cool young people drank martinis."

She was all graceful movement despite the high color in her cheeks and a little flare of temper in her eyes. He hated being distracted by that, but he couldn't help himself. There was something soothing about the turn of her head, the flutter of her hands.

"You're young and cool," she said, "and you didn't order one."

He almost laughed aloud at that. Young and cool. "I haven't been young in a long time," he said. There was a bowl of mixed nuts on the table instead of the usual peanuts. Jackie Whitcomb ran a classy establishment. He pushed the bowl toward Kay.

"You're thirty-six," she said with certainty. "That isn't old."

"Ah," he said. "Part of your investigation?"

"Yes. And just because you were a minister doesn't mean you can't be cool. Father Chabot is one of the coolest men I know."

He shouldn't be surprised she knew about his past. She admitted she'd been investigating him, and he was sure she was thorough.

"Yes. He's one of the coolest people I know, too."

"I know that your wife died in a single-car accident on a lonely road," she went on, her tone growing gentle, "and that Ron Milford was her employer." She leaned toward him on folded arms, her eyes touchingly intense and urgent. "You're right. I can't read your mind. But it doesn't take a genius to conclude that you're here for revenge. Just—please. Don't do anything stupid."

Stupid. It was difficult to hear his plans described that way when he remembered the frightened entries in Julia's journal.

"Do you know about my hospital stay?" he asked.

She nodded, then leaned back when the cocktail waitress brought their drinks. The moment the woman was gone, Kay said quietly, "You had a shattered femur from a firefight in Baghdad the day before you were to go home. You were three months at Walter Reed, two months in the hospital at home, and three months in rehab."

He accepted that his life was an open book to her. Only his heart was his own. "All that time I was recovering," he said, "I read my wife's journals so I could be close to her. I used to tease her before I went to Iraq that one day she was going to be to our generation what Mary Chestnut and her journals were to the Civil War. When it was all I had of her, I drank in every word."

SHE SAW LOVE for his wife in his eyes and that ever-present pain. If there was anything she understood, it was loss and pain. Her pain, though, was a child's pain that had grown up with her and was inextricably woven in her being. She'd been hurting for so long, she didn't know what a life filled with happiness could be like.

Jack's pain had slammed into him after years of a happy marriage and two little children, a life dedicated to God and his congregation. It must be a terrible burden, something he had to fight against, something that could make him do the unthinkable.

She wanted to touch him in sympathy, but was afraid that would cross a line that might further complicate an already tangled situation. "Are you blaming him because she had to work late?" she asked gently. "Because she was driving home in the dark on an icy back road…'?"

"I'm blaming him," he corrected, "because he killed her. In the last few weeks of her journal, Julia talked about suspecting that he was taking in money from clients that was never being invested. She began to keep a personal log of who came and went and tracked down what happened to their money. She began to see a pattern. Small amounts were invested to bring in just enough to report some activity on clients' quarterly statements. But the bulk of the money taken in disappeared."

She watched him take a deep drink of his Scotch and water. Her frivolous strawberry margarita suddenly didn't seem adequate to deal with what she was hearing.

"In her last entry," he went on, "she wrote that she was going to stay late that night to copy some documents and the next day she was going to take what she knew to the district attorney."

"Oh, God."

"Yeah."

Kay could imagine Julia working stealthily in a dark office, finding records, making copies, all the while her heart thudding with the possibility of being discovered.

"My guess is, he was on to her for a while," Jack said, coolly dispassionate. Then his eyes lost focus as though he was seeing an image of her. "She never kept a secret very well and always looked guilty if she knew something she hadn't shared. Like when she became pregnant with Paul at one of the worst financial periods in our lives." He smiled fondly, still lost in his memories. "My congregation was made up of lower middle class people with very little money. We shared what we had, but you know how things are at a time like that. The car dies, or the plumbing needs work." He thought about that a moment, then shook his head and refocused on Julia's last day. His jaw hardened and misery filled his eyes.

"Anyway, I can just imagine that while she thought she was being cagey and surreptitious, Milford probably read her face and knew exactly what she was doing. Either he hid out and let her leave the building, then followed her and drove her off the road. Or—" his hand tightened on the glass "—he was in the building, confronted her, she ran to the car and tried to escape, but he caught up with her and pushed her off into the lake."

Kay's vivid imagination saw Julia's car rolling down an embankment, bashed by rocks and trees before it fell into the lake. It would be difficult for anyone to tell that her car had been struck from behind and forced off the road. The unfortunate truth was that, unlike television, investigators didn't always get to the bottom of real life accidents.

"Did you see the police report?" she asked.

He nodded. "There was nothing about it to make anyone suspicious."

Kay shifted in her seat, as though she could physically draw herself out of the web he'd spun. She took a sip of her drink. It was cloyingly sweet, but her mouth was dry and she needed it.

"I know you have her journals," she said, "but it's hard for me to believe that Ron Milford was capable of murdering anybody. I mean, you've met him. He's a nice guy."

"I know that's the way he appears." Jack leaned against the back of the booth and propped a foot on the seat beside her. "But thieves and murderers wouldn't get away with their crimes if you could recognize them on sight for what they are."

"I've spent time with him," she insisted. "I interviewed him in his home. I've walked around town with him while we talked about the various community projects he's gotten involved in. Wouldn't someone who'd committed murder keep a low profile? I mean, if you're going to escape with stolen money after you've killed someone to cover your tracks you'd go to Bora-Bora, or somewhere else far away. You wouldn't come to Maple Hill, Massachusetts to retire—only a couple of hundred miles from where you'd done all that. And then you wouldn't start another money management company."

Jack shrugged. "Bold innocence is a good cover."

Kay pushed her drink away. This was all too unbelievable, too…awful.

"Your wife actually named Ron Milford in her journal?"

He shook his head. "She simply refers to him as Ron. And, coincidentally, both owners of the company are named Ron. But Ron Scieszka, Milford's partner, is still involved with the company and while he lives in a very elegant home, he's done nothing else to suggest extravagance. While Milford's retired, gone on a cruise, moved away and bought a new home and is going into business again in an office that looks like something out of *Architectural Digest.*"

"Well…that's not really proof of anything," she argued.

"He left the company and Haverstown," Jack insisted, "and he's spending wildly. He's probably opening another office to start bilking people again."

"You can't prove that, either."

"I'll get the proof. You want to make a wager that I'm right?"

She looked into the pain in his face overlaid with anger and a grim determination and felt serious concern. "What do you intend to do if you get proof?"

He held her gaze for a moment then gave a single shake of his head. "Put him away."

"You have two little kids," she reminded him, trying to stack up facts that would make him see things her way. "And most of a life ahead of you. You were a minister, for heaven's sake."

He was quiet one telling moment. "I'm not a minister anymore," he said finally.

"You're still a father."

"I am. But when the day comes that my children learn about what happened to their mother, they're going to know I did something about her death."

"How will it help them if you do something that separates you from them?"

"I said, 'put him away,' not 'blow him away.'" Something changed in his expression as he narrowed his focus on her eyes. "It's curious that you're worried about my children. I got the impression you didn't like them very much."

She folded her arms, stacking up her own defenses. "Then your claim that you know what you're doing is faulty. I thought they were very beautiful and very bright."

He pinned her with his look. "Then, why did the sight of them horrify you?"

"I'm...I...have my own problems. But I'm working on them. I help a little boy in second grade with his reading every Friday. I bought him a Spider-Man..." She stopped abruptly. She was babbling. "We were talking about you, weren't we?"

"I'm talking about *you*."

She stood, suddenly tired of the whole discussion. "Well, I'm not talking anymore. Would you please take me back to my car?"

He complied without protest, looking tired himself. It was a brief ride back to the *Mirror* office. "Have you lost a child?" he asked, pulling up in front of the Porter Building where the office was located. He turned off the motor and waited for her answer, his expression gentle, sympathetic.

"A little sister," she replied.

"Recently?"

"Eighteen years ago." She pushed her door open. She wasn't talking about Betsy tonight.

"I'll follow you home," he said.

She leaned into the open passenger door. "That's not necessary. I've been going home alone since I've lived here."

"I'll do it anyway. Good night."

Fine, she thought, slamming the door and walking the short distance to her car. She climbed in and left the exit, and saw his truck fall in behind her on the highway. He pulled up beside her while she parked, then idled there while she went to her front door and unlocked it. Then he was gone with a tap of his horn.

The chivalrous gesture left her feeling cared for, even spoiled. She had to remind herself that he had two children. She went to bed in a very bad mood.

BUSTER GREETED Jack at the door, tail wagging, lanky body jumping up and down with genuine excitement. Jack appreciated his enthusiasm but couldn't help but wonder what piece of furniture or clothing he'd eaten today. He ruffled his ears and told him he was a good boy, hoping that the words would inspire the dog's behavior.

Calpurnia sat up under a blanket on the sofa where she'd obviously just awakened. "Kids are fast asleep," she reported. "Amanda has a permission slip for school that you have to sign. I found it in her backpack when I cleaned it out for her. I left it on the kitchen table. And your parents called to talk to the children. They wanted to know where you were, and I told them about the meeting. They said they might want to come down for the Fall Festival."

If he was making any progress with Milford by then, that might not be a good idea. He didn't want his mother worrying, or his father with his bad heart in the middle of a confrontation between Jack and Milford. "Thanks, Cal," he said, helping her to her feet. "You're welcome to stay the night if you're too tired to go home."

She shook her head. "Thank you, but Pookie's waiting for me." Pookie was a thirty-pound white Persian with psychotic tendencies. "There are refrigerator cookies cooling on the kitchen counter. You might want to put them in the jar before you go to bed. I got restless around nine o'clock and made two batches."

He helped her on with a very staid blue wool jacket. "Ah, you're a good woman, Calpurnia. What would I do without you? Thanks for working so late."

"Happy to be of service," she said. "See you tomorrow. Are you working this weekend?"

"No. I'm off both days, so you are, too."

"Good. I've got to get moving on my popcorn balls for the Altar Society booth. Buster has to go out, by the way. I'm afraid I fell asleep on the job."

"Okay. Thanks, Cal."

As she drove away, Jack hooked Buster's leash to his collar, a ritual the dog already understood meant fun. He began to leap and pant and dragged Jack out the door and toward the trees. The job over in a moment, the two raced back to the kitchen.

Silence filled the house as Jack went to the box of dog treats in the cupboard. Buster waited intently and Jack appreciated his incandescent happiness. This time of night had been difficult for him since he and the children had moved to Maple Hill. Daytimes were tolerable because there were people to talk to, issues to deal with. But nighttimes were ugly in their melancholy stillness.

Buster sat for his treat, a trick he'd learned in the last few days, and Jack congratulated himself on his newly acquired dog training skills. He had no shoes to speak of and Cal had had to make new cushions for the sofa, but Buster had learned to sit.

Jack sat in the living room with the cordless phone and called his parents. He'd called once a week when he and the children had first moved to Maple Hill, but since he'd met Milford and gotten involved with the Wonders, and since his father had been doing so well, he'd called less often.

John Keaton's robust voice was a relief to hear.

"Hey, Dad," Jack said. "How're you feeling?"

"Jack! Emmie, it's Jack!"

His mother's high, cheerful voice came on the line. "Hi, Jack! We spoke to the children tonight. They sounded wonderful!"

He assured them that they were doing well.

"So the move to Maple Hill was a good thing?"

His parents were unaware of his real reasons for coming, knew only that he'd wanted a change of scene, to find a new way to make a living.

"Yes. It's a great place to live."

"We want to come and see for ourselves. Cal says the festival is the second weekend in October?"

"Right." He didn't have the heart to discourage them, but asked cautiously, "You're sure you're up to a trip, Dad?"

His father told him that seeing him and the children could only do good things for his heart.

"How are you and God, Jack?" his mother asked gravely.

He knew she hated his spiritual defection, but he was fairly sure she didn't know how complete it was.

"We're coexisting." That was noncommittal.

He was grateful that she let the matter drop. They talked about Buster, he promised to e-mail them a map to the house. They told him they loved him and said good-night.

He missed being told he was loved, he thought as he turned off the phone. The children told him every night and he valued that enormously, but it was somehow validating to hear it from another adult.

He went into the kitchen to see if there was coffee left and to snag a cookie when he noticed that the counter was covered with sheets of tin foil. The foil was covered in crumbs, not cookies. He looked around quickly, thinking he'd misunderstood where Cal had left them. But they were nowhere to be seen.

The old bench pulled up to the counter told the story. It was a simple rustic thing that had been left in the place and usually sat near the back door for pulling off boots. But Cal always drew it up to the counter for the children to stand on when they helped her cook or bake. Buster apparently also found it useful.

Sensing he was in trouble, the dog attempted to run off. Jack caught his collar, told him he was a bad dog and pushed him into his crate and closed him in.

Buster whined and lay down morosely, clearly crushed.

Jack walked away, hard-hearted. Buster was getting no sympathy from him; now he had no shoes *and* no cookies.

He went upstairs to check on the children and found them both asleep as Cal had promised. Amanda was curled in a tight ball, the blanket pulled over her head, and Paul had tossed his pillow on the floor and most of his blankets. Jack covered him up again, and placed the pillow beside him.

He took a leisurely shower, thinking about Kay Florio and her reaction to his children. He wondered if her little sister had died of an illness or in an accident, and just what it was about the incident that had traumatized her so much that she associated it with all other children.

He considered that all-together demeanor she worked

so hard to portray and imagined how difficult that was for her under the circumstances. Loss of anyone close required a major retooling of one's life to be able to go on. He knew that firsthand.

She didn't seem to have quite managed that and he couldn't stop speculating on what had happened. He, at least, had been an adult when the tragedies had ganged up on him. Kay claimed she'd lost her sister eighteen years ago. She'd have been a child of seven or eight at the time, and what was closer to you at that age than a sibling? Were coping skills even acquired that young?

For the first time since he'd gotten the news about Julia's death and ended up in the hospital, he felt sorry for someone besides himself and his children. He'd counseled members of his congregation in their grief when he'd been the old Jack Keaton. He knew what was happening. He was trying to adjust, to see beyond his selfish circle of pain to the rest of the world.

To someone needing only to find his way through life again, that was a good thing. But for someone with a plan that required he keep his grief in view, his hatred honed, it wasn't. So he steeled his resolve. He liked Kay Florio. He was sorry she'd been hurt. His mind tried to create an image of her as a little girl and he tuned it out, concentrating instead on pulling on the old shorts and T-shirt he slept in, turning off the light and finding his way into bed.

He pictured Ron Milford and mentally put bars in front of his face. In the old days, he'd preached against the death penalty, but now he wished he could picture him strapped to a chair while lethal poisons were injected into him.

A single, plaintive bark from downstairs interrupted his dark scenario. He tried to dial up his resolve a notch, then remembered the importance of maintaining perspective. He climbed out of bed, went downstairs and let Buster out of his crate.

The dog danced around him all the way up the stairs, and licked his face madly when he put him on the foot of Amanda's bed, but jumped down and followed Jack into his room.

He leaped onto the foot of his bed and curled up behind his knees. Jack woke up once and felt the dog's closeness a comforting presence. Until he awoke at 6:00 a.m. to find a few dozen cookies regurgitated on the foot of his brown-and-beige coverlet.

JACK SPENT the first three days of the following week painting two rooms in Jackie Whitcomb's inn, then two days painting Mrs. Milford's shop across the hall from her husband's office. He was halfway through the trim on the windows and doors when Evan came to tell him Friday that there'd been a change in the schedule.

"Crisis in the mayor's office," he said, helping Jack wash his brushes as he spoke. "An upstairs bathroom sink overflowed and left stains on the ceiling and one wall. Which we could just work on when we could fit it in, but Jackie's giving citizenship awards to some school children in her office early next week, and she wants it in good shape for them. And she says you've done such a great job at the inn. I'll clean up for you here."

"That's good, but I promised Mrs. Milford…."

"Hank spoke to her. She understands. She and her partner are off buying office furniture anyway. I'd promised you'd go now."

Jack complied, happy to discover perks to working in the mayor's office. There were always doughnuts or bagels left over from the city staff meeting, always someone running for coffee and happy to take one more order for an Americano, and everyone was so busy with affairs of the city, that no one hung over him, ready to criticize.

Added to the ease of his day was the fact that Cal and a friend of hers had taken his children and the friend's grandchildren to Springfield to see a college production of *Alice in Wonderland*. They wouldn't be home until midnight, leaving him an entire evening to himself.

Jack had dinner at the Barn, went home to walk Buster, then spent much of the evening on the floor with him, reviewing his investments book. Around ten, he went into the kitchen to make coffee and turned on the radio. Statewide high school football scores were interrupted by a special news report.

This close call just in from downtown Maple Hill. Newcomer Ron Milford, who recently opened a money-management office in Porter Building II on the Common sustained a concussion, two broken fingers and a bruised shoulder when the chandelier over his desk fell on him while he was working late. Sergeant Ray Machado, who responded to the 911 call placed by a janitor, said he was coherent and responding to questions when the EMTs arrived. A Maple Hill Hospital spokesperson says the new Health Insurance Portability and Accountability Act created privacy laws that prevent him from giving us any information on the patient's condition, but Mrs. Milford reports that he's expected to be released tomorrow. Dry rot in the two-hundred-and-seventy-year-old building is blamed for the accident.

Jack stood for a long moment with a coffee filter in one hand, and a bag of ground coffee in the other. An accident, he wondered, or someone Milford had cheated out of their life savings also trying to work a plan something like his?

And Kay had doubted his research.

He put the filter and coffee down, grabbed his jacket off the hook and hurried to the door. Suddenly remembering Buster, he came back to put the cooperative but bewildered dog in his crate, then ran out to the truck.

CHAPTER ELEVEN

THE COUSINS NIGHT, Kay concluded after the ribs and sauerkraut she'd slow-cooked all afternoon remained untouched on the table, was turning into a disaster. And that wouldn't have been so bad, because their mercurial temperaments often brought about grand displays of temper and emotion, but this one beat anything she'd seen in twenty-six years of being a Florio cousin.

The reason for the discord might be because Rachel had called them together on a Friday night, worried about Agnes's worsening confusion when she'd come to fill their aunt's pillbox that morning. She wanted her cousins to agree to having a neighbor check in on her several times a day, and to try to speed up the plan to get her into an assisted living situation. Helping Agnes was the last thing they'd agreed on that evening.

Charlie, whom Kay had thought would love the low-carb dinner hadn't touched a bite. She was anxious because Sam Cavalleri had invited her to dinner. And Rachel, who'd arrived in a nasty mood anyway, was angry at her for it.

"You sit at home night after night doing nothing, and

now you're upset because a gorgeous man has asked you out on a date? That's sick, Charlie."

Charlie tossed her long hair over her shoulder. "I'm not upset because he asked me out, I'm upset because…I'm nervous! And because I'm nervous I had pasta for lunch, sneaked a candy bar between classes and had a vanilla shake on the way here!"

Rachel rolled her eyes with complete lack of sympathy. "Well, if you'd learn to exert a little self-control…"

"If *you'd* learn to exert a little self-control," Charlie countered in a shout, "and tried to be a little understanding instead of judgmental, maybe your daughter wouldn't think of you as a bitch, and your husband wouldn't…"

"Stop!" Kay shouted, knowing what Charlie intended to say would be irretrievable. "We get together to support each other, remember? Not to bring each other down. So, you had a few carbs. You've lost twenty-one pounds. You're not going to gain that back with a plate of pasta, a candy bar and a milkshake."

Charlie shook her head. "I gained four pounds. I went home and weighed myself before I came."

"Who in God's name weighs themselves at dinnertime? You blew your diet because you were upset, and now you're trying to punish yourself for it by weighing yourself. That's absurd. And I'm sure Sam is not going to see a difference of four pounds anyway."

"I'll know the difference."

Kay turned on her, completely forgetting the lecture she'd just given her cousins on mutual support. "Well, that's what you get for making every waking moment of your life about your weight. Good Lord! You're a beautiful woman, a great teacher and apparently the school thinks you can be an administrator. Either accept yourself as you are because everyone who knows you has, or do something about it without obsessing or making all of us pay when it's hard on you."

Charlie was offended. "I've worked very hard…"

"I know that," Kay retorted. "Sam noticed. And I don't know if it was because you're twenty-one pounds slimmer, or because it made you feel good enough about yourself that you're showing some confidence. Whatever it is, he wants to spend time with you. That's so nice. I'd love it if someone wanted to spend time with *me*."

"You don't need a man to be happy," Rachel declared as though separation from Gib had taught her some new truth. She'd rejected the ribs because she claimed to have had a late lunch.

Kay turned on her. "Oh, give it a rest, Rache. No woman *needs* a man, but some of them are damn good company. Like your husband. Stop torturing him for needing someone else and talk to him. Try to see yourself from some point of view other than your own. You don't run the universe, you know."

Charlie and Rachel stared at her. Agnes, who'd been in a foggy theater world all evening said in a remarkable Betty Davis imitation, "Fasten your seat belts. It's going to be a bumpy ride." That was the diva's famous line from her role as Margo Channing in *All About Eve*.

Rachel finally blinked. "And what's wrong with you? Is the book going badly? Maybe you should go back to your fictional world if it's more to your liking than we are."

"Nothing means more to me than this family," Kay said, gathering up plates. "But the urge to beat you two up is overwhelming. So, I'm going to take my Crock-Pot and leave early. I'll do *all* the cleanup next time." She stopped to hug Agnes. "I'll come by tomorrow with your groceries, Auntie."

Agnes patted her arm, suddenly lucid. "Okay. I'll be here." Her bright dark eyes studied Kay with under-standing. "The book will come, sweetie. If the people in it are hard to understand, that's only because you have to take them from real people, and we don't even un-derstand ourselves."

Kay was distracted on her way home, her little car filled with the sweet-and-sour aromas of her rib and sau-erkraut dish. Agnes's words played over and over in her mind, contributing to her sense of being completely lost in her own life. Not a good situation for a reporter, who was supposed to investigate the world around her until she understood it, or a novelist, who was supposed to lay out what she knew for her readers' enjoyment and education.

Instead, she'd accomplished none of the things she'd come to Maple Hill to do, both her cousins were in per-sonal quandaries that made them difficult to enjoy time with, and her aunt was slipping more deeply into her dreamworld. Added to that, her mother would soon be coming to upend Kay's life for the space of the Fall Festival weekend, and the one and only man she'd been interested in for years was very possibly bent on mayhem—or, at the very least, the personal and financial destruction of another human being.

At home, she poured the contents of the Crock-Pot into a large pottery bowl and put it in the refrigerator, then went upstairs to change into grubbies and work on her novel. It would be interesting to see if her arguments with her cousins were as good for emotional dialogue as contact with Jack was.

She'd been working on the book in spare moments, deleting the lines about the baby, starting over, only to have it reappear as Greta and Tom argued anew. Characters taking charge of their fictional lives was usually considered a good thing, but the "baby" was becoming spooky.

She was pulling on a yellow sweatshirt over matching bottoms when she noticed the light blinking on her answering machine. The message was from Haley.

"Hi, Kay," her breathless voice said. "You've probably heard by now that Ron Milford is in the hospital."

Kay gasped aloud and sank onto the edge of her bed to listen to the rest of the message. "He was working late in his office and the chandelier overhead fell onto his desk. He's not badly hurt, but the hospital wants to keep him overnight. I got a shot of him being carried out of the building into an ambulance, and WMHH was kind enough to share some of what they knew since there's no way we can scoop a radio station, but I wondered if you'd give Joanne Milford a call sometime tomorrow so we can incorporate her comments into the story. I want to give Joanne a little time to recover from the shock, anyway, but you know her better than I do. And maybe get us some information on the last time the building was inspected. Somebody checked the wiring all right, but apparently there was dry rot in the ceiling. And what's the status of the other residents of the building? Are they worried? What's the city's take on it?"

There was a sigh and the distant sound of a baby crying. "Gotta go. I know you know what you're doing here, just had to empty the thoughts from my head into yours. Don't worry about coming into the office Monday morning. I'll get the obits and the police blotter done this weekend. I imagine a lot of the city people you'll want to talk to and most of the other business owners in the building won't be reachable until Monday. Bye, Kay. Call me if you need me."

Kay saved the message, grabbed her purse and jacket and drove to town, determined to invade the scene. If she could find anything to link the accident to Jack Keaton, she intended to call Gib and tell him everything she knew.

JACK USED THE KEY Milford had given him to get into the building, then crawled under a length of crime-scene tape stretched across the hallway in front of the open door of Milford Money Management's office. He played the flashlight around the floor and walls in the front, and found that area undisturbed. But Milford's office was a mess. The chandelier remained on the desk like an overturned birthday cake. Jack's flashlight picked out crystals that had flown around the room when the fixture fell.

Everything that had been on the desk was strewn around; Milford's chair lay on its side, and there were a few small spots of blood on the carpet.

The chandelier covered most of the desk and hung over the front in a delicate rain of crystal. Still attached to it was the thick chain from which it had hung, and the chunk of plastered ceiling covering the board to which the fixture had been screwed, and several other pieces of splintered board that had fallen with it. Judging by the fixture's central stem driven into the wood of the desktop, he guessed it was heavy enough to have done far more serious damage to Milford than it did. He was a lucky man.

It crossed his mind that God should be more selective about whom he allowed to be lucky, but decided not to indulge the thought. Theologians had been arguing the justice of that point for centuries.

He ran the light over the ceiling and saw the ragged hole and the attic beyond. As he lowered the light, it picked out a twelve-foot ladder leaning against the wall in a corner of the room. He recognized it from the building's utility room because he'd used it to paint the picture rail in Joanne Milford's office across the hall. He imagined the police had used it to climb into the attic to reach their conclusion that dry rot was to blame.

He set up the ladder under the hole to check it out for himself. The hole was a little bigger than the width of his shoulders and allowed him to wriggle through with relative ease. Unwilling to lean his weight on the edge of the hole for fear it would give, he climbed carefully to the top step of the ladder, set his light down, then reached out for an iron bed frame nearby and used it for support as he took a wide step out of the hole.

The attic stretched the length of the building and was a warehouse of old signs and antiquated office and retail equipment. There was a stack of storage boxes, old home furnishings, and the iron bed with its ornate brass headboard. He saw an old baby bonnet on a hook. He had to look at that twice before he could refocus on the matter at hand.

He stretched out on his stomach on the floor of the attic, approaching the edges of the hole with great care. He shined his light on the splintered wood, wishing he knew what he was looking for. His congregation had always taken care of his residences as a supplement to the meager salary. He'd never had to deal with problems like dry rot.

There was a sudden sound from the office below and he quickly doused his light and shrank away from the hole while trying to stay close enough to identify the new arrival. But the darkness made it impossible. He lay still, trying not to breathe.

He decided he was going to have to have that "luck extended to the undeserving" talk with God after all because whoever had walked into the office was climbing the ladder.

KAY COULDN'T BELIEVE she was doing this. When Haley had hired her, she'd made it clear that the best way to earn cooperation from the police department was to be cooperative in return. She said she'd learned that the hard way several years earlier.

But Kay wasn't doing this to tamper with evidence or learn details the police were unwilling to share. She was trying to decide if it was time for her to tell them the things she knew about Jack Keaton's past and his mission to Maple Hill.

If Ron Milford had been hurt because she'd kept quiet about what she knew, she'd never be able to forgive herself. Granted, he hadn't been seriously hurt, but the sight of the chandelier smashed on the desk was enough to make her see that he could be dead right now.

Her heart in her throat, the small flashlight usually on her key chain now caught between her teeth, she climbed the ladder she imagined the police had left. She was three steps from the top when she caught her first glimpse into the dark attic. Her flashlight was weak and lit only a very small space, but she could see boxes in the corner and…was that a hat on the wall?

Without warning, a shadow rose right in front of her face and she looked into a pair of intense brown eyes lit by her flashlight. She opened her mouth to scream, dropping the flashlight, but a hand closed over her mouth before any sound could escape.

"Be quiet!" Jack Keaton's voice whispered.

She heard a sound behind and below her. Footsteps in the hallway!

"Get up here!" Jack pulled on her arm as she leaped up the last few steps. She fell into him where he knelt at the edge of the hole. They clung together, she breathing heavily, he holding her so tightly she couldn't have made a sound if she'd wanted to.

Below them the footsteps grew louder, there was a small squeak as someone pushed or pulled on the office door. The footsteps moved around the office, there was a small tinkling of sound as though the intruder had touched the chandelier. A moment's silence was followed by a step on the ladder.

She looked around for somewhere to hide but without her light, couldn't see a thing. Jack, though, seemed to know where he was going. He dragged her with him along the floor to the shelter of what appeared to be a stack of document boxes. She couldn't imagine they were wide enough to hide them, but they were something.

Her heart thumping frantically, Kay clung to Jack as the footsteps drew closer to the top of the ladder. Frightened, she waited for that telling step on the floor when Jack suddenly caught a fistful of her pant leg.

Startled and confused she pushed against him, then realized that the bright yellow of her sweatpants was the only thing visible in the darkness. But the footsteps were now in the attic and Kay was afraid her movement would be heard.

Jack leaned over her to lay his arm along her leg, his leather jacket concealing the bright color of her sweatpants. His hand manacled her ankle for purchase.

The footsteps moved ominously across the floor. As they moved past the boxes, Kay saw a weak and familiar little swath of light moving ahead of them. He'd found her flashlight! She started when she saw that, certain that meant he knew she was up here. She strained her eyes to try to make out anything familiar, but since she could see little above shoe level, and even that was in darkness, she gave up.

Jack held her more tightly, either encouraging her to remain still, or wanting to suffocate her so that if he had to run for it, he could do it alone.

Kay closed her eyes, thinking remaining still would be easier if she couldn't see the light approaching. If only she could hold her hands over her ears to block the sound of the footsteps.

And then, incredibly, with death or injury or whatever threat the intruder posed only inches away, her heightened senses made her aware of Jack, as well. She felt his heartbeat against her back, the warmth and strength of the hand wrapped around her ankle, his knee bent up protectively against the other side of her body, his free arm holding her to him as though they'd been lashed together.

Her heartbeat threatened to choke her. And there was a little tick of sexual awareness gaining strength and speed right in the center of her being.

This could not be happening! Celibate for two years, and now inches from death, she wanted to jump Jack Keaton.

The tension of imminent death and sexual discovery was about to strangle her when the footsteps began to retreat. The light disappeared and the sound of footsteps receded as the intruder made his way down the ladder.

"Don't move," Jack whispered into her ear. His breath seemed to find its way right inside her, ruffling the contents of her brain and sending shock waves to her heart.

She remained still, knowing Jack was right. If the intruder suspected they were here, he might be waiting for them to move, thinking he was gone.

Finally there was a small squeak of the door, then footsteps in the hall. Jack straightened away from her and leaned back against the wall with a groan. She sagged against him in relief.

"Oh, my God!" she exclaimed. "Who was that? Did you see anything?"

"No, I didn't see anything," he replied testily. "I was bent over trying to prevent him from seeing *you*. Next time you go out in the dark to sneak around, don't do it dressed like a lightbulb!"

She sat up and turned to him in annoyance. Unfortunately, she couldn't see him. "At least I've never sneaked around to hurt anyone!"

He dug something out of a pocket and the glow of a flashlight appeared between them. "You think *I* did this?"

"Didn't you? How did you get in here if you haven't gotten in before?"

He held up a ring with two keys on it. "Milford gave it to me because I've started painting early and sometimes stay late."

"I thought you were working on Joanne's place across the hall."

"I am. But her single room has no restroom, and the one in the building is locked up at night. So Milford lets me have access to his. How did *you* get in?"

She tossed her head, trying not to look sheepish. "There's a connection on the second floor between this building and the building I work in next door. It's from the turn of the century when the two buildings were a department store and an apartment building owned by the same man. That's why this is Porter Building II. He used to leave his office on the second floor of the store and cross a small catwalk to his apartment."

"And those doors were never locked with the change in ownership?"

"On our side, it's a door, but in this building, since the renovation, it's now a window into a janitorial closet. Easy to get through." She smiled. "There's little concern about the theft of cleaning supplies." She sobered quickly. "You've had ample opportunity to…"

He frowned impatiently. "Give me credit for some precision," he interrupted. "A chandelier on the head is a little iffy. Particularly if you're counting on dry rot to make it fall."

She used his thigh to push herself to her feet. Even angry, she noticed that it was warm and muscular. "You're probably smart enough to know how to make it *look* like dry rot."

He got lightly to his feet. "Thank you. But I don't know what dry rot looks like, do you?"

"Actually, I do. I replaced my basement stairs because of it."

He pointed his light at the hole and moved toward it. "Then, tell me if that's what you see."

She went near the edge and knelt down. He grabbed a fistful of the back of her jacket as she leaned over to check the rim of the hole. She put her fingers to it and snapped off a small piece of wood. He shined his light on it. It was porous and seemed to have been compromised by something, but didn't crumble in her hand like the stuff under her porch. "It sort of does," she said, thinking that it looked like dry rot, but felt curiously different. "Dry rot leaves the wood so spongy you can make a powder of it in your hands. This feels different. Maybe it's a different kind of problem. Termites, or something."

Jack took the piece from her and shined his light on it in the palm of his hand. Then he shook his head. "No tool marks. Or are those drilled holes?" There were several close together in the spongy wood, then another on the other side of the broken beam.

She leaned over him to look. "The building inspector drills holes to test for dry rot. Could be that. Or wormholes. They're always so perfectly round in antique furniture. Just like that."

"I'll bet someone weakened the beam. Probably whoever just came up here looking around."

"It suggested to me that *you* did," she said, resisting her memories of being wrapped against him, her desperation to know that he hadn't done this in spite of suggestive evidence to the contrary. But she was a reporter. She had to face facts. "You've been working right across the hall for two days," she said, then added intrepidly, "and frankly, your intentions are suspect."

He stared at her bleakly for a moment. "If you believe I did this," he said, "then aren't you afraid to accuse me of it here in the dark with no one else around? I mean, you're at my mercy. If I wanted to keep you quiet, I could strangle you up here and hide you behind the boxes. Or push you through the hole and be out of town in minutes."

He was absolutely right. A little ripple of fear bumped along her spine, but she tried not to show it. "That's a charming way for a minister to talk."

"I'm a housepainter," he corrected.

"Whatever led you to the ministry doesn't just go away because you decide to do something else, does it? Faith isn't a simple talent that you can suppress because another kind of work will make you more money or less bored."

"I have no faith."

"You're raising children. Can you really do that without faith?"

He seemed annoyed that she'd posed the question. Then he climbed onto the ladder. "Come on," he said. "Let's get out of here. Show me the path to your building."

She followed him down, determined to ignore the suggested threat and show him that she considered him incapable of doing her harm. Physically, anyway.

JACK FOLLOWED HER down the stairs to the second floor and lit a dark corridor with his flashlight as she turned in one direction, then another. The cleaning closet was relatively small and stacked with all the usual stuff— two brooms, a mop, a mop bucket, stacks of hand towels, toilet tissue, various cleaning products.

The long window was behind a high-back sink with ancient faucets. Kay stood on a box of towels and climbed into the sink. She reached behind it to push open the window.

"Careful," she cautioned as she prepared to step out. "The trick is to pull your leg over the back of the sink without turning on the hot water."

He followed her onto the narrow catwalk with a mercifully high railing on both sides, thinking what a weird path his life had taken. He just had to keep the plan in mind.

The catwalk spanned a mere ten feet at the most, and

led to a door in the Porter Building that Kay opened easily. Jack trailed her to the stairs, then down and into the back room of the *Mirror*'s office.

The smell of ink assailed his nostrils. Hank had told him that the little weekly was printed in Springfield because it was simpler and even less costly to outsource the job than to maintain a press and a printer. Many small papers made the press pay by opening a print shop, but Haley didn't want to have to deal with it.

"Funny how it smells like ink when you don't even print the paper here," he said.

She flipped on a light to reveal the comfortable clutter of the usually busy front office. "The back room's filled with old copies, and every week we bring in three thousand of the current edition to mail out. Ink's in the air."

"Isn't mailing more expensive than using paperboys?"

"Yes, but apparently far less trouble. I've only been here a year and the newspaper business is a new experience for me. But apparently boys—and girls—have a busy after-school life with sports and clubs and it's hard to find dependable kids to deliver and then collect for subscriptions. Mailing's easier."

She pressed a button on her answering machine, and Haley's voice told her about Milford's accident. She turned it off and took a look around the office. "Got the same message at home. Well. Anything else you want to know?"

There were a hundred things he wanted to know

about her. She looked like a daffodil in her bright sweats, the wild curl in her hair further rumpled by the evening's climb into the attic next door, into the sink and out the window. Despite her suspicions about him, she was like a little ray of light in his world. He hated the thought of leaving her.

"If you want to follow me home," she said abruptly, startling him with all the possibilities that could have followed that suggestion, "I'll make coffee and we can go over what we know about Milford's accident."

"Ah…"

She noted his hesitation, then tried to negate the offer by shaking her head. "Of course you can't. Your children…"

"Are out with the nanny and some friends at a play in Springfield," he said, reaching for the phone and dialing. "I'll see if they're back yet."

Cal answered immediately—apparently in the middle of a yawn. He asked how the evening went.

"The kids loved it!" she said happily. "And so did Jean and I. The kids are already in bed and I'm too tired to go home. Do you mind if I stay over?"

"Of course not. I'm going to be another hour or so— is that a problem for you?"

"Depends," she said, sounding suddenly wide-awake. "Work or woman?"

"I'm going to have coffee with a friend."

"Male or female?"

He ignored the question. "How's Buster?"

"He's fine. Didn't even eat his blanket this time. I've already taken him out."

"You're irreplaceable, Calpurnia."

"Thank you, Jack. Enjoy your coffee. I'll be here, so don't worry about what time you come home."

Jack put the phone down and nodded. "I'm available for coffee if the offer still stands."

She looked pleased. He liked that. Sort of.

CHAPTER TWELVE

HE FOLLOWED HER through the dark and quiet streets of Maple Hill to the turn on Adams and pulled up behind her in front of the pretty saltbox, lit by two carriage lights on either side of the front door.

She put her key in the lock, then smiled at him in sudden embarrassment before opening it. "I'm afraid it's kind of a mess," she said. "I've been getting some things ready for my booth at the festival, and it's sort of all over the place."

He shrugged. "I live with two little children and a dog. I'm accustomed to things being all over the place. Sometimes some not very pleasant things."

She laughed lightly and opened the door.

There was stuff everywhere, but it was the most fragrant and beautiful stuff. The coffee table and the sofa were covered with wreaths and garlands of dried flowers, herbs and leaves. The rustic and comfortable room smelled like a meadow and made him feel as though he'd walked into the colonial past. She looped four wreaths off the sofa and onto one arm like a set of giant bracelets and disappeared with them.

"Sit down," she called from somewhere beyond, "I'll put the coffee on. Want a brownie? Or a pecan roll?"

"Sure," he shouted back. "Whichever." He sat in the middle of the sofa and studied the wire and leaves strewn over the coffee table. She'd wound what looked like eucalyptus leaves into bunches, ready, he guessed, to form them into a wreath. He was a little surprised that her slightly tense and efficient nature had this artistic side. Well, he knew she was working on a novel, but the wreaths were extravagantly graceful and colorful.

He saw photos on the mantel over a fieldstone fireplace and got up to inspect them, interested in the people who'd populated her life. In one, she was a toddler sitting in a wagon with her arms wrapped around a baby. A lively looking woman knelt near the wagon, smiling for the camera. Kay's wild hair was evident even then.

In another, taken possibly a year later, she stood with her hand holding on to a stroller in which the younger child sat, now a toddler with a wide smile and the same curly hair Kay had, only the baby was a redhead.

In yet another picture a nice-looking man with a serious face posed with both girls in his lap. Cinderella's castle was behind them and all three wore Mickey Mouse hats.

There were several more photos with the four of them, then, as Kay grew taller and more serious—just three of them appeared in the pictures. The red-haired baby was gone.

Jack remembered asking her if she'd lost a child and

she'd said, "my little sister." He felt her sadness in the images of her flanked by her parents at her high school graduation, and of her and a young Charlie in ruffly lavender dresses standing on either side of Rachel dressed as a bride.

In the last two photos, probably on a college campus, and at the top of the Empire State Building, the serious man was now missing.

Kay walked into the room with a tray bearing steaming cups and two plates. She stopped when she saw him studying the photos, then went to the coffee table.

"Handsome parents," he said, moving the wire aside so she could put the tray down.

"Thank you." She sat and he sat, too, leaving a small space between them. "My father was a surgeon. He was very serious and very brilliant. Whenever he denied me what I wanted, I threatened to release that photo of him in Mickey Mouse ears to the hospital's publication. Brownie or pecan roll?"

He had a feeling she was suddenly forcedly cheerful, and he wondered if that had something to do with his study of the pictures.

"I guess I'll get to meet your mother in person." He reached for the brownie. "Unless you'd rather have it?"

"No. I love pecan rolls. I was going to fight you for it."

That was an interesting prospect.

He waited to feel guilty for having the thought, but that didn't happen. His life, which, for a year now, had been all about Julia and his need to avenge her, was now very immediate—all about this moment. He didn't understand why precisely, he just understood that it was significant—and thought Kay's sudden tension was because she knew it, too.

"I can't believe how quickly it's all happening. Two more weeks and Mom will be here." She smiled wryly at him as she handed him a fork. "She's very charming, and she's the most wonderful cook, but she won't hesitate to tell you what's on her mind."

"Honesty's good."

"Then, my mother's a downright saint. Do you need cream for your coffee?"

"No. I take it straight."

"Taste it to be sure. I make it strong."

He complied. It was perfect. "Just the way I like it."

"Thank you. Rachel says I should serve it with an antibiotic."

He laughed. She seemed to relax a little.

"Did you make the brownie?" he asked. "It's delicious."

"No, it's from Perk Avenue. I didn't inherit my mother's genius in the kitchen. I cook passably well, but I don't particularly enjoy it."

"My wife loved to cook." The words came out before he had time to think about them. When Kay looked interested rather than offended, he went on. "I probably have the only children in the country who'll eat asparagus, brussels sprouts and sauerkraut without complaint. They're fearless when it comes to food."

She leaned back with her coffee, and he wondered if

she'd withdrawn. She was uncomfortable with the topic of children. He remembered the redheaded child in the photos and knew she had to be the sister she'd lost.

"You'll have to introduce them to my mother," she said, that edginess coming over her again. "She wrote a book on cooking for children. Also, did I tell you the *Mirror*'s having a contest for kids during the Fall Festival?" When he shook his head, she went on to explain. "The week before, Haley's going to include a sheet in the paper for children to color. There's a pumpkin, a cat, a spider and a ghost."

"Amanda loves to color. But she has to have markers rather than crayons."

Kay nodded with a phony smile. He found it difficult watching her pretend to want to talk about his children. She had a death grip on her fork, but she had yet to take a bite of the pecan roll.

She'd invited him into her home, he told himself, so that gave him a small right to assume a little familiarity. "Kay," he asked gently, "what happened to your little sister?"

He'd expected resistance to the question, or at least reluctance to answer it. He hadn't expected her to turn in his direction, to look at him with a thin smile and pleading in her eyes.

"I think I invited you here to tell you," she said, her voice strained. "I've been sitting here wondering why I asked you to come for coffee when I knew you'd see my photographs. I also knew that you'd mention your children because…they're obviously very important to you." She swallowed noisily and put her plate and fork on the coffee table. "And I just realized that it was because I thought I was ready to tell you."

He'd experienced this particular situation many times in his career as a pastor. Most people who came to him for counseling wanted to talk, but occasionally someone came to him who wanted to share their pain but had buried it so deeply, the conversation was like an excavation.

"Are you thinking you aren't ready after all?" he asked.

She frowned over that. "No. I guess I just don't want to after all."

"Because you're afraid I won't understand?" When she shook her head at that, he turned slightly toward her, resting his elbow on the back of the sofa cushion. "You know about Julia, about the time I spent in Iraq. My losses are huge. That doesn't mean I think I'm the only one suffering, but I know how personal the burden is, and how big."

She put a hand to her mouth, almost as though she wanted to prevent the words from coming out. Every line of her body was tight with pain, and her face was pinched with it. Her mouth trembled and her eyes were filled with misery. "You know what it's like to lose someone you love," she said, her voice just above a whisper, "but do you know what it's like to be responsible for the loss?"

The question shocked him. At the age at which she must have lost her little sister, she couldn't possibly be responsible. But she clearly felt she was. The burden of her guilt was almost visible on her shoulders.

"Of course you don't," she continued, sniffing. A tear escaped and she swiped it away, falling back into the corner of the sofa. "You were a pastor, then an army chaplain."

He put a fraternal hand to her shoulder. "I was shot at in Iraq, and I shot back. I know I've caused injury and death."

She dismissed that with a shake of her head. "You were fighting for your country. Defending the marines you were sent to help."

"Tell me," he insisted softly, "what you did."

THAT WAS THE FIRST TIME she could ever remember the question being posed that way. When she'd first had to explain to the nanny, then to her parents, then to the police and all the other law enforcement people, then to shrinks and priests and anyone else her parents thought might help her, the directive had always been, "Tell me what happened."

She knew the question had been deliberately phrased to be nonjudgmental, but it made her feel as though they thought she'd watched the kidnapping happen, as though it had occurred to someone else and hadn't affected her at all. Instead of ridding her of the blame, it heaped it on.

She began haltingly, telling Jack about the hot day at the beach cottage on Long Island. "We went to New

York that summer because Mom was working on a new show with a new format and she was trying to work the bugs out. Daddy stayed in Boston. We rented a beautiful cottage just a block from town."

She explained about the impromptu desire for candy, and about Betsy, who had to follow her everywhere.

"The shop was just a block from the house. We went every other day for something or other. Sometimes the nanny came with us, sometimes she let us go by ourselves. She'd been with us about a year; since Mom had started working longer hours. You could see the store from my bedroom window." She shook her head. After all this time she could still be overwhelmed by the fact that it had happened. "That particular day, the nanny wasn't feeling well. She sometimes got migraines and controlled them with medication, but nothing was working for her that day. So Betsy and I went alone."

She closed her eyes, hating the memories, but they were so much a part of her that nothing shut them out. And now that she'd started the story, it kept reeling itself out, like the strip of scarves up a magician's sleeve. Only these weren't bright and pretty, but dark and ugly.

"She usually held my hand, but after picking out her candy, she went across the store to look at a display of stuffed animals. I was busy trying to decide between a chocolate bar and a bag of sour candies." Her jaw went rigid and a single sob moved her entire body. "By the time I decided, she was gone."

"Oh, Kay." He understood in that moment how

deeply his relationship with this woman had developed. He'd been a minister; empathy was second nature to him. But he felt the shrapnel of her pain as though it was ripping into him.

"I can't tell you how that felt," she said, her eyes staring at the memory. "I was only eight, but I was a smart little kid, and I knew...I *knew* she wouldn't have just run off. I knew she wouldn't have left me willingly. I started to scream for her. The owner of the store called my home and the nanny came. I can still remember the expression on her face. She looked like I felt, only it was almost as though she feared for her life where I already knew that if Betsy was lost, my life was over. My parents loved me, but they adored Betsy."

He tightened his grip on her shoulder as she went on. "My mother was still at work. The police sent a car for her. She came home in a complete panic. A friend of my father's flew him from Boston to Long Island. Everyone looked everywhere. My father fired the nanny on the spot. I tried to tell him she'd been sick, that it was my fault and not hers, but he wouldn't listen. He was like someone else." She dragged in air and continued.

"No one ate, no one slept, no one spoke. Then one day, the police detective who'd been working with us came over with a priest and I heard my father scream, as though he'd been cut into without sedation. And I knew I'd killed Betsy."

He drew her into his arms, words of comfort eluding him. For the first time since he'd lost faith, he wished things were different. Belief in God was a handhold when overwhelming grief sucked you down. It gave you things to say when someone else was drowning. "God's in charge." "She's with God now." "Though we don't understand what's happened or why, God knows what He's doing."

Now all that flashed through him were the anger and sense of injustice he'd lived with for the past year. But he had to do something to help her. He knew that was why she'd asked him here.

"Kay, you know in your heart that wasn't your fault." She leaned into him, her cheek against his shoulder and he wrapped both arms around her. "Predators are insidiously clever in how they grab victims."

"I should have made her hold my hand."

"Little children are explorers by nature. And you were eight. You thought you were safe in the neighborhood store. It wasn't your fault."

"I wish she had screamed for me."

"She probably didn't understand she was in danger." She raised her head to look into his eyes. Hers brimmed with misery and tears. "My parents blamed me." He opened his mouth to dispute that, but she shook her head to stop him. "They said they didn't. I'm sure they thought they had to be supportive of me, but I know deep down they thought it was my fault. They showered attention on me, they sent me to therapy, but no one was ever the same again. The killer was caught and went to jail, but all three of us were broken."

"Tragedy changes us. And this is hard to understand, but though it causes us great pain, the change it makes in us isn't always bad. The loss is forever, but so is the strength we find in ourselves to carry on."

She studied him frankly. "Tragedy made you angry and vengeful."

"Yes." He couldn't deny that. "But the perpetrator of my tragedy wasn't brought to justice. That's up to me."

"Yeah," she said grimly. "I guess I'm the perpetrator of my own..."

"No!" He cut her off firmly. "Don't do that. You're blaming yourself as a way to hold on to the grief because the grief keeps Betsy near you. It wasn't your fault. I'll bet if you accept that, you'll see that your mother doesn't blame you, you'll get your novel written, and the whole world will open up to you."

She leaned a companionable elbow on his shoulder, that frank look still in place. Their relationship had crossed a line tonight that put them on different terms. "You haven't let *your* grief go," she challenged.

"Yes, well." Her face was so close to his he could see the purity of her complexion, the flecks of gold in her eyes, a small scar just above her eyebrow. "This is one of those do as I say and not as I do situations."

SHE COULDN'T LET HIM get away with that. In fact, she knew with complete conviction that she couldn't let him get away at all. She didn't know what to do about his worrisome intentions toward Ron Milford, about her own unwillingness to get serious about anyone, about all the issues of her life dangling out there without solution.

Yet, despite herself, she didn't care. He understood her in a way no one else did, and now that they'd gotten over their need to antagonize one another, she was very comfortable with him. He made her feel secure— even if he did have a six-year-old daughter.

She looped her arms loosely around his neck. She saw an instant's trepidation in his eyes, but he didn't move. "Do you feel stronger since…Julia?" she asked softly.

"In some ways," he replied. "I've always tried to be a good father, but I counted on her to know how best to deal with the children on tough, sensitive issues. Since she's been gone, I've had to do it, and I'm better than I thought I'd be."

"So, you're a stronger father. What about…you?" She tapped his shirtfront right over his heart. "Is the man stronger?"

"That's hard to say. Everything about me is different than it was before she died. Before I went to Iraq."

She saw horror way back in his eyes. "Have you talked about it?" she asked, realizing for the first time how much anguish he'd probably had to squelch in order to deal with the death of his wife, the recovery from his injuries, and the well-being of his children.

He shrugged. "I talked to a psychiatrist while I was

in the hospital, but it would probably take years of just letting the memories come out when they want to. And there isn't time for that. So it's all in here, just a part of me that has to be there. I've just accepted that I don't know who's right or wrong. Loss of life is still horrible whether it's for a good cause or bad, and I am comforted that all the guys there were just doing the best job they could in an ugly situation. And when God brings them home, He knows that."

She knew he didn't realize what he'd said. He raised an eyebrow in surprise when she gasped and smiled.

"What?" he asked.

"You said, 'when God brings them home,'" she repeated for him.

He didn't react for a moment, then shook his head. "I meant when…"

She put her hand over his mouth. "No, don't change the image for me. I got a picture of God reaching down from heaven and scooping them up. I like it."

In a tender gesture that took her by surprise, he kissed the tips of her fingers, then drew her hand away. "I should go," he said briskly.

She had no intention of letting him. "Why? Because you've discovered you're not as Godless as you think you are?"

"Because it's late," he corrected.

"What if I invited you to stay?" She sat eye-to-eye with him, waiting for his answer.

He met her gaze, then closed his eyes for an instant.

She didn't know if he was considering her invitation, or trying to fight it.

"Thank you," he said at last with an apologetic little stroke of her arm. "But I've always counseled against careless sex. It makes problems, it doesn't solve them." Then he tried to push her away so that he could stand.

She put an arm around his neck and held on. "Who said it would be careless?" And then to prove that she had real feelings for him, she held his face in her hands and kissed him, the gesture filled with the bud of excitement building in her, and the promise of discovery.

His response convinced her that he could be swayed.

"We understand each other," she whispered against his lips. "You're going to live with Julia, at least until you've carried out your plan. And I...I don't have a plan. So let's let this be all the night is about—a reaffirmation of life for two lost souls who could really use it."

She half expected more argument. Instead, he picked her up in his arms and headed for the stairs.

"The bedroom..." she began, pointing upward in the general direction.

"I know where it is," he replied with sudden single-minded focus. "I've been here before, remember?"

That's right. He'd come to pick up a change of clothes for her when she'd been splattered with paint.

She wasn't sure when she'd lost the initiative in this encounter, but he strode into the bedroom, clearly taking charge.

"There are wreaths on the bed, too," she said on the chance he intended to drop her in the middle of it.

He set her on her feet and she reached to a bedside lamp. It flooded that corner of the room and a small section of the bed with soft light. Here she had more eucalyptus wreaths, star flower and gypsy grass wreaths, a mountain ash wreath complete with berries. She carried them to the other end of the room and lay them down in a row in front of her closet.

She turned back to Jack to see that he'd pulled off his shirt and was tossing it at a chair. She watched his back muscles ripple and experienced a small sense of trepidation.

No one would ever suspect he'd spent a year in the hospital. As he turned back to her, his shoulders were broad and square, his pecs well defined above a washboard stomach. His will, she knew, had the same level of fitness. For a woman who liked to do things her way, this was a moment of truth.

He must have seen her hesitation. "Second thoughts?" he asked. His voice held a suggestion of disappointment but not impatience.

Deciding that was a telling revelation about him, she shook her head without hesitation.

He held a hand out to her. "Then come to me," he said.

She put her hand in his and let him draw her into his arms.

JACK HAD FIGURED OUT how to rid himself of feeling guilty for making love to another woman. Julia was gone, but their love for each other retained a tight hold on him and always would. He'd been two long years without her, without a release for all he'd seen and felt, without someone to hold for comfort and simple body contact. Pretending Kay was Julia would give him back what he'd lost—at least for tonight.

Kay would never know. He used to be good at this and he'd see that she didn't regret a moment. She'd have the life-affirming, lost-soul renewal she sought, and he…he'd have…

She was making it hard to think. Her fingers were at his belt buckle, then she stopped to plant a kiss in the middle of his chest. There was a sincerity about the simple gesture that filled him with shame for wanting to use her.

Then she pulled off her sweatshirt, apparently eager to follow through, and he tugged on the hem of it to help her. She stood in front of him in a lacy, pale blue bra, her breasts fuller than Julia's, her manner a little embarrassed.

"It's been two years for me," she said quickly, her fingers knotted together. "I work a lot, I'm…I…it's hard to get close to anyone with my childhood in the way."

He understood. "It's been that long for me. I was in Iraq and sustained by the thought of going home to Julia. Then she was gone, I was in the hospital…."

Her eyes went to his leg in sudden concern. "Are you okay to do this?"

"It was just my femur, but it's hard to say what might or might not affect performance." He smiled. "And I probably shouldn't do anything acrobatic. Are you still willing to risk it?"

She laughed lightly. "I'm a little disappointed we won't be using the trampoline, but yes, I am." She stepped out of her slip-on shoes, then pulled off her sweat bottoms. He sat on the edge of the bed to remove his shoes, then his jeans.

Her panties matched her bra, and that brought Julia to mind again. She never had the budget for fancy undies, buying them instead in four-packs at a discount store.

God, he was hopeless.

God, again, he thought, disgusted with himself. He was closing in on Milford, and he was about to go to bed with a woman for the first time in a very long time. Fine time to be ambivalent. Fine time for old loyalties to intrude.

He had to stop worrying about it. If he'd survived the last two years, he was damned near invincible.

She came near to study his injured leg, the weird puckered scar near his knee where the doctor had had to graft skin to close the wound because it had been blown away. "Vitamin E is supposed to make that less ugly in time," he said when she put her fingertips to it.

"I'm sorry that happened to you." She looked into his eyes and said with the sincerity that seemed to guide her tonight, "I'm sorry about all that's happened to you."

Jack stood up to toss the blankets back, caught Kay's hand and brought her into the bed with him. "Let's forget what's happened to us," he said, kissing the swell of a breast, "and be those lost souls who've found each other."

She whispered a *yes* as she wrapped herself around him and kissed him.

He unhooked her bra and tossed it over the side. Her panties and his shorts went next.

It began as a turbulent lovemaking. Jack was aware of a certain greed in her to be filled with him, and that spurred his desire to lose himself in the physical fervor, to put Julia in her place and recapture, if only for this small space of time, all that had been taken away from him.

Their coming together was quick, hot, and as he prepared to move astride her, she pushed against him. He hesitated for a moment, wondering if she'd changed her mind after all. And in the time he took to assess her mood, she pushed him onto his back and climbed over him.

He realized with a jolt of surprise that she hadn't been resisting him, but simply fighting him for who would be on top. As loving and passionate as Julia had been, she'd never tried to wrest control from him—in or out of the bedroom.

That was the last time he thought of Kay as taking Julia's place in this encounter.

He gave himself over to her and discovered that abandoning control could be a delicious thing. She was nimble, artful, single-minded in her determination to torture him with her exquisite touch.

When he reached for her, she caught his hands and pushed them down beside him.

"Later," she said softly. "Right now, let this just be for you."

That was contrary to the way he lived.

"I can't…" he began to object, but she held his hands firmly away and kissed him to silence him.

"I know," she said. "First a man of God, then a man in service to his country, now a man raising children. Accept this moment, Jack."

Stunned and humbled, he allowed her to explore him with her fingertips from his shoulder to his knees. She planted kisses across his shoulders, breathed a line down the middle of his chest, ran a soothing hand over his scar then up again, stopping just short of that part of him that begged for her.

She leaned over him to ask in a whisper, "Am I hurting your leg?"

"No," he said in a strained voice, his hands moving to her thighs. "But you're torturing every other part of me. Can we get on with…?"

She kissed his lips. "I just want to make sure you're with me."

"With you?" he asked. "I don't think we could get any closer."

"With me…emotionally."

"Oh, I'm with you."

"Good, then just let me…"

Unable to bear another moment, he caught her waist, lifted her over him, and entered her with a single shift of his hips.

She uttered a soft, high-pitched cry of surprise, then settled on him, tightened on him as he ran his hands up her sides to cover her breasts. She braced her hands on his arms, her body opening and closing on his like a morning glory.

He burst inside her—life, love, memories, old worries, new concerns—his whole world blowing apart in that moment. He sat up to hold her, she clung to him with a little sound of anguish—or was it discovery?—and time stopped and stretched. When it began again and his world settled back into place, something was different. He couldn't pinpoint the change, but he felt it.

And he'd learned that he wasn't as invincible as he'd thought.

KAY COLLAPSED on top of him, physical and emotional satisfaction cranking up the volume of her life. Moonlight thundered through her window to the sounds of Wagner, Jack's heartbeat was Ringo Starr, playing counterpoint.

Before she could analyze the new music in her life, Jack cupped her head in his hand, turned their bodies and rose over her. She wanted to organize her thoughts, to ask him if his knee was all right, if he had to call home, if…

Apparently seeing the questions in her eyes, he put a fingertip to her lips to hold them back. "Just be quiet," he whispered. He kissed her eyelids. "Close your eyes and just let yourself feel."

She settled back with a sigh, willing to do as he

asked. She'd proposed this night, unsure whether it would be a good thing or bad, but willing to take the risk. Now, it seemed, the risk had taken her far beyond where she'd intended to go.

What she'd hoped would be a reaffirmation of life felt instead like a renewal of it. She'd read about this in books—that a man's touch could turn a girl into a woman, a nonbeliever in romance into a lover—she just hadn't believed it could happen to her. Soft sentiment had died in her when she was eight.

Yet she heard music, felt starlight on her body, believed in the future.

She opened her eyes to tell him that, but he kissed them closed again. "Shush," he said gently. "Let me work."

She felt his hands slowly explore her. They shaped every curve, traced every plane, charted every hollow until her life was deafening with promise.

He entered her and climax crashed upon them like cymbals and reverberated for a long, long moment. Finally surfacing as he lay beside her and drew her into his shoulder, she felt as though her lost soul had been found.

CHAPTER THIRTEEN

"NOW, THIS IS THE LIFE," Jack said, sitting at Kay's kitchen table with a plate of country ribs and sauerkraut at 8:00 a.m. "Breakfast with substance. I can't believe your cousins didn't like this." He was on his second helping.

In the light of day, it was hard for her to believe what had happened last night. She didn't regret a moment, didn't want to change a moment, didn't doubt for a moment that he'd been as sincere as she had, and she knew without question that the whole foundation of her life had shifted and nothing would ever be the same.

She just didn't know what to do with it—or about it—or him.

Jack had awakened in a warm and cheerful mood, had kissed her good-morning, suggested he'd put on the coffee while she showered first. When she came downstairs, he was inspecting the casserole she'd made yesterday and looked interested. He was gorgeously disheveled in his T-shirt and slacks.

"I was looking for bacon or sausage," he said, "and found this. Can we have it?"

"Please," she'd said, getting plates. "And what you don't eat, you can take home. I made it for dinner last night with my cousins and they were all upset about other stuff and never touched it."

"What other stuff?"

She spooned the casserole onto two plates and pointed him to a drawer. "Utensils are in there. Men. You know about Rachel and Gib. Well, that situation's not improving very quickly. And Gib's partner, Sam, asked Charlie out and she was so traumatized, she couldn't eat at all." As she put the plates one by one in the microwave, she told him about their argument and her eventual explosion.

He looked up from setting the table, a grin in place. "You lost your temper?" he teased, pretending surprise. "No. I don't believe it."

She removed his plate with a hot pad and put it at his place. "I'm usually very patient with them, but…" She stopped short of telling him she'd been in a complete dither about him and had no idea what to do.

He glanced up from pouring coffee and must have read her expression. "You blew up because you were mad at me, didn't you? Or because you didn't trust me?"

"I wouldn't have made love with you if I didn't trust you."

"I mean that you don't trust my plan for Milford."

That was partially true, but she'd been mad at herself for being interested in him, for caring about him even though his intentions were suspect—and he had children.

Now that she'd made love with him, she had little choice in her feelings. He'd been tender, generous, passionate. She was in love, damn it.

But he hadn't mentioned their lovemaking this morning, and though he'd behaved in an affectionate and familiar way, he'd made no declarations, offered no promises. He was behaving in the way she'd offered when she'd invited him to stay—as though all he'd wanted with her was last night.

"I was tired and overstressed," she said. The microwave timer dinged and she took the second plate to the table. "I get cranky. I can't help it. But, we were all cranky, so it didn't end well."

"Lucky for me," he said, tucking into the ribs. "I thought you told me you didn't inherit your mother's cooking skills."

"No, I said I can cook, I just don't like to. Do you cook for you and your children?"

"We have a wonderful nanny, cook, housekeeper who has saved my life. Do you know Calpurnia Jones?"

"Oh, sure!"

He nodded. "She'd love your wreaths. She has a garden that's unbelievable." He pointed to the wreaths she'd hung from a rack over the stove. All the pots and pans that should have hung there were piled on a corner of the counter. "When did you have time to do that if you're always working or writing your book?"

"When I have trouble with my book," she admitted, "I work on the wreaths. That's why I've finished so many."

He looked sympathetic. "Hard to focus?"

"Oh, I don't know. I guess I just don't know as much about life as I thought I did." She pointed her fork at him. "Actually, time spent with you is usually very good for the hostile dialogue between my hero and heroine. You used to inspire me to be snappy and smart."

He nodded as though he understood. "I usually sand or power-wash very thoroughly after you and I have talked."

"Mmm." She wondered how he would react to a reference to last night. "Do you think we've changed that in each other?"

He studied her across the table. She guessed he was debating with himself on whether or not to be honest. The old pastor in him must have won out. "Oh, most definitely," he said.

Then before she could say any more, or encourage him to, the kitchen door flew open and Rachel and Charlie burst in.

"Come on, Kay! We're…" Rachel was saying as she led the way, dressed in brown corduroy slacks and an orange denim jacket. She stopped abruptly at the sight of Jack at Kay's kitchen table.

Charlie, coming up behind her, put a shocked hand over her mouth. "Oh, Kay," she said, trying to pull Rachel back. "We're so sorry."

Rachel yanked out of her grasp. "No, we're not," she

denied with a bold smile. She came to Jack and offered her hand. He tried to stand to accept it, but she pushed on his shoulder. "No, don't get up. I'm Kay's cousin, Rachel Whittier." She pulled Charlie forward. "Charlene Florio, also a cousin."

Charlene nodded shyly. "Hello."

"Hello," Jack replied. Then ignoring Rachel's directive, he stood anyway. "I'm Jack Keaton. Nice to meet you."

Rachel frowned down at the food on the plates. "I'd prefer to think that you're really slow eating dinner, than that you're having this for breakfast."

"Oh, be honest!" Kay said, going to the cupboard for two cups. There was no way to hide the robe she wore, so she didn't bother. It was clear her cousins had reached the obvious conclusion. "You'd rather think I threw this away and that we're eating egg-white omelets. But, we're not. We're enjoying every cholesterol-laden bite of it. Aren't we, Jack?"

"Yes, we are," he said staunchly.

"And no carbs to speak of," Charlie contributed.

Kay expected Rachel to frown at Charlie. Instead, Rachel focused on Kay. "We're on a mission to find something for Charlie to wear for her date with Sam," she said, waving a catalog in her hand. "And we were hoping you could come with us. But it seems…"

Kay leaped at the opportunity. It was a simple way to end this morning-after situation without having to speak of what had happened, without Jack having to pretend that it had been anything but the one night they'd intended.

She poured coffee into the mugs. "Of course I can come. Jack has to go to work after breakfast. Right?" She gave him a smile that absolved him of all responsibility.

He gave her a look that surprised her in its disappointment.

"Right," he said after a significant pause.

"We'll take our coffee in the living room." Rachel took a cup and handed one to Charlie. "While you two finish breakfast. We want to look over Prue's catalog one more time, anyway. Sorry for the interruption."

Kay knew that was just good manners for Jack's benefit. The moment he was gone, she was going to have to explain.

After her cousins had disappeared, she went to top up Jack's coffee. He put a hand over it. "No, thanks. I'll just finish this and take off. But, thank you. It's delicious."

The warm affection of the morning was gone and in its place was a cool courtesy.

"I'm sorry they intruded," she said, keeping her voice down as she put the pot back. "But you do have to go to work, don't you?"

"They didn't intrude, they're your family," he corrected with that same tone. "And it's Saturday, and I don't have to go to work. But, it's that look on your face that's trying to pretend nothing happened that I object to."

Now she was hurt as well as confused. "What did happen?"

"I don't know. Something." He pushed his plate away and pinned her to her chair with his eyes. "Just don't pretend it didn't happen to you, too."

"I didn't want you to think I was expecting you to stay," she explained, "or to declare yourself, or anything like that."

"I won't try to read your mind, if you don't try to read mine."

"There's no reason to get testy."

"Maybe I'm just tired and overstressed." He quoted her with a superior glance as he stood. "Excuse me. I'll go up and get my things."

"Fine. I'll pack up the casserole for you."

"Thank you."

"I JUST DON'T UNDERSTAND," Rachel said as the three cousins rode in her white Crown Victoria to the Prudent Designs studio in the old Chandler Mill Building outside of town, "how come you've known him long enough to be intimate with him, and we've never even met him."

"I know about him," Charlie said importantly. "I saw him at the last Fall Festival meeting. He works for Hank Whitcomb."

"I've never seen him until today."

"Well, you were busy hiding from Gib at the last Fall Festival meeting. That's what you get."

Rachel gasped. Charlie, apparently high on the prospect of shopping, was taking no prisoners. "So, is this the first time?" she asked Kay.

She wanted to tell her it was none of her business, but they'd been nose deep in each other's lives since they were children.

"Yes. It's nothing serious, just…" She'd been about to add that it was just something that happened, then remembered Jack's expression at the kitchen table. "I don't know what it is," she amended. "It just is."

"Well." Rachel sighed. "You could keep us informed."

"You can't inform about an impromptu night together."

"Morning-after reports are acceptable, also."

"Why bother with those. You could just barge in on me on a regular basis and save us all a lot of trouble."

Her cousins laughed, and that made her laugh. It was impossible to feel badly about the morning even if she didn't understand where her life was going.

HIS HOUSE WAS QUIET when Jack walked in with Kay's leftover casserole. Buster was in his crate, probably a sign that Calpurnia intended to sleep in a while longer after the late night. The dog's tail thumped at the possibility of release.

Jack stuck a finger in the cage to rub Buster's snout. "Hang in there," he said. "I'm going to check on the kids, then I'll take you with me for a walk around the lake." He needed fresh air to clear his brain.

Both children were still dead to the world, Amanda in her burrow, and Paul with arms and legs hanging out of the covers. Jack raised an edge of Amanda's blankets to make sure she was still breathing and left it up. Then he covered Paul, freed Buster, grabbed his leash and ran with him out to the truck.

He used to run regularly in the old days before his injury, but it was too hard now to accommodate the limp. His left leg reacted a little more slowly than the right, and he couldn't seem to find the right rhythm when he ran. So he walked instead, the slower pace easier to react to if he got out of step.

Buster was ecstatic with a whole new world to investigate. He sniffed everything, ran to the end of the leash then back to Jack with a spring in his gait Jack envied.

Hearing footsteps behind him, he called Buster to him so that he didn't trip anyone as they passed.

"Hey, Jack!" Two men in shorts and sweatshirts caught up with him but adjusted to his slower pace rather than passing. He recognized Hank Whitcomb and Gib Whittier. "We were just talking about you," Gib said. "We need a couple of hands to help with Father Chabot's jail for the festival. He didn't dig it out of the basement until last night and discovered that it's not going to make it another year. So, Evan Braga volunteered us to build a new one. Can you paint it?"

Gib was jogging at Jack's walking pace, but Hank had stopped to pet Buster.

"When?"

"A week from Tuesday evening. My house," Hank said. "There'll be edibles."

"If my babysitter can stay, I'll be there."

"Good. Seven-thirty."

Hank straightened and was jogging in place, ready to sprint off again when the roar of a distant motor made all three men turn in the direction of the sound. A young man in leathers on a motorcycle, fringe flying, approached at high speed, then slowed to the speed limit when he saw the joggers. The bike passed them with a roar, the driver's identity concealed by sunglasses and the brim of a pulled-down cap. Buster hid behind Jack.

Gib stopped jogging to watch him, then whistled as the bike disappeared toward town. "I wonder how he got those?" he asked no one in particular.

Hank frowned. "Who? Got what?"

"That was Derek Slocum." Gib refocused on his companions. "Always in trouble. That was some set of leathers he was wearing. Two weeks ago when we stopped him, he was wearing jeans and an Army surplus jacket. What the hell is he into now?"

"Obviously something that's paying well," Hank said. "He even had the custom fenders and tank cover."

Gib started jogging again. "I'm sure whatever he did to get those will show up on my desk eventually. The Springfield Harley-Davidson outfitter is probably reporting a B and E as we speak. Let's go. I've got a lunch date."

Gib and Hank set off again, and Jack promised to call about Tuesday. He continued on his walk with Buster, and eventually passed Cam Trent's place where he'd been painting window frames a few weeks ago and noticed little Misty O'Neil floundering in the lake.

As Buster stopped to explore the base of a large maple tree, Jack remembered the horror he'd felt at the sight of her with no one around for half the length of the lake, remembered his swift but slightly uneven sprint into the water, watching her go under and trying to memorize the spot. He could still feel the fabric of her clothing against the palm of his hand when he caught her, the exhilaration, the prayer he'd muttered to himself out of long habit.

He put a hand to his aching head, wondering what in the hell Maple Hill and its people were doing to him. He'd come to avenge Julia, to be completely hardhearted about making Milford pay. And here he was walking a puppy around the lake while his children slept at home and while he tried to adjust to the meaning of a night of lovemaking that had been supposed to simply relieve tension but had knocked him to his knees with its power. An almost spiritual note to it had tapped a tenderness in him from his pre-Iraq days that he'd thought had died with Julia.

But he didn't want to be on his knees. Seems he couldn't trust himself not to pray.

He tugged on Buster's leash and headed back toward the truck. He'd take the kids to a cartoon feature at the movies today. That was good for distracting him. And he was going to stop and buy shoes. He'd been charmingly coerced by Father Chabot into buying tickets for the Festival's dinner dance, and he couldn't wear his tennis shoes with a suit.

"THAT'S BEAUTIFUL on you," Rachel said to Charlie, startling both her cousins with that generous observation. "I like the red rather than the purple, though, don't you think, Kay? And it'll be perfect through the holidays."

Kay met Charlie's astonished gaze with her own wide-eyed surprise. Charlie did look beautiful in a calf-length red wool skirt and a matching jacket with a pearlescent silk camisole visible at the neckline.

Something had put Rachel in a thoughtful mood and Kay couldn't help but wonder if it had anything to do with Gib. She'd been hurrying them along this morning, glancing at her watch as though she had another appointment.

Kay nodded. "I like the red, too. Charlie?"

Charlie's face was flushed with color, her eyes bright with excitement as she did a turn in Prue's three-way mirror. Then she swept both hands over her generous posterior and frowned. "I'd like it better in a size six."

Prue came to her to smooth the shoulders and smile at her reflection. "Fashion isn't about size," she said. "It's about womanliness rather than femininity, about the hutzpah to have the personal style to make the dress do its work for you. And you have that if you stop thinking you should look like a model. You're beautiful. You and the dress are a dynamite combination."

Charlie patted Prue's hand on her shoulder. "I'll take it in red. What'll I do for shoes?"

"Flats would be fine with this, or shoes with a little wedge. Even three-inch heels would be good, but why put yourself through that."

Rachel glanced at her watch again and shouldered her purse. "I'd love to be in on the shoe shopping, but I've got a lunch meeting at Perk Avenue." She gave Charlie a quick hug. "Have a wonderful time, and let me know how it goes."

She blew Kay a kiss. "You've already had a wonderful time. See you both next week."

Charlie stared at the door Rachel closed behind her. "What's with her?"

"Hmm." Prue prepared a box with tissue while Charlie went behind the screen to change into her street clothes. "I happen to know that Gib has a lunch meeting today. He was supposed to meet my husband to talk about the possibility of leaving the force to join the Wonders' security team, but had to change the date because of another commitment." She grinned at Kay. "Could Gib and Rachel be meeting each other?"

There was a gasp from behind the screen as Charlie handed the clothes over the top. Prue went to take them from her. "You think they're finally talking?" Charlie asked, her eyes appearing above the screen.

Kay held up crossed fingers. "We can only hope. She certainly was in a good mood."

"Yeah. That's a little unsettling. If it *doesn't* go well…"

Kay silenced her with a hissing sound. "Don't even let that thought form."

"I've made an appointment to have my hair cut," Charlie announced over lunch at the Barn.

Withholding a "Wahoo!" of approval, Kay asked, as though it were no big deal, "What brought you to that decision? We've talked about it so often…"

Charlie picked at the strips of grilled chicken in her Caesar salad. "I've just finally decided to be brave, I guess. I thought my weight and my hair protected me from inspiring a man's interest. But they didn't. Sam's interested anyway. I mean, I know I'm a good person, a good teacher, and I think I might become a good administrator, but I never thought of myself as an attractive woman. I *want* to be, but I'm taking a chance. Rejection is very scary, and so is the possibility that he'll want to be intimate and I'll hate it."

Kay caught her hands and held them tightly in her own. "Charlie, there's no reason to think you'll hate it."

Charlie doubted her with a look.

"I know. You told me the rape was painful and scary, and made you feel like you'd never be clean again. But that was a long time ago. Making love with a man who thinks you're wonderful would be a completely different experience."

Charlie nodded, squeezing her hands in return. "I'm just worried about going to that same place in my head. What did you do? " She looked into Kay's eyes, needing an answer. "It's not at all the same, but you've been as desperate as I've been to find your way out of the past. What did you do when Jack

Keaton made love to you? How did you forget…
Betsy?"

Kay realized with sudden surprise how easily she and
Jack had gone from heavy discussions about Betsy and
Julia, to finding solace in one another. Had that graduation from sharing souls to sharing bodies not happened
to her, she'd have considered it impossible.

"I…I was in the moment," she said, wanting to explain in a way that would free Charlie from her concerns. "We'd talked about what happened to Betsy, then
about…about his wife dying, and suddenly… I think we
just wanted to help each other. I may have been able to
let Betsy go because my thoughts were for him rather
than for myself. And I wanted to give him…a whole and
caring woman."

"That's good." Charlie absorbed that information.
"But Sam's life is perfect. He loves his parents and his
married brother and little sister. He's never been married, so he has no old baggage I can help him through.
He might not even understand what I'm afraid of."

"Everyone understands fear," Kay insisted. "Be honest if you think it's too soon. He might appreciate it."

Charlie looked more relaxed. "How did we get from
a haircut to how we put the past away to make love?

"Cutting off old dead ends, I guess," Charlie laughed,
answering her own question. "If we skip dessert, I have
time to buy shoes before my hair appointment."

Kay wandered around the store while Charlie tried on
shoes. She heard a child's shrill scream of excitement

then was startled out of a scream of her own when a display of walking shoes fell off a shelf behind her. Several
men's shoes and a bare plastic foot bounced off her head.

"Ouch! Ow! Owww!" she complained, sinking onto a
chair during the barrage, covering her head with her arms.

"Amanda!" a familiar male voice said sharply. "Paul!
I told you to stop running!"

A concerned clerk came to fuss over Kay, picking up
the plastic foot that had landed in her lap. "Are you
okay? I'm so sorry. We…"

A pair of very familiar hands took hold of her arms,
one hand going to her face to lift her chin, then turn it
right, then left. Jack's dark eyes scrutinized her. He
knelt between her knees, inspiring a sharp image of one
of her favorite memories of the night before.

"How many of me do you see?" he asked.

She smiled, the very sight of him brightening an already nice but curious day. Things as she knew them
were changing. Rachel had been cheerful and possibly
meeting Gib. Charlie was having her hair cut and going
on a date, ready to step over her past.

It was odd that seeing him should make her feel better when he represented a change in her she had no idea
what to do about.

"One of you," she replied with a dry smile, "is usually too many."

He pinched her shin punitively. "Feel okay? No
dizziness?"

"No." She rubbed her head where the thud of one of

the big shoes still reverberated slightly. "I'm fine. But I'll bet my hair's a mess."

He grinned as his eyes went over her hair. She wondered what that meant.

"It's always a little…undisciplined," he explained. "Curls going this way and that. But somehow appealing."

Before she could decide what to say to that, she noticed the two children standing on either side of him, looking contrite and concerned.

The little boy came to lean an elbow on her chair and said conversationally, "Buster ate Daddy's shoes." On his hand was a fuzzy slipper with an alligator head.

"Yeah." The little girl came and wriggled her little bottom between Kay and the other arm of the chair to make room for herself. "And he ate the sofa and my Barbie. She has to be in a wheelchair 'cause he bit her knees off."

Kay flinched at the child's closeness. Betsy had had that same confidence that her company was welcome, that everyone would want to know what she knew. She hoped Jack would interpret the flinch as a reaction to the poor Barbie doll's condition.

"I'm sorry to hear that," Kay said, hoping the child would move. But she appeared comfortable. "I met Buster and he seems like a very nice dog."

Amanda insisted that he was. "But we're having trouble making him eat food instead of stuff. I'm sorry we bonked you on the head."

"It's all right. I'm not hurt."

"Paul scared me with the alligator slipper."

Jack took the slipper from Paul's hand and got to his feet. "They were fooling around when they shouldn't have been." He gave each of the children a stern look that they accepted soberly.

"Sorry," Paul said.

Amanda repeated the apology. But she still hadn't moved.

Jack offered his hand to Kay to help her up. "Can we buy you coffee in apology."

"Ah, no thanks," she said, grateful to have an excuse not to have to be with the children. "I'm here with Charlie. She's buying shoes." Afraid he'd seen she was happy to have a good reason to turn him down, she got nervous and chatty. "Well, of course she's shopping for shoes. That's what you do in a shoe store. What kind are you getting? What did Buster eat?"

She got the feeling he knew exactly what was going on in her mind. He was the kind of man who paid attention; she'd had good evidence of that last night.

"He's eaten every pair I have except my tennis shoes," he replied. "I have to get shoes I can wear with a suit for the dinner dance."

"Ah," she said, pretending not to notice his knowing look. "Hot date?"

That teasing question seemed to annoy him.

Amanda caught her hand. "I'm in first grade, and I have a Shrek lunch box."

It was Betsy's touch, small but firm. Taking charge.

Kay wanted desperately to pull her hand away, but guessed Amanda was probably as sensitive to subtleties of mood as Betsy had been, and her hang-ups weren't worth hurting her.

"I used to have a Tinkerbell lunch box." Kay was aware of sounding breathless, of Jack watching her.

"Okay, let's let her go," he said to Amanda. "She has things to do, and we have, too."

Amanda squeezed her hand, then dropped it. "Okay. Bye."

"Bye, Amanda. Bye, Paul." She looked up from the children to say a polite goodbye to their father and saw that he was staring at a table bearing a display of boots. He turned to glance at her, then looked back at a pair of half boots in black leather with shiny silver eyelets. "These look familiar?" he asked.

They were the same boots they'd seen on the intruder last night. "Yes, they do," she said.

The clerk who'd fussed over Kay had apparently been hovering. "Those are very popular," she said. "Wear like iron. I swear every other man in town has a pair. Women, too." She pointed to a shelf behind the counter with dress shoes. "When you're ready, we'll find something for you to wear."

She picked up another tennis shoe that must have fallen off the display Paul and Amanda had knocked over, and walked away with it.

"Just our luck about the boots," Kay said. "In the movies, when the person hiding in the dark catches a glimpse of the perpetrator's shoes, they're always boots with a silver toe, or some other identifying detail."

He smiled wryly. "Nothing's going to be easy for us. You may as well accept that right now. See you."

"Yes," she said, and she had a pretty good idea that he wasn't talking about shoes.

CHAPTER FOURTEEN

LIFE WAS GOOD for Jack most of the week. The children were happy and cooperative, and the sudden appearance of Halloween items in all the stores had them planning costumes and looking forward to raiding the neighborhood for candy. Amanda brought home from school a cat mask made from a paper plate, and Paul's kindergarten class made construction-paper black cats with whiskers made of small drinking straws. The refrigerator looked like the basement of some alternate-reality Louvre.

Calpurnia was in a fall cleaning frenzy and had washed curtains and shampooed carpets and resisted Jack's efforts to pay her extra. "I have to be here anyway until it's time to get Paul and wait for Amanda," she said. "I might as well make myself useful." He solved the problem by paying off a bill he knew she had at the auto shop.

An item in Thursday's *Maple Hill Mirror* said that Ron Milford had been released from the hospital on Sunday, and that Whitcomb's Wonders had been hired to repair the damage in his office and rehang the mercifully undamaged chandelier. He was already back to work.

Hank called Jack on Thursday to ask him to run by the Milfords' on Friday to do an estimate on painting their Dutch Colonial home inside and out. It was a beautiful structure with an old barn-style roof, shutters and window boxes and a beautifully landscaped lawn with fruit trees and an old-fashioned privet hedge.

Jack measured the outside on Friday morning since no one was home, then returned Monday after lunch when Joanne was there to let him in to estimate repainting the inside. It was huge, the interior complex, and his notes extensive. He took them home to calculate and promised to return with a quote after dinner.

Meanwhile Father Chabot had scraped the rectory's main corridor wall when he'd brought the old jail up from the basement and wondered if Jack could do a quick repair since the Bishop was coming to visit.

Jack complied, certain he would have to deal with the old priest's charming but prying questions, but he'd been called to the bedside of a sick parishioner and Jack was able to work in silence. In the absence of the priest, he let his mind wander, thinking about his past and how his plan of action would affect his future.

He reminded himself that he no longer believed, so whatever he did was only between himself and his own conscience. And he'd seen Kay's expression when Amanda took her hand last weekend in the shoe store. She'd been horrified and desperate to be free of her. She'd been cool enough not to yank her hand away, but Amanda was very smart. Prolonged exposure to Kay's attitude could only do further harm to a child who already had to live without the mother who'd adored her, and whom she'd adored.

So, that was it between him and Kay—one perfect night that had shaken loose the man he used to be and, to be honest, a little of what he used to believe.

The classic picture of Christ with the children that hung in the meeting room visible from the hallway where he worked had been following him since he'd first worked here. He kept his eyes averted from it, but in his mind's eye he could see the smiling face and, contrary to everything he thought he believed, he wanted to look at it, wanted to feel the comfort it used to give him in the old days.

He made himself finish his work without looking in that direction, cleaned up, then locked the door behind him. Putting Milford away would give him comfort.

He brought Chinese takeout home for dinner at Cal's request because she was cleaning kitchen cupboards and had stuff all over the stove, the counter and the table. Then he went back to Milford's after seven, assuring Cal he'd be home in time to put the children to bed.

Of course, when he'd made that promise, he hadn't counted on seeing Milford's house on fire, and his wife in the yard calling 911.

THE *MIRROR* OFFICE was a hub of activity while Kay tried to focus on profiles of the various people in charge of the Fall Festival. Computers that allowed writers to place type, add photographs, make up a page and place headlines had taken much of the pressure and excitement out of the newsroom, but a special page was being prepared tonight to advertise the festival, with a long list of sponsors. Jed Warton, the advertising director, supervised Haley's creation of the page while Priss Adams fielded phone calls, checked details with committee members and did all the other work needed to make up the page.

A little self-satisfied that she didn't have to be involved because of several important stories underway, Kay kept her mind on her task. Her heart, unfortunately, was still in her bedroom pressed against Jack Keaton's.

She survived last week heroically because she'd helped Charlie with her shopping, then listened for several hours the following day while her cousin rhapsodized about her evening and the fact that it had ended with an impressive good-night kiss.

The day after that, Kay had run into Rachel at their aunt's when Kay had filled a special request for chocolate cake. Rachel had been there because Agnes's neighbor called, saying Agnes had spilled her pillbox.

"She is not eating that!" Rachel said firmly, pointing to the cake. She was her old self again—suggesting that her lunch with Gib had not gone well. "She takes Lipitor for cholesterol and doxazosin for high blood pressure. Why would you bring her chocolate cake with inch-high frosting?"

"Because she called and asked me to," Kay replied.

Agnes took it away from Rachel and went to the kitchen with it. "I'm drowning my sorrows. Elliott Whitman accepted my invitation to dinner and never came."

Rachel and Kay exchanged a glance. "He's in Hollywood, Agnes." Rachel snapped the lids closed on the seven-compartment pillbox and placed it in the middle of the table.

"I know. Liz told me he got a new series. But you'd think he'd make time for old friends." Agnes forked a bite of cake into her mouth and savored the flavor. "Mmm. I want chocolate cake at my wake."

"We wouldn't have to plan a wake if you didn't eat that stuff."

Agnes waggled her eyebrows at Rachel and continued to eat. "Someone's going to call, 'That's a wrap!' over me one day soon. But I'm going to throw a wonderful party before I go." She patted Rachel's cheek. "When you're in a better mood you can help me plan."

Rachel seemed suddenly defeated. She pulled a chair away from the table. "Well, if you insist on eating that, sit down and I'll bring you some coffee."

Kay followed Rachel into the kitchen. "Are you okay?" she asked, hating to see her cousin looking beaten.

"Oh, yeah." Heaving a gusty sigh, Rachel put the few dishes from the sink into the dishwasher. "I met Gib for lunch the other day as you suggested, but it didn't go well. It started out okay, but then I wanted him to admit that he'd hurt me, and he wanted me to admit that I'd made his life hell. We were shouting at each other in no time. I left before they threw us out of Perk Avenue."

Kay wrapped her arms around her, at a loss to offer advice. She thought it unfortunate that loving someone didn't come with the ability to solve their problems. "I wish I could fix this for you."

"I know." Rachel held her closely, then pushed her gently away. "When you and Charlie were kids, I wished I could bring Betsy back for you, and erase that awful day for Charlie." A pleat appeared between her eyebrows and she looked into Kay's eyes with confession in hers.

Kay waited.

"Did you know," Rachel asked, "that the day that happened to Charlie, I was supposed to take her to lunch and shopping?"

For a moment Kay couldn't make a sound. "No," she whispered finally. "I never heard that."

The guilty look in Rachel's eyes was such an anomaly in the usually responsible and confident woman, that Kay could only stare.

"Aunt Sylvia asked me if Charlie could spend that day with me and I agreed, but it was a tough week at work and I was fanatical about keeping a perfect house and organizing my life. That was my one valuable day off. So I called her the night before and asked if I could spend the day with Charlie the following week. You know how I have to be organized." She sank onto the top of Agnes's step stool. "So, the creep woke up that day, found Charlie home and…" Rachel stopped abruptly.

"Rachel." Kay put a hand to her cousin's shoulder. "Come on, now. You're not shouldering blame for that?"

"I always took care of the two of you. It was expected of me and most of the time I loved it. But that day...I had other things to do. I hate that."

Kay wrapped her arms around her again. "Well... Charlie doesn't blame you. She's never told me she was supposed to spend the day with you."

"I'm not sure she even remembers. You know how shock can make you forget incidents that surround an accident or a trauma. I see it all the time at the hospital."

Kay experienced sudden enlightenment. "Is that why she annoys you sometimes? Because she doesn't hate you, and you think she should?"

Rachel sighed and pushed herself to her feet. "I think so. And in my effort to make sure that my neglect never harmed anyone ever again..."

"You've gone over the top, been overprotective, overly organized, demanding more of yourself than anyone can give without something suffering." Kay smiled. She couldn't help it; she finally understood. "You can't forgive Gib for cheating on you, because you can't forgive yourself for thinking that you made him do it."

Rachel considered that and frowned over it, then finally nodded. "Yeah. That may be it."

"You have to try the talking thing again, Rache."

Rachel glowered at Kay. "It doesn't work for me. I get angry and I don't hear what I want to hear and I start blaming..."

"Look. You have a right to be mad and deeply hurt. It's just that if you want to fix it, tell him what's in your heart. Admitting to fears and weaknesses is okay. Pull it all out for him to see and tell him how it's tortured you all this time. Let yourself need him, Rachel. Please. Let him help you."

"I don't know…"

"Give it another try. If it doesn't work, you can blame me for all eternity." Kay hugged her quickly and grinned right in her face. "You know how much you'd love that."

Rachel swatted her arm. "Okay, okay. God, you have one night of passion in two years and you think you can solve the world's problems."

The world's problems, Kay thought as Rachel helped tidy up. But not her own.

Wednesday had been uneventful except for the stories she was trying to pull together by deadline. She was able to enjoy Thursday despite the chaos going on around her because she was flush with self-satisfaction over the week's successes. Charlie had had a great date, and Rachel had faced a truth about herself.

On Friday, it was clear Jordie had been reading his Spider-Man book over and over. She rewarded him with a copy of *Amazing Grace*. He looked less than thrilled.

"It's about a girl?" he asked, his nose wrinkled in distaste.

"Yes." She opened the book to show him the illustrations. "When the kids in her class tell her she can't be Peter Pan, she proves to them that she can do whatever she decides to do."

"What happens?"

"You have to read it."

With her family's lives showing promise, and Jordie doing well, Kay was beginning to feel confident that she might be able to do something about her own. Then the police scanner near her desk crackled to life.

"Station 255," a calm voice said, "you have a structure fire at 1221 Peabody Road. Flames showing. Cars in the driveway, people possibly inside."

"1221 Peabody," she repeated to herself as she quickly saved her story and reached for her purse. "Why is that familiar?"

It occurred to her as she raced out to her car. She swore and picked up speed. It was Milford's house.

Jack could not be responsible she told herself over and over while maneuvering through the light dinner-time traffic. The man who'd made such thoughtful, delicious love to her could not harm another human being.

It was dusk by the time she arrived at Milford's home. Hoses crisscrossed the yard leading from three fire trucks whose bright lights lit the area. She saw Gib and a uniformed officer talking with Ron Milford, who was dressed in a robe. He held his weeping wife in one arm.

Kay climbed onto the doghouse roof and took pictures of the crowd. Photographing onlookers was fire investigation policy, and she was convinced it might help her figure out who was after Ron Milford.

If it wasn't Jack Keaton.

And she told herself it couldn't be.

She snapped photos in a systematic grid pattern. Her

heart sank to her shoes when she spotted Jack's face right in the middle of the crowd near the gate. She lowered the camera and stared at him, suddenly sick. He couldn't have done it. And yet here he was.

He met her gaze from across the strobe-lit darkness and began to cross the space that separated them. She leaped off the doghouse to confront him.

JACK HATED the doubt in Kay's eyes. He did want revenge on Milford, but he wanted him to see it coming.

"I can't believe," he said, maintaining a foot's distance between them, "that after the night we spent together, you consider me capable of setting Milford's house on fire while he's still inside."

She folded her arms over the camera sling. "And yet you're here…watching."

"I had an appointment."

"To do what?" she asked, obviously upset. "To set a fire?"

Shaking her would have been so satisfying, but he'd always preached that a man was strongest when he was kind. And it probably did look bad that he was here. He had to count to ten, though.

"No," he answered calmly. "To give them an estimate on painting the house."

The doubt flickered, but she tipped her head back. He now recognized that gesture as her stubbornness taking a stand. "So, you've been around."

"I have. I was here Friday measuring outside, and this

morning, doing the inside. But Mrs. Milford was with me the entire time I was in the house. You're welcome to check with her."

"As soon as Gib's finished with them, I'm going to offer them a place to stay for the night," Kay said.

"Good. I'll come along. Just in case you'd like to apologize to me after you've spoken to them."

She said nothing to that. Jack hung around while she took more pictures, then followed her to the Milfords when Gib left them.

"Ron, I'm so sorry," she said, taking his free hand. His wife still clung to his other arm, dabbing at her eyes. She wore a business suit in dark blue. "Joanne. Thank God you're both all right. I wondered if you'd like to stay with me until the mess is cleaned up."

"Thank you, Kay," Joanne said. "But Hank sent someone from the Yankee Inn to tell us they've reserved a room for us until we can get back into the house." She looked mournfully behind her at the now smoldering and waterlogged mess. "I'm sure it'll be a couple of weeks."

Kay commiserated. "Do you think it was something electrical?" she asked with uncomplicated interest. Jack was sure it never crossed Milford's or his wife's mind that she was after a story. Or maybe she just wanted to assess whether Jack was involved.

Milford shook his head. "I don't see how it could be. We had everything looked over when we bought it. That was just three months ago." He drew his wife closer and looked troubled as he added, "After what happened in my office, this can't be coincidence. I was in the shower, but thank goodness Jo came home an hour earlier than she'd expected, saw the fire and called 911. I guess I have an enemy, though I have no idea why. We don't know where it started yet, but our bedroom's destroyed and most of the back of the house. I was obviously the target."

Then, as though Jack had personally directed this part, Milford noticed him and offered his free hand. "I guess that estimate to paint will change considerably," he said with a somber grin, "and we'll have to talk about it another time."

Jack manfully resisted a self-satisfied smirk in Kay's direction. "Of course," he said politely because he had to. "I'm sorry about what's happened."

"All our clothes were destroyed," Joanne said, on the brink of tears again. "My good jewelry's in the safety deposit box, but I just bought a few things from Prudent Designs, and they're gone. My lambskin jacket, my..."

Milford squeezed her to him. "On the other hand, your designer husband is safe and sound," he said. "And we're well insured, so just relax. You're going to have a few weeks' vacation at the inn, and you can go shopping in Boston for a couple of days if you want to. And take your business partners with you."

"That would be nice," she said, perking up.

"If I can do anything—" Kay gave Milford her business card "—give me a call."

"I will. In the meantime, I guess I should advertise for more clients. My office is almost ready for business again."

The limo used to pick up and deliver guests to the airport from the Yankee Inn arrived. The Milfords climbed in and were whisked away.

Without prompting, Kay turned to Jack in the rotating red light of a fire truck and said gravely, "I apologize."

While Milford's remark did prove that Jack had been invited to the house, it failed to prove that he hadn't set the fire. She must have come to that conclusion on her own.

"Apology accepted," he said. "I think this corroborates my suspicion that he's cheated people in the past. Someone hates him as much as I do."

Kay rolled her eyes impatiently. "Jack, for God's sake. You just saw him be strong about what happened, be charming and sweet with his wife and courteous to us when he must have wanted to rant and tell nosy me to take a hike."

"That never works with you," he said distractedly. "He must know that, too." He saw Gib walking back and forth near the hedge, then following it behind the house. Jack caught Kay's arm. "Come on. I think Gib's got something."

They found Gib on his haunches, studying a flower bed of chrysanthemums.

"What is it?" Kay hurried to his side and leaned over him.

He straightened and frowned at her. "It's a police investigation. Who do you think you are? Go home. You can come to the station for the daily report in the morning."

She gasped dramatically. "I'm your cousin."

"You're my ex-wife's cousin," he corrected. "Get out of here before I have you arrested for that alone."

Kay glanced at Jack, her expression an apology for what she was about to do. He drew a little closer, fascinated by her approach.

"Ex-wife? You've filed for divorce?"

"Don't be stupid."

"You mean, she's filed?"

"Not to my knowledge."

"Then she's not your ex-anything. And I don't suppose you want to hear that she's very upset your lunch didn't go well."

The remark was tauntingly pointed and Gib rose to the bait. "How did you know we had lunch?"

She gasped again. "Hello!" She pointed to herself. "Investigative reporter here."

He leaned over her grimly. Jack stepped closer, prepared to interfere if he wasn't teasing. But he was.

"How upset was she?" he asked softly, glancing surreptitiously around.

"Very upset."

"She admitted this to you?"

"Soulfully."

"Don't fabricate, just tell me the truth."

"I am. The day the two of you were meeting, she was cheerful and hopeful. Since then she's been cranky."

"God. Cranky's become her middle name."

"She's had something bothering her none of us knew anything about."

"What?" he demanded.

"She's going to tell you. Be understanding."

"So help me God, I always try to be, but she starts railing on me and I…I lose it."

She was nodding before he'd finished.

"Try extra hard this time," she suggested.

He was silent for a moment, then he sighed and promised, "I will." He pointed toward something in the flower bed. "Make yourself useful and take a picture of that tire track."

"Ah. Evidence." She leaned over the bed, poised the camera, then looked up before clicking the shutter. "Gib," she said urgently. "That track's from Derek Slocum's bike."

Gib glanced at Jack as though soliciting sympathy, then said, his voice high with disbelief, "I know that, but how the hell do you?"

"I was there the day he was speeding and you were in pursuit. Remember? He took a tumble, you called for an ambulance…"

He nodded understanding. "That's right. And I am in the presence of an investigative reporter. You saw the tracks that day and memorized the pattern?" The question was a little snide. She replied seriously, "Yes, I did. Well. They are distinctive with that sort of Celtic Knot middle." She asked under her breath, "You think Derek did this? Why?"

"Possibly," he replied impatiently, "and I don't know why. Unlike you, I'm not an investigative reporter, just a lowly detective, and I actually have to collect data and sort through facts before coming to a conclusion. And what I think really doesn't matter. It all has to go to court, be presented to a jury…."

"Gib."

He drew a long-suffering sigh. "I saw him decked out in leathers the other day that had to be worth a mint. I wondered at the time where he got them. This may explain it."

She was puzzled. "But, what does he have against the Milfords?"

"Probably nothing. He's done work for hire before."

"Somebody paid him to do this?"

"I wouldn't be surprised."

She went from puzzled to worried. "You know, if you pick him up, chances are their mother's off somewhere drinking, and Jordie…"

"I'm way ahead of you. Jordie will be taken care of. Will you take the damn picture?"

She turned away from him, shot the tracks twice. "If you're working tonight, I'll bring prints right over."

"I'd appreciate that."

"I also shot the crowd. Maybe whoever hired Derek is in there somewhere."

"Thank you." He glanced at his watch. "When can I have them?"

"Half an hour?"

"Okay."

Kay started back to her car and Jack fell into step beside her. "I'll wait while you print the pictures," he said.

"Why?"

"It's dark and quiet, you're alone. Whatever's going on, I don't like it. If someone in the crowd is responsible for the fire, they saw you taking photographs."

She looked around at the still-lively scene around Milford's house, and the shadowy darkness that stood between her and the *Mirror* office. She tucked a companionable hand in his arm. "Thank you," she said. "That's very old-fashioned of you, but I appreciate it."

He pretended shock as they walked on. "I've never known you to be amenable," he teased, then something softened in his eyes and he added with a grin, "Oh, wait. Yes I have."

"You were less quarrelsome, yourself," she said, a little unsettled by his reference to the night they'd spent together. "Don't you have to get home to your children?"

"I do. But the nanny's there for the moment."

He waited at Priss's desk, looking through last week's paper while Kay enlarged the photos on her disk and printed them out. She packed them into a folder, and Jack followed her in his car to the police department.

Gib was grateful to have them, then noticed Jack waiting in the doorway. "Is Jack your bodyguard?" he asked Kay.

"Just my friend," she replied with studied nonchalance.

Gib looked into her eyes, then up at Jack, who leaned

a shoulder in the doorway. "Don't con me, Kay," he said absently as he looked through the photos. "Reading people goes with my job. He has more invested in you than friendship."

She thought that might true—even *hoped* it was. But Gib's use of the word *invested* reminded her of all the problems inherent in her attraction to Jack. He had a little girl who reminded her so much of Betsy.

She patted his arm, unwilling to discuss her relationship with Jack. "Just make sure you put that skill of reading people to good use when you meet Rachel again."

Jack followed Kay home. When she got out of her car, she thought he might walk her to her door as he'd done the last time. A kiss would be welcome tonight, when she didn't understand what was happening or who was involved. Being with him, touching him, always lent her a sense of security her life generally lacked.

But he simply waited in his car until she opened her front door and flipped on the inside light. She waved, he tapped the horn, and after she closed and locked the door, she heard him drive away.

AMANDA, PAUL and Buster were desperate for Jack's attention when he got home. Calpurnia tried to take him to task for paying her auto repair bill. He told her he didn't know what she was talking about.

"Clete said a Good Samaritan paid my bill." She studied him suspiciously.

He shrugged. "Maple Hill's full of them."

She tried to question him further, but he'd gotten down on the floor with the children and they already had him pinned. The dog barked excitedly and kissed his face. The children laughed hysterically, and Cal couldn't have been heard if she'd shouted, so she gave up. As the children and the dog attacked him, Calpurnia leaned over him to say goodbye.

He suddenly remembered the work party for Father Chabot's jail. He sat up, a child in each arm, his hand covering their mouths. "Can you stay late tomorrow so I can help with a project for Father Chabot's festival booth?" he shouted at Cal's retreating back.

She turned at the door with a nod. "That'll give me time to flip the mattresses."

"Don't do that," he said while the children wriggled and laughed behind his hand. "I'll do it."

"Okay. Anyway, I can stay."

"Great. Good night. Okay, you little beasties. I'm going to feed you to this little monster here, starting with your toes, then your fingers, then your nose!"

They thought the threat hilarious and screamed as Buster kissed and nibbled them. Jack felt their laughter in his heart, realized that he was coming to love the silly mutt and experienced a heightened sense of…happiness?

That couldn't be.

He analyzed his feelings again as he picked up a child under each arm and headed for the kitchen and the carton of blueberry swirl ice cream in the freezer. Knowing the kitchen meant begging treats, Buster ran ahead of them, tail high.

Yes, Jack thought, opening the freezer as Amanda climbed onto the kitchen stool for bowls and Paul reached into a drawer for spoons. He was happy.

Not a laugh-out-loud, complete-faith-in-the-future happy. But a sort of trust-the-moment happy. Tonight was good, and that gave him hope that there might be other good times, as well.

It didn't diminish his desire for justice, or the need to figure out who else was after Milford besides him. It did contribute to his confusion because somehow, all entangled in the plan to avenge Julia, were growing feelings for Kay Florio. So, he was still in a terrible mess, but he was hopeful about it.

That was the scariest part of all because it was a little like having faith.

Which he didn't.

HE ARRIVED at Hank's Tuesday night with a luminescent orange paint Evan had suggested to make the jail visible from all over the Common. He knocked on the front door and was totally surprised when Kay opened it. She looked as shocked as he was.

"What are you doing here?" he asked a little ungraciously. He'd been hoping to figure out how to proceed with her before seeing her again.

She stood a little taller. "Jackie has maple leaves for

my wreaths," she replied defensively. "I'm stealing them from everyone. Should I have asked you if I could come?"

"Of course not. I just didn't expect you."

She stepped aside to let him in, then pointed to the open basement door. Loud voices and laughter could be heard from downstairs. "Follow the noise," she advised. "Unless you'd like me to check first if there's someone down there who might surprise you again?"

He'd been heading for the stairs, but came back to her with a frown. "Now, that was just plain sarcastic," he accused.

She looked a little uncertain, but held her ground. "Yes, it was. You should remember that you're not alone in the world. It's filled with people who get to come and go, invading your space whether you like it or not. Whether…"

She wore a silky pink scarf over a gray sweater and he hooked a finger in the knot at her throat and pulled her to him. He saw an instant of alarm in her eyes that was quickly replaced by interest and complete attention.

He kissed her to quiet her—and to have an excuse for the contact he needed. One of her hands went to his waist, the other to his arm. He thought she intended to stop him with it, but it simply fluttered there without purpose while his kiss told her in no uncertain terms that he claimed a right to be wherever she was.

When he drew away, he saw in her face that she understood his message.

"Well," Jackie said with a gasp, one of the twins in

her left arm, the other holding her right hand. "I had no idea, and I usually know what's going on all over Maple Hill." She smiled widely as she started up the stairs. "I apologize for intruding. I was on my way to put the twins to bed. Wow."

When she was out of sight, Kay stared at Jack a long moment, then turned without comment and disappeared through a doorway at the back of the stairs. Jack went down to the basement.

Hank, Gideon and Cam were nailing together the pine walls of the jail. Someone had already installed real bars. While they worked, they talked about Ron Milford.

Jack was beckoned to Hank's side to hold the walls together while he hammered. "...can't imagine who'd want to hurt him," Hank was saying. "I know everyone has a past, and he's been here only a short time, but he's gotten right into the community and treats everyone with consideration."

Gideon nodded, standing ready with the barred wall. "I know. He seems like such a nice guy. But a falling chandelier and a house fire can't be coincidence."

"Maybe someone out there knows something about him we don't," Jack suggested. He shimmed the walls together with a deft kick as Hank prepared to put in the last nail on that side. "Ivan Boesky probably seemed like a nice guy."

Cam held his wall up against the other side and Hank moved to it and put in the first nail.

"It's not as though Ron could be doing insider trading in Maple Hill," Cam contributed. "Everybody likes him. Her, too."

Jack felt sure that was part of Milford's plan. It was entirely possible Milford's wife had no idea what he'd done in Vermont. Coming to Maple Hill had allowed him to escape without going too far away to raise suspicions, and his community involvement and personal likability would make everyone doubt any possible allegations of criminal misconduct. He'd pulled off his assimilation into Maple Hill society with the same skill he'd used to rip off his Vermont clients.

"He's working on my portfolio," Gideon said. "And I've done some research myself on the investments he's made for me. It looks like the best possible risk-return combination to me. I think he knows what he's doing."

Jackie brought refreshments down on a tray and winked at Jack before going upstairs. "Just give me a shout if you need more coffee," she said.

Hank raised an eyebrow at Jack. "What was that all about?"

"We're seeing each other on the side," Jack said with a straight face, unwilling to discuss his relationship with Kay. "That wink was code for 'I'll meet you at midnight under the clematis.'"

Hank's expression also remained sober. "She's bossy, you know. And your entire income will go to shoes and makeup."

"She's staying with you," Jack clarified, giving the wall a straightening kick when Hank reached the bottom nail. "She's just fooling around with me."

Gideon laughed as he helped Cam put the fourth wall in place. "Hank used to work for NASA, you know. You could disappear on a ship bound for Mars and no one would even know where to look for you."

Jack had to grin. "There've been times when that would have sounded good."

Hank pointed to a pair of hinges on the worktable nearby. Jack handed them to him. "She winked at me," he said, "because I knew something she didn't."

"That never happens. The woman has an internal satellite dish."

Jack tried to let it go at that, but he should have known better.

"So, what was it?"

"A...romance," he said—cagily, he thought.

"You mean, you and Kay?" Gideon asked.

Jack turned to him in astonishment.

Gideon made a point of squaring up the door Jack had let slip in his surprise. "What? My job is security. I saw your car in her driveway weekend before last. Did you think no one would notice?"

"I thought," Jack returned with mild annoyance, "they'd have better things to do."

"It's a small town." Cam held the hinge in place while Hank drilled holes. "We wouldn't interfere, but we like to know what's going on."

"We're guys!" Jack reminded his companions with exasperation. "Guys don't discuss other people's affairs."

"We live with women who do." The holes made, Hank hammered in the nails. "So, we're also in the loop. Congratulations, by the way. Kay's a smart and beautiful woman."

"Yeah," Gideon said. "But what does she see in Jack?"

There was laughter over the friendly barb, then conversation changed to other subjects and Jack was mercifully off the hook.

The walls all finally in place, they sat on workbenches and talked further over coffee and brownies.

The sound of feminine laughter on the stairs announced the arrival of Jackie and Kay.

"Don't mind us," Jackie said, waving in their direction. "We're just looking for picture wire."

"On the hook near the fuse box," Hank called across the basement.

"Does she know," Gideon whispered to Jack, "that you can't bowl worth a damn?"

"It's my bad leg," Jack replied. "And I don't think she cares."

"I think it's your lack of skill and talent. How can she not care?"

Gideon's harassment was ended by the ring of Jack's cell phone. The caller ID told him it was a call from home—Amanda wanting to stay up later, no doubt.

"Hello."

"Daddy?" It was Amanda's voice, but he heard the

fear in it. He put down his brownie. "Yes. What's the matter?"

"Something's wrong with Cal, Daddy," she said anxiously. "She was working upstairs and she fell down and now she can't get up again."

He stood, wondering if she'd simply fallen or collapsed. "Is she conscious?" he asked, realizing when he got no answer that Amanda didn't know the word. "Is she awake? Can she talk to you?"

"Yeah, she just can't get up. And she says her back hurts."

"Okay." He started for the stairs. "You stay with her and I'll be right home."

"What is it?" Jackie asked, intercepting him. He realized that everyone had followed him. Kay stood worriedly beside Jackie.

"My daughter said that Cal's fallen and hurt her back," he explained. "I've got to go."

"I'll go with you," Kay volunteered.

He wasted a moment staring at her.

"Well, if you have to take Cal to the hospital," she said practically, "you can't leave the children alone. I'll just take a minute to get my things together, then I'll be right behind you."

IT WAS THE RIGHT THING to do, Kay told herself as she quickly gathered up some of her creations that she'd brought to show Jackie. Jack would need help, and though she wasn't anxious to spend time in close proximity with the little girl, it was late and Amanda would probably be sleepy and go to bed.

She realized later that she had a lot to learn about Amanda.

Calpurnia lay on Jack's bedroom floor, the mattress half on, half off the bed. She'd been trying to flip it, something Jack had told her not to attempt without him, she admitted to Kay as Jack lifted Cal carefully into his arms. But she tried it anyway and that was when she hurt her back and fell.

"You're supposed to do what Daddy says," Amanda told Calpurnia as she ran ahead of her father and opened the door. The dog followed them, barking anxiously. "'Cause he says it for your own good."

"Thank you, Amanda." Jack smiled down at her. "Kay's going to stay with you while I take Cal to the emergency room. You be good, okay? You, too, Paul."

Paul nodded worriedly. "Is Cal gonna be all right?"

"I'm sure she will be. I'll tell you what the doctor said when I come home."

"You should cover her with something." Kay stopped his forward progress at the bottom of the stairs and went to the sofa where a granny-square afghan lay over the back. She opened it out and covered Cal with it, then followed Jack out to the truck to open the passenger door.

She pointed to the children to stay inside. "It's cold out here," she cautioned.

When the dog tried to follow her she pointed him

back to the house and told him firmly to "Stay!" He looked undecided for a moment, then complied.

With Cal sitting up in the seat, her face white with pain, Kay put the blanket around her like a shawl, then fastened her seat belt in place while Jack ran around the truck and climbed in behind the wheel.

"Be careful," she said, meeting his eyes in the dark cab of the truck. There was something in his that felt like a touch. She closed the door and waved them off.

She stood just inside the front door and finally had time to realize what she was up against—two little children, one of them a little girl, a Betsy kind of little girl—who did not seem the slightest bit tired.

"We can make hot chocolate," Amanda said, then put her arm around her brother. "Dad makes it for Paul when he's upset."

Paul shook off her arm. "I'm not upset. I just want Mom." He sighed and shook his head at Kay. "But she died and she can't come back."

Kay understood the look in his eyes. She reached for his hand. "Well, let's go see if hot chocolate can help all of us. I'm not upset, either, but I am a little worried."

Paul put his hand in hers, and presuming she should be allowed the same privilege, Amanda took Kay's other hand as they walked into the kitchen. Kay experienced the bittersweet memory of her sister's hand in hers.

"My mom was prettier than you," Amanda said candidly, "'cause she had long, long hair. And yours is kinda funny."

Kay had to agree with that. "I know. It wants to curl one way and I try to make it go another and it never works. Someday I'm going to get it cut really short."

Amanda pointed to a cupboard over the sink. "That's where the cocoa is. You just put two spoons of it in boiling water. Then you have to put an ice cube in Paul's 'cause he's little and we don't want him to burn his mouth."

Paul didn't like being called little. "Daddy says I'm going to be tall someday, just like him."

Kay pulled down the carton of cocoa. "Yes, you are," she said, thinking that he reminded her a little of Jordie. He'd been more indulged, obviously felt better understood, but the loss of his mother lent him a similar vulnerability to that of the neglected Jordie. "I can tell by your feet."

Paul bent double to look at his teddy-bear-slipper-clad feet. He looked up at her again. "How come?"

"'Cause they're long for a five-year-old boy. That means you're going to be tall."

That pleased him. "Cool."

Amanda tossed her long curls. "I'm going to be pretty like my mom."

Kay glanced at her as she put the kettle on to boil. "I can see that. I saw a picture of her once, and you already look like her."

Amanda beamed. "I do?"

"Yes, you do."

Amanda dragged a kitchen stool beside Kay and climbed onto it until she was as tall. "I can measure the cocoa into the cups."

"And I know where the cookies are." Paul dragged a kitchen chair to the counter, climbed onto it, then onto the counter. Kay hurried to spot for him, holding her breath while he reached as high as he could for a bag of sandwich cookies on the third shelf. "Cal puts them up here so we won't eat them all," he announced, handing them to Kay. He reversed the process and climbed down.

When the water had boiled, Kay filled their cups, adding an ice cube to Paul's as instructed. Amanda insisted she didn't need one until Kay added one to her own.

"Do you have kids?" Amanda asked conversationally, as they all sat around the kitchen table.

Paul took a fistful of cookies out of the bag and passed it on to Kay.

"You're only supposed to have one!" Amanda was quick to correct him.

"I wanted…" He looked at the bounty in his hand and counted. "I wanted five. Can't I have five?" he asked Kay.

Surprised at being consulted, she stammered. "Ah… well, yes. But it's usually polite to take only one at a time."

"Okay." He made a face at Amanda, then put an entire cookie in his mouth.

Amanda ignored him. "Are you Daddy's girlfriend?" She leaned toward Kay, her feet in wooly pink socks under a fleecy pink robe kicking back and forth.

"No," Kay replied, taking a cookie and passing the bag to Amanda. "I'm just his friend." Then she asked casually, "Why? Does he have a girlfriend?"

"I don't think so. But Erica Whitcomb says her mom says he should get one. That he should stop being sad about Mom."

On one level, this intimate conversation with this little Betsy-reincarnated was torture, but on another, it was a lot like having the chance to talk to her sister again.

"Do you think he should have a girlfriend?" Kay snapped her cookie in half and gave one piece to Buster, then dipped the other in her cocoa. She knew she shouldn't have asked the question, but thought it was something she should know.

"Well. Mom can't come home. And he misses her a lot." Amanda sighed philosophically. "Would the girl-friend be like our mom?"

"Maybe. If she was somebody he loved, and if you liked her, too."

"What if we *didn't* like her?"

"Then, you'd have to tell your dad that."

"I want us to find a girlfriend who makes cookies," Paul said. "Amanda says Mommy's cookies had great big raisins."

"Doesn't Cal bake cookies?"

Amanda shook her head. "She cooks really good stuff, but not cookies. She buys them at the store, or she makes the kind you cut with a knife and put them in the oven."

"Refrigerator cookies?"

"Yeah. They have cute faces, but no raisins. Can you bake cookies?"

It was a woman-to-woman challenge. Amanda rested her chin in her hands and watched Kay analytically.

"I haven't made any lately," Kay admitted, wishing she could boast about her cookie-baking prowess.

"'Cause you don't have any kids to eat them?"

"Because I have a job that keeps me really busy, and I don't have a lot of time."

"What if we bought raisins," Paul suggested, his eyes closing sleepily, "and you came over and we helped you? We used to help Mom."

Kay nodded. "If I came over again and you had raisins, we could try it. But I just came over tonight 'cause your Dad needed someone to stay with you while he took Cal to the hospital. So I don't know if I'll be coming again."

Paul rested his head on his folded arms and yawned.

"Why don't you two go on to bed," Kay suggested, gathering up their cups, "and I'll tuck you in."

Paul sat up and opened his eyes wide. "I want to stay up. Daddy said he'd tell us what the doctor said about Cal."

"Yeah," Amanda confirmed. "And I want to keep you company."

Kay put the bag of cookies in the cupboard and shepherded them back to the living room. "Then, what if we all get comfortable in the living room and wait?"

Buster got up and followed them to the sofa, falling

down near the coffee table and going right back to sleep. Paul took a pillow with a Tigger face on it and curled up in a corner of the sofa.

Kay intended to leave the rest of the sofa for Amanda to stretch out, but the little girl caught her hand and pulled her with her to the sofa. "We can sit together," she said with a yawn, "and watch TV."

"Okay." Kay put it on at low volume, found an old musical she guessed wouldn't harm or horrify Amanda and sat beside her.

She snuggled close. Kay had already inured herself to the memories of Betsy this child inspired and sat stoically as she remembered hours spent with her little sister watching cartoons.

Amanda wrapped both arms around Kay's elbow and leaned her head against her. Paul was already asleep.

Certain it wouldn't take Amanda very long to drop off, Kay pretended interest in the film, thinking that the instant the child fell asleep, she would move to the big chair.

Amanda sat up abruptly, as though she'd read the thought. Her eyes heavy, her cheeks flushed, she smiled winningly at Kay. "Could I sit in your lap?"

Unable to refuse her, Kay lifted her into her lap and let her get comfortable. That seemed to involve a side-saddle position, a bent knee that dug into Kay's side, then the sudden abandonment of her position as she ran upstairs then returned at a run with a floppy-eared bunny made of muslin. It was naked except for a tissue folded like a diaper around it.

Amanda quickly resumed her place, her knee in exactly the same spot, but her bunny clutched in her arms. She wriggled a few times, finding just the right spot on Kay's breast for her head, then breathed a heavy sigh.

"'Night," she said.

Kay stroked Amanda's hair, unable to stop herself.

Amanda snuggled closer, then fell asleep.

Kay was curiously peaceful. Or maybe she was just exhausted. Her memories still hurt abominably, but there was comfort in knowing that Amanda was relaxed and happy. After all the child had been through in her young life, she deserved to be.

Paul sat up abruptly, looking disoriented. Then he spotted Kay, grabbed his pillow, propped it up against her and lay down again. He went right back to sleep.

With a hand on his shoulder and an arm around Amanda, Kay tried to get interested in the movie to distract herself from the fact that she was wrapped in children. But her own eyes grew heavy. She rested her head against the back of the sofa and fell asleep to the tinny sound of the old 1940s musical.

CHAPTER FIFTEEN

JACK RETURNED home just before 1:00 a.m. He'd spent three hours in the hospital waiting room after Cal was taken into the E.R. to see a doctor, when the physician appeared to tell him she'd suffered a lumbar strain, been given strong pain medication, a muscle relaxant and shouldn't be left alone for a few days. Fortunately Addy Fortin, Hank's mother and Cal's longtime friend, had heard about her accident through Hank and had come to the E.R. to keep him company and await the diagnosis.

"No problem," she said. "I'll take her home with me."

"What'll Hank do without you?" Jack asked. It was well-known that Addy answered most calls to Whitcomb's Wonders and was a very well-organized dispatcher.

"I'll have the calls switched to my home," she said with a shrug. "And Adam's there to help me." Adam was Jackie's father. Adam and Addy's wedding had delighted all of Maple Hill the year before Jack arrived.

"Then I'll follow you home, and help you get her inside."

"That would be very nice of you."

That task finally accomplished with help from Adam

Fortin, Jack drove home and walked into his living room, expecting to find it dark and quiet. His mind formed an image of Kay in his bed, but he knew better than to even indulge it and shook it off.

What he saw was almost more mind-bending. Kay and his children sat in the middle of the sofa, all entangled like a pile of puppies. Paul was propped against her with his Tigger pillow, a fist clutching the hem of her sweater. Amanda lay stretched out in Kay's lap, her head lolling back in Kay's arm, one leg extended over her, the other dangling between her knees.

Buster came to him, tail wagging, his expression a little desperate. Jack had to drag his eyes from the picture of Kay all wrapped up in his children, and took the dog outside for a quick walk into the trees.

Back inside again, Jack scooped Paul into his arms and carried him upstairs. Buster followed him up and then down again.

Jack tried carefully to extricate Amanda, but she made a sound of disapproval in her sleep and clung. Afraid of hurting Kay or his daughter, he decided to let them be. He took a pillow from the big chair, propped it against the corner of the sofa, then cupped Kay's head in his hand as he tipped her toward it. Supporting Amanda's weight in his other hand, he slipped her onto the sofa beside Kay whose arm was still wrapped around her. He covered them with the afghan he'd brought back with him and sat in the big chair to admire the picture they made.

Stirrings of old emotion rose to cloud and confuse the moment. Julia should be there, with her arms around Amanda. She'd died trying to right a wrong, and Jack had yet to correct that injustice.

When he'd been in the hospital, hatred had fueled him and revenge was all he'd thought about—except the children.

He hated to admit, even to himself, that he was changing. He was still driven to prove that Julia had been murdered, and to bring Milford to justice. But that desire no longer took up every corner of his being.

His heart took more space now. When he'd come back from Iraq to a life with a large hole in it, his heart had been small and shriveled. But Kay and Maple Hill had reconstituted it. He wanted to think ahead, make plans, indulge dreams he'd once thought dead that had taken shape again. Hope warred for space with the old hatred.

He could only imagine what this night with his children had cost Kay. Being with little girls tortured her because of her sister, and yet she'd volunteered to come home with him, knowing he'd need help. She'd extended herself for him despite her own issues and the endless squabbles that peppered their relationship.

She loved him.

The realization fell on him like a net. He couldn't escape it no matter which way he turned.

He had strong feelings for her, but there was a lot to

do before he dared think of it as love. He smiled at her sleeping figure as he wondered if she even knew how she felt. She was always so busy explaining herself to him or him to himself, that he wondered if she ever just let herself feel.

He remembered with a rush of warmth the night they made love. She'd been all passion and sweetness and he hadn't been able to pretend she was Julia as he'd hoped. She had a lot of qualities in common with his wife, but she was unmistakably unique.

He relaxed in his chair, laid his head back and started to murmur a prayer before he caught himself and snapped his eyes open. He looked around, so surprised at himself he felt sure someone had witnessed what went on in his mind.

The room was quiet, Kay and Amanda still asleep arm in arm. A little unsettled, he closed his eyes again, and tried to close his heart to that prayer.

But it was now as big as his hatred and harder to control. He could feel it opening, blossoming, seeking sunshine. He went to sleep, unwilling to think about it.

KAY SURFACED from sleep to the aromas of bacon frying and coffee dripping. Caught somewhere between dreams and wakefulness, her senses accepted those smells as familiar, interpreted them to mean security and comfort.

There was sunshine beyond her closed eyelids and the quiet sounds of conversation came to her ears. Dad was in the kitchen, probably on the phone; he was always on the phone to the hospital. Mom was making breakfast and Betsy was snuggled up to her as she always was. She could feel her breathing, taking up the whole bed.

Kay stretched and let a fizzy happiness take over her being. The whole kidnap-murder thing had been a dream; she knew it! It went on forever, but she'd known all along that it wasn't possible that Betsy had been taken, that her parents had become lifeless clones of the people they used to be and that she had to live day in and day out with the knowledge that it had been her fault, that she should have been more watchful. That was unthinkable.

Then Betsy stirred, but Kay felt too happy and lazy to open her eyes. She heard her scamper off and guessed she'd gone into the kitchen, or to the bathroom. In either case, her parents were in the kitchen and Kay could just stay… She heard a dog bark and smiled. Jethro was a yellow Lab with a big voice. He loved Betsy.

"Kay!"

It took Kay a moment to realize that that wasn't Betsy's voice. She let herself float to wakefulness, wondering curiously who it was. Charlie? No. Charlie had a quiet, raspy voice. This one was all power and volume.

"Kay, wake up! Daddy's making pancakes and bacon for breakfast! He says it's ready if you're awake."

Kay opened her eyes, still wondering about the mystery voice. Then she focused on an unfamiliar textured ceiling, the tops of beige curtains she didn't recognize. A large tongue bathed her in kisses. It belonged to a black dog and not a yellow one. She apparently wasn't quite awake yet.

Suddenly a child's face appeared before her eyes, upside down. She saw pink lips, blue eyes and masses of blond curly hair. Betsy.

No. Blond hair. Not Betsy.

"Kay?" Amanda asked.

The dog barked and kissed her again. Buster not Jethro.

The blissful eight-year-old child's world Kay had occupied for a moment collapsed on top of her in a rain of pointed memory shards; blunt, hurtful images of reality; hollow-point bullets of the ugly truth. Betsy was gone. Her father had died, never recovered from the loss. Her mother hated her, and it was all her fault.

Kay sat up abruptly and Amanda dodged her just in time. She ran for the bathroom off the kitchen and vomited those few moments of blissful, carefree happiness. Beside her, Buster whined.

She flushed and leaned over the john as guilt settled on her again like an old robe she'd worn for years and was comfortable in, despite the hair shirt lining. There. That was better. Awful, but better.

Jack appeared, gently stroking her back, then running a facecloth under cold water with large competent hands. She remembered how tenderly they'd explored her body and experienced a moment of abject misery as she realized that that couldn't happen again.

Amanda had forced herself into Kay's personal space and made her deal with her memories of Betsy. She'd discovered that she wanted to come to terms with her memories, but they still made her go to pieces. She could never be responsible for a child. She would drive herself and the child insane with needing her within sight at all times.

She looked up into Jack's eyes, saw compassion there and the same misery she felt. Somehow, from all the way in the kitchen, he'd read her mind. She opened her mouth to tell him that the tenuous relationship they didn't even really have was over.

But he cupped her head in his hand and put the wet cloth to her face, swept it over her mouth, folded it over and ran it down her throat.

"I have to go," she whispered, and tried to move past him.

He caught her arm and tossed the facecloth in the sink. Buster, disliking the tension, ran out into the hall.

"You have to understand something," Jack said quietly. She could hear the children giggle just beyond the half-open door. "Amanda isn't Betsy, and this is your adult life, not your childhood. You volunteered to come home with me, Kay. You want to be with children. You're going to want them in your life."

She shook her head adamantly. "I'm not strong enough after all."

"Yes, you are. You held her. She slept in your arms. You're alive. You can't expect it not to hurt."

"When I woke up," she admitted in a broken voice, desperate to make him understand, "I thought she was Betsy and I was so happy. I thought the past hadn't happened, that I'd dreamed it. When I saw that the child I held wasn't Betsy, but Amanda I...I..."

He nodded, not horrified as she'd expected, but unsettlingly understanding. "I know. The night I made love to you, I wanted you so much, but Julia's been gone less than a year and I felt guilty that I needed another woman in my arms. So I justified it to myself by planning to pretend you were her."

That hurt only momentarily because she was sure he'd known who she was that night.

He nodded, smiling grimly. Their energies collided in the confines of the small room. "But there's no mistaking you for someone else. You're very loudly you. Amanda is the same way, an individual whose identity is clearly her own. Neither one of us can go back, Kay. There's no recapturing our innocent pasts."

"The difference," she said firmly, "is that you were an ocean away when Julia died. You aren't responsible. I was holding Betsy's hand minutes before she was taken. I got involved in what I wanted for me and...and *forgot* about her."

She reached for the door and he pushed it out of her hand, closing it. "You were just a kid picking out some candy," he said, emphasizing the words for the innocent act he seemed to believe it to be. "No one would blame an eight-year-old child for that. You're holding on to this guilt without encouragement from anyone. Maybe because it's easier than having to get married, raise a family, face the horrible chance that something like that could happen to you again?"

She considered that and admitted that it could be true. "I'd drive my husband and my children insane with my paranoia. What kind of life would that be?"

"For whom?" he asked. "For you?"

She knew how it would be for her. What she meant was...

"Or what kind of life would it be for me? Assuming I'd proposed and you'd accepted?"

She couldn't even answer. There was no air in her lungs.

"It'd be a hell of a lot better than the last couple of years have been," he replied. "And I guarantee I could bring you more happiness than you've had in a long time."

The arrogant claim was made without apology. And she believed him completely. But she was beginning to believe Florios weren't supposed to be happy. It wasn't in the cards.

"I have to go," she said again. "Please."

He hesitated, seeming to debate the wisdom of further argument, then apparently deciding against it. He pushed the door open to let her out.

She found herself face-to-face with his children. They'd obviously heard raised voices and were concerned. Buster looked worried, too.

Kay took her courage in her hands and kissed Amanda's cheek, then Paul's and ruffled the dog's ears.

"Thank you for being such good company," she said as they followed her to the sofa where she collected her purse and pulled on her jacket. "It was very nice to have cocoa and cookies with you."

"Aren't you gonna stay and have breakfast?" Paul asked.

She shook her head. "I have to go to work." Putting her purse strap on her shoulder, she suddenly remembered the nanny. "How is Cal?" she asked Jack.

"She's at Hank's mom's and will be for a couple of days. She just pulled a muscle in her back, but she's in pain and has to rest."

So, he was without anyone to stay with the children. She couldn't do it. She needed out of his life.

"Who's gonna take me to school?" Amanda asked Jack.

"I will," he replied without hesitation. "I'll have to change my schedule a little bit, and we'll miss Cal's company, but we'll get everything done."

"But she used to pick us up at lunchtime." Amanda, keeper of all details, was worried. "Now where're we gonna go?"

He did hesitate an instant over that. "I'll take care of it," he said. "We'll get it all worked out."

"I can pick them up," Kay heard herself say, "if you let me know where to take them." She wouldn't have to see Jack, she told herself reasonably, only Paul and Amanda. "Day care? Jackie's house? I know her nanny watches Henrietta for Haley sometimes. Maybe she wouldn't mind adding them to the mix."

Jack seemed confused by her suggestion and her offer to help. "Thank you," he said, following her to the door. The children danced along beside her. "I'll call you tonight after I've put something together. If it works for you, that's great. If it doesn't, that's all right, too. Will you be at home or at work?"

She drew a business card out of her purse and handed it to him. It listed her cell phone number as well as her office and home numbers.

"Thank you." He opened the door for her and grabbed Buster's collar to prevent him from following her. "I'll be in touch."

Amanda followed her to her car. "I want you to come back," she said authoritatively.

"I'd love to." Kay aimed her remote at the door. "But I have a lot of things to do. And the Fall Festival is coming up, you know. I'll bet you're going to really like that."

She giggled excitedly. "Yeah. Daddy says we're gonna color pictures and make pumpkins and win a cake!"

Right. The cakewalk. She had to get on that. All the life events she'd been keeping at bay for weeks were barreling toward her and she wasn't ready. She had to finish her wreaths, get more cakes for the walk, prepare for her mother's arrival.

"And I'm gonna be a princess for Halloween," Amanda announced as Kay opened her door and placed her purse-camera bag on the passenger seat. "Who do you like better? Cinderella or Belle?"

"Ah…Belle is…?"

"Beauty," Amanda replied. When Kay remained clueless, she added with benevolent impatience, "And the Beast, silly."

"Of course. Beauty and the Beast. I forgot." She smiled, remembering the heated discussions she and Betsy used to have about the respective virtues of Cinderella and Snow White.

"I like Cinderella," Kay said, "because she worked so hard, but my little sister used to like Snow White."

"I like Cinderella, too." Amanda frowned at Kay. "Where is your little sister?"

"She…died a long time ago."

Amanda surprised Kay by lifting her arms to her and when Kay leaned down, she hugged her tightly. When Kay finally drew away, Amanda explained with a smile, "When I tell people my mom died, that's what they do to me. It makes me feel better."

Kay gave her a quick, unsolicited hug, then got into her car. Jack came to take Amanda back to the porch. Kay drove away without looking back, just giving that light tap of her horn Jack always did when he followed her home after a meeting.

She wept like a fool all the way home, her feelings complicated, but soothed by the child's comforting embrace.

Charlie called that evening. "Kay, I'm so sorry to bother you on a Wednesday," she said urgently, breathlessly, "but Gib just called me. He picked up Derek and he doesn't want to talk to him, but he asked for me. So I jumped into my car to go see him, but it won't start again.

Clete did the simple fix for me that night I got stuck because I was broke, but now I guess I'm going to have to bite the bullet. Can you come for me and wait for me while I talk to Derek? I'll owe you big, I promise."

"I'll come right away. But, do you know what happened to Jordie? Was their mom home?"

"No. I asked Gib about that. He says Rachel has Jordie. The other two foster homes in town are full, and Rachel and Gib were approved before they split."

"Right." Kay knew that. Gib had taken children home before. But she couldn't wait to hear details about why Rachel agreed to help him, or just how he approached her. "Well, that's a relief. I'll be right there."

Kay waited several hours on a bench in the office while Charlie was led through a locked door and disappeared. She worked on her novel on a yellow pad for some time, the words flowing with an ease that was not surprising considering how her problems with Jack seemed to spur story and dialogue. The events of the morning had been good for several pages.

She looked up at the sound of Gib's voice in time to see him walk out of an office and move toward the desk he occupied in the middle of the room. She was always surprised by how lethal he looked in a shoulder holster and with a badge fastened to his belt. He no longer appeared to be the kind member of her family who was always available when she had to move something or needed legal advice.

She waved at him and he dropped a sheaf of papers

on his desk and crossed the room to sit beside her. "Hey, cuz. What's going on? Did you come with Charlie?"

She explained about Charlie's car. "She told me she talked to Rachel this morning and she's watching Jordie?"

He nodded. She knew he couldn't discuss the case with her, but the situation between him and Rachel wasn't directly involved in it. "How'd you get her to help you?" she asked baldly.

Gib smiled wryly. "She made it clear she's doing it for Jordie. But I am invited to dinner tomorrow night, so I may get to talk to her after all." Before she could speak, he forestalled her with, "Yes, I know. Be quiet and listen to her, then be patient. Or sensitive. Or something I know I'll find hard to do if she goes off on me." He pointed to the yellow pad in her lap. "Working on your book?"

"Yes."

"Am I in it?"

She patted his shoulder. "It isn't science fiction, Gib."

He pretended hurt feelings. "I share pertinent case information with you," he said softly, an emotive hand to his chest, "so you can have firsthand information, and this is the thanks I get? I'm suddenly Godzilla?"

"Gib!" Another detective beckoned him. "Come on back. Slocum kid wants to talk."

"All right! Excuse me, Kay." Gib strode away, leaving her to her book and the hundred questions she was mentally gathering for Charlie.

When Charlie appeared again an hour later, flanked by Gib and Sam, she looked tired and worried.

"You've got to get those boys away from their mother," she said to Gib as they approached Kay. "This is the second time he's been picked up and you've been unable to find her. And this Brownie Burns he's been working for sounds like a real lowlife and someone he shouldn't even *know,* much less hang with."

Gib nodded. "He won't be going home for a while anyway, but the caseworker's not going to be able to get the mother out of this one. Thanks for coming, Charlie."

"Well, of course. Thanks for taking good care of Derek. He said you're always hassling him, but you're always straight with him, too."

"I was the one who was kind to him," Sam corrected. "I'm the one you should be thanking." Sam's remark was deliberately suggestive. Gib rolled his eyes. "Why don't you two take it outside? And hide behind the rhododendron. I don't want to have to explain my partner fraternizing with a witness."

"You're just jealous," Sam said quietly, following Charlie toward the door, "because nobody likes *you.*"

Gib turned back to Kay with a groan. "I'm hoping he's wrong about that."

Kay punched his arm. "I like you."

"Thanks, but you don't count. You like me for my muscle and my moving skills."

"I also like the way you swung from the Empire State Building before you ate Manhattan."

CHAPTER SIXTEEN

JACK WAS INSPIRED to visit Kay rather than call her Thursday evening. He was sure it would have been easier to telephone than to look into the "I-love-you-but-I-don't-see-how-we-can-be-together expression in her eyes, but he'd been on the phone with Jackie and Glory for the better part of an hour and the kids were restless. He piled them into the jump seat of the truck, put Buster in the passenger seat and drove to Adams Street.

Kay was shocked. She stood on her doorstep in baggy gray sweats, little stems of things sticking out all over her. In her hands was a half-assembled wreath that smelled richly of its eucalyptus components. She smiled warmly at his children, but he couldn't tell if she was pleased to see him or not.

"I just wanted you to know," he said, picking a sprig of lavender off her shoulder, "that I've got the kids' routines handled until Cal comes back, and you don't have to pick them up from school. Glory's going to do it. They'll stay at Jackie's until I pick them up when I'm finished. No more overtime for me until Cal's back."

"But I *want* Kay to do it," Paul whined.

"She's a very busy lady. We'll have her do something more fun with us. Like have dinner, or something."

She cast him a punitive glare. He stared it down and she finally relented and opened the door wider. "Come on in for a minute. I've got some ice cream Amanda and Paul might like, and I have something to tell you. You didn't leave Buster home unattended?"

"No, he's in the truck."

She sat the children at her kitchen table with bowls of something with chocolate chips and nuts. Laid out on the table were long strands of dried flowers woven in a colorful string. Amanda was fascinated by them.

"What is it?" she asked, reaching out to touch. Jack gently pulled her fingers away. They looked like something that had required a lot of effort.

"I'll show you." Kay chose a short length, nimbly manipulated both ends until they were connected, then placed the coronet it made on Amanda's hair. His daughter with royal tendencies was thrilled.

Then Paul wanted one. Kay repeated the process with a string of dark straw flowers and Jack suddenly had two children in line for a throne somewhere.

The children happy and now focused on their ice cream, Kay drew Jack with her into the living room filled with her wreath-making operation. Many of the wreaths and swags were now finished, some decorated with ribbon, others made colorful with berries and fall leaves. He was surprised by the effect the homey skill had on him. He imagined a fire in her fireplace, Rod

Stewart singing Sinatra on the stereo, and rain hitting the windows.

"I just wanted to tell you," she said, turning to him in the middle of the room, "that my cousin Charlie—you know, the teacher?—was called to the jail by Derek Slocum. At first he didn't want to talk to the police, but asked for Charlie. Only her car couldn't start, so she called…" She stopped in the middle of that and erased it from between them with a swipe of her hand in the air. "You don't need to know all that, just that I drove her. Anyway, after she talked to him and tried to convince him that he's better than his situation, that he can rise above his mother and her boyfriend and be somebody if he admits what happened, he told her. Remember that Gib suggested someone had paid him?"

"Yes."

"Well, it's apparently this small-time crook he's worked for before. Brownie somebody. Burns, I think. Derek told Charlie someone paid Brownie to see to Milford's house. Brownie has a numbers operation, pimps a couple of girls, uses Derek and some other kids for burglary to keep ahead of his 'investors' when the other operations aren't going well. Anyway…he hired Derek to set fire to the house."

"But who hired Brownie?"

"Derek didn't know. He says Brownie doesn't even know, that somebody left him a message in a disguised voice, and when he agreed, the money was in his bank account within an hour. He paid Derek, and that's how he got his leathers."

"*Before* the job was done?"

"Charlie asked that same question. It's one of those honor-among-thieves things. Derek's done work for Brownie before and he's dependable."

"Did he have any idea why this mysterious client of Brownie's wanted to toast Milford?"

"No."

"So he set fire to a house with people in it without qualms?"

"I think the situation at home is so bad he's convinced he has no value, so he values no one else. Except Jordie."

"God."

"Yeah." She acknowledged the grimness of the situation, then focused on him with interest. "You know, for a Godless man, you certainly invoke Him a lot. I know that was more a curse than a prayer, but He's obviously on your mind."

That was true, but he wasn't happy with her pointing it out. He felt himself slipping back, yearning for that peace he used to know when he was comfortably wrapped in his belief in God and His wisdom, and was able to see His hand in all things.

But the last couple of years had killed that belief forever—or so he'd thought. Yet he found his reconstituted heart wanted to replace all the love and faith it once held. But if he believed again with the old faith, he couldn't exact his revenge for Julia. He had to, or he wouldn't be able to go on.

And obviously someone else out there whom Milford had bilked hated him, also. Jack wanted to get to Milford first, and believing again would take the teeth out of his plan.

He shifted his weight and paced to the window just to be able to evade Kay's eyes. He still knew enough about the faith he used to have to understand that he couldn't calmly decide *not* to believe now, so that he could take Milford down later, and *then* consider restoring his faith.

God knew what was going on in his mind.

Well, there was nothing damning in gathering knowledge.

As he stared out the window at the darkness, a cab pulled up in front of the house. In the light from the porch, the driver, a dark-haired woman, got out to help an older woman out of the back. Then she went to the trunk to retrieve the woman's things.

Jack saw the physical resemblance instantly. The cab's passenger had to be the famous Brenda Florio. She was small and dark in a very elegant black skirt and jacket. Her hair was salt-and-pepper gray. She had the air of a woman accustomed to taking charge of a situation, and yet she had a bright smile for the cabbie and, judging by the smile on the cabbie's face, she tipped well.

"I think your mom's here," Jack said, instinctively going to the door. The woman was overburdened with luggage and his intention was to help.

"Wait! Let me…"

If Kay was trying to tell him not to open the door, she was too late. The woman stopped in her tracks halfway up the walk and stared at him, her mouth open.

"Hi," he said, going down the walk to take the bags from her. "Let me help you with those."

Kay forced a smile. So, her mother was a day early. She could deal with this. They would eat, talk about frivolous things, skirt all important issues, and then the festival would take all their time and energy and it would be time for her to leave.

That might have worked if Jack hadn't answered the door. And if his children hadn't heard a newcomer arrive and stormed out to investigate as though they were comfortable here, spent a lot of time here.

Now her mother would be wanting details, offering criticisms, suggestions, admonitions. And Kay just knew that the fact that she'd made love with Jack Keaton would be visible on her face. That complicated an already difficult situation.

Jack followed her mother in, carrying her bags, chattily discussing the suddenly cooler weather and how good that would be for the Fall Festival. The children skipped around them, showing off their coronets to Brenda's admiration.

"Kay made them for us," Amanda boasted, "and she stayed with us when Calpurnia hurt her back. But she couldn't stay for breakfast 'cause she's very busy."

Brenda turned to Kay with a look of surprised delight. Oh, no. She couldn't stay for breakfast....

Kay put on a bright smile and ignored her mother's shock. "Hi, Mom," she said cheerfully, opening her arms to her. "How nice that you could come a day early."

Brenda tossed her purse and a plastic bag from a Bergdorf Goodman store onto the sofa and walked into Kay's hug. "We wrapped the French street market show early, so I thought, why not get a head start on our preparations for the festival?"

"Why not? Mom, I'd like you to meet Jack Keaton." Kay drew the children to her. "And his kids, Amanda and Paul. Jack, my mother, Brenda Florio. Kids, this is my mom."

Jack put a bag down to shake hands. "I'm happy to meet you, Mrs. Florio. And everyone's excited that you've come to help the festival."

Brenda took his hand, shaking it with enthusiasm. "I was flattered to be asked. And it's nice to have time to spend with Kay. We're both usually too busy to get together. Hi, kids. I'm very happy to meet you."

They giggled.

"I'll carry these up for you." Jack pointed upstairs with his chin. "Which room?"

"The pink one opposite mine," Kay said.

It didn't occur to her until the words were out of her mouth that she'd just made it clear to her mother that he knew where her room was—and all that suggested. Of course, Amanda had just made it sound as though she and Jack had slept together at his place the night she "couldn't stay for breakfast."

Not that anyone should be horrified, but that was a detail she'd have liked to keep to herself. It still resonated inside her like the music of flutes and cellos.

Amanda and Paul followed Jack up the stairs.

The moment they were out of earshot, her mother waggled her eyebrows at her. "What a gorgeous man!" she said in a whisper. "And what beautiful children. How long has this been going on?"

"It's not really going on," Kay denied and headed for the kitchen. "I'll bet you could use some coffee."

"He knows where your bedroom is," her mother disputed, following her. "How can it not be going on? I know everybody has sex with everybody else today for no reason other than fun, but you don't. In fact, you told me the last time we talked that you were too busy for men."

"I was." She measured coffee into a filter then placed it in the brewing basket and poured in water. "But he was part of a story I was working on."

Brenda pulled up a kitchen chair, eager to hear more. "What kind of story?"

"He saved a little girl from drowning. Then…well, we have some things in common." She turned on the coffeepot, regretting the words the moment they were out of her mouth, sure her mother would ask the obvious question.

She did. "What things?"

Kay struggled for a way to explain without having to share all she felt. "We…he…was a minister. He was sent to Iraq with the Naval Reserve and then his wife died…."

Brenda made a small sound of distress. "How awful." She sat back, looking concerned. "But, please tell me you have more in common than grief."

Before Kay could comment, Jack and the children appeared in the doorway. "We're off," he said, raising a hand to stop Kay when she would have come to him. "We'll see ourselves out. Enjoy your visit. Call me if there's anything I can do."

Kay went to him anyway. "You're sure you have the kids' schedule handled?"

"I'm sure." And then in a gently familiar gesture, he took her chin between his thumb and forefinger and leaned down to kiss her lightly on the lips. "Bye." He turned to Brenda and said warmly, "It was nice to meet you, Mrs. Florio."

Brenda waved. "I can't tell you how nice it was to meet you," she said significantly. "Bye, kids."

They all returned her wave. After the door closed behind them, the house fell quiet.

"That was a sweet kiss," her mother said.

Kay nodded, refocusing her attention on finding two coffee cups. Her mind full of that little kiss, she had trouble remembering where she put cups. "He's a sweet man."

"Beautiful children."

"Yes."

The serious interrogation was about to begin, Kay was sure. Had she finally put Betsy behind her? How was she coping with Amanda and Paul? Just how seri- was this?

Her mother shocked her by asking instead about the recipe in the old diary belonging to Caleb and Elizabeth Drake's daughter.

"Philly Potter," Kay said, removing the carafe and letting the coffee drip into a cup. She reached into a bottom drawer and withdrew the journal she kept wrapped in archival paper. The silk cover was tattered and frayed, the binding coming apart. She placed it on the table in front of her mother, who touched it reverently.

"My goodness," Brenda said breathlessly. "The daughter of the two people so important to Maple Hill that we have their statues on the Common wrote her thoughts in this book."

Kay sat at a right angle to her and carefully turned a few pages. "Read this passage. She sounds like quite a woman."

Brenda carefully picked up the book and held it at a distance. The page was yellowed and dotted with age, but the writing was elegant and very legible.

"I so wish there was more time to enjoy the autumn days but so much effort and energy must go into preparing for winter that I scarcely see the beautiful leaves or smell the fragrant breeze. Except for the time when I go out to bring in another basket of fruit or vegetables to prepare, all I see are the contents of the pot I'm stirring, and all that fills my nostrils now is the smell of apples. I know

I will love having applesauce in January, but right now I am sick unto death of apples.

There are pumpkins growing big and fat in the back garden, and I'm anxious to try a new recipe that Mother's Braintree friend, Abigail Adams, has given me."

Brenda's voice quieted as she read the ingredients for the recipe that followed.

She looked up at Kay with excitement in her eyes. "Rum and pecans. Yum! Have you seen cooking pumpkins in the market?"

Kay nodded. "The Farmers' Market has small sugar pumpkins."

"Great. Can you come shopping with me in the morning, or do you have to work?"

"I have to take pictures of the Kiwanis and the Wonders volunteers building booths in the morning." Kay went to get her mother's coffee, then put her own cup under the stream of brown liquid. "But I could go with you after that. Or meet you there."

"Great. We can meet there and that'll give me time to take in everything without keeping you waiting. Then we can have lunch at Perk Avenue. Do you and your cousins still have dinner with Agnes once a week? I'm anxious to see them."

"I'm sure everyone will love to see you."

Brenda smiled, then looked around herself at the old kitchen as she sipped at her coffee. "This is quite a place," she said. There was respect in her tone, but the suggestion that she'd never want anything like it. She had an affection for comfort, convenience and practicality. Except for an interest in vintage recipes, she was a very contemporary woman. "And a lot to keep up. With all your preparations for the festival—" she fingered a wreath made of dried hydrangea hanging on the back of an empty kitchen chair "—have you had any time for your book?"

"Not much," she admitted, "but it's iffy at best. I mean, it goes well in fits and starts, but I keep running into walls."

Her mother nodded. "I think that's the way creativity works. It makes a slave of you, it doesn't let you have continuing success so that you don't get cocky and think you're better than the process."

That was insightful and understanding. Kay went for her own coffee then sat at a right angle to her mother in mild surprise.

"Do you struggle with creating recipes?"

"Yes, but after all these years I understand how it works. When it fights me, I just let it be." She smiled across Philly's diary at Kay. "But that's hard for you, isn't it? You've always been a problem solver, had to make things come out right."

Kay leaned back in her chair—worried about the direction the conversation was taking. They were skirting dangerous ground. "I probably get that from Dad. It's preferable that surgeries *do* come out right. Can't just let those tumors and aneurisms be."

It *was* a snide response on her part, Kay realized, and regretted it instantly.

She saw the disappointment in her mother's eyes. "I meant it as an observation," she said. "But you interpreted it as criticism, and you don't take that very well. That you get from me." She put her coffee down. "Can you show me where my room is so that I can lie down for a few minutes?"

Kay led the way upstairs, thinking that mother-daughter relationships had a lot in common with the creative process, at least as far as the scarcity of success was concerned.

FRIDAY MORNING, Jack helped set up the booth site on the Common. He'd been working with Hank and Cam, but the two of them had to leave when a crisis at the Maple Hill Manor School required their rescue. It seemed some pipe had burst in a dorm building and shorted out the wiring. Maintaining the school buildings, Hank claimed, accounted for a good percentage of his payroll.

Jack worked on with help from other community groups. The day was beautiful and crisp, the leaves enveloping the Colonial buildings crimson and gold. The sound level was high as the festival physically began to take shape. Drivers honked and waved and passersby on foot stopped to watch or lend a hand. In the middle of the morning, Jack stood over several boxes of lights to be strung around the Common. They were so badly tangled that it reminded him of Christmas lights at home. Julia had always been careful to loop them so that they would separate freely when it was time to put them on the tree. But somehow, between the basement where they were stored and the tree, the string knotted and he would have to fight it yet again. Julia and Christmas in the same thought darkened his mood.

"Need a hand with that?" a familiar voice asked.

Jack looked up to find Ron Milford standing on the other side of the boxes with that good-citizen smile he always wore.

"They won't let me move or carry," Ron explained, "because of my arm, so Jackie suggested I see if you needed help."

Jack knew Milford fairly well now, and though he presented a "jolly good fellow" face to the world, Jack was convinced he had a line on the real man.

"Sure." Jack handed him one end of a string of lights, still playing his own role as detective. "Hold this while I see if I can get them untangled. We've got about thirty of these and they've all been put away by a knitter, apparently."

Milford laughed. "I thought this only happened at my house. When I *had* a house."

Jack expressed concern. It wasn't entirely phony. He liked Milford's wife and hated to think of how close she came to being burned to death in the fire. "How's the insurance claim going?"

"Got that taken care of right away. And I've hired Hank

and your guys to rebuild for me. It's just—" Milford's expression grew grim "—a little weird to think someone hates me that much. And I can't even imagine why. Cathy always used to say that I built the business on being a nice guy. Apparently someone doesn't think so."

Jack was so struck by that seemingly convincing claim of innocence that it took him a moment to notice the unfamiliar name.

"Who is Cathy?"

"My first wife. She died of cancer four years ago." Milford looked up and Jack caught a glimpse of an emotion he knew very well—a bottom-of-the-heart sadness. It knocked him off balance, made his brain hesitate. He had to say something that didn't require thought.

"I didn't realize Joanne was your second wife."

Milford came out of his thoughts. "Yeah. Great girl, but she's a lot higher maintenance than Cathy was. Anyway…I talked to Sergeant Whittier about the boy who set fire to our house. He said someone he doesn't know put him up to it."

Jack nodded, trying to stabilize his thoughts and feelings, find order in his confusion. He hated thinking he had *anything* in common with Milford.

"That's what I heard."

"They've apparently been trying to find his mother for a week. She and her boyfriend were in jail in Gloucester. Took them three days to sober her up." Milford shook his head with what appeared to be genuine concern. "I'd almost feel sorry for the kid if he hadn't destroyed the old belt ball my father left me. It's been in the family since it was given to my great-great-great-grandfather as the winning pitcher in a game played during the Civil War."

Jack tried not to be interested. "Must have been worth a small fortune."

"Yeah. And just as valuable emotionally. My father died a year ago and left me a small fortune besides the ball." He took several steps away as Jack, absently fiddling with the lights, managed to untangle a couple of inches of cord while keeping an eye on Milford. "Things weren't going well with my money management company. It was becoming more stressful and less profitable. The inheritance made it seem like a good time to get out. Joanne had been talking about going to Europe, maybe taking a cruise...."

He'd taken the trip and the cruise on his inheritance?

"I don't understand why the investment business isn't lucrative," Jack said, puzzled.

Milford shrugged, helping Jack undo a loop of cord. "I made the mistake of taking on a partner after the technology market slump of 2000. I'd been working myself to death trying to save my clients money. Scieszka, my partner, knew his stuff, so we split the duties. I dealt with the client end of things and Ron took care of the investments. It worked at first, but he's also the one who taught me about looking like you have money to convince clients that you can make it for them. I can afford to do that now, but I couldn't then. He got us into an office building where the overhead was too high, the market was still iffy, then one of our employees embezzled from us."

Jack's fingers froze on the lights. He'd been trying to unravel the mystery of Julia's death for so long, that though that remark didn't even seem to relate on the surface, he sensed that it was going to. "Embezzled," he repeated.

"Yeah. A lot. And we didn't know what to do about her because she had two little children and her husband was serving in Iraq."

Jack's heart slammed into the back side of his ribs. He couldn't breathe.

Milford was still talking. "Before we could even decide what to do, she was killed in an automobile accident."

The only thing that prevented Jack from knocking him out cold was that he needed him talking. He took Milford's good arm and dragged him inside a nearby booth where they were somewhat obscured from the view of the other workers.

"What are you…?" Milford demanded, apparently too shocked to struggle.

"You're talking about Julia Keaton," Jack said, pressing him into a corner of the booth.

"How do you…?"

"Because I'm *Jack* Keaton!" he snapped, tightening his grip. "The husband who was in Iraq!"

"My God!" Milford gasped, eyes wide and frightened. "You're the one who's trying to kill me!"

"No, I'm not. But I would be if someone wasn't beating me to it."

Milford looked genuinely confused. "I don't understand. She died in a car—"

"She left a diary." Jack loosened his grip on him as a group of laughing, talking women walked by with armloads of stuffed animals. When they'd passed, he pinned Milford with a glare. "She had proof that money was taken from your clients but investments were never made. I think whoever's trying to kill you is one of those clients."

Milford's eyes lost focus as he thought about that. "But…that can't be. I brought in people I knew, old friends, and told Scieszka what I thought we should do with them—who needed quick cash and who could afford to wait and let an investment build. We had a money management seminar at the library! I…" He stopped talking, a look of disbelief moving across his face. "It didn't occur to me to check on him," he said after a moment, his eyes still unfocused. "I saw the monthly statements and they were fine, all the usual things." He snapped out of those thoughts suddenly, grabbed Jack's wrist and yanked it off his arm.

"What kind of proof did Julia have?"

"Photographs of the books," Jack said. "An altered document with your signature on it."

"I never prepared reports or any documents. Scieszka did that."

"It has your signature."

"I swear to you I never cheated a client or played tricks with the books. If my signature was on your document, it was forged!"

While Jack considered that possibility, Milford went on.

"You know me, Jack. I have *your* money! I'd met with you, explained everything I was doing for you, hired you to work for me!" His eyes were dark with emotion—panicky, angry, indignant—and alarmingly innocent.

He shook his head and turned in a circle, clearly trying to reason through what he'd just heard.

"So," Jack proposed quietly, "are we talking about your partner, then?"

Milford stopped, closed his eyes and drew a breath. Then he fell onto a bench built into the side of the booth. "Ron Scieszka has two ex-wives, four kids in college, one of them in Europe and he'd lost everything in the market when he came to me looking for work. He was the one who proposed splitting the duties. He made sense. He knew what he was doing." He hesitated then added bleakly, "It would take someone who knew what he was doing to pull that off. If it is true. And if it is, why haven't all our clients complained? Why haven't I been called back for an investigation? Why isn't—?"

Jack interrupted calmly. "It'd be hard to prove right away, wouldn't it? He'd only been with you a year, just long enough to take in a lot of money, but too soon for the lack of performance to show. And, by your own admission, you brought in friends of yours, old acquaintances. They'd trust you. Probably even wait patiently for their money to grow."

Milford's expression darkened further. "You're suggesting Julia was killed for what she knew?"

"I'm sure of it. The entry in her diary the night before she died said she was going to the District Attorney with what she had. I think he followed her home and ran her off the road."

Milford shook his head in disbelief. "I can't believe he could do that."

"Is there any way you can find out what's going on at his office without him knowing you've called?"

The disbelief changed slowly to acceptance. "I called a couple of days ago to talk to him about a buyout payment he owes me and was told he'd taken a couple of weeks off."

Jack hated the thought that Scieszka might get away. "I'll bet he's gone for good."

Milford seemed to vacillate. "But, if he did kill Julia, wouldn't he have left then? Why wait a year?"

"Because Julia's death was presumed to be a simple one-car accident on the ice. The car was so banged up from the rollover, the police couldn't tell if she'd been bumped by another car—at least not without a CSI-type investigation, and the road conditions made them presume it was an accident. He was in the clear to make all the money he wanted until someone caught on."

"Okay." Milford apparently seemed to see the sense in that and said again, "Okay."

"Will you come with me to tell Gib Whittier what we know?"

Milford's mouth twisted in grim amusement. "Have you already told him you suspected me?"

"No." Jack put the boxes of lights out of the way against the side of the booth. "I have the disk Julia left with the photos on it, but…I don't know. I had to see you in action for myself. I thought working for you would help me find out if you were up to the same thing here. Then your chandelier fell and made that difficult. Then I thought painting your house would give me access to information, but someone burned down your office and your bedroom. So I think someone's on to what M & S was doing, only like me, they have the wrong partner."

Milford drew a ragged breath. "I'll drive. The other guy obviously requires less proof than you do. Let's clear this up before he kills me."

CHAPTER SEVENTEEN

"I'LL GET RIGHT ON THIS," Gib said a few hours later after a long discussion with Jack and Milford. Jack had given Gib Julia's diary and the disk.

Milford, shaken, went home to retrieve his records of the sale of his half of the business to Scieszka. Jack left the police station and stood in front of it for a moment, mentally pulling himself together. Going over the details of Julia's death with Gib, rereading parts of the diary to point out her concerns made the old pain fresh again. He felt his love for her and the enormity of the loss sucking him back to the darkest depths of his grief.

"Hey! Jack Keaton!" A strong baritone pulled him back to the moment. Father Chabot stood beside him, the door to the police station swinging closed behind him. "How are you?"

Jack tried to dredge up a smile, but what formed instead felt like a grimace of pain. He could only guess by the priest's frown of concern that it had looked like one, too.

The priest, a head shorter than Jack, put a hand on his shoulder. "You appear to be a man in need of church coffee," he said.

So Catholics called it that, too. Church coffee, for economic reasons, was weak and looked like tea.

Jack looked into Chabot's eyes and recognized, even in his anguish, the need, the training to help. He opened his mouth to refuse, but the priest was already pulling him toward the parking lot. "I'm on foot. Can we take your truck? I was visiting an incarcerated parishioner. Had dinner with the Bragas last night and I'll be walking off the calories for days. Ah. There it is." He'd spotted Jack's truck and climbed into the passenger seat before Jack could stop him.

Jack slipped in behind the wheel. "I can't be saved, Father," he said candidly.

Father Chabot smiled. "Neither can my coffee. You just looked like a man who needs to talk."

It was a short drive to the rectory and Father led him into that quiet room with its print of Christ and the little children. Something raced in Jack's chest—hatred and anger, he guessed, trying to escape their impending assault on him.

Chabot pointed to an overstuffed chair. "Relax. I'll be right back. Cream and sugar?"

"No. Straight up. Thanks."

The chair faced the print. Jack sat in it intrepidly, convinced the picture couldn't affect him. The last two years of his life had been too dark and cruel for him to ever think of it as a road to salvation.

The priest was back in a minute with two steaming

mugs. It worried Jack that the contents smelled like burned toast.

"I made it early this morning," he said, "and it sat on the heat plate for a while. I microwaved it."

Microwaved church coffee ten hours old. He took a sip and struggled valiantly against a wince. It was coffee brewed to drive out the devil.

"Tell me, Jack," the priest encouraged.

Jack breathed in and started with his decision to follow several of his congregation and all the other brave young men he didn't know to Iraq. He talked about the initial euphoria to do good, the effort to make connections, the understandable anger they encountered, then the terrible emotional and political tangle it all became.

He said that comforting the dying and those left to fight took parts of his own life, and only the thought of going home to Julia and his children kept him sane.

Then he unreeled everything about Julia's death just before he was to come home, the firefight that hospitalized him for months, about her diary and how he'd come to Maple Hill to take Milford down—only to discover he'd been wrong about which Ron was the guilty one.

Father Chabot sipped at his coffee and listened patiently. When Jack was finished, he asked gently, "Are you afraid you left her alone to go and heroically save souls, selflessly willing to die to serve your fellows— only she was the one who sacrificed her life?"

Jack stared as that rushing feeling accelerated inside him. The priest was good. Father Chabot had focused on the very thought that had plagued him often in the middle of the night. Had someone stuck a hot poker into the wound he'd sustained that night in Baghdad, it could not have hurt more than he was hurting now.

He put a hand over his mouth to stifle a sob.

Chabot leaned toward him. "You're wondering how God could have made such a mistake. You were the one ready to offer your life, but He took your innocent wife's instead. Cruel. Mean. Useless."

"She didn't want me to go!" he heard himself scream. "She said she didn't know what she'd do if I didn't come back. That the children needed me and the rest of our congregation who had to stay behind needed me."

"You had to do what you considered the right thing."

The truth came out of Jack like poison bubbling out of a witch's cup. "I was bored with life in a small church," he said. "The job was too small. I thought I was suited to do big things, assume big responsibilities, take big risks. And to do that, I had to leave Julia alone— and she died."

The priest leaned toward him. "Jack," he said gently, "I'm sure you made a difference. I'm sure…"

Jack denied that with a vicious shake of his head. "No. I served no one. Men still died in pain and misery, their friends were still inconsolable, and Julia died alone."

"Jack," Chabot said, and when Jack didn't respond, he said his name a little louder. When Jack looked up, the priest asked gravely, "Are you mad at God," he asked, "or mad at yourself?"

In that instant, he felt as though his own rage could kill him. "Had God meant the futility of the whole experience to be a lesson to me—that would have been one thing. But taking Julia instead was just cruel!"

Chabot moved his chair to sit beside him and placed a hand on his arm. Jack felt it weigh through the sleeve of his sweatshirt. Sound and light seemed magnified. He was too aware to survive.

"You've decided Julia's death was God's punishment because you suspect your own motives. Don't do that. You don't strike me as a careless man. We all have a tendency to beat ourselves up when we fail at something, but I think God appreciates the effort and blesses us anyway."

Jack tried to resist absorbing the words, but he could feel them trickling into his consciousness anyway.

"We know a loving God, Jack. Go back to the basics. 'God so loved the world that He gave His only begotten Son.' It's an unfailing truth. Julia's death was a sad and horrible thing, but God didn't do it *to* you, He just let it happen because, for reasons you may never understand, it was part of His plan for you."

Jack shook his head, resisting, remembering the dozens of times he used those words to comfort.

"I know it's hard to think of pain and loss as part of a plan, but they're as important to it as your children, your friends, all the things in life that give you joy. He let those happen, too."

Jack had once believed all that, now he wasn't sure what he thought. Grief and frustration lay over everything.

"Maybe I've just lost Him," Jack admitted.

The priest slapped his shoulder. "Live with confidence, Jack. He knows where *you* are. He just asks that you be open to Him."

Jack pointed to the print on the wall. "Like the children."

"Yes."

He took one last look at the loving, benevolent face, then put his cup on the low table in front of him and stood. "Thank you for caring, Father." He smiled wryly. "And for the coffee."

Father Chabot walked him to the door. "You're welcome to both anytime."

Jack wrapped him in a quick hug, then hurried away.

He climbed into his truck and glanced at his watch. He had an hour before he had to pick up the kids. He dialed Kay at the office, needing to catch her up on what he'd learned, needing to put this emotional tempest behind him. He didn't have time for it.

When she didn't answer, he called her home, and when there was no answer there, concluded she was setting up her booth on the Common. The festival committee had hired Hank's security team to protect the premises over the weekend, particularly at night when the vendors left their booths.

He turned in the direction of the Fall Festival.

"A KISSING BALL?" Rachel held up a ball Kay had made with dried pink rosebuds, turning it as though that would help her determine its purpose. Kay's mother and cousins had come to help her put up her booth. She'd rented a large, waterproof pavilion for the show. They'd brought Agnes with them, hoping she'd enjoy the change of scene. She sat on a chair with Charlie beside her, making tags for the wreaths and garlands Kay would bring tomorrow morning. "You kiss it instead of a man?"

"No," Kay corrected, determined to remain in good humor. After that small but mean exchange with her mother, she'd apologized and been the epitome of patience and cheer while they shopped this morning at the Farmers' Market. Even when her mother told her she should eat eggs, parsley and chestnuts for more controllable hair, she kept her smile in place. "You stand under it and kiss a man. It serves the same purpose as mistletoe, but is more interesting. And you can use it all year around. I brought one for each of you."

Agnes, looking wonderful if a little vague in brown slacks and a green sweater patterned in fall leaves, took one of the other two kissing balls Charlie was tagging and putting back in a box.

"When Elliott Whitman comes," she said. "I'm going to kiss him silly."

The cousins smiled at her and carried on with their work. Rachel helped Kay hang the pipe filled with sand at each corner for stability. She'd brought Jordie with her and he sat under a table playing with a toy truck.

Brenda asked quietly, "Elliott *Whitman?*"

"She has a crush on him and, in her imagination, she thinks he's coming to visit."

"Elliott Whitman."

"Yeah. I think he was a handsome young star at the time she was fading out of the business. He seems to represent some kind of ideal for her, or something. Some proof that her world remains intact."

"I was on…"

"He's bringing the wine, you know, for our next dinner together," Agnes shouted out to everyone.

Brenda heard that and asked worriedly, "Is she safe alone? I didn't realize dementia was setting in so noticeably."

Kay explained how all the cousins split the duties to help her stay in her apartment as long as possible. "And Annette Bleaker, a few apartments over, comes to check on her a couple of times a day." She sighed sadly. "Rachel's looking into assisted living for her, but we're waiting for an opening."

Brenda smiled fondly at her sister-in-law. "I know it's the way of it, and we all come to this if we're lucky enough to live this long. But it hurts to see. She was such a lively young woman. Reminds me of our reunions when your father and your uncles were young and our lives were all whole and…"

When our lives were whole. Before I ruined them. Kay could hardly remember that far back.

Brenda stopped herself and looked directly into

Kay's eyes. "Everyone's life changes from the ideal projection it seems in the beginning—those of us who are lucky enough to have good beginnings. I didn't mean…"

Kay shook her head to stop her, unable to hold back what had been on the tip of her tongue for years. "It's all right," she said softly. Rachel was busy straightening the scalloped top of the tent while Charlie and Agnes looked for the right place to put a tag on the kissing balls. "I know you've never forgiven me."

Brenda's eyes widened; she opened her mouth to speak, closed it, then opened it again, pinching Kay's arm with trembling fingers. "I never forgave you," she said under her breath, enunciating every word, "because I never *blamed* you!"

Rachel tugged Jordie out from under the table as she prepared to leave.

"We're going to go buy a Shrek costume for Halloween," he announced excitedly.

"Shrek?" Agnes asked.

"He's green," Jordie explained, "and his buddy is Donkey, and he loves Fiona. Just like Gib loves you, Rachel."

The tent fell silent. Everyone glanced at everyone else in surprise, afraid to comment on or question the boy's remark because of Rachel's apparent astonishment. Brenda busied herself with straightening the twisted ribbon on a kissing ball, obviously waiting for the right moment to resume her conversation with Kay.

"He told me," Jordie said, obviously feeling he had to validate his claim.

"When?" Rachel breathed.

"Last night when he took me to get ice cream. He asked me if I wanted to talk about my mom 'cause…" He hesitated, then looking around at the watchful faces of his companions, decided they were friendly enough to share confidences. "Well. She's gonna go to jail, too. Just like Derek has to go to jail 'cause of the fire. But, I don't think my mom likes me, so it's okay if she's gone. But Derek does, so I wish he didn't have to go. I asked Gib if I could stay with you —" he smiled winningly at Rachel "—'cause I like your house. And if I did, if he could live with us 'cause I know he's your husband. But he said he loves you, but you don't love him 'cause he did something bad. But doing a bad thing doesn't mean you're bad. It just means you're a good person who decided to do the wrong thing. That's what you told me about Derek. Remember?"

While Rachel stared at him, Kay and Charlie pretended to be busy.

"That was probably worth more than any nagging we could have done," Kay said quietly.

Charlie nodded but looked glum.

"What is it?" Kay asked, pulling her outside the pavilion. The air was cool and perfumed with fall.

"I told Sam I didn't want to see him anymore," Charlie blurted.

"What?" In her exasperation with her cousin, Kay forgot to lower her voice. Fortunately Agnes and Brenda were involved with Rachel and Jordie's conversation. "I thought you were having a good time. He treats you like he adores you."

Charlie angled her chin defensively. "Well, doesn't it make you wonder? What if he just has some freaky thing for fat girls? I can't believe he's serious about *me*."

"He's going out with you."

"I know. I mean, I've gained three pounds because we've been out to dinner three nights in a row."

Kay shook her head impatiently. "And you don't think that means he likes you? You think it's part of some bizarre fetish?"

Charlie shrugged. "I don't understand it."

"Did you tell him about what happened?" She didn't have to explain what she meant.

"Yes."

"Did he react badly?"

"No. He said he was sorry for me that I had had to endure that experience, but it didn't affect the way he felt about me."

Kay swatted her arm. "Then what, please God, is *wrong* with you?"

"Well…" Charlie tried to speak, but simply expelled a gasp instead. Kay instinctively put a comforting hand to her arm. "I mean…all my life I've felt dirtied by what happened. But he doesn't think of me that way. So…what if I can't be the whole, perfect woman he thinks I am?"

Kay opened her mouth to scold her for that silliness, then remembered that she, herself, was afraid of her relationship with Jack. Old guilt plagued her just as old memories hurt Charlie. It was so easy to talk about putting the past away and moving ahead, but even when there was a good reason to do it, it was harder than it seemed. Still—Charlie bore no blame for what happened to her.

"I swear, Charlie…" Kay began, then changed tack, realizing her cousin was in a fragile state. "What did he say when you said you didn't want to see him again?"

Charlie's face crumpled. "That neither my body nor what happened to it would ever put him off, but my brain would, because I was thinking like an idiot."

Kay had to remember to shake Sam's hand the next time she saw him. She wrapped Charlie in a hug. "I think he's a very smart man, and you're just feeling panicky because the man likes you as you are—and you don't. Maybe you were right to break up with him. I think you have to find a way to be happy with yourself before you can expect a man to be happy with you."

Kay began sending her cousins home, even though she realized that would leave her alone with her mother and their unfinished conversation. "I so appreciate your help," she said, hugging them, then Agnes, then Jordie. "Shall we meet at the Barn for breakfast in the morning before we come to the Common?"

The agreement was unanimous. Kay and her mom walked them to their cars and waved them off.

Change was in the air. Fall was definitely here. The wind stirred the leaves and carried the perfume of wood smoke and mysterious, musky fragrances picked up from far away.

Her cousins' lives were changing. Rachel seemed to love having Jordie with her, had been shaken by what he'd said about Gib.

Charlie had placed a call on her cell phone the moment she got into her car. Kay hoped she'd been calling Sam.

For the first time, she wondered what she would do without her cousins if they resolved their romantic differences. Well, she wouldn't be without them; Rachel had been married for a long time and she'd still managed to hang out with them regularly. But since she and Gib had been separated, the three of them had been a small army against their particular problems, and the progression of Agnes's dementia.

If Rachel and Charlie solved their problems, they'd have other priorities, and she'd still be chasing small-town news stories, grappling with her novel and making wreaths out of dried things and nature's extras.

"You just sit, Mom," Kay said, indicating the only chair. "I'm going to make sure everything's tagged, close up these boxes, zip the tent closed, and we can go." She hung a camp lantern from the overhead support.

"Is Betsy what this is all about?" her mother asked, ignoring the chair and facing her.

Kay pretended innocence. "What what is all about?"

"This animosity between us. I know I'm not the ___ iest person in the world to get along with, but I ___ more trouble with you than with anyone. And everyone else tells me that you're the most delightful and charming woman they know. So…despite all the therapy we've put you through, all the pains I've gone through to make sure you didn't have survivor guilt…you think I *blame* you for Betsy?"

Kay was amazed that she'd studiously avoided the topic all these years, then just forced it out, made it visible. It hurt abominably, but it wouldn't go away.

She tried to lean against the table, but it was too unsteady. "Your eyes were always averted when we talked," she accused her mother in a quiet voice, standing in the middle of the shadowy tent. "I know you were always careful about what you said or did in regard to Betsy, but I got the feeling you couldn't stand to look at me."

Brenda gasped in pained disbelief. "Kay, I was so full of grief, but I swear I never blamed you for it. If I averted my eyes it was because I didn't want you to see what her loss had done to me. I wanted you to grow up to be a normal, functioning person."

Kay spread her hands to show off her normal appearance. "I function very well, and I can act normal most of the time. It's just lately—"

"You've always been so responsible," her mother in- "I suppose in your young mind, blaming r what happened to Betsy was one way to a horrible thing understandable. But I never . I swear to you I didn't."

Kay wanted to believe that, but for most of a lifetime she'd been convinced otherwise. "Daddy did," she whispered, remembering with a broken heart that the last word on his lips when he died had been her sister's name. Kay had let herself think that it had been a greeting—that Betsy had appeared in his last moment to take him home.

Brenda's face contorted with old grief and she sank onto the chair as though she couldn't stand another moment. "He didn't blame you," she said finally, her voice ragged. "He blamed me. I hired the nanny, stayed in the city because of my show. He said that would never have happened if I'd been home."

Kay knelt in front of her, speechless. In all this time, she'd never suspected her father had felt that way. Her parents' grief had been so profound, yet they'd seemed to gain comfort from each other.

"Oh, Mom." She took her hand, surprised by how cold and frail it felt. "That was just pain talking. I'm sure he didn't mean it."

Brenda nodded. "I know that, and he said it only once. But that he said the words at all meant to me that somewhere inside him, he believed that." She placed her other hand on top of Kay's. "He loved all of us so much, but Betsy was his angel." A loud sob erupted from her. "What a horrible, horrible way for an angel to die."

Kay wrapped her arms around her and held her while she wept.

HER MOTHER'S PAIN mingled with her own and in this little shelter redolent of eucalyptus and lavender, it seemed so wrong.

"Kay?"

She was startled to look up and see Jack standing in the opening of the pavilion. "Hi," he said, taking a step into the shelter. "I thought you'd be here." His eyes went from her to her mother with a frown. "What happened?"

"Nothing new," she said, arms still around her mother. Even in the anguish the two women shared, she was aware of a leap in her heart at the sight of him, a yearning to touch him. "We were talking about Betsy and how guilty we both feel about her."

Kay knew for a fact that most men confronted with the sight of two weeping women would have been happy to walk away. But Jack seemed to grow an inch or two, then came toward them to get down on one knee beside them.

"You know what happened to Betsy wasn't your fault, Brenda," he said in a gentle but firm tone she'd never heard him use before. In fact, he didn't *look* quite like the man she knew, either. The fire usually present in his eyes had abated, and he was less edgy. He leaned toward Kay's mom, elbow on his knee, and took her hand. "But hurting yourself by taking the blame makes you feel better—like some sort of self-flagellation. It's the same thing Kay does."

Kay might have objected to his statement if she hadn't been so completely fascinated by the sudden change in him. She just kept watching her mother's hand in his, and the steady look in his eyes.

"God doesn't want that from you," he said. "He wants you to accept that He's taken her home and to be at peace. He doesn't want either of you to suffer like this. He wants you to be kind, to do good, to alleviate other people's suffering, but not to perpetuate your own. He wants you in service to Him, not in bondage to old guilt that was never yours to claim anyway."

Kay's mom looked at him. Kay saw in her face the eagerness to believe him—coupled with the fear that he was wrong. "How do you know, Jack?"

"Because trying to interpret what God wants of us is what I do. Or what I used to do. I was a minister before my wife died and anger killed every joyful thing inside me."

Suddenly Kay recognized who he was. He was the Jack she'd never seen before—at least not to this degree—the Jack who nurtured and comforted. Jack, the minister, in service to the God he thought he no longer believed in.

"Our priest," Kay's mom said, taking a tissue Kay handed her, "told me the same thing. So I tried not to feel like it was my fault, but then Kay felt *she* was responsible. So, now I think if I'd assumed responsibility for it, she'd have felt differently. She was only eight. If I'd blamed myself, she'd have known it wasn't *her* fault."

"It's nobody's fault," he said patiently, gently. "If

theology could answer the question of why God allows horrible things to happen to those He loves, I could make a fortune on tour. But we don't have all the answers. We live in and on faith. What both of you have to hold on to is that Betsy is Home, and your suffering—" he glanced in Kay's direction with that solemn face "—serves no good purpose."

Kay was shaken by the look in his eyes. "And neither does your suffering," she reminded pointedly.

He gave her one single nod. "And neither does mine," he repeated. He squeezed her mother's fingers and looked into her eyes. "Kay needs you whole and happy." His face transformed again suddenly into the face of the man Kay knew as he added with a light laugh, "The Maple Hill Fall Festival needs you whole and happy and cooking pumpkins."

Tears streaming down her face, Kay's mother stretched her arms toward him and he leaned into her hug.

Kay felt as though someone had taken hold of the axis of her world and spun it around. Her mother had felt responsible for Betsy's death and had lived all these years with the thought that her husband blamed her?

And Jack had regained his…faith?

And where was she in the midst of these personal epiphanies? Still guilty? Still afraid? She wasn't sure. Any sense of truth was still tumbling like a planet out of orbit.

Kay's mother drew back and looked into Jack's eyes. "Are you in love with my daughter?" she asked candidly.

Kay groaned and closed her eyes.

"I am," Jack replied instantly.

Kay's eyes flew open as she experienced equal parts of joy and terror.

Her mom patted his cheek. "Then, I'd better let you have some time with her." Jack stood and helped her to her feet. She hugged Kay and picked up two empty boxes. "I'll carry these to the car."

Kay didn't know what to say, where to start, how to tell him that she loved him, too, but...

"I came to tell you," he said, cutting off her thoughts, "that Milford didn't kill Julia—Scieszka did. Milford and I had a long talk, then we spent a couple of hours with Gib. I gave him Julia's diary, and Milford told him how Scieszka set up their partnership so that he did all the actual investing while Milford gathered clients, answered all their questions."

She opened her mouth to comment, but had no idea what to say. "Where is he now?" she asked finally. "Scieszka, I mean."

Jack shook his head. "Not sure. Milford called the office and was told he was on vacation. I imagine he's left with the money for parts unknown. That's why I finally went to the police."

"But...why did Scieszka wait so long?"

"No one suspected him of anything. He probably got enough money together to disappear in style, decided he was tempting fate by hanging around and took off."

Kay was both relieved and dismayed. Justice for Julia was in sight. Jack would be able to put that behind him and get on with his life.

She shook her head against the thought. Over the past month, she'd alternately toyed with the idea that they could make a life together and been certain it would never work. She'd hated being around children since Betsy was lost, but his children had taught her that if she opened up to them, they offered more comfort and laughter than grief.

She'd just learned that her mother blamed herself and not Kay for what happened to her little sister, and Jack had somehow reached out of his own anger and grief to comfort her.

She wondered what could possibly happen next.

"What's…happened?" she had to ask.

Jack spread his arms in a gesture of helplessness. "I can't say, exactly. I had a talk with Father Chabot. He knows where I am."

"Father Chabot?"

"God."

It wasn't the time to be light, but she didn't know how she could fit into Jack's life if he reclaimed God.

"He's not coming for you, is he?" she teased.

He laughed lightly. "He knows where I am, but that doesn't mean He wants me."

JACK HAD A CURIOUS, almost unsettling sense of peace. Even as he formed the thought, he realized it was a contradiction in terms, but that was precisely where life stood at the moment—old, deeply rooted beliefs dragging him back to faith, opposite emotions at war inside him, his future filled with sun and shadows. How could he possibly explain that to Kay?

"I came to tell you what I'd learned about Milford and his partner," he said, deciding it was best to start simply, "and then I heard someone crying." He drew a breath, suddenly realizing himself what had happened next. "Offering comfort started out as old habit. I've comforted many members of my congregation, many dying friends in Iraq, many grieving friends of the dying, and…I couldn't let the two of you be in pain without trying to help. And what came out of me was everything I thought I'd lost hold of, but apparently haven't. And…the weird thing is, I sincerely believe every word I told you." He tapped a fist softly against his heart where a pain lingered. "And strangely, it comforted *me*. That's what it's all about, you know—the circle. The love that links us all together and is never ending. One hand reaching for another hand and another until we're an unbreakable bond of love and trust. Like your wreaths. A beautiful loop you can look at every day to remind yourself of life everlasting."

His heart thudded against his chest and he had to reach deeply for a breath. He felt the air move through his lungs and, as he breathed it out, he seemed to expel much of the darkness of the last two years. Love had brought him back—Julia pushing and Kay pulling. He might explode with the wonder.

And the generosity of a God who would give this to him a second time.

Kay wrapped her arms around him. "Jack. I'm so happy for you. I know the whole thing with Scieszka isn't over, but I'm sure the police will find him and Julia can rest in peace." She kissed his cheek and took a step back from him. And he saw something in her eyes he didn't like.

DEAR GOD, she thought.

She glanced quickly heavenward, afraid she'd offended Him. That had been less a greeting than an oath. And with Jack on his old path again, she was sure God was listening.

But... *Dear God!* She couldn't be in love with a minister! She wasn't spiritual enough. She went to church, but she'd been doing it so long it was habit rather than choice, and sometimes her mind wandered.

"Why do you look so sad?" he asked, reaching for her arms. His eyes were scanning her face. "I heard your mother say she didn't blame you for Betsy. You're only going to make her feel worse if you continue to blame yourself. If you'll let go, she will, too. It was an ugly and horrible thing that neither of you is to blame for."

She wanted to find a safe, quiet place for her memories of Betsy. She felt such relief that her mother *didn't* blame her, that it was going to take her a while to find her feet, to grasp where she stood.

She just couldn't imagine taking her place next to a

man who stood at a pulpit. Particularly one with two children. It would be one thing to let go of the guilt, but quite another to take on the care of two little children without being terrified for their safety every moment.

And she didn't think she was taking too much for granted; he said he loved her and there was love in his eyes. She could have swum in it.

"After Gib finds Scieszka," Jack said, firming his grip on her, "we have to talk."

"Okay." Agreeing to that was safe enough. A million things could change between now and then.

His gaze sharpened on her as though he'd read her mind. "You're humoring me. You don't want to talk about us?"

She smiled innocently. "Talk never hurt anyone."

He caught her arm. "Unless they're talking to *you,* and then it's like physical combat. What's the matter?"

"Jack." She shook his hands off and took several steps back until she hit her head on the camp light. He reached up for it and placed it on the table. It made a bright light in one corner and long shadows in the rest of the area.

"Just tell me." He stood a small distance away from her, arms folded, and waited for her to explain.

She could put this off—as she wanted to do—or she could make it clear now that their fragile and turbulent relationship could go no further. It was difficult to admit to that in the fragrant shadows of night, but it was true. She hoped he'd understand and make it easy on both of them. But there was dark emotion on his brow and he didn't look as though he was in a mood to make anything easy.

"I can't be serious about a minister," she said firmly, searching her mind for reasons he'd understand. "I'm Catholic, for heaven's sake!"

He shrugged that off. "So I'll be the first Path of Light minister with a Catholic wife."

Wife? "Wife?" she asked in a high whisper.

He grinned. "It's generally frowned upon for ministers to have lovers. Sets a poor example. You can help me with whatever part of the church schedule you're comfortable with, then go off to Mass on Sunday. I'd have no problem with that."

Okay. She made the large leap in her mind to *wife* for the sake of argument. "The kids would be confused."

"How can watching two people live good lives in their own way confuse them? It reinforces the fact that it isn't the path to doing it that matters, but the doing it."

That was so sane. But she couldn't let it draw her into his way of thinking.

"No." She said it firmly and with finality. "When you were Jack, the…the Milford stalker, you thought you knew everything, and now that you're Jack, the man of God, you're sure you have the answers to everything."

His smile was beautiful—and just a little scary. "That's the thing, Kay. I do. Finally, I can accept all that's happened. I understand that I wasn't mad at God,

I was mad at myself. I left Julia and the children and my congregation to go do big and important things."

"But you didn't do it selfishly." She rose quickly to his defense, forgetting she was trying to keep her emotional distance. "You did it to serve…"

"I did it partly to serve," he interrupted, "but partly because life in a small congregation was predictable and comfortable and I thought I was capable of bigger things—forgetting that all the little jobs have to be done, also."

"You did a brave thing," she insisted. "And much as you make me insane, I've never known you to be thoughtless or careless."

He nodded. "I don't know about that, but I know that I can finally accept my losses and live the rest of my life."

Good. She liked hearing that. She folded her arms to hold herself together and prepared to say goodbye. "You're going to be fine. Everyone in Maple Hill loves you…."

"*You* love me."

"Yes, I do, but I just don't see it working between us, Jack."

He caught her arm and pulled her to him. He held her tightly, caught a fistful of her hair with unclergy-like force and kissed her until she couldn't remember her name. Every nerve ending wanted more.

"I beg to differ," he said, raising his head. She was grateful to be able to breathe. "I think it works very well between us." Then he released her. "Anything else going in the car?"

She had to give herself a minute to translate the practical question. The sensory impact of the kiss still overrode the workings of her brain.

"Ah...no."

"All right. I'll follow you home and see you in the morning."

She opened her mouth to protest, but he said with weary patience, "Oh, stop it."

He drove behind her, waiting until she and her mother had the door open, then tapped the horn and drove away.

Kay kicked off her shoes.

"That is the sweetest man," her mom said, heading for the kitchen. "Don't get too comfortable. You have to help with the pies for the raffle."

"Yeah," Kay grumbled wryly, following her. "Sweet."

CHAPTER EIGHTEEN

KAY STARED at the Common and couldn't quite believe her eyes. Maple Hill had been transformed. Vendors were filling the booths they'd set up last night, and twinkle lights strung back and forth across the space lit up the dawn. The statues of Caleb and Elizabeth Drake had been festooned with bright leaves by the school children, and bundles of wheat tied with plaid ribbon marked the perimeter of the vending area. Uncarved pumpkins were everywhere.

Kay had had to park several blocks away, but her cousins and Jordie were strung out behind her like bearers on a safari carrying wreaths and garlands. Gib and Sam had volunteered to help carry before going in to work, and she was happy to see chatty good humor between Gib and Rachel, and Charlie and Sam, rather than the tension she'd expected. Her mother had already reported to the contest area where tables were being set up for carved pumpkins, and the pie contest. Agnes's neighbor would be bringing Agnes to the festival later in the morning.

What could have been a lonely job for Kay of walking miles back and forth to the car—not to mention several trips back and forth in her small car to the house to pick up her products—had turned into a cheerful, convivial experience.

"Oh, smell that coffee!" Gib exclaimed as they walked down a long line of booths filling with every imaginable craft. "Where's it coming from?"

Rachel, wearing wreaths on both arms, pointed in the direction of the next aisle. "Perk Avenue's set up a booth to benefit the homeless shelter. All charity and information booths are in that aisle. I'm going to need a cup the minute I can put these wreaths down."

"I'll pay you all off with coffee," Kay promised as they reached her pavilion. She handed a bill to Gib and sent him and Sam off to get drinks for everyone. Jordie insisted on going along.

"He's really attached himself to Gib," Kay observed as she took wreaths from Rachel's arm and placed them on hooks she'd put up last night.

"He was a good father," Rachel said, with a glance toward the men walking away. "And he doesn't seem to have lost the skill."

Kay caught Charlie's eye as Rachel turned away to hang the last wreath she carried.

Charlie grinned widely.

Kay handed Rachel two more wreaths. "Will you hang these, then hook that utensil ring from the middle support so I can put all the kissing balls on it?"

"Sure."

Kay handed Charlie one end of a garland made of berries, leaves and wheat. "Will you help me drape this in front?"

"So you can interrogate me about Sam?" Charlie did as she was asked, handing Kay a roll of wire.

"That was the plan, yes." Kay cut off a length with the snips in the pocket of the apron she wore and stretched up to fasten the end of the garland to the side pole of the booth. She glanced down at her cousin without remorse. "So, did you talk to him?"

"I explained my hang-ups. He said we all have them in one form or another, but he didn't see why we couldn't work on them together, and…all is well."

"All right!" Kay moved to fasten the other side and while Charlie held it for her, she asked quietly, "What happened with Rachel and Gib?"

"I don't—"

"They had a long talk," Rachel interrupted, coming up behind them. "Gib apologized abjectly. Rachel was able to admit she'd been very difficult and had to find a way to handle her stress, and is moving back home tomorrow. Anything else you want to know?"

Charlie screamed and wrapped her arms around Rachel.

"You're just happy I'm moving out."

"Yes, that, too," Charlie laughed. "But I'm so happy you're going to be back together. Think of all the fun things the four of us can do with the holidays coming up."

Kay hugged Rachel, then as the men arrived with

coffee and the couples naturally paired up, Kay sent them off to look around, assuring them she could handle the rest by herself.

Rachel checked her watch. "I'll be back at ten to man the booth so you can do your cakewalk thing."

"Okay." Kay shooed her away.

Think of all the fun things the four of us can do.... It was already happening. Her cousins had solved their romantic problems, and though Kay wouldn't have it any other way, she knew everything would be different now. With Gib and Sam working together, it would be only natural for the two couples to gravitate to each other in their spare time.

Well, that was good. She'd have more time for her book.

She hung the last few kissing balls Rachel had missed and admitted to herself that that was bunk. She didn't care about the book right now. She'd tossed and turned most of the night, thinking about Jack and his kids and her firm rejection of his offer of love.

When she thought of her life without them, she began to wonder how hard it could be to make the adjustment to life as a wife and mother. So she had to learn to compromise. So she had to offer the best wisdom she could then trust the children to remember it when she wasn't there to guide them. Every parent in the world must face the fear of what could happen, then trust in guardian angels, or Providence, or whatever protected the vulnerable.

Only it didn't always protect them. And no one knew that better than she did.

Still. Life alone was beginning to make life as a mother seem worth the risk.

But then, she was considering life as the wife of a *minister.* That made it hard to be philosophical.

Rachel was back at ten as promised, and Kay hurried to the east end of the booths where the cakewalk area had been set up across from where her mother was placing pie contest entries. Her mother looked up and waved. Kay waved back. Her mother looked serene this morning, Kay thought. Usually, when she was in celebrity mode she was a bundle of chatty energy, but she'd had a new calm about her when they'd driven to the Barn to meet everyone for breakfast.

"You look fresh," Kay had said as they got into the car.

Her mother had drawn a deep breath and looked up at the sky. It had still been dark, the stars fading but the moon a perfect crescent above the spire of a church.

"I feel fresh," she said. Then she'd looked into Kay's eyes, and Kay had known that something essential had changed between them and the old animosity was gone forever. "I hope you do, too."

She opened her mouth to lie, to say that she did, but the needs of their new relationship stopped her. "I feel…scared," she admitted.

Kay's mom nodded as though she understood. "Knowing you're in love is terrifying. It means you are not the single most important person in your life anymore. It means you owe someone else all the best you can give." Then she'd pinched Kay's arm. "But you were never a coward. You're up for it."

Kay had little time to think about her personal courage as cakes began to arrive. The bakery had lent the committee a cooler case, and it was full by the time the cakewalk was open for business at eleven.

Claire Bell came by, checking things off on a clipboard, looking like a Ralph Lauren ad in a long skirt and tweed jacket. She observed the full case and the people already lined up to participate.

"Your music's all set?" she asked.

Kay indicated the boom box on a table beside her. "John Philip Sousa," she said. "Best cakewalking music in the world."

"Excellent. According to Jackie, this year's admissions exceed all expectations already and it isn't even noon yet."

Kay nodded. "It's my mother." She pointed across the lawn where cameras were clustered around her mom as she spoke to a group of women gathered at the entries table.

Claire gave a little jump of excitement. "I *know*. I have to win one of her pies. Good luck. I'll be back later to check on you. Perk Avenue says they've made a few extra double chocolate cakes if you need backup."

"Great."

"You have my cell phone number."

Kay patted her pocket. "I have."

Claire left and Kay went to work. By noon, Kay could think of nothing but escaping the Sousa music and having a *carne d'espeto* sandwich. An early-afternoon breeze carried the aroma of marinated beef cooked on a skewer over a brick-oven grill. The Portuguese Club prepared the favorite treat, then served it on a Portuguese roll or sweet bread. It was a taste of heaven and something her father had always adored. Her mother refused to make it, insisting she couldn't top the club's offering.

And then something flung itself at her waist and held on.

"Hi, Kay!" It was Amanda. She caught Kay's arm and dragged her toward a small crowd of people. Lunchtime had thinned out the cakewalking crowd, so Kay stepped away for a moment.

Jack stood with a strong-looking man as tall as he was, and a small, slender woman in sneakers and blue jersey pants and jacket. The man carried Paul, and the woman wore a bright smile.

"Kay, I'd like you to meet my parents." Jack placed an arm around his mother's shoulders, and caught Kay's arm to draw her closer. "Emma and John Keaton. Mom, Dad—Kay Florio."

Emma nodded at Kay. "I understand you've been distracting my son."

Kay gasped and then laughed at the woman's candor. "I thought it was the other way around," she said, offering her hand.

Emma Keaton hugged her instead. Paul pointed to the cakewalk circles and while he and his father and grandfather explained how the game was played, Emma took advantage of the moment to pinch Kay's cheek. "Whatever you're doing, keep it up. He's alive again, and there was a time when I was sure that couldn't happen."

Kay wanted to explain that she wasn't responsible for that, that he'd somehow found his way back to the man he used to be before Julia died—but Paul and Amanda were already standing on circles, waiting for the music to start. Emma and John also claimed circles and were quickly joined by Hank and Jackie and all of their children.

Kay started the music. Jack went to stand beside her while it played.

"So, YOU WERE TRYING to tell my mother that you haven't hounded me, followed me, accused me of terrible things and spurned my advances?"

She gave him a dry look. "I slept with you. That's hardly spurning your advances."

She stopped the music and a jubilant Amanda won a cake. She selected one from Perk Avenue with a lot of cream and cherries. John Keaton paid for another round and so did Hank. Kay started the music.

"I'm in love with you," Jack said.

Kay glowered at him. "Don't you dare say that."

JACK RAISED an eyebrow at her tone, then repeated intrepidly, "I'm in love with you."

She stopped the music again; Erin Whitcomb won this time, and they all stepped away to give the gathering crowd a chance to play.

Kay made a production of helping Erin choose a cake, then explaining the rules to the newcomers. She started the music again.

"I said, I'm—"

"I heard you!" she snapped under her breath. "Jack, we've had this conversation. I made a point of being firm."

He had to make a point of being patient. "And you think that somehow makes your opinion law?"

"No, but you can't be serious! It's too soon for you, too late for me and…and…"

The words cut the ground out from under him, but there was a completely different message in her eyes. "So, that's a no, to your loving me, then?" he asked. He had to make her say it. She was a journalist dedicated to the truth.

Her shoulders sagged and her eyes condemned him for forcing the issue. "I do love you," she replied, "but I know it's the wrong thing to do."

All right. He had something to run with. "Wrong for whom? My kids, who like you? For me, who loves you? Or for you, who loves me?"

"Hey!" somebody shouted good-naturedly from the cakewalking circle. "We've walked around ten times!"

Kay stopped the music, announced a winner, presented a cake, then pushed Jack away. "Stop it!" she said, her eyes filled with tears. "I have a job to do here, and you're getting in my way."

"That's my plan," he said quietly, staying her hand before she could start the music again. "I'm going to be in your way until you stop being afraid. That's all it is, you know. Fear of being happy."

She turned her back on him and started the music.

"Daddy, can we go on the rides?" Amanda pointed to the Ferris wheel visible across the Common.

"I'll take them," his mother said. "Why don't you buy your father a funnel cake and a cup of coffee and sit him down somewhere." She looked at Kay. "He has a heart condition and he's supposed to relax every afternoon, but he won't do it unless I nag."

His father rolled his eyes. "She thinks the world runs on her nagging. But the funnel cake sounds like a good idea."

Jack took his father to the food area, bought a plateful of treats, then found a table where they had a clear view of the carved pumpkins lined up on a long table.

"What're those pies for?" his father asked.

"Kay's mom is judging the best pie." He pointed to her, talking to Jackie Whitcomb. "That's her."

"Your mother says she's watched her on television." He studied Jack warily. "She seems to think we're going to be in-laws. But she imagines a lot. She think she has powers of perception but is wrong a lot more often than she's willing to admit. And, didn't I see the lady shove you away?"

Jack nodded morosely. "That's her style. Makes me crazy."

"She looks at you with that—" his father bobbed his head from side to side "—you know...your mother used to have it for me forty years ago. Lust."

Jack wanted to believe that was true.

"And it's all right that the time is short since Julia died." That was Jack's one haunting thought given voice.

"Why is it all right?"

"Because grief doesn't have a set time or a given ritual. You loved each other the best you could, and there's nothing unresolved between you. She'd want you to be happy again, to make someone else happy. And it'd be good for the kids. They seem to like Kay and I watched her eyes when Amanda ran to her. She has a soft spot for children."

"Yes." Jack explained briefly what had happened to her little sister.

His father looked stricken. "My God."

"Yeah."

As far as nothing unresolved between Jack and Julia, his father still thought her death had been an accident.

Jack was considering sharing the truth about that when Evan Braga dressed in a comic-opera sheriff's uniform appeared at their table. "I arrest you, Jack Keaton," he said, both thumbs hooked in red suspenders on which was pinned a toy star-shaped badge, "in the name of the Maple Hill Fall Festival. Seems your fellow Wonders pooled their money so you'd be put away for a long, long time."

Jack got up from the table while his father laughed.

"Don't worry, son," he said as Evan caught Jack's arm. "I'll put a file in your half of the funnel cake."

"Thanks, Dad. There'd better be some of that left when I'm paroled."

"Don't count on parole," Evan said, hauling him through the crowd enjoying the festival. The jail was in the middle of everything for the best visibility—and the best fund-raising—possible. Those he knew cheered his arrest, those he didn't, smiled at the playful spectacle. "We've made so much money on you, we may have to put you away for life."

Jack grinned at him as they approached the jail. "Are you susceptible to a bribe?"

Evan pushed him behind a nearby booth and looked around surreptitiously. "Talk," he commanded.

Jack pulled a bill out of his pocket. "Can you get me a conjugal visit?"

Evan looked horrified. "Jack, we're in front of the Altar Society booth."

Jack lowered his voice. "Can you arrest Kay Florio and let us serve our time together?"

"Promise you won't do anything foolish to embarrass me?"

"Just how sensitive are you?"

"Jack…"

"All right. All right. We'll keep our clothes on. Just get her here." He slapped the bill into Evan's hand.

Jack found Gib already serving time when he was pushed into the cell.

"Where the hell have you been?" Gib demanded, making room for him on the single bench. "We pooled our money to have you put away ten minutes ago."

Jack frowned at him as he sat beside him. "I don't know. Maybe I was hard to find. I thought the Wonders had me put away."

Gib nodded. "With my encouragement. Listen, I have to talk to you and I needed a place where we could be private."

He looked serious. Jack turned toward him.

"I've learned some interesting things about the fire and the falling chandelier."

Hilarity went on outside the booth. There was excited conversation, laughter and a call for all entrants in the pumpkin pie contest. Jack had to lean closer to tune out the noise. "What?" he demanded.

"You told me when you arrived on the scene the day of the fire, that Mrs. Milford was calling 911."

"That's right."

Gib shook his head. "I was looking through the files late last night and discovered that the call was made by a passing motorist."

It took Jack a minute to grasp the importance of that detail. "But she was on a cell phone…"

"Yes. At 7:12 p.m. she called a number in Haverstown, Vermont."

Haverstown… It suddenly all came together. "Ron Scieszka."

"Yes. And I had the lab in Boston check out a part of

the beam around the chandelier. A piece with one of those drilled holes you were worried about. Guess what it contained."

"What?"

"Stump-Gone."

"Ah…"

"It's a Bonide used to get rid of tree stumps. You drill holes into wood, pour this stuff in, and outside, you pour kerosene into it and set it on fire, but in the building, she just let it eat away at the wood. It was easy to get at from her shop across the hall that shares the common attic."

"I didn't know that stump stuff existed."

"It dissolves the lignin binding between cellulose layers of wood."

Jack stared. "What's lignin binding?"

"No idea," Gib admitted. "I memorized that part. Bottom line is, it makes the wood porous, causing it to lose its strength. Joanne Milford knows what it is. She and Gary Warren cleared a tree out of the middle of the high school's courtyard when they redesigned the landscaping."

"So you can tie her to it?"

"She confessed. She waited in the attic for Milford to sit as his desk, then applied enough pressure to break the support that held the chandelier. She rolled on Scieszka, said she's been in league with him all along since she managed the office for her husband and Scieszka joined the company with big ideas. He liked nice things and was determined to get them despite the ex-wives that were getting most of his money. Joanne was tired of Milford losing money and saw an ally in Scieszka. They fell in love and hatched a plan to steal from their clients."

"That's when Julia came in."

"Yes. Joanne insists Scieszka didn't tell her what he was planning, but then blithely agrees they'd planned their comfortable future too carefully to let anyone interfere. When Milford decided to retire, she was still pretending to be happily married while Scieszka socked away money. She considered staying with Scieszka at that point, but he told her it would look suspicious after Julia's death and someone might decide to investigate. So she moved to Maple Hill with Milford, still pretending, while Scieszka squirreled away the fortune that would keep them like royalty in Mexico."

Jack puzzled over that. "Okay, but why kill Milford if Scieszka was collecting all that money?"

"Greed. They wanted the key-partner life insurance Milford took out when they went into partnership. And everything else he had."

"God."

"Yeah. Apparently she got nervous when she found out I'd sent a chunk of the fallen beam to the state lab. She probably figured we'd connect the Stump-Gone to her. We caught her packing."

"I don't understand why she confessed. She brazened it out this long."

"She called Scieszka this morning to tell him we were suspicious.

"When he told her to relax, that he'd covered all the tracks, she told him that a man named Keaton—" Gib pointed to Jack "—was working for Milford. She said she didn't suspect you of being related to Julia when she first met you because she thought it completely impossible that that could happen. She'd heard that you'd come home near death and weren't expected to walk again. Then she and Milford moved here. But she's seen you with Kay—a reporter—and was beginning to wonder if we were related.

"He got angry, told her she was foolish for not having told him. And I guess suddenly the love affair was over. She'd helped him conceal a murder, tried to murder her own husband for him and he called her a brainless idiot. Hell hath no fury and all that." Gib put a hand on Jack's shoulder. "I'm sorry, Jack. But it means it's over. I've got someone picking up Scieszka as we speak."

Jack squared his shoulders against the shudder running through him. "You found him?"

"No. But he has an antitheft device on his car. We're getting connected to the company that manufactures it to see if they can locate him for us."

A hundred thoughts went through Jack's head. At last! It was over at last! He'd done his job; Julia was avenged. And then he thought about poor Ron Milford. "She's a great girl," he'd said of Joanne, "but a little higher maintenance than Cathy." He had to be hurting like hell.

There was the dramatic clatter of keys, then the jail

door opened and Kay stood there, Evan's hand on her arm. She frowned at Gib and Jack.

"When you told me to come peacefully," she complained to Evan, "you didn't tell me this was a coed facility."

"Never fear," Evan said, pushing her in and pulling Gib out. "This one's coming with me, and Jack's promised not to do anything to embarrass me."

"Oh, good." She sat on the far end of the bench and studied Jack warily. "What had you been considering?"

"He bribed me," Evan informed her as he closed the door, "to bring you for a conjugal visit."

Kay turned on Jack. "You *paid* to have me arrested? After I made it clear…?"

"Yes," he replied. "You're going to pretend you don't want to do time with me? Forever?"

KAY SUSPECTED she'd just received a proposal. She tried to think, to form words, but nothing would come. Her thinking processes had shut down. All she could do was feel.

A proposal. From a man she loved. She'd been so sure there was no room for something so normal in her life. It was obviously very special but also…blessedly normal. Other women were proposed to and got married. Women who had uneventful childhoods and ordinary lives.

And now Jack Keaton was asking *her*.

She continued to stare at him with her mouth open.

He took her hands in his and drew her to him. "I'm convinced we can do this, Kay. I'll love Julia always, but that'll make me a better husband than I'd have been without all she taught me about loving and giving. And it's different that we're not the same faith, but it's nothing we can't work around. We love the same God."

"So…you're going to have another church?"

He nodded. "Word is there's a little one standing empty a few blocks from downtown. You can keep writing or stay with the paper, or both, whatever you want."

"I'm about to give up on the book," she grumbled. "All I seem to be able to do is write combative dialogue. And this baby keeps appearing in the story."

"What baby?"

"My hero and heroine's baby. They blame each other for not being able to recover from its death. But I never wrote them a baby."

"Ah." Jack nodded sagely. "Maybe it's Betsy trying to get you to work her out of your system through your book. Or maybe you're trying unconsciously to do that."

She considered the possibility.

"And about the dialogue." He kissed her. "You just need a little personal research into the loving kind. I'll help you. And if you want to help me with church programs and activities, you can. If you don't, that's okay, too. We can make it work."

A life spent with him was everything she'd ever wanted. But she had to think about… "The kids…." she said with a worried shake of her head. "What if I stunt their emotional growth, or…or…retard their social development with my fears for their safety. What if they…?"

He stopped her by catching the hand she gestured with. "Kids want someone to love and understand them. That's it." He grinned suddenly. "Okay, mine want somebody who can bake cookies, too, but I don't think it's a deal breaker."

A picture formed in her head of the four of them around a big table, along with her mother, her cousins and Agnes as well as his parents and Calpurnia. Buster chewed on a table leg.

"Oh, Jack." She heard the yearning in her own voice.

It matched the longing in his eyes. "If you don't say yes," he threatened, "I'm going to regress so far back into grief…"

She didn't let him finish the thought. "Yes," she said firmly. "I'll do time with you. Forever."

"Dear God!" she heard him mutter as he crushed her in his arms. She knew that wasn't an oath, it was a thank-you.

CHAPTER NINETEEN

"JACK, I NEED AIR!" Kay pleaded, wedging space between them. They'd been kissing for ten minutes and she was intoxicated with her status as an engaged woman, with the news he'd revealed to her about Joanne Milford in hurried bursts between kisses.

"No, you don't," he insisted, kissing her again. "I'll call for oxygen. I'll…"

The door to the jail burst open again and they looked up, smiling unashamedly, prepared to welcome a new "prisoner" in the name of St. Anthony's library.

Jack stood up at the look on Gib's face. Kay read the same thing. Something was wrong.

"What is it?" Jack asked. She felt his tension as he braced himself for the answer.

"One of my guys just called me." The cell phone was still in Gib's hand. "Scieszka's here."

That announcement had an audible sound beyond the words. Kay heard the knell of danger right behind him, felt it creeping along her spinal chord.

"In Maple Hill?" Jack asked stiffly.

"Yes, but…" Gib looked grim. "On the Common."

Kay couldn't believe that. "But he'd gotten away. He was 'on vacation.' Why would he come back? For Joanne Milford?"

Jack and Gib shook their heads at the same time. "She's in jail, not on the Common," Gib replied.

"He's coming for me," Jack said. "Because I ruined it all. He committed murder to keep his secret, bided his time for nine months, then was about to escape with Joanne when you and I found him out."

He pushed Kay toward Gib. "Take her into custody, or something. I've got to find my parents and my kids."

"Just a minute," she protested, evading Gib's hand and chasing Jack as he headed off toward the food area. She heard Gib behind her, shouting orders at someone.

John Keaton sat at a picnic table with an older couple, talking and laughing over coffee. Kay recognized Addy and Adam Fortin.

Jack ignored them and turned his father toward him. "Where's Mom?" he demanded. "Where're the kids?"

"What's the mat—?"

"Where are they, Dad?" His voice rose a decibel.

John pointed in the direction of the distant Ferris wheel. "I guess they're still on the rides. I haven't…"

Jack took off at a run in that direction, Gib following.

Remembering what Jack had told her about his father's heart condition, Kay stopped long enough to try to reassure him.

"Don't worry," she said, patting his arm, ready to sprint off after Jack. "Everything's going to be all right."

The man caught her arm in a steel grip. "Tell me what's happened." He climbed laboriously out from between the bench and the table, looking agitated.

How did one tell him succinctly that Julia had been killed and the man who'd done it was now nearby somewhere and Emma and the children were in danger?

And then like a miracle, she saw Rachel wandering by with a soft drink and beckoned her frantically. "This is Jack's dad," she said breathlessly, "and he has a heart condition. John, this is my cousin Rachel. She's a nurse."

"All right. My heart's already stopped beating." John put a hand to it, looking pale. "What's wrong?"

She pushed him gently onto a bench. "Julia's death wasn't an accident. Jack knows who did it, and that man is here, looking for him. That was a police officer following him, and I'm going after them. And if you have a heart attack, I'll never forgive you. Rachel, keep him well."

As Kay took off after Jack, she heard Rachel's authoritative voice giving John instructions. "Deep breaths…"

Kay had completely lost sight of them but headed for the Ferris wheel and finally found them stopped in the middle of the midway, Jack looking one way, Gib the other. Kay spotted Jack's mother the same moment he did. She intercepted Jack and Gib at a small gift concession where Emma waited, the children's jackets over her arm.

"Mom, where're the kids?" Jack asked, catching her shoulders.

The smile on her face died at the look on his. "On the merry-go-round." She tried to point, but her arms were full. "What? Why?"

As though some evil force had orchestrated the event, the wheel of painted wooden horses had stopped and the few children on it leaped off except for Amanda and Paul, still laughing gleefully though the music had stopped.

"They have two tickets," Kay heard Emma breathe, but her attention was on Jack, who was running for the merry-go-round. He'd also spotted the man coming from the side with a purposeful step. He was tall and fair-haired in black slacks and a black T-shirt. There was a telltale arrogance in his bearing and a frightening determination in his headlong stride toward the children. He was a good three yards closer than Jack and had a hand on each of them before Jack even reached the platform. She heard a primitive sound in Jack's throat.

Her own terror made it impossible to breathe and it felt as though she'd swallowed tinfoil. Around them, other rides rose and fell and flew while those aboard laughed, screamed and shouted to friends and family on the ground.

Kay heard her inner self—the eight-year-old who'd been powerless and would live with her forever—deny the moment. No, no, no! This is not happening to Jack, and it is not happening to me a second time.

Scieszka opened his jacket slightly so that a shoulder holster with a large, lethal-looking gun was visible. He smiled at Jack, clearly enjoying the moment of power.

He was handsome and looked coldly evil, pale blue eyes showing detached calculation. "Jack Keaton," he said in a clear, unhurried voice. "You're a stubborn man. Jo should have told me about you. I'm not going to let you ruin everything."

"I'm coming up there to get my children," Jack said to Scieszka in a voice that surprised Kay with its calm strength. "And I'm going to send them down to my friend." He indicated Gib.

"Jack…" Gib said softly.

Scieszka picked up Paul and slung him on his hip. Paul pushed against him and began to cry.

"Daddy!" Amanda pleaded, knowing something was terribly wrong.

"You're going to stay where you are," Scieszka said. "I came here looking for you and asked a man buying a candied apple if he could point you out. I told him I was an old friend from Vermont. He hadn't seen you, but he was happy to point out your children, and to tell me that you'd saved his daughter from drowning." He shook his head, as though pitying Jack. "Taking your children from you seemed like a better idea than simply offing you for ruining my plan. So the children and I are going to take a ride. First, though, I'd like to know how you *knew* the accident wasn't."

"Julia kept a diary," Jack replied, taking a step toward

Scieszka. "She took photographs of your books and the police have the CD."

Scieszka warned him to stop with a hand around Amanda's throat. She wept noisily. Kay saw Jack's agony, though he looked away from the children, probably to be able to focus.

"Julia was the most efficient secretary I've ever had," Scieszka praised cruelly. "But too smart for her own good."

"You killed her," Jack accused.

"Yes. I knew she'd been looking into the books, but when she left in such a hurry that night, I thought whatever she'd taken was in the car with her."

"Like you said, she was very efficient. She must have delivered the CD to our safety deposit box earlier in the day."

Scieszka nodded calmly. "I had a long lunch with a client and Jo and Milford came along. She probably stayed late that night to reinforce her case against me. Bad mistake."

Kay's heart thudded in her throat so loudly, she was sure it was visible. In books and movies, she thought, this was the point at which the heroine grew angry and, tired of being terrified, took command of the situation.

While the men talked, she inched behind a small knot of teenage girls who were exclaiming over a piece of jewelry one of them had won at the ring toss booth. Kay was tired of Betsy's kidnap coloring her whole life, and though her terror had turned to anger, she hadn't noticed courage rising to take control of her. She was still

ruled by fear—fear of losing Jack, fear of harm be-
falling the children, fear of having to live without them.

"Look, there's got to be something we can do here," Gib
said reasonably. "You'd probably like safe transport to..."

Kay lost track of what he was saying. She was moving slowly from the knot of girls to a woman with a dog
on a leash and a little boy beside her with a pumpkin-
shaped balloon.

Scieszka snapped back at Gib and Kay kept moving,
from the boy with the balloon past an old couple moving slowly. Then she was around the back of the merry-
go-round and climbing quietly onto the platform. A
weapon! She needed a weapon!

She had nothing, no purse, nothing around she could
use for a weapon. Then as she looked for something, she
spotted her big-soled shoes. She pulled one off, noticing that her fingers shook. It was because she needed a
plan, she told herself bracingly, making a fist with her
free hand. She had nothing in mind beside smacking
Scieszka as hard as she could.

All right. It wasn't a sophisticated plan, but it *was* a
plan. Her fingers stopped shaking. And she became
aware of just a hint of courage surfacing to stir her anger
at Scieszka for the grief he'd caused Jack and his family, and for ruining her engagement.

Gib continued to talk to him while Scieszka wrapped
his free arm around Amanda, pulled her off the horse
and set her on her feet. Kay crept up behind him, intent
on using his distraction with Amanda to strike the back

of his head. She saw Jack's eyes widen at the sight of her and Gib's face tighten. Emma stood back, both hands over her mouth.

It was Amanda who spotted her and said tearfully, "Kay!"

Scieszka spun around. Paul slithered out of his arms as his other hand reached across his chest to draw the gun. Kay was still terrified, but inspired with a vengeful wrath because now that she loved Jack, the tragedy that had befallen him and all that had happened to her were somehow entangled. Scieszka represented all her own demons, too. She swung the shoe with all her might right across his face. The gun flew out of his hand.

He cried out, clutching both hands to his mouth, the children screamed, then Jack was on him, driving him to the platform.

He struck him again and again. Kay caught the children to her and held them away. Gib stood aside for a moment then tried to pull Jack off of him.

"Hey," he said picking up the gun. "Come on. I need something left to arrest."

Jack held on to the black shirt, Scieszka's bruised face lolling lifelessly backward. "Let me enjoy the moment," he said.

He did, then something changed in his expression and he let his burden fall.

Gib turned Scieszka over and cuffed him just as Sam arrived at a run, leading the backup he'd apparently called for. Scieszka was hauled away.

Jack got down on one knee and opened his arms to the children, who ran into them. He held them tightly to him. Kay imagined Julia joining their embrace, then leaving them to her and going Home. She let herself think fancifully that Julia had Betsy by the hand.

Jack finally stood and Kay went to wrap her arms around him, the children caught between them. "Thank you," he whispered into the curve of her shoulder. "I'd yell at you for taking that chance, but...you saved them for me."

"I saved them for us," she corrected. "We are still engaged?" She felt drunk with her own good fortune, happy to be alive. She couldn't remember feeling this happy since before Betsy died.

He squeezed the breath out of her. "Yes, but not for long. Let's get married while my parents and your mother are still here."

She took his face in her hands and looked into his eyes. She'd intended to ask him if he was sure, but could see that he was.

Her happiness swelled. "Yes," she agreed. "Let's do that."

"I'm *right* here," Emma declared, standing beside them and still clutching the children's jackets, fear lingering in her expression. "What was that all about?"

They were suddenly surrounded by more family and friends. John had dragged Rachel with him in pursuit of Jack and Kay despite being told to sit still. Addy and Adam had rounded up as many of the Wonders as they could find, convinced that Jack was going to need help and Father Chabot had followed them.

Jack explained to everyone about Julia's discovery while he'd been in Iraq, and how he'd learned about it when he'd been recovering. He also told them how he'd come to Maple Hill to settle the score with Milford, only to discover he'd been wrong about who was responsible for Julia's death.

Everyone expressed shock at Joanne Milford's involvement. There was a moment of quiet while they absorbed the news.

"On the good side," Emma put in, "I just heard a proposal made and accepted." She grinned broadly. "They're getting married."

There were cheers and congratulations. While the Wonders surrounded Jack, Rachel and Charlie wrapped Kay in an embrace.

"I'll still help with Agnes," Kay insisted, thinking a little sadly about the single lives that had brought the cousins together so often.

Rachel shook her head, looking uncharacteristically emotional. "Don't worry," she whispered. "Woodlake Village Seniors Residence just called me. They have a room for Agnes. Perfect setup. Room for a lot of her things, beautiful setting. I told them we'd take her there Wednesday. We need a couple of days to get her things together."

JACK AND KAY were married on the Maple Hill Common on Wednesday morning with Father Chabot and a friend of Jack's from his divinity school days officiating together. Though all the festival booths were gone, the pumpkins and wheat bundles remained.

Amanda tossed rose petals, Paul carried the rings and Gib and Rachel and Sam and Charlie stood up for them. Agnes sat on a bench with Kay's mom and John and Emma Keaton. Friends surrounded them and Caleb and Elizabeth Drake looked on, still wearing their festive garb.

Agnes insisted on hosting the reception and didn't seem to mind that it had to be held at Perk Avenue rather than her apartment. "I'm moving," she explained to Kay, convinced in her dementia that Kay didn't know, "and all my things are already on their way." That was true. Everything important to her had been moved during the wedding, and after the reception, the cousins, Sam and Gib, along with Brenda and Jack's parents and the children, were taking her to Woodlake.

In a cream wool suit, Agnes wandered among the tables, looking vital and animated, clearly delighted to be a hostess again.

Kay, Rachel and Charlie stood together in a corner of the room, watching her. Jack, Gib and Sam sat at the counter over soft drinks, deep in conversation.

"It was thoughtful of you to get married," Charlie said, her voice raspy with emotion, "so that Agnes could reign over a party one final time."

Rachel squeezed Charlie's shoulders. "I think she'll like Woodlake Village. There's a lot going on she can take part in or not, however she feels. And she'll be well taken care of."

Charlie nodded. "I know. I just wish that her fantasy world could be real for her just once—that Liz and Richard and Bogie and Bacall could have come to the wedding."

At that moment, the door to the tea shop opened and a tall gray-haired man in a dark suit walked in and stopped just inside the door. He carried a wine bottle in one hand, and a bouquet of flowers in the other. Kay's mom, who'd been talking to Emma and John, left them and went to greet the stranger.

"Who is that?" Rachel asked.

Charlie's eyes were enormous. "Oh, my God," she gasped.

"What?" Kay asked.

Agnes looked up from a conversation with Prue and Gideon Hale.

"Elliott Whitman!" she cried, and went across the room, arms extended toward him, a girlish smile on her face.

"Agnes, darling," he said in a deep baritone, opening his arms to her. He embraced her gently, then handed her the flowers.

"I knew you'd come!" she said, clutching them, her cheeks pink with excitement.

Kay's mom led them to a table. Bridget Malone who owned the tea shop brought them cake and two glasses. Kay's mom slipped away and headed for the kitchen where Kay and her cousins intercepted her.

"Mom!" Kay caught her hand. "That's Elliott Whitman? *The* Elliott Whitman?"

Kay's mom smiled smugly. "*The* Elliott Whitman."

"And he really knows Aunt Agnes?" Rachel asked.

"I explained about her dementia, and he remembered that she'd encouraged him once when he was making his first movie and some bully of an actor no one's heard of since harassed him unmercifully. He said she told him she'd seen a lot of stars come and go, and that to endure, he should just continue to be as good an actor as he could be and not get involved in the politics. 'Take the work seriously,' she said, 'but never yourself.'"

"You know him?" Charlie's voice was high with disbelief.

Kay's mom feigned a superior attitude. "I'm much more of a celebrity than you girls realize. Just because I'm Kay's mother and your aunt, you think…"

"How do you know him?" Charlie wanted to know.

Kay's mom shrugged. "We did a week of *Hollywood Squares* together. He's very charming."

"*You* arranged this!" Kay studied her in amazement, then hugged her fiercely. "What a sweet, sweet thing to do, Mom!"

Brenda dismissed the praise with a toss of her head. "It's this town, these people." She pointed to Jack, Gib and Sam. The children had now invaded their male circle. Jordie drank from Gib's soft drink glass and Jack had slipped off his stool so that Amanda could occupy it and pick off his plate. Sam held Paul, who seemed to be telling him a long story that involved broad arm gestures. "These men," she added with a wistful sigh. "Nothing in the world like the right man, and Maple Hill knows how to grow them—or help them along once they're here."

WHEN IT WAS TIME to leave, Gib, Rachel, Jordie, Sam and Charlie went together in Rachel's car, and Kay's mom and Elliot Whitman took Agnes with them. Jack's parents took the children, and Jack helped Kay into his truck. He'd washed it inside and out for the occasion, and placed a towel on the passenger seat to protect her ivory wool suit.

"You okay with doing this?" he asked, thinking she looked emotional.

"Absolutely." She put her flowers down on the floor and pulled off the fussy little hat she'd worn down the aisle. Her curls were in disarray, just the way he liked them. "I've been happy to share the good times with her. I can't let her down because this is hard."

"It is your wedding day. Rachel and Charlie insisted they could do this without you."

"No. We'll leave for Niagara Falls after we see her settled." She leaned over to kiss him after he climbed in behind the wheel. Then she asked in concern, "Are you okay with it? It's your wedding day, too."

"Of course. I'm your support through thick and thin."

She smiled widely, apparently liking that answer. He put the key in the ignition and she reached for her seat belt and turned to him in surprise when she produced only a ragged half of it and no buckle.

He laughed and pulled her to the middle of the bench seat. "Use the lap belt. Buster ate the other one."

Everything you love about romance...
and more!

Please turn the page for Signature Select™
Bonus Features.

Bonus Features:

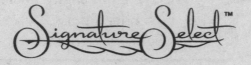

BONUS FEATURES

SEASON OF SHADOWS

EXCLUSIVE BONUS FEATURES INSIDE

Maple Hill Family History
A brief history
by Muriel Jensen

When Caleb Drake married Elizabeth Waltham in 1770, Maple Hill was a small collection of farms with a church, a school, a dry goods store, a blacksmith, a doctor's office and a tavern making up the small town. Caleb and Elizabeth had no idea they would be heroes in the War of Independence, or that they would provide the foundation of a family that would live and love several hundred years into a future beyond their imagination.

Henry Knox's famous trail from Fort Ticonderoga in New York to Boston, Massachusetts, intersected the Drakes' lives at Westfield in the snowy January of 1776. Caleb and the local militia provided cattle and provisions for the men moving fifty-nine various artillery pieces by ox-drawn sleds from the fort to the heights overlooking Boston, where they would be used to dislodge the British entrenched in the city below.

Caleb had gone home to retrieve a jug of brandy to celebrate with Knox and the militia the progress on the trail when he saw a deployment of British troops lost in the bad weather. With Knox and Boston's rescue moving slowly just beyond the trees, Caleb gathered his militiaman Fowler, powder and shot, determined to prevent the soldiers from meeting Knox—even though he had to do it alone. He had no time to argue with Elizabeth when she fell into step beside him, expert with her own fowling piece.

Local legend says they were out of powder and down to Caleb's knife and tomahawk when the militia working with Knox arrived to help. The Drakes were credited with saving the mission.

Caleb and Elizabeth had seven children, four of whom survived into adulthood. Philomena was born in 1777, and married a handsome young lawyer named Matthew Potter when she was seventeen. She was beautiful and headstrong, but Matthew was patient and quiet and accustomed to argument in the courtroom. He was also very much in love.

Waltham Drake, born in 1778, was brilliant but shy, and often overlooked because of William and Robert Drake, his lively and mischievous younger brothers.

Still, he caught the eye of Martha Dartford, the daughter of a successful sheep farmer. They raised twins, George and Ethan Drake. George studied at Harvard, but Ethan, too lighthearted for serious study, stayed home to care for his widowed mother and enjoy the life of a country gentleman.

When Martha died in a riding accident, and a

harsh spring destroyed crops and took a toll on livestock, tiny Maple Hill's survival was at stake. Starting over required capital no one had. Ethan decided to "borrow" it from the gentry and the merchants who traveled the Post Road.

The Berkshire Highwayman became a familiar nuisance in the area for the next year. Almost everyone who traveled the road experienced an encounter. The highwayman's habit of taking only half the contents of a victim's purse, or of leaving beautiful women or the clergy unmolested, gave birth to a legend.

During that year pastor Philip Montrose was able to put a new roof on the church thanks to a generous and anonymous donation, the widow Bourgeois found a bundle of bills in her well bucket that allowed her to save her farm from foreclosure, and there was suddenly enough money in the town's meager budget to pay the salary of the teacher, Miss Arliss, so that she didn't have to return to Boston.

Ethan's career in crime was cut short when Annabel Montrose, the pastor's daughter, confronted him in a grove of maples off the road where he awaited his victims. She'd seen him sneak the stack of cash into her father's collection basket and threatened to reveal him as the Berkshire Highwayman unless he agreed to marry her. Her mother had died when she was twelve, and her brothers had taken off for parts unknown. Annabel wanted a husband and children, but life as a pastor's daughter left her little opportunity to socialize with young men. She'd been admiring Ethan for some time.

When Ethan protested that he might be a little unorthodox for a clergyman's daughter, she insisted he was just right. Her aunt had left her a large home in Maple Hill and she had a plan to turn it into an inn, and take more *legal* advantage of the traffic on the Post Road. Thus the Post Road Inn came into being.

Ethan and Annabel raised five daughters.

Elizabeth, born in 1825, was clever and temperamental. She married Robert Bourgeois, who had few visible prospects but a million ideas and a winning disposition.

Studious Beatrice fell in love with Joseph Childress, a professor from Yale who was writing a book about the War of Independence. They were married in Maple Hill and she returned with him to Connecticut.

James Dancer, a frontiersman, captured Dorinda's adventurous heart and took her to Missouri.

Amelia Drake, considering her sister foolish to leave such a wonderful place as Maple Hill, married banker Thomas Whitcomb, a newcomer to Maple Hill. He'd fallen in love with the town and wanted nothing more from life than his work, his property on the lake and Amelia.

Josephine, the spirited youngest of Ethan's daughters, fell in love with Daniel Fortin, who owned the dry goods store.

The community eventually combined financial

forces and erected a statue on the common to Caleb and Elizabeth Drake.

Adam and Charles Fortin, Josephine and Daniel's twin sons born in 1845, developed reputations as outrageous pranksters when they painted their aunt Amelia's chickens when they were seven years old. Their pranks continued with the release of frogs in the classroom, worms in the collection basket and a skunk in Esau Milton's tavern.

The firing by Confederates on Fort Sumter in 1861, however, forced them to grow up. They enlisted in the 10th Massachusetts Regiment Volunteer Infantry.

Adam died at Gettysburg, but Charles returned home much decorated and married Catherine Milton, who'd been in love with his brother. Charles's grandparents' inn was so successful that he and Catherine went into the hospitality business, as well, turning her large home into the Yankee Inn.

The story went that Catherine's great-grandmother, Jane Wolfe, had discovered a wounded British soldier in her father's barn during the War for Independence, and had hidden him there until her parents went to church. Pleading a headache, she stayed home and helped the soldier up to her room, where she hid him for three days, tending to his wound and feeding him with leftovers from the dinner table.

Her family finally discovered him, but saw that he was so ill he was little threat to them, and Jane's pleas that they not turn him over to the local militia were so heartfelt that they sheltered him. Love for the Wolfes caused him to switch allegiance, and he and Jane eventually raised eight children in the house.

Charles and Catherine's marriage was never a happy one despite a son and daughter and the inn's financial success. Charles rejoined the army and went west with General George Custer in the campaign against the Sioux. He died with him at the Little Bighorn in 1876.

A guest at the inn that same year was a Portuguese whaler from New Bedford who came to Maple Hill to open a fish market. Tibero Florio was handsome and likable and soon charmed Jocasta Robidoux, who cooked at the inn, into becoming his wife.

Charles and Catherine's daughter, Charlotte, as restless as her father, went to Oregon on a wagon train with Jamie Whitcomb, a neighbor boy. Her brother, Drake, maintained the inn, though he hated the confining nature of the work. Until he met Prudence Benedict, a barmaid who was always sweet and smiling, but who repeatedly spurned his advances. Will Anselmo, who'd recently purchased the tavern, explained to him that she had a young daughter born out of wedlock and was determined to save Drake from the embarrassment of her situation.

Drake took great pains to convince her that he adored her and found nothing even remotely embarrassing about her beautiful daughter. They were married in 1894. He no longer strained against the life of an innkeeper, but added onto the house, landscaped the grounds and added a bridge over the small creek that ran beside the property.

Maple Hill now had paved streets, electricity and a telephone in the dry goods store and the bank. There was a police station and a fire department, and the school moved into a new two-story building. The old Bourgeois home became City Hall.

Drake loved four-year-old Belinda like his own child, and he and Prudence gave birth to four boys, two who died in the Ardennes in World War I, one who fell victim to the influenza epidemic and the youngest son, Ben, who took over the inn.

Meanwhile, several descendants of former Maple Hill residents returned home. Robert Childress, a successful doctor in Connecticut, brought his family to see the place where his ancestors had lived and they all loved the beautiful setting so much that they stayed.

Elaine Dancer, who'd grown up in St. Louis on journals the women in her family had kept for generations, visited Maple Hill to see where nineteenth-century Dorinda had lived. All Elaine had left were the memories of a broken love affair, and a new pregnancy. She was desperate for a connection with the part of her family that remained in Maple Hill.

She was disappointed to find that the family home was now known as the Old Post Road Inn. A young woman behind the desk was happy to tell her about the highwayman in the inn's past, but apologized for being unable to provide her with accommodations. She referred her to the Yankee Inn, and suggested she try the new Breakfast Barn for good food. Her brother had just opened it for business, she said.

Ben Fortin, running the inn, was a happy bachelor determined to steer clear of women and marriage. Until Elaine Dancer approached his desk, explained she was a long-lost resident of Maple Hill and asked if he had a room.

On her second night at the Yankee, he invited her to dinner. She explained that she was pregnant with the child of a man she hadn't known was married. Ben told her about his mother and the half sister he loved dearly.

Ben and Elaine were married two months later, and when Elaine's child was born his name was Fortin—Adam Fortin.

Meanwhile, several generations of Florios had flourished, every eldest son bearing the name Tibero. The current holder of the name ran the fish market still in the family and fell in love with a French girl from New Bedford.

The United States became involved in World War II the following year and Ben Fortin joined the army. Elaine ran the inn in his absence and raised Adam with the help of old Jamie Whitcomb, who'd returned to Maple Hill after losing Charlotte to a long illness. Two of his great-nephews ran an appliance repair shop.

Jamie lived at the inn and kept Adam occupied

when Elaine got word that Ben was missing. She died a thousand deaths until he was located two weeks later. He'd become lost after sustaining a head injury in heavy fighting and joined another unit.

Eventually he returned safely; Adam attended Southern Massachusetts University and married Deborah Eldredge from an old Cape Cod family.

Their daughter Jacqueline was born in 1968.

The Florios had four children—Agnes, who horrified everyone by going off to work in Hollywood; Manny, who became an architect; Joe, who dealt with health problems most of his life, and Michael, who became a surgeon.

Agnes remained single, but each brother had a daughter who grew up to live for her family and friends—and perpetuate the code of Maple Hill.

They are Kay, Charlie and Rachel, who in the fall of 2005 were living a *Season of Shadows*.

Fall Festivals

Why I love them
by Muriel Jensen

I succumb to Fall Fever every September, even before the weather cools or the first leaf falls. It must be a cellular memory of some female ancestor gathering wheat in a field somewhere and stopping to catch a whiff of that indefinable something-different in the air. I feel the quickening of her heartbeat.

For her, the approach of autumn meant a hundred tasks ahead to prepare her family for winter. For pampered twenty-first-century me, it means lush produce during the last few weeks of Astoria's Sunday market, truckloads of pumpkins appearing in the parking lot of every grocery store, Halloween costumes in shop windows, recipes for all those cold-weather comfort foods—chili, stew, onion soup with a cheesy crust.

Despite all the work facing that woman in the past, I like to think she still felt excitement at the prospect of the approaching holidays. All the indoor chores of winter had to be easier than spring and summer's backbreaking labors.

In my modern world we're taking brisk walks to enjoy fall's beauty, but daily life is moving in from the garden and the pool. (No, I don't have a pool. I'm writing from Oregon, where even a sunporch is an exercise in optimism.) We turn up the thermostat, the cats curl up on the floor registers and radiate heat. The family knot tightens.

Celebrations of fall began when primitive man thanked the gods for a good harvest. Our own Pilgrims' Thanksgiving was a Christian evolution of that gratitude for God's bounty. Today's community festivals with their food, crafts and games echo that grateful sentiment.

All across the country, in small towns and big-city neighborhoods, people are cordoning off streets or taking over town squares or fairgrounds to share the fruits of their summer labor and celebrate their common struggle—and their survival.

There's a turkey trot in Arkansas, yo-yo championships in California, coffin races in Colorado, a festival of scarecrows in Maine, the Kit Carson Trail Ghost Walk in Nevada and a national storytelling festival in Tennessee.

Games and contests are often an important part of such festivals. There are pumpkin-carving contests, cook-offs using pumpkin, apple, or other seasonal favorites, scarecrow-decorating competitions, cakewalks. Children compete for prizes shooting hoops, tossing beanbags, dunking for apples, decorating cookies, or showing off their Halloween costumes.

In New England you'll find ethnic foods offered by the excellent cooks of Portuguese, Italian, French and Irish descent. In the Midwest good old American food predominates, and in the Southwest it's Tex-Mex and barbecue. The Northwest and the Great Lakes region with their Scandinavian ancestry tantalize with favorites. Both coasts and the Gulf states offer wonderful seafood dishes. My favorite is crab cakes.

I'm a terrible cook but an accomplished guest at the table, and I find festival food among the best tasting. Nothing is more cozy than sitting in a crowded place, sharing a table with family and friends, and the opportunity to get to know people you pass on the street every day but seldom get to chat with.

Zoe Alter, Signature Bonus Feature Editor, spoke with Muriel Jensen in the fall of 2004.

RECIPES:

A sampling of some of Muriel's favorites.

My mother was French-Canadian, my father Portuguese, and I am Danish by marriage. There are several recipes I've enjoyed at fall festivals and I'd like to share them with you.

MY MOTHER-IN-LAW'S FRIKADELLER
(Danish meatballs)

1 large onion
1 tbsp butter
¾ cup soft bread crumbs
¾ cup milk
1 ½ lb ground beef
2 beaten eggs
1 ½ tsp salt
pepper
1 cup warm milk
2 tbsp oil
¼ cup flour

Chop the onion, cook in butter until soft.
Soak bread crumbs in milk, then combine crumbs
with onions, meat, eggs and seasonings. Mix well.
Gradually add as much milk as mixture will take.
Chill and form into 12 meatballs. Brown in butter
and oil. Dredge in flour, make gravy and allow meatballs to simmer in it 5 to 10 minutes.

MY HUSBAND'S EASY AEBLESKIVER

1 cup flour
2 tsp baking powder
2 tsp sugar
dash salt

Sift dry ingredients together and put aside.

Separate *2 eggs* and whisk whites in a copper bowl
until frothy, put aside.

Add egg yolks to *1 cup of milk* and mix together.

Add *2 tbsp melted butter.*

Add wet ingredients to dry and mix together.

Fold in egg whites.

Grease an aebleskiver pan generously so that small
amounts of shortening remain in the bottom of
each depression. Spoon batter in about ¾ full.
Stand by with a skewer or the traditional steel knit-

ting needle. As soon as you see browning around the edges, give the dough a quarter turn with the needle. At this point you may add a 1/2 teaspoon of applesauce if you like. If not, the aebleskiver is still delicious without it. Turn once or twice more until you have a round shape, browned on all sides.

Serve immediately with powdered sugar and raspberry or strawberry jam.

PORTUGUESE CARNE D'ESPETO
(Meat on a spit or skewer)

5 lbs of sirloin tips marinated overnight in wine or beer in which you've placed 2 heads of chopped garlic and salt and red pepper to taste. Place on skewers and grill to desired doneness.

At the Portuguese feast in New Bedford, Massachusetts, visitors buy a skewer of meat and cook it themselves over a long open grill. The experience makes for great fun and conversation.

TOURTIÈRE (French-Canadian meat pie)

1 lb lean ground pork
½ chopped onion
1 clove garlic, finely chopped
⅓ cup chopped celery
1 tsp salt
¼ tsp nutmeg*
1⅛ tsp ground mace*
2 tsp cornstarch
1 cup water
pastry for 2-crust, 8-inch pie

Combine all ingredients except pastry, simmer in covered pan for 30 minutes, stirring frequently. Pour into one pie crust and cover with other, making slits or pricking with a fork to let steam escape. Bake at 425°F for 10 minutes, reduce to 350°F for 35 minutes.

* ¼ tsp each of cloves, cinnamon and marjoram may be substituted for nutmeg and mace.

Festival Crafts
by Muriel Jensen

The crafts found at such events are often old-fashioned, homespun skills still appreciated today.

Wreath making can be a minimum-skill, maximum-yield project. You can start with a basic twig or straw wreath that can be purchased in any craft store. Or if you're lucky enough to have a friend with grapevines, you can start from scratch and create a final product that will allow you to impress yourself with your own prowess.

This is a project that can be accomplished solo, but is best done with friends. Trim vines as long as you are able to get them, then soak them in warm water. (The tub works very well.)

Retire to a friend's living room to drink wine or coffee and snack as you look over the objects you've collected to decorate your wreaths. Dried or silk flowers work beautifully, fall leaves are absolutely gorgeous (did you know you can dry them in your microwave between two paper towels?), sprigs of berries are beautiful and organic, or strings of shiny and get together somewhere to play games, listen to music, or just talk. If you're so inclined, make a plan to meet once a month over the winter to celebrate each other and nature's generous bounty.

beads make your wreath catch candlelight or the glow of your fire.

In an hour or two your vines will be pliable. Wind them into circles three or four times then tuck the end in between two of the turns. When the wreath dries, the end should stay firmly in place. If it doesn't, tie it with wire or a twist tie that can be covered by the decorations.

KISSING BALLS can be made with fresh or silk flowers of almost any description. Those with small "faces"—roses, straw flowers—look prettiest. Simply cut the stems short and stick them into a foam ball, completely covering it. Add a length of pretty ribbon or cord to hang them in a doorway or from an overhead light.

DRIED HYDRANGEAS make a beautiful fall arrangement. There are none in my garden, but my neighbor has two large bushes and is generous with the flowers. She cuts them after they've turned color and before they begin to brown. I cut the sprig apart so each flower is separate on its own stem, tie cord or twine to each stem and hang the flower upside down from a line in the basement. Though I've never tried this method, I understand you can place a bouquet of hydrangeas in water and simply let the water evaporate over time and the flowers will dry beautifully. They look lovely in an arrangement with greens or tucked into your Christmas tree.

If there is no fall festival i̶n̶ ̶y̶o̶u̶r̶ ̶a̶r̶e̶a̶ ̶c̶o̶l̶l̶e̶c̶t̶ ̶y̶o̶u̶r̶ neighbors and their favorit̶e̶

AUTH̶